Carnal Gift

by
Pamela Clare

CARNAL GIFT

Kenleigh-Blakewell Family Saga, Book II

Print Edition
Published by Pamela Anne Clare, 2013

Cover Design by Seductive Designs
Cover Photo by Jenn LeBlanc of Studio Smexy™

Originally published in 2004 by Dorchester Publishing Co., Inc.
Reprinted by Dorchester Publishing Co., Inc. in November 2008.

ISBN-10 0983875960
ISBN-13 9780983875963

Acknowledgments

Special thanks to Mick Bolger of traditional Celtic band Colcannon for giving my characters their Irish voice. (Check the band out at www.colcannon.com.)

Additional thanks to my agent Natasha Kern for hard working in getting back my rights to this book and to my son Benjamin for his help in getting the novel reformatted for print on demand. Many thanks to my sister, Michelle, for her help in editing.

Dedicated to my sister, Michelle, for a lifetime of laughter and friendship. Everyone says I laugh all the time when I'm with you. All I know is that I love you and feel happy when we're together. So let's spend more time together during the second half of our lives than we have in the first half.

AUTHOR'S NOTE

This book was my heartbreaker. I spent months researching Ireland during the penal era, then threw myself into writing the story for more than a year. When I was done, I had a manuscript that was almost five hundred pages long. I cherished the story even more than the first book in this series and felt it was much better written. I was so excited when I turned it in to my editor.

I got a phone call about a month later. The publisher informed me that the book far exceeded their maximum word count. I was shocked and deeply upset to hear that the book would be cut—by at least one hundred pages. I couldn't imagine what the story would be like without those pages and asked that the publisher make an exception in this case. After all, no one had told me there was a maximum word count.

I was told that no exceptions could be made. After all, page count determines how many books fit in a box, how heavy those boxes are, how high shipping costs become, etc. I could understand why such things matter to a publisher, but they didn't matter to me as the author. I was telling a story that needed precisely this many words; to cut it would be to irrevocably change the story. In the end, the cuts were made.

I cried for a month. The book that was released didn't feel anything like the book I'd written. Perhaps the colder corners of the publishing industry can look at a novel and just see a product, but for me, a book is about the characters. The hero's character in particular suffered from these cuts. I hated it.

My editor suggested I save the manuscript for the day, many years in the future, when I would be a bestselling author and the publishing house would feel it worth the investment to put out the original version of the story. That's what I did.

But something happened that no one could have predicted: the ebook revolution. That very revolution brought about the end of that publishing house's print publication program. They no longer publish print novels. However, it also gave me the ability to dust off the manuscript and share it with readers.

As I read through Jamie and Bríghid's story, I fell in love with it again. I never read the cut version, and I never allowed myself to think about the original version. Reading it again was like discovering lost friends.

And now I share it with you. For the first time, readers can read the novel I wrote, not the butchered version. For those who read the original release, it ought to feel like a completely different story and a new reading experience. For those who haven't, you'll never know what you missed—and that's a good thing. Enjoy!

Pamela Clare
Aug. 7, 2011

A word about Irish Gaelic...

When I wrote this story, it was very important to me to give the Irish characters an authentic Irish identity. I opted to give them very Irish names and to include Irish Gaelic in the story. However, most of us don't have access to Gaelic-speaking friends and neighbors. To make reading the story a bit easier, here's a quick guide to pronouncing the characters' names and other words that are repeated throughout the story.

I've translated all of the Gaelic except in places where the story is being told from the point of view where the character doesn't know Gaelic. In those few places, the text remains untranslated. Sometimes in life we just don't know what's being said.

Bríghid — BREEDGE = Brigid in English

Ruaidhri — RO-ry = Rory

Finn — Finn (from Finnegan) in English, too

Aidan — AY-den = Aidan in English, too

Muirín = MWIR-rin = This has no equivalent in English. It's a very old Celtic name.

iarla — EEER-la = earl

Ailís — eye-LEESH = Alice

Seanán — SHAWN-on = Shannon

Niamh — NIEVE or NEEVE (There's really no English equivalent.)

Ní — NEE = "Daughter of"

Maelsechnaill — MALL-shek-nyall

Uí — for the men (Fionn and Ruaidhri). This means "son of" and is pronounced somewhat like "oy" or the French word "oui."

Bainne clábair — Bonnie clabber, a food made of soured milk

Mo Aisling ghael — Mo ASH-ling GELL = My beautiful dream or vision.

The Rs are lightly rolled, not the heavy roll you hear in Spanish or Scottish.

In direct address, the word "a" goes before some names, and the spelling of the name changes slightly in those cases. In the case of Bríghid's name, it looks like "a Bhríghid."

Prologue

Skreen Parish
County Meath, Ireland
January 30, 1751

*B*ríghid Ní Maelsechnaill put the bacon and oatcakes on the table, her heart humming with excitement.

Her father stepped out of the back room, dressed and washed for the day. His gaze met hers, a special twinkle in his blue eyes, and a smile on his face.

They shared a secret, and soon her father would tell her brothers.

She smiled back, reached for the butter crock, put it next to the oatcakes, and smoothed her apron. She wanted the breakfast to be perfect, and it was. The oat porridge was thick and hot, but not lumpy. The oatcakes were cooked, but not burnt. The bacon was crisp, but not blackened—just the way her father liked it. There were eggs, fried potatoes, *bainne clábair* and a pot full of hot tea.

Her father pulled out his chair, sat, motioned the boys to the table. Like a swarm of locusts, they descended—Finn, Ruaidhrí, and little Aidan. Though not kin, Aidan had lived with them for two years now and was one of the family, as sure as he'd been born into it.

Bríghid helped Aidan put a napkin around his neck, took her seat, slapped Ruaidhrí's hand as he reached for the bacon. "Not yet, Ruaidhrí."

When all were seated and quiet, her father bowed his head, folded his hands, prayed. As excited as she was, she heard scarce a word of it, but crossed herself when it was done—and waited.

Her father didn't serve himself as he usually did after the prayer, but gazed intently at Finn and Ruaidhrí. "Finn, Ruaidhrí, I've news for you. Your sister has become a woman."

Finn's blue eyes widened, and he smiled at her. "Well done, little sister."

She smiled back, her heart filled with a warm rush of love for him.

"But, Da', how can Bríghid be a woman? She doesn't have big dugs like—"

From the sudden silence and the pained look on Ruaidhrí's face, Bríghid knew Finn had pinched him good under the table. She'd pinch Ruaidhrí herself later. She'd have breasts one day. They just needed time to grow.

Her father fixed Ruaidhrí with a gaze that spoke trouble. "Your sister is a woman now, a maiden chaste and fair as ever there was in Ireland. You're to show her respect and courtesy, or I'll know the reason why." He took a gulp of tea. "She shall have ribbons and lace for her hair—and a trip to the fair come May Day."

Bríghid's heart soared. She might have squealed aloud at this news, but she was fourteen now and mustn't behave like a giggling girl of seven summers. Instead, she smiled. "The fair!"

The boys' faces brightened as well.

"The fair!" Aidan bounced up and down in his chair.

"I expect the two of you to protect Bríghid and to guard her virtue, as I've no doubt the lads will soon swarm to her like bees to honey. She's got her mother's look about her. There isn't a prettier lady in the county, nor all of Ireland I'd wager. Her safety and happiness depend on the menfolk in her life, and we shall not fail her."

Finn nodded, his expression grave.

Ruaidhrí, looking contrite, nodded. "Aye, Da'."

Bríghid felt herself blush to the roots of her hair, but couldn't hold back a smile.

"And, Bríghid, you're to have the back room now. A young lady needs privacy in a household of men."

For a moment, Bríghid was speechless. How could her father have known? She'd felt so uncomfortable lately, trying to dress and undress, bathe and sleep with her brothers in the room. "Thank you, Da'."

"You're welcome, *mo Aisling ghael*." A smile on his handsome face, he reached for the bacon. "Now let's eat the fine breakfast you've set before us."

The food was gone in less than half the time it took to prepare it, but Bríghid knew that meant they'd liked it. She kissed her father on the cheek as he headed toward the door, his lesson books tucked under his arm. His whiskers were rough against her lips, his skin warm with the smells of pine and tobacco—her father's own special scent.

"Are you off to gather rushes today, my Bríghid?"

"Aye, I am. There's much to be done before tomorrow night."

He nodded his approval, started out the door. Then he turned back to her. "Your mother would be right proud of you, so she would." He tickled a finger under her chin, smiling down at her. Then he turned strode out the door, calling to the boys. "Come along, Ruaidhrí, Aidan. Let's not be late."

As she watched him go, Bríghid felt a pricking behind her eyes, but refused to cry. She barely remembered her mother, as she'd died, weakened by famine, when Bríghid was only three. But Bríghid had tried to be a good daughter, one her mother would have been happy to claim had she lived. To hear her father say such words ... The midwife had told her she might have confusing feelings or want to cry more now that she was a woman.

Bríghid cleared the table, made quick work of the dishes. She placed more peat on the fire—the hearth fire could not go out until after May Day—then took off her apron, put on her cloak and scarf, and set out.

The day was mild and sunny, as if nature itself shared her joy. Winter seemed to know there was no point in fighting the approach of spring and was in retreat. In places where the sun stayed longest, the grass was beginning to green. The night's frost had melted into dew on the bare branches of the apple trees. Some ewes had dropped their lambs, and the cows would soon calve. In a matter of weeks, there would be milk, cheese and butter in plenty, and flowers would begin to bloom.

Bríghid walked down the lane that came up to the door and set across the field to the edge of the lake where the rushes grew tall. As a virgin—and especially since her name was Bríghid—she was the one who must gather the family's rushes for Imbolg, blessed Saint Bríghid's special day. The rushes must be pulled by hand by a maiden, not cut with iron. They must be gathered in silence and hidden from the rest of the family until tomorrow night, when they would be woven into crosses for the house and cowshed, made into girdles for the cows and used to make the *Brídeog*—the little St. Brighid doll—and a little mattress for the Brídeog to sleep on. Extra rushes would be strewn on the floor and the table to welcome the Saint into the home and hearth.

"Go down on your knees and do homage, and let blessed St. Brighid enter the house." She mouthed the words she would say tomorrow night before the prayers and feasting, wanting to get them right and make her father and brothers proud.

She knelt in the frozen marsh, began to pull rushes out of the ground. Their edges were sharp, but she had done this many times and knew to wrap a scarf around her hand. They broke free easily, and soon she had a goodly pile. But many more were needed if there were to be enough for both the floor and the table, as she intended. She didn't mind the work. It was good to be outside, and the day was too lovely for any but happy thoughts.

The spring fair! She almost laughed out loud with delight, then remembered she must be silent. She'd never been to a fair. She wondered what colors of ribbons the merchants would sell. She wanted blue ribbons and white ribbons and white lace. Perhaps red ribbons, too, if her father had the coin. She would braid her hair, work the ribbons into her braids, tie bits of lace at the end of each.

She wondered, too, if her father spoke truly. Was she pretty? Would young men be drawn to her like bees to honey? The thought made her belly tickle, her heart beat faster. Perhaps she would meet a handsome young man at the fair. Perhaps she would meet the man destined to become her husband.

She knew her father wouldn't allow her to marry until she was sixteen. She'd heard him tell the midwife he felt fourteen was still too young for motherhood. The midwife told him she helped girls of thirteen and fourteen birth children all the time, but her father had stood fast. She would not wed until she was sixteen.

Because she trusted her father, she was not angry with him. Most country girls were married before they were sixteen, and many had children. But her father was the wisest man she knew. He was a teacher and had read all manner of books. He taught boys and girls to read, do math and to love Irish history. If he believed it best, she would wait until she was older and not complain.

She wanted a husband, to be sure, a man brave and fair to woo her with sweet words, stolen glances, and wreaths of flowers. He would be strong and tall like Finn. He would be kind and gentle like her father. He would work the land, not spend his days at sea. He would not raise his voice to her or hit her. Nor would he waste himself in drink.

And they would have children, as was their duty. She wanted four girls and four boys, and she had already chosen their names: Róisin, Ana, Meallá, and Laoise for the girls, and Ciarán, Breacán, Lochlann and—

She stopped, listened.

Someone shouted her name. She stood, rushes bundled under her arm, saw Ruaidhrí running down the road, Aidan lagging behind.

They spied her, dashed through the grass toward her.

She motioned to Ruaidhrí to stop, but he paid her no mind. She was to gather rushes in silence, and no one was to see them. But now they had come along, and she would have to start over. She started to scold Ruaidhrí, saw the terror on his face, little Aidan's tears.

Her stomach lurched.

"They took him!"

No. It couldn't be. "What?"

"The *iarla's* men took Da'!"

Aidan dashed forward, clutched Brighid's hand, sobbing.

There was a buzzing sound in her ears. The rushes fell, forgotten, at her feet. "What happened?" Her words were a whisper.

"They found us sittin' along the hedgerow. They dragged him away in chains! Oh, Brighid, they beat him!" Tears poured down Ruaidhrí's cheeks. He dashed them away. "I could not stop them. I tried. They laughed and kicked me."

She felt tears gather behind her eyes, felt the tripping pulse of panic in her veins. Then she saw her little brother was bleeding from a cut on his lip. She was a woman now. She must not give in to her own childish tears, but must comfort the others.

"You were very brave, Ruaidhrí. And you, Aidan." She wiped the blood from Ruaidhrí's mouth with her scarf, tried to ignore the sick feeling her stomach. "Come. We must find Finn."

Chapter One

November 10, 1754

"*Cén fáth a' chuirfeadh Dia a smacht ar bhás linbh?*"
Why would God let a baby die?

Bríghid slipped the worn leather brogues onto Aidan's feet, distressed to see how big the holes in the toes had become. "Only God and His saints know the answer to that, *a phráitín.*"

She stood, took the little woolen coat from its nail in the wall, and helped Aidan put it on. Its sleeves were too short by several inches. She'd taken the hems out as far as they could go last winter. He was almost ten now, she reminded herself. He'd need a new coat, and a warmer one, as he now spent more time outdoors with Finn learning men's work. He'd need a new pet name, too. A young man would hardly find it fitting to be called "potato" in front of the other boys.

"I feel bad for the baby." Aidan wrapped his red woolen scarf around his neck.

"Aye, me too." She felt just as bad for the babe's young mother.

Muirín had labored two long days to bring her first child into the world. Bríghid, though unmarried, had gone to help, bringing herbs to soothe and calm the mother. There had been little the women could do to ease Muirín's suffering. They'd held her hand, given her sips of tea, wiped her brow, offered silent prayers, called for the priest. But the child had slipped into the world blue and lifeless, the cord tight around its neck. Muirín's husband had died some months back of a fever of the lungs, and the child was all she'd had of him.

The babe's stillbirth had touched Aidan deeply, and no wonder. His mother had died in childbed. His father had been killed in a skirmish with the hated English when Aidan was four. Only twelve at the time,

Bríghid had taken him in and had raised him with the help of her brothers—and, for a time, her father.

Now it was time to bury the babe and consign its soul to God. With no church, Father Padraíg had called a Mass at the Old Oak. It was remote enough that their chances of being caught and punished were slim. Mass was usually said discreetly in someone's home or in a cowshed, but all the neighboring families were coming to pay their respects to the child they never knew—and to help Muirín cope with her grief. There wasn't room for them all indoors. Though Bríghid had seen a church from the outside—a grand building that seemed to reach up to Heaven itself with windows of precious colored glass—she had never been inside one. She'd been born long after the *Sasanach* had taken away the churches and made it a crime for a Catholic to pray.

It was a long walk to the Old Oak, but it was the safest place for so many people to gather, and it was holy ground, consecrated by priests and the Old Ones who came before. The ancient remains of a holy well stood near the base of the tree, where some women still left offerings. 'Twas said Saint Padraíg himself had prayed beneath its branches when Ireland was a pagan land.

Finn wouldn't be joining them, as one of the cows had taken sick with the milk fever. They needed her milk, and the butter, curds and cheeses that came from it, to make it through the winter. Finn would spare no effort to see the cow cured. He would pay his respects later.

Bríghid put more peat on the fire. Finn would grow chilled working in this weather, and she didn't want him to find the hearth grown cold when he at last came in to rest. Poor Finn did the work of two men now that Da' was gone—or three, as he had taken on Muirín's outdoor chores when her husband died. He never complained, never said an angry word. But Bríghid could see how tired he was each night. She fed him the best pieces of meat from the stewpot to help him keep up his strength, but often he was so weary he could scarce finish his supper before falling asleep.

Aye, Ruaidhrí did his share of hard work, too, but at sixteen he hadn't the patience for farm work that Finn had, nor the knowledge. Hot-tempered and restless, he hurried through his chores, his mind always somewhere else. Ruaidhrí had been hit hard when the *Sasanach* took Da' away. The happy and gentle boy he had been had vanished overnight.

Bríghid and her brothers had never seen their father again. The breakfast she'd cooked with such care that morning had been the last meal he'd shared with them. Soon after, he'd been put on a ship and taken to Barbados to be sold as a slave alongside other Irish the

Sasanach deemed criminals—teachers, scholars, priests, fighters. 'Twas said plantation owners worked their slaves to death in the cane fields, and that if hard work didn't kill them, strange and terrible fevers would.

But Bríghid would likely never know what became of her father. He'd been a man of one-and-fifty years when they'd taken him, no longer in his prime. She couldn't even be certain he'd survived the long journey. She could not bear to think of her father in such horrid conditions, his back bent in the fields, his skin marred by the lash. A strong but gentle man, he'd always been more poet and dreamer than farmer. He'd never raised a weapon against the English invaders, never raised a fist to any man nor his hand to his wife or children. That his life could come to such an end bespoke *Sasanach* cruelty.

She missed her father, missed him so fiercely she felt at times as if her heart were being torn from her breast. She missed his sense of humor and gentle teasing. She missed the deep, warm sound of his voice. She missed the way he'd always made her feel safe, loved, special. *Aisling*, he had called her. His dream. His vision.

When she was little, he'd held her on his lap and read to her until late in the night. He'd told her stories of the old days in front of the hearth, taught her to sing the old songs. He'd comforted her in sickness. He had been her world. She'd felt protected knowing that, no matter what came with the sunrise, her father would be there.

But that was long ago.

Every day since they'd taken him, she'd prayed to God and all his saints to watch over Tommán Uí Maelsechnaill and spare him from loneliness, disease, cruelty, death. Every night, she'd gone to sleep wondering whether he yet lived, whether he was suffering, whether he knew how much his children and the people of Skreen parish missed and loved him.

How different their lives were without him. Without his teaching to bring in calves, chickens, honey, hay and woolen cloth, they were poorer than ever. Finn worked until he was exhausted. Ruaidhrí was consumed by rage at the *Sasanach*. Aidan had lost another father.

Had her life been changed?

Aye, it had. By now, her father would have found a husband for her, someone to love her, give her children, be a man for her. She was, after all, almost 18. To be the wife of a man who cherished her, a man she cherished in return, and to raise his children had been the only dream she'd allowed herself. 'Twas the only dream a poor Irish girl could hope to see come true—that and perhaps the dream of a full belly.

Her heart ached for the loss of that dream.

She swallowed her sorrow, feeling ashamed. Finn at 26 was of an age to marry as well, but he never complained about it, or the deep loneliness Bríghid knew he felt, as he was now the man of the house. So much depended on him. If Finn could put aside his own dreams, then so could she. Her brothers and Aidan needed her. Who else would cook their meals, darn their socks, heal their sicknesses?

She turned to Aidan. "It's cold out today. Are you sure you won't wear your cap?"

Aidan shook his head, ran his fingers through his unruly red hair.

Bríghid donned her cloak, fastened it with her grandmother's dragon brooch. Taking Aidan's hand, she opened the door and stepped into the cold autumn air.

Ruaidhrí was waiting for them outside by the barn, slapping his arms to warm them. He hadn't had the sense to wear a cap either, his blonde hair tousled by the wind, his cheeks red from the chill. He scowled at her. "So it *was* today you were plannin' on leavin'?"

Her little brother had virtues, but patience was not among them.

Jamie Blakewell reined his stallion to a halt and surveyed the surrounding countryside—or what he could see of it. He'd ridden to the crest of a broad hill. Beneath him, a cold, white mist spread like a blanket across the rolling landscape. Only hilltops and the bare treetops of the forest were clearly visible, though Jamie thought he could make out the shapes of hedgerows and tenant cabins in the distance.

Strangely, something about this country, so foreign to him, reminded him of his home in Virginia. Perhaps it was the open and untamed feel of the land. Despite the patchwork of fields and low stone walls that crisscrossed the countryside—proof that people had worked this soil for centuries—it seemed wild, unspoiled.

He patted Hermes' neck with a gloved hand. The stallion's breath lingered in clouds of white, rising and dissipating in the chill air. Jamie was grateful for the thick warmth of his woolen greatcoat, which kept out both wet and cold. Winter was coming, and fast from the feel of it.

For the first time since he'd come to Ireland, he felt the tension begin to drain from his body. It felt good to be outdoors. He'd spent the past five days arguing with Sheff in the manor that served as Sheff's hunting retreat. The board had been lavish, the wine excellent, the company insufferable.

Although Sheff had welcomed Jamie openly, he was not the man Jamie remembered. Where he'd once been a bit arrogant, he was now pompous and cruel. His skin wore a sickly pallor, and he drank far more than was good for him. There was a sharp edge to Sheff now, a darkness. Jamie had recognized it immediately.

He knew a thing or two about darkness.

The sound of hooves approached from behind, slowed, stopped beside him.

"You call this hunting?" Jamie's tone was light, but his disdain was not entirely feigned.

"It is what gentlemen call hunting." Sheff retrieved a small flask from a pocket inside his greatcoat, pulled out the cork, drank deeply.

"The hounds do the actual hunting, whilst we gentlemen ride along, talk politics and drink, then shoot whatever the dogs drag down. Hand me that, will you?" Jamie accepted the flask and drank. The liquor scorched a path to his stomach, warmed him. "To whom will the trophy belong—us or the hounds?"

"I had forgotten you had a Red Indian for a nurse. I suppose you think it more manly to crawl through the muck on your belly clad in animal hides with a knife between your teeth."

Jamie handed the flask back to Sheff. "I don't know about the knife between the teeth, but the rest of it sounds good."

"You are a savage, Jamie, old boy. Whatever shall I do with you?"

Servants hurried past them on foot and on horseback, barking commands to the hounds, which bayed and strained against their leashes, already hot on the scent.

A ruddy-faced man with broad shoulders rode up to them. "This seems as good a place as any to release them, my lord."

"Very well. Get on with it, Edward."

Sheff's father had passed on only two months past. With his father's last breath, Sheff had become Sheffield Winthrop Tate III, Lord Byerly, an earl with a host of estates and titles that read like a map of Britain. As much as Jamie had known his friend would one day assume his father's noble titles and lands, Jamie was still entertained by the stiff formality that made up Sheff's existence. He was, after all, still Sheff. Jamie had known him since their college years at Oxford, where they'd drunk too much, lost immoderately at cards, and spent innumerable nights between the thighs of lovely courtesans.

It was Sheff who'd taught Jamie the joys of debauchery when Jamie had been nineteen and new to England. While Jamie had already discovered the pleasures of a woman's body, there had been much about life he hadn't known. England had seemed a different world from his tobacco plantation on the banks of the Rappahannock River. Sheff had introduced Jamie to that world, and the two had become friends despite the fact that Sheff was the heir to an earldom and Jamie merely the well-to-do owner of a tobacco plantation.

Six years had passed since they'd completed their studies at university. Jamie had spent those years in Virginia, and Sheff had joined his father in London. Now Jamie had come back to Britain to handle some delicate business on behalf of his brother-in-law, Alec Kenleigh. Alec had stayed behind in Virginia to be with Cassie, Jamie's sister. Cassie was deep in mourning, her grief largely Jamie's fault. She was also with child and nearing her time. Despite the pressing nature of this business, Alec had refused to leave her.

Jamie had used the trip as an excuse to arrange a visit with his old friend. Truth be told, Jamie needed Sheff's support—and his connections. The Colonies were at war. Ever since the French had forced Washington's surrender at Fort Necessity last July, the call from Pennsylvania to Virginia had been "Join or Die."

Jamie had been there, had fought in the hail of French bullets that had turned the hastily built stockade into a hell of blood-soaked mud. While he had escaped with a minor wound where a bullet had bit into his shoulder, a third of their company had died. Sometimes at night, he could still hear their agonized cries, smell the blood and the gunpowder, hear the *crack* of enemy gunfire.

And then there was Nicholas, his nephew and Cassie's and Alec's oldest son.

Some months after his terrible loss at Fort Necessity, George Washington, a fellow Virginian and a friend, had asked Jamie to march northward with him and his party of one hundred thirty as a scout and sharpshooter in hopes that Jamie's knowledge of Indian customs and tongues—backed up by his deadly aim with his French flintlock rifle—would help turn the tide should they encounter any foe. Jamie had agreed, and, despite Cassie's protests, Nicholas, at four-and-twenty an accomplished marksman in his own right, had insisted on coming along.

They'd been encamped near the banks of the Ohio when a war party of Wyandot had attacked under cover of night. Jamie and Nicholas had been discussing the next day's march with George over a bottle of Madeira when they'd been interrupted by the sounds of war cries, shouts, and gunfire. Jamie had stayed with George and caught a stray ball in the arm. Thankfully, George had been unhurt. But Nicholas had fought his way across the camp toward the worst of the fighting. Witnesses had later told Jamie how Nicholas had tried to save two young militiamen from being taken captive by the Wyandot, only to be wounded and taken captive himself.

As soon as Jamie had been fit to leave the camp, he had tracked the Wyandot, stopping neither to sleep nor eat, but he'd been too late. The Wyandot had celebrated their victory by burning their captives alive. Jamie had reached the village in time to see flames lick at three charred shapes that had once been men.

Christ, how Jamie wished it had been he who'd been taken!

Every moment of his life since then had been a living hell. He would never get the reek of burnt human flesh out of his nostrils. He would never forget his sister's anguished cry or the look of anguish in Alec's eyes when they'd learned of their eldest son's fate. He would never forgive himself for failing to bring his nephew home alive.

Jamie had loved Nicholas like a brother.

He had not saved his nephew, but he would do all within his power to save the colonies. While many people still felt the war could be fought and won on land, some prominent colonists—Benjamin Franklin among them—felt sea power would be the key. Control the great rivers and lakes of the north, and Britain could cut off French supply lines. Waging war on the water would also draw French troops away from the frontier, where unprotected British families farmed the land. Alec was ready to provide specially built ships for the endeavor, but so far Parliament seemed more concerned with affairs on the Continent and had little consideration to spare for the Colonies. Jamie had come as an official representative from Virginia to encourage the use of naval vessels and to urge Alec's contacts in Lords and Commons to move toward a declaration of war in the Colonies.

Jamie forced his thoughts away from war, back to the landscape. "The countryside is more fair than I'd imagined from your stories of it."

Sheff gave a noncommittal grunt, adjusted his hat and the powdered wig beneath it. "It would be fairer still were it not full of barbaric Irish. It's a pity Cromwell didn't kill them all. Then again, who would pay my rents if he had?"

Jamie bit back his retort, chose his words carefully. "I've met my share of Irishmen in the colonies. They seem as civilized as Englishmen of their class."

Sheff chuckled. "I knew you'd say something like that."

Edward shouted commands to the servants who restrained the deerhounds, and the dogs were loosed. Amidst a din of yaps and howls, the animals dashed downhill toward the forest.

They'd ridden far from the manor this morning on the trail of servants who'd been tracking a suitable stag all night. Their path had led them to this hilly region with hedgerows and patches of dark forest. Jamie enjoyed the sport of hunting. Even more, he enjoyed what it brought to his table. But growing up in Virginia, he'd learned a very different type of hunting, one that pitted hunter against prey in a contest of skill. To chase an animal down with dogs and dispatch it from horseback hardly seemed worthy of a grown man.

"Jamie, my friend, tonight we shall dine on venison." Sheff smiled and spurred his mount forward with a shout.

Jamie loosed his stallion's reins and urged him on. "Time to show him what you can do, old boy."

The stallion lunged forward and within seconds passed Sheff's mount. Arabian blood flowed through Hermes' veins. He loved nothing more than to run. Jamie felt cool air rush over his face as Hermes raced downhill in pursuit of the dogs. Mist closed in around them, cool and wet against Jamie's skin. The fog was not as dense as it had seemed from above, and he found he could see some distance through the trees. Still, Jamie gave Hermes his head, knowing the horse would better sense unseen obstacles than he.

He felt the stallion's stride shift and instinctively bent low over Hermes' back as the horse leapt over a fallen log. The horse's muscles tensed, and Jamie tightened his grip on the animal's flank as Hermes swerved around a deep thicket of gorse. Jamie felt a smile spread across his face. He loved to ride as much as Hermes loved to run. He'd grown up on horseback, learnt the skill from the age of four. He'd inherited the best stables in Virginia from his father, stables Alec, as Jamie's guardian, had done much to expand. Together, he and Alec spent much time, endless talk, and no small fortune on horseflesh.

And this was why, thought Jamie, as wind whipped through his hair.

From ahead came the sound of splashing water. Jamie thought he could make out the dark shadow of a creek's bank. He felt Hermes' stride shift again and bent low. The horse soared over the water as if on wings.

The sound of hooves approached from behind.

The hooves faltered, stopped.

Jamie grinned.

The air was sharp with the sound of Sheff's curses and splashing as Sheff's mount waded across the stream.

Jamie rode over hedgerows and through islands of forest for what seemed the briefest time, but which might have been ten minutes or more. The stag was seeking shelter, trying to go to ground. Jamie knew it would be allowed no such reprieve. He rode just behind the hounds now, Hermes at a comfortable gallop. The dogs disappeared into a dark growth of forest just ahead, and Jamie ducked to avoid overhanging branches.

Women and children screamed.

Men shouted, cursed.

Hounds growled.

Jamie urged Hermes forward. He broke through the trees into a clearing and reined the stallion to an abrupt stop.

There before him, huddled together in the shelter of an ancient, gnarled oak, stood a group of frightened peasants—men, women and children. Some of the peasant men gestured excitedly toward the south, the direction they said the stag had gone. But most stood as if frozen, a mix of dread and loathing in their eyes. Standing in front, arms spread as if to shelter the rest, stood an old man clad in black.

A Catholic priest.

On a crude table beside him sat a wooden goblet, a basket, and a tiny, wooden coffin.

Some of the hounds had closed in on the little crowd and growled menacingly. The rest meandered through the clearing, noses to the ground, sniffing. Through it all rode Edward, Sheff's man, shouting angrily at people and dogs alike.

Jamie had just enough time to take in the scene when Sheff rode up behind him.

"I was about to tell Edward to call off the dogs," Jamie shouted over the clamor.

Sheff's face was pinched with rage. "Call off the dogs? They're bloody fortunate I don't command the dogs to rip them to pieces! They've interfered with the hunt."

"Not intentionally, I'm sure. It appears our hunt has ridden into them and interrupted a funeral mass."

Sheff glanced coldly at the priest. "So much the worse for them."

That's when Jamie saw her.

Chapter Two

S he stood not far from the priest, clad in a grey, woolen cloak, her arms wrapped protectively around the shoulders of a frightened, red-haired boy. Though her head was partly covered by a hood, a single dark braid as thick as a man's wrist fell out of her cloak and hung nearly to her waist. Her skin was as fair as cream, except for the rosy pink of her cheeks. Her features were those of a porcelain doll, delicate with high cheekbones, her lips full and red as if swollen from a man's kisses. Even from a distance, Jamie could see her eyes were a deep blue. She leaned down and spoke in the child's ear, and Jamie found himself wanting to reassure them both they would come to no harm.

What was her name?

Before he'd realized what he was doing, he had urged Hermes in her direction.

She looked up.

Their gazes collided.

Her eyes burned with contempt.

Stung by the venom in her gaze and the stupidity of his own actions, Jamie stayed the stallion, jerked his attention back to Sheff.

Sheff was shouting directions to Edward and the other servants, who by then had gathered most of the hounds and were leading them to the south side of the clearing in search of the stag's scent. Then he turned to the priest. "You've made a grave mistake, old man." Sheff walked his mount toward the priest, slowly, menacingly. "Not only have you and your *flock* interfered with the hunt, itself a crime, but your presence here is treasonous. Papist priests have long been banished, or hadn't you heard?"

The old man, arms still spread protectively before the frightened crowd, craned his neck to meet Sheff's gaze. His wrinkled face wavered between defiance and dismay. "We ... we meant no harm, my lord. We're only consignin' the spirit of this poor babe to God."

"You needn't fear I will harm these pitiful creatures, old man. They are my tenants and therefore my responsibility."

The priest slowly lowered his arms, a look of wary hope dawning on his face.

"No, it is you alone I hold responsible. Do you know the punishment for treason? I could have you hanged, drawn and quartered."

Stunned, Jamie objected, but his voice was drowned out by cries from the crowd.

"Mercy, Your Lordship! Mercy!"

This seemed to enrage Sheff, who lifted his attention from the priest to the crowd. "You ask me for mercy who should have sent your priest to France long ago had you any concern for him? You dare ask me for anything who plot against England on my lands?"

"These are Uí Naill lands, *Sasanach!*" A young man, fair-haired and strongly built, glared fearlessly up at Sheff out of angry blue eyes.

"*Ná déan, a Rhuaidhrí!*" The cry came from *her*. Her eyes were wide with fear, her gaze darting between Sheff and the young man who'd spoken so foolishly. Face pale, she clutched the young, red-haired boy to her as if to shield him from death.

For a moment, there was silence. The forest seemed to hold its breath.

Sheff stared contemptuously down at the young man who had defied him.

Jamie had seen that tight-lipped look on Sheff's face before and knew Sheff was beyond fury. "Sheff —"

Sheff ignored him. "Percy, bind the old man, and take him to the gaol in Skreen."

Gasps and cries of outrage rose from the crowd.

Jamie felt hatred surge from the Irish, felt the balance of emotion tip from fear to rage. Hermes shifted nervously beneath him.

Edward obviously sensed the change, too, and directed his men to train their hunting muskets on the crowd.

Stunned silence fell over the clearing.

"Sheff, a word with—"

"Have the rest of your men tear down this heretical altar, and take the child to the lawful church for burial in a paupers' grave."

"My baby!" A pretty young woman with a tear-stained face would have rushed forward to claim the coffin had other women not held her back.

"Bring the rapparee to me."

The dark-haired beauty cried out in dismay at these last words, her voice all but drowned out by angry cries and shouting. "He's no rapparee, my lord! He's barely more than a boy!"

The terrified expression on her face tore at Jamie's gut.

"My lord!" Jamie shouted this time. "A word with you—now!"

He'd never called Sheff "my lord" before, not even in jest. His use of the term now startled them both.

Sheff's gaze fixed on Jamie, dark and angry. He turned his mount, and the two rode a short distance away from the crowd.

"This is a baby's funeral, Sheff! Have you gone mad?"

"Jamie, I'm warning you not to interfere." Sheff spoke quietly, but his voice was steel, cold and hard. His brown eyes flashed fury. "You are my friend, but I will brook no challenge to my authority on my lands!"

"You cannot expect me to sit idly by and watch as you terrify and provoke innocent people!"

"Innocent? There's no such thing as an innocent Irishman." Sheff laughed a cruel, hard laugh. "Your breeding is showing, my colonial friend. Don't let your vulgar sensibilities lead you astray. You wouldn't want me for your enemy."

"So you threaten *me* now?" It was Jamie's turn to laugh. "I might be as common as a blade of grass, my noble friend, but I recognize the seeds of an uprising when I see one. Push this crowd one step further, and you'll find out what I mean. How many shots do you think your men will get off at such close quarters before we're overpowered? Have you noticed some of the men have picked up stones?"

Jamie did not truly fear the crowd, but he'd needed some reason to stay Sheff's hand. It was clear Sheff would not be swayed by a call for compassion.

Sheff glared at him, lips pressed together in a grim line, but his eyes flickered nervously to the Irish beyond. "What do you suggest, Colonial?"

"Find some excuse to show leniency—a holiday, a saint's day, your mother's birthday, anything. Release the priest with a warning, ignore the young hothead, and for God's sake return the baby's body to its mother."

Rage flared anew in Sheff's eyes, and for one long moment, his gaze locked with Jamie's in a battle of wills. Then he jerked on the reins and rode back to confront the crowd.

"Damn it!" Jamie swore under his breath. He felt powerless, furious.

Sheff was acting worse than a tyrant. Draw and quarter a priest? Jamie knew the penal laws as well as the next Englishman, but no one actually executed priests unless they were caught fomenting insurrection—or so he'd thought.

But Sheff was an earl and lord of these lands, and as such his orders were beyond contestation. Jamie would have to find a way to stop him, their friendship be damned. He turned Hermes' head back toward the crowd, urged the stallion forward at a walk.

The dark-haired woman now stood a short distance from Percy's men. Her head was bowed as if in sorrow, and Jamie imagined she was crying. She still held the red-haired boy in her arms, his freckled face pale and frightened. The men had seized the hothead and were binding his wrists with a length of rope, taunting him. He made no effort to resist, though Jamie could see he was enraged.

Sheff again spoke to the crowd. "My ... friend has just reminded me that today is my departed mother's birthday. In remembrance of her, I shall answer your pleas for mercy and grant you a boon."

*B*ríghid held tightly to Aidan's chilly hand and hurried down the rutted road behind Ruaidhrí. She couldn't wait until they were safely home again and sitting in front of a warm fire with Finn.

Ruaidhrí was in a rage, but all she could feel was overwhelming relief. When the *iarla* had told them he'd return Muirín's poor babe to her and release Ruaidhrí with no more than a warning, provided Father Padraíg agreed to leave his lands under escort, she'd thanked the Blessed Virgin and any saint who'd been listening. It was almost too good to be true, given the young *iarla's* liking for cruelty. He was worse than his father.

She knew she'd come horribly close to losing her brother. She was so relieved he was safe she didn't know whether to hug the life out of him or slap him soundly. He'd let his tongue get the best of him again and had almost paid the price. The *iarla Sasanach* would surely have had him beaten—perhaps even hanged—had the other *Sasanach* not intervened. She had watched as the strange, fair-haired Englishman had argued with the *iarla*, though she hadn't been able to hear their words. Both men had been angry.

She didn't want to think about the other *Sasanach* lord, the one with the fine, grey horse. She'd been taken aback when she'd looked up to find him staring at her with his green eyes. Her breath had stopped. His gaze had seemed to pierce her, to slide beneath her skin. No man had ever looked at her that way before. He sat tall and proud on a beautiful grey stallion, dressed in his fine, warm clothes. But he was different from the other lords she'd seen. He wore no hat, no silly wig, his fair hair ruffled from his riding. And his face was bronzed like that of a man who worked the fields or spent his life at sea. She'd found herself staring back at him, and she'd been furious with herself.

Why had he stayed the *iarla's* hand? She didn't believe the story the *iarla* had given them in his attempt to save face. He had been arguing with the other Englishman, not talking about his dead mother's birthday.

"Ruaidhrí, slow down!" She glanced down at Aidan, who was fair running beside her. "We can't keep up."

Ruaidhrí stopped, glanced back, then froze, his eyes wide. "Run! Into the trees!"

Bríghid whirled about, saw riders in the distance. They were the *iarla's* men, and they were riding hard up the ribbon of road. A thin stand of trees ran along the north side of the road, but it was a good fifty paces away up a steep hill.

Ruaidhrí scooped Aidan up and dashed uphill toward the dark line of forest.

Bríghid lifted her skirts and ran after him as fast as she could. She could hear the approaching thunder of hooves.

Had the riders seen them? And if they had been seen, would it matter? Just because these men worked for the *iarla* didn't mean they were after Ruaidhrí. The *iarla* had set him free. But Bríghid knew better than to trust English promises.

Her heart hammered in her breast. Harder she ran until trees surrounded her.

Ruaidhrí had hidden behind a low hedge of gorse, Aidan in his arms.

Bríghid fell flat on the cold earth beside them, tucked her red skirts in.

Aidan's eyes were round with terror. Bríghid stroked his cheek. The boy laid his head trustingly on Ruaidhrí's shoulder. Their heavy breathing mingled, slowed.

The hooves drew near.

She watched as Ruaidhrí held a finger to his lips, his signal to Aidan not to make a sound. Her brother's gaze met hers, and she saw the fury that boiled inside him—and the fear he tried valiantly to hide. She wrapped her fingers around his and squeezed, feigning a calm she did not feel. He might be on the verge of manhood, but he was still her little brother.

A group of four *Sasanach* rode into view on the road below. They slowed their mounts until they rode at a walk. The man in the lead reined his horse to a stop.

"They've disappeared," he shouted back to the other men. "I swear I saw them walking along this stretch."

"I saw them, too."

Bríghid watched, her heart in her throat, as the men scanned the horizon, then turned their eyes toward the trees.

One of the men laughed, a low hissing sound. "I think it's time for another hunt. We'll flush them out like bloody pheasants."

The four riders turned their horses off the road and started slowly up the hill. The man in the lead drew his pistol, cocked it.

Panic pulsed in her veins. There was no way they could avoid being discovered. The gorse grew low to the ground and sheltered them only on one side. As soon as the riders reached the trees, the three of them would be sitting targets.

Her gaze darted to Ruaidhrí's, and her fear grew stronger. She could tell he was plotting something. His hand slipped to the waistline of his breeches and grasped the hilt of a dagger. She swallowed hard. She knew what she must do.

Ruaidhrí had just closed his fingers around the hilt of his dagger, when, to his horror, Bríghid spoke—in *Béarla*, in English.

"Please. Don't shoot." Her voice quavered. Slowly, she stood.

"Drochrath air!" Ruaidhrí cursed under his breath, released the dagger.

What was she doing? Had she gone daft?

The *Sasanach* were startled, but only for a moment.

"Oh, we would never shoot a lady," said one.

"Not one as pretty as you," said another.

The men laughed.

Ruaidhrí heard the lust in the men's voices, slowly stood. It was him they wanted. If they got him, they'd leave his sister alone.

Aidan leapt up, wrapped his arms around Brighid's waist.

"What did I say? Flushed out like pheasants."

Cruel laughter filled the air.

Then Brighid spoke, the fear in her voice adding to Ruaidhrí's anger. "Why are you followin' us? The *iarla* showed mercy and released my brother."

The man who seemed to be the leader of the group rode over to Brighid, began to dismount. "He didn't send us to fetch your brother, poppet."

The realization hit Ruaidhrí like a blow to the stomach. They were here for Brighid.

This could not be happening.

Not again.

In a flash, the dagger was in his hand. He pulled Brighid behind him, barked at Aidan to lie flat on the ground. "You'll not be takin' her."

For a moment there was silence. Then he heard the metallic clicks of three more pistols being cocked. He looked about. All were aimed at him.

"The rapparee thinks he's a cat with nine lives." The leader smiled, revealing a row of rotted teeth. "You've already used up one today, boy. Are you sure you want to use another?"

Rage. Desperation. Helplessness. Raw emotion surged through Ruaidhrí until he thought he would explode. He was outnumbered. They had pistols.

But Brighid was his sister. He loved her. He could not bear to think of what they would do to her. "You can't be takin' her!"

The nearest man lifted his pistol, aimed it at Ruaidhrí's chest.

"No!" Brighid broke free from Ruaidhrí's protective grasp, shielded him with her body. She turned to face Ruaidhrí, cupped his cheek in her palm. Her gaze met his, her eyes a mirror for the turmoil within him. Her face was pale. *"Staon, a Ruaidhrí." Now is not the time.*

She peeled the knife from his fingers and dropped it on the ground, then turned to face the *Sasanach.*

The *Sasanach* leader wasted no time. He reached out, pulled her to him.

"Bríghid!" Aidan cried out, ran forward, and would have been kicked by the *Sasanach's* cruel boot had Ruaidhrí not pulled him back.

The child's desperate tears tore at Ruaidhrí's gut. They reminded him of another time years ago, another act of English cruelty. "Tell the whoreson you call a lord he's dead if he touches her! May God curse all English!"

"No one's going to harm a hair on her pretty head." The *Sasanach* who had Bríghid mounted his horse, pulled her roughly into the saddle in front of him. "The lord simply wishes to have a word with her."

Ruaidhrí didn't believe that for a minute.

"Farewell. May God bless and keep you all." Bríghid's gaze met his once more before the *Sasanach* spurred his horse down the hill, taking her with him. The sadness in her eyes tore at his heart. And Ruaidhrí knew.

She didn't expect to see him again.

"*Coinneaoidh mé leat, a Bhríghid!*" He shouted, his words following the horses up the winding road. *I will come for you. If it's the last thing I do.*

Chapter Three

*B*ríghid clasped the horse's mane and held on tight. She would not cry. She would not. She tried to breathe deeply to calm herself, but couldn't seem to fill her lungs.

Sweet Mary, what was she to do?

They rode forever—across the stream, over countless hills and past the sacred hawthorn grove that had always marked the edge of her world to the *iarla*'s manor. She was so stiff and sore when they arrived she hadn't the strength to dismount without help. The despicable man whose groping hands she fought off for the length of their journey took advantage of the situation to fondle her breasts.

"Just give good Edward here a little feel, poppet. That's nice."

His touch and the lecherous grin on his face left her feeling sick.

She was taken to a servant's chamber upstairs where a bath was waiting and knew from that moment that the *iarla* wanted far more than a word. The feeling of sickness in her belly grew, and she felt she could not breathe. A young servant girl, a Dubliner by the sound of her speech, was sent in to help her bathe and dress in fancy clothes that lay on the bed, but Bríghid refused to cooperate. When the servant tried to undress her, Bríghid slapped her and cursed her in Gaelic. The girl's wide eyes as she fled the room proved she still understood her mother tongue.

Then the *iarla* himself arrived, the servant girl behind him. He was tall and thin with features that reminded Bríghid of a Roman, or a rat— small, brown eyes, a long, thin nose and high, harsh cheekbones. He stank of drink and something she thought must be men's perfume. Without his wig, he was all but bald. What little hair he had was clipped short and mousy brown. She forced herself to meet his gaze, though the lust in his eyes repulsed her.

"You are surpassing fair." His cold fingers traced the outline of her cheek. "What is your name?"

"Bríghid Ní Maelsechnaill." She spoke her name as clearly and proudly as she could. It was an ancient name, a noble name. Nothing this outsider did could besmirch it.

He laughed. "That's certainly a mouthful."

"Brigid, my lord." The servant girl gave Bríghid a look of bitter triumph, a pink palm print still on her cheek.

Bríghid bit back the curse that leapt to mind at hearing her name twisted into loathsome English. Now was not the time.

"Thank you, Alice." The *iarla* smiled to the servant girl, but his hand dropped to caress Bríghid's shoulder. "My friend is quite taken with you, Brigid. I saw how he looked at you this morning."

Whatever Bríghid expected him to say, it was not this.

"I can see you remember." The *iarla* smiled. "It was at my friend's request I spared your young rapparee. What is he to you, your lover?"

Bríghid refused to answer the question directly. The less this *Sasanach* pig knew about her family the better. "I am a maid." She meant to sound unafraid, but her words were unsteady.

"Then your brother, or perhaps your cousin?" He waited for her reply. "Well, no matter. Thanks to your beauty, your rapparee is safe tonight. Do as you're told, and he'll stay safe."

Then Bríghid understood.

She was to buy her brother's continued freedom with her virginity.

"I expect you to show my friend just how grateful you are. Your willingness is everything." He tucked a finger under her chin. "Do you understand?"

Bríghid choked back tears, looked him in the eye, held her tongue.

*T*wo hours later, Bríghid sat before the fireplace in a long hallway awaiting the *iarla's* command. She wore a gown that a whore might have found immodest, her hair twisted atop her head. A crackling fire had been lit, along with a few candles on the mantelpiece, but neither managed to chase away the shadows that hovered in the corners. Empty chairs lined the walls of the hall, which was so large it could devour the cabin Bríghid called home with room to spare. Carpets the color of blood and decorated with exotic flowers stretched across the wooden floor.

In the next room, the *iarla Sasanach* and the man she was to be given to were eating their supper. Servants bustled in and out of the large, oaken doors carrying platters of meats, tureens of soup, bottles of wine, loaves of bread. No one spared a glance for her.

She was tempted to run, but where could she go? She wasn't sure how to find the door, and surely someone would see her. Even if she did make it outside and into the forest, she would freeze without her cloak. She wasn't even sure which direction would take her home again. And then there was Ruaidhrí. The *iarla* had made it clear that her little brother was safe so long as she did as she was told. She had no choice but to bear whatever horror this night thrust upon her—and to survive.

Never had she felt so helpless, so alone.

Angry shouts came from the room beyond. She couldn't make out most of what was said. Something about the French and war and ships. A servant hurried from the room struggling to balance two trays. When one threatened to topple onto the floor, he placed it on a nearby chair, rushed off to the kitchen with the other.

On the tray sat a knife.

Brighid's heart beat faster. The tray was a good twenty paces away. If anyone caught her, she'd surely be punished. What good would a knife do her anyway? Did she think she could get away with killing either the *iarla* or his friend? She'd be hanged and her family made to suffer. Besides, could she really take a life?

Then she thought of the man who'd fondled her breast, remembered the sickening feel of his hand on her body, the leer on his face. *Aye.* Without thinking further, she stood, walked as swiftly and silently as she could across the room. The knife lay on the tray, small and silver. She hesitated, took it. She had just taken her seat again and was smoothing her skirts when the servant returned. Without seeming to notice the missing implement, now tucked into the waistline of her petticoats, the servant hoisted the tray and raced back toward the kitchens.

She tugged at the silky cloth of the blue gown they'd made her wear, tried to pull it up over the bared tops of her breasts, which had been shaped into deceivingly large mounds by the corset. The white lace bodice did nothing to conceal her nipples. Her shoulders were all but bare, and the roll of cloth beneath the skirts made her hips and bottom seem larger—and her waist smaller—than they really were. She felt naked.

Fears she'd tried to quell uncoiled one after another like snakes in her belly. Would it hurt? Would he keep her for more than one night?

Would he plant an English bastard in her belly? Would the good people of Skreen parish accept her when she returned, or would she be forever shamed? With Father Padraíg gone, who would hear her confession and absolve her of so great a dishonor? Would she ever find the husband she so desperately wanted, a man who could love her despite her shame?

Her fingers instinctively reached for her throat, but they'd taken her cross, the little iron cross of St. Bríghid, after whom she was named. She had worn it around her neck suspended on a leather thong since she was a child, and it had always made her feel protected. Now it was gone, and her grandmother's brooch with it. Shaped like a twisting dragon with open jaws and garnet eyes that gleamed red, the brooch was the most precious thing she owned. It had passed for generations from mother to daughter, staying within the Maelsechnaill female line. Now Bríghid had lost it.

"*Sé do bheath' a Mhuire, atá lán de ghrásta, tá an Tiarna leat ...*" The prayer spilled from her lips of its own accord. *Hail Mary, full of grace, the Lord is with Thee...*

Light poured into the hallway, and a servant motioned for Bríghid to come.

"No!" The word was a whisper, a plea. Bríghid stood on trembling legs and forced herself to take a step toward the doorway. *For Ruaidhrí.* Another step. *For Finn.* And another. *For poor little Aidan.*

Her fingers rose to her waist, felt the hardness of the knife. She'd been foolish to take it. She'd never be able to use it.

Just in case.

In the doorway, her steps faltered.

He stood on the far side of an enormous, dark table, staring at her just like before. Again Bríghid found she could not breathe. His gaze met hers and held it. His green eyes, cold and hard, seemed to see inside her.

Bríghid instinctively lifted her arms to shield her breasts, looked away.

"This is Brigid. She's a bit shy, Jamie, but I've no doubt you can cure her of that affliction. The ladies at Turlington's always had good things to say about your abilities." The *iarla* rose from his chair and strode toward her. His hands grasped her shoulders, and he forced her further into the room. "When she heard how you'd intervened on the young rapparee's behalf, she wanted to thank you personally. Isn't that so, Brigid, my dear?"

Bríghid tried to speak, could not.

The man the *iarla* had called Jamie was still looking at her, a brandy snifter in his hand. He drained his glass, put it down, his gaze never leaving her.

The *iarla* fingered the ribbons of her bodice. "You always did have an eye for the most beautiful women. She's yours, if you want her."

"A gift?" The man's eyebrows rose, his gaze shifting at last to the *iarla*.

"Consider her a renewed pledge of friendship. I would set things aright between us. You know as well as I things have been strained since you arrived. We scarcely agree on anything it seems. I want things to be the way they were years ago."

"I see. How … thoughtful."

"I must say, if you don't want her, I certainly do." The *iarla* pulled slowly on the ribbons of her bodice until they came undone and the lace parted. "What do you say we unwrap your pretty package now and share what delights she has to offer?"

Bríghid felt the heat of both men's gazes on her bared breasts. She heard herself whimper, stifled the sound. They were going to rape her together right here. Now. In this room.

The man with the green eyes rounded the table so quickly she gasped. Before she could take a step backwards, he stood before her and began to remove his frock.

Icy dread flowed through her veins.

The *iarla* reached for the fall of his breeches, began to free himself. "You can take her maidenhead, of course. I did offer her to you."

Bríghid felt her legs begin to shake. There was a ringing in her ears. This could not be happening.

"Sorry, Sheff, old friend." The man draped his frock over her shoulders, covered her nakedness. "I prefer to have my sport in private nowadays."

The *iarla* froze in the midst of unbuttoning his breeches and gave a disappointed groan. "Come now! She's far too fair a flower to be plucked by only one man, and my cock is rock hard!"

Bríghid shuddered at the vileness of his words, tried not to hear them.

The fair-haired lord placed his hands around her waist and propelled her out the door. "Be that as it may, I'm of no mind to share her tonight. She's been in my thoughts all day, and I intend to savor her."

Strong hands guided her down the long hallway to a staircase on the other side. The man was very tall and walked quickly, and Bríghid was forced to hurry beside him, taking two strides for every one of his.

The *iarla Sasanach* followed. "You are a cruel man, Jamie. I suppose I shall have to wait until you've gone back to England for my taste of her?"

The other lord laughed. "That depends. If she's as fair as she seems, I shall find it hard to part with her."

They talked about her as if she were nothing, a possession to be used as they saw fit, with no wishes, no life of her own, her body a toy. Her rage—and her dread—grew. Would she be used, then traded from one to the other? Would she be spirited to England never to see her family again?

"So now you threaten to steal her from my service?" The *iarla* sounded both indignant and amused.

"You did say she was a gift, did you not?"

"Aye, but I didn't mean for you to take her from under my roof."

They climbed two flights of stairs to another long hallway, this one lined with doors. The man stopped in front of one of the doors and opened it. Light from several candelabras filled the room. Inside stood an enormous canopied bed with thick, carved posts that jutted toward the ceiling.

Bríghid's stomach twisted in a painful knot. She took an involuntary step backward, collided with the hard body of the Englishman behind her.

I will not cry.

"Good night, Sheff." The man forced her inside, turned to the *iarla*. "Thank you for the lovely dinner—and the delightful gift."

He started to close the door, but the *iarla* stopped him with the squared tip of his black leather shoe.

"Friends then?"

"Friends." With a smile, the man closed the door.

Bríghid was alone with him.

For a moment, he stood, arm around her waist, head cocked as if to listen. "Damn!" He swore under his breath and left her side to blow out the candles.

The room fell into shadow. A log settled in the fireplace, sent up sparks.

Bríghid started at the sound, clutched the frock tighter around her.

"I won't hurt you, Brigid." His features were lit by light from the fire as he came to her. Long lashes framed his eyes. His skin was bronzed, his cheekbones high, his chin strong. His honey-colored hair had been gathered in a ribbon at the nape of his neck. It might have given him a boyish look were he not so tall and his shoulders so broad.

"Th-that's not my name." She fought to still her trembling.

He pried the cloth of his frock from her fingers, slipped it from her shoulders. His gaze fixed upon her. "Then what is your name?"

She shielded her breasts, tried to lift her chin. "Bríghid. Bríghid Ní Maelsechnaill."

To Bríghid's surprise, he carefully repeated what she'd said, though his tongue stumbled a bit over her ancestral name. "My name is Jamie Blakewell, Bríghid. And I won't hurt you."

"So you say."

"By the end of this night, you will know I mean what I say." His warm hands settled on her arms and slid up to cup her shoulders. He drew her to him, enfolded her in his embrace, forced her stiff, resisting body to mold to his.

She did not want this and would have turned her head away were it not for the strong hand on the back of her neck. He was going to rape her, rob her of her virtue, steal from her the only gift she could ever give a man, the gift she had saved for her husband. A whimper of dread escaped her, as he lowered his lips to hers.

His lips brushed softly over hers once, twice, three times, then slanted to take hers in a gentle kiss. She'd never been kissed before, not really. She had expected to feel disgust, loathing, revulsion. Instead, she felt out of breath, warm. His mouth was a brand, hot and persistent. His lips coaxed and caressed hers, sent shivers down her spine. He smelled of fresh air, tasted slightly of brandy. When his lips parted hers and his tongue stroked inside her mouth, the shock of it sent her senses reeling.

Alarmed by her body's response, Bríghid balled her hands into fists and pushed against his chest. But he was a man, full-grown and strong, and she knew she would not be able to resist him.

He held her fast, his body hard and hot against hers. His kisses captured her cries of protest, as his hands sought the fastenings of her gown. "I know you're afraid. I know you don't want to share my bed."

The words were whispered against her cheek so softly she wondered if he'd really spoken. Why had he told her this? Did he want her to know he had no qualms about taking an unwilling woman? Hatred surged from the pit of her stomach. "I'm not afraid, *Sasanach*."

But she was.

He pulled the gown down over her shoulders. It slid to the floor, puddled at her feet.

She stood now, breasts bare, dressed only in her corset, petty coats and chemise. In her fear, she struck at him—hard. "No!"

Neither the blow nor her plea had any effect. He captured her wrists in one hand, pinned them against his chest.

She struggled to pull away, but found herself hauled up tightly against him.

His lips brushed over hers, then began to taste her cheeks, her hair. "You smell like roses." His voice was thick, husky. Then it again dropped to a whisper. "I'm not going to force myself on you, Bríghid, but you must play along. I fear he is watching."

Chapter Four

Jamie felt her stiffen, saw her gaze dart to the corners of the room. "Wh-where –?"

He held her still, brushed her lips with his, whispered. "Shh, love. Say nothing. Trust me."

Fury flashed into her eyes. "Trust you –?" She tried to pull away.

"I warn you not to fight me." This he said aloud. "You cannot win, and I've no wish to use my strength against you."

She stilled.

Jamie could see the confusion and fear in her eyes and felt an unexpected stab of tenderness. It had been years since he'd felt anything for a woman. He cursed Sheff for putting him—for putting *her*—in this position. Then he cursed himself. It was his unexpected and unfathomable reaction to her that had drawn Sheff's attention to her in the first place. He bore at least some responsibility for her safety.

He turned her around, began to unlace her corset. Bending down, he kissed the tender flesh of her nape and spoke for her ears alone. "These walls are riddled with holes. I will do all I can to help you escape, but you must play along. I am not your enemy."

The corset fell to the carpet.

She quickly covered her breasts with the cloth of her chemise. "You are English." Her voice was barely a whisper. "Why would you help me?"

Jamie turned her to face him again, pulled her against him so he could speak to her without being overheard. She was a little thing, barely coming to his shoulders. How old was she? Fifteen? Sixteen perhaps?

Her skin was creamy and youthful, but her full breasts and the swell of her hips spoke of ripe womanhood.

He traced the delicate shell of her ear with his tongue. "I have never taken a woman against her will, and I don't mean to start with you."

He felt a tremor pass through her, felt the heat within him rise in response.

This was not going to be easy.

His gut told him Sheff was watching from the room next door. Jamie thought he'd heard the door to the room, where no one was staying, open and close just after he'd pushed Sheff out. He remembered well enough the stories he'd heard of Sheff's father. The elder Lord Byerly had watched his guests and servants disrobe, bathe, and tup through small openings in the walls and had been sexually gratified. He'd watched his wife and servants give birth and had enjoyed that, too. He'd eventually shared his secret with his eldest son, who had told Jamie, as if spying upon the private moments of others were some grand lark.

Jamie hadn't found it funny. And he hadn't forgotten.

Somehow he had to convince Sheff his gift was being well used so that Sheff would seek his own sport elsewhere. Then he had to spirit Bríghid away from here. She was not safe. Jamie knew as soon as he was gone, Sheff would do whatever he chose with her.

Jamie couldn't let that happen.

For now, however, he was a player on a stage. He needed to remember his lines.

"That's better." He spoke aloud for the benefit of his audience. "I will try to give you pleasure if you let me."

"'Tis only shame you'll bring me." Her voice quavered.

"You're sure of that, are you?" He drew her earlobe into his mouth, nibbled the exposed flesh of her neck.

He felt her quick intake of breath and knew she was not sure.

But he felt no sense of triumph, only fury at the circumstances. When Sheff had said he had a special gift for Jamie, Jamie thought perhaps Sheff was giving him a pup from one of his prized bitches or a fantastically expensive bottle of cognac. Then the servants had opened the door, and she'd walked forward out of the dim hallway, a look of terror on her young, pale face.

At once, Jamie had been struck by two overpowering emotions.

The first was rage as hot as any fire in hell. He'd never imagined Sheff could treat an innocent maid like a whore, like chattel to be given away against her will. Sheff was no better than a colonial slave owner who abused the women under his power. Jamie had wanted to slam his fist into Sheff's arrogant face, but he'd realized almost immediately he'd have to claim her if he hoped to spare her endless misery in Sheff's bed.

The second emotion was lust, as primal as the ocean tide. Dressed in a gown of light blue silk, the dusky rose of her nipples visible behind the lace of her bodice, she was the most desirable woman Jamie had ever seen. He'd wanted her then.

He wanted her now.

He set her from him, removed his stock, and began to unbutton his waistcoat.

She clutched her chemise to her breasts, looked at the floor, stepped away from him.

"You are beautiful, Bríghid. But I'm sure you've heard that before." He tossed his waistcoat carelessly onto a nearby chair, bent to loosen the buckles at his knees. Why he should waste time on such words was beyond him—he wasn't really making love to her, after all. Then again, he'd only spoken the truth.

"Father Padraíg says beauty is a curse for Irish women." There was fear in her voice, but her words were lilting, her accent enticing.

Jamie removed his shoes and stockings, tossed them aside. "Then you are likely the most cursed woman I've ever seen."

Her head snapped up. There was anger in her eyes, behind it desperation. "'Tis no laughing matter, my lord. I am here against my will, a prisoner."

"I'm not laughing." Jamie reached for the fall of his breeches, began to unbutton them. "And I'm no lord."

She looked at him curiously for a moment before her gaze fell to what his hands were doing. She gasped, looked away.

Jamie pulled his breeches down over his thighs. They joined his waistcoat on the chair. Then he realized the men in her life were likely unable to afford linen for drawers. She probably thought he was standing before her bare from the waist down.

He removed his shirt, tossed it aside. "Bríghid, look at me."

She shook her head.

He ran the back of his hand down her cheek, tucked a finger beneath her chin, forced her to meet his gaze. "You're trembling again."

"I ... I cannot help it. I've ne'er been so near a man. I want to go home."

Her fear, her unhappiness tore at him. "How old are you, love?"

"Almost eighteen."

"In all your years, has no man ever kissed you?" His fingers sought the pins that held her hair and began to remove them one by one.

She shivered. "No."

"Has no man even tried?"

"A few have tried."

Her hair fell in a glorious mass to her hips, thick, dark and soft as silk. The warm scent of roses filled the air. The feminine sweetness of it was torture.

"And did you make them suffer?" He ran his fingers through her tresses.

Her eyes closed. "M-my brothers did."

"I see." He pulled her close against him. "And what would your brothers do to a man who kissed you like this?"

He kissed her again, deeply.

This time she melted against him, her palms flat against his chest. A little moan escaped her throat, her breath warm and sweet. Her lips yielded to his, as his tongue sought union with hers. She was soft and pleasing and utterly innocent.

Jamie felt himself grow hard, his body more than ready to mate with hers. He was getting lost in her. He was forgetting. This was an act. It wasn't real. He couldn't let it be real, for her sake. She did not want this.

He pulled his mouth from hers, looked down at her face. Her eyes were closed, her lips swollen, wet. Her cheeks were flushed. Then her lashes fluttered open, and she glared at him.

"You lied! You are trying to seduce me!" She trembled, her breathing rapid.

He lowered his voice. "If that were my plan, I would already have succeeded."

He reached down to untie the lacings of her petticoats. His hand touched something sharp and hard. She gasped, reached for the hidden object, but he was quicker.

He caught her wrist with one hand, pulled the knife from the waistband of her skirts with the other, whispered. "Was this intended for me?"

Her petticoats slipped to the floor with a rustle.

She looked up at him, met his gaze, whispered. "If that were my plan, I would already have succeeded."

Her words showed spirit, and Jamie almost laughed. But he could see the terror in her eyes. He raised a hand to brush the hair from her face.

She shrank from him.

He spoke aloud again. "I'm not going to strike you, Bríghid." He kissed her, his lips just brushing hers. "I'm going to do everything I can to keep from hurting you."

He reached over and pulled down the coverlet on the bed. He let the knife fall into the folds of cloth, where it lay hidden. It would come in handy later.

He turned back to her, lifted her into his arms, lay her on the plush feather mattress.

She lay shivering, her dark hair draped in waves of ebony across the pillows. Her slender legs, held fast together, were hidden beneath gossamer silk stockings tied into place with blue ribbons. The thin chemise she wore could not fully conceal the dark thatch of curls at the apex of her thighs or the dusky tips of her breasts.

He knelt by the bed, slipped the soft leather slippers from her feet, trying to ignore the persistent throb in his groin. To gaze upon her lovely body, to feel her ready softness, to smell her skin, all without being able to take her, was torture—a pleasurable sort of torture, but torture nonetheless.

But he knew that she suffered truly, and suffered far more.

He lifted one slender leg, reached for its ribbon.

She cried out, pulled the cloth of her chemise down over her thighs.

"You've a beautiful body, Bríghid. There's nothing of which to be ashamed." He rolled the silk down her smooth thigh, over her shapely calf, down her ankle, and slipped it off her dainty foot. Then he lifted the other leg.

"M-must you really undress me like this?"

Jamie chuckled for the benefit of his audience, but he understood her question.

If this were just pretend, why couldn't he just get it over with? Why take it this far?

There was no script, so he improvised. "I suppose I could just toss you on your belly, lift your gown and get on with it. But it's better this way, isn't it?"

This time, his lips followed his hands as he slowly slipped off the stocking. He tasted her creamy thigh, nibbled the sensitive skin above her knee, sampled the white smoothness of her calf, kissed the daintiness of her ankle, licked the delicate arch of her foot. He felt her body tense, heard her breath catch in her throat.

She trembled anew, and he knew it was not from fear alone.

Why *had* he taken things this far? He could have pretended to take her at any time. He could have left her fully clothed and pretended to rut between her thighs without prelude, yet he had insisted on this mockery of seduction. Was he taking advantage of her plight, enjoying her while pretending to play the hero? What good was it to save her virtue if he left her feeling sullied?

He dismissed his doubts. While he couldn't deny there was pleasure in this for him, it was also more than a little awkward. He had no more chosen to be in this situation than she. If he opted to feign seduction it was to spare her the memory of something rougher and more vulgar. From her untrained responses, he knew she had experienced nothing of the passion between men and women. Whatever he did tonight would stay with her and color her feelings about men for years to come, perhaps for life.

It would be so different if he were truly making love to her—slower, more tender, much more ardent, more thorough. He would touch and taste every part of her until she opened to him like a rosebud opens for the sun. He would make her ache for him, make her think of nothing but having him inside her. He would take her, gently and slowly at first, until she cried out for release. Then he would thrust into her hard and fast, give her what she wanted, take what he needed. But she had no way of knowing that. She would never know. To her, he would likely never be more than a hated Englishman who had shamed her.

But Sheff was watching. Jamie was certain. And the only way he could keep her safe was to convince Sheff he had claimed her fully as his own. If it offended her maidenly sensibilities, so be it.

He stood, untied his drawers, let them fall.

Bríghid gasped, closed her eyes, turned her head away. She felt the mattress yield to his weight, felt the heat of his body as he lay next to her and pulled the covers over them. She tried to cease her trembling, could not.

What was wrong with her? She wanted to scream. She wanted to hit him. She wanted him to kiss her again. Her skin tingled where his mouth had touched her. Her lips ached, and her belly felt as if a fire were blazing deep inside her. If only she could close herself off. If only she could stop feeling altogether.

The mattress rocked, and she felt his weight settle on either side of her and knew he was above her now. She squeezed her eyes shut. But when he began to lift her chemise, her eyes flew open. "No!"

He spoke aloud. "I've respected your maidenly shyness long enough, love."

"Please, don't!"

The weight of his body held her down as he slipped the soft cloth up and over her head, tossing the garment aside. He held himself above her, like prey poised to strike. "Most women say it hurts the first time. I will do what I can to spare you, but it depends in part on you. Don't struggle."

At his words, raw panic seized her. What if he had been making sport of her just to pacify her? What if he had been lying all along and intended truly to bed her? She struck at him, tried to twist away, pushed against the hard muscles of his chest.

"Don't fight me, Bríghid." His voice was sharp this time. He captured her wrists in one hand, pinned her arms above her head, held her motionless.

She felt overpowered by his size, his male strength, overwhelmed by his presence. She was helpless, trapped.

His lips found hers again, ravished her mouth, leaving her unable to breathe or think. His tongue explored her, twined with her own. The hard wall of his chest brushed her nipples — a new sensation, both disturbing and seductive. She felt her nipples tighten, begin to ache. Then she knew.

Some part of her desired him. Him. Her enemy. A hated *Sasanach*. The man whose attention had made the *iarla* notice her.

The man who'd saved Ruaidhrí.

His knee nudged hers apart and his weight settled between her thighs. He reached down between her legs with his free hand.

She froze, heart pounding. But instead of his using his hand to guide himself into her, she felt cloth settle against her. Somehow he'd maneuvered a bundle of blanket between her thighs.

He'd been telling the truth.

She gaped at him in astonishment.

His pupils were wide, his eyes dark with some emotion she didn't understand. "I want you." His lips traced a line along her throat. Then he whispered for her ears alone, "Cry out. Now."

She felt his weight shift, felt his body thrust against the cushion of blanket that separated them. Startled by the intimacy of his motions, she shrieked.

He moaned, rained kisses across her cheeks. "Shh, love. The pain will pass."

Instead of pain, Bríghid felt sweet relief wash through her. He'd been telling the truth. He *wasn't* going to rape her. He *was* trying to help her escape.

"You feel so good." He moaned, began to move between her thighs in a rhythm that needed no explanation.

Relief turned to mortification. She felt her face burn with embarrassment. She squeezed her eyes shut, would have turned her face away had his lips not reclaimed hers.

He kissed her forcefully. His tongue probed her mouth, searched for her secrets. She succumbed to his invasion, discovered she was kissing him back. Through a haze, she struggled to regain control of her emotions.

What magic did he use to make her feel this way? What was wrong with her that any part of her responded to this man? Though he had spared her the worst, he was touching her in ways no man should. He was a stranger. He was a *Sasanach*.

Just then, he arched his back, called her name, groaned. Then he was still.

For a moment there was no sound but their mingled breathing.

"Oh, Bríghid." He kissed her lips lightly, brushed the hair from her face. "I don't think I shall ever let you go."

She could not meet his gaze. The fire burned inside her still, and she felt ashamed and furious—ashamed of her body's response, furious that he had forced so much upon her. Hadn't he done everything a man could do to a woman but take her virginity? He'd made her feel things she shouldn't. His touch was now a mark upon her soul, for surely what she'd felt had been sinful and wrong, even though she hadn't meant to feel it.

He rolled off her, pulled her into the crook of his arm, stroked her hair. "Sleep, love."

She lay stiffly beside him, her head resting on his chest. She would never be able to sleep like this—naked and so close to him she could hear his heart beating. Something tickled her cheek, and she found her gaze inadvertently drawn to his body. Crisp gold curls were sprinkled lightly across the planes of his chest, which rose and fell slowly with each breath. His nipples were flat and sandy-brown, his skin smooth and kissed by the sun.

Bríghid closed her eyes. She'd seen men's bare chests before. Why did the sight of this one make her blood grow warm?

And that other part of him. She'd gotten only a glimpse. It was the first time she'd seen a fully naked male, or at least a naked male over the age of five. There were some clear differences—first and foremost size. His sex had stood huge and rigid against his belly. The sight of him had left her ...

She felt his body tense. Then she heard. The door to the next room squeaked on its hinges, closed almost silently.

From the hallway came the sound of approaching footsteps.

Chapter Five

*B*ríghid felt her heart lurch. She would have sat bolt upright had he not held her tightly against him.

He pressed a finger to her lips. "Shh."

The footsteps drew near, stopped outside the bedroom door.

Her breath froze in her chest.

The silence pressed against her. Seconds passed with agonizing slowness.

Then footsteps. They moved away from the door, grew distant, faded.

Bríghid felt the Englishman's body relax, released the breath she didn't know she'd been holding.

"I would not have let him take you, love." His voice was deep, resonant in his chest.

"Don't call me that." She pushed away from him, more than a little distressed to discover that she'd been clinging to him in her fear, heedless of the way her breasts pressed against his side and her thighs stretched alongside his. She gathered the sheets and pulled them up to her chin, scooted to the far side of the bed. Rage, shame, fear, relief churned through her, mixed, entwined. This *Sasanach* had seen her naked. He had touched her in the ways of a husband. He had forced her to feel things she should not.

He would not have let the iarla take you.

He turned on his side to face her, folded one strong arm beneath his head. "You're not still afraid of me are you?"

She'd taken most of the covers with her, leaving him exposed to the hips. Try as she might to avert her gaze, she couldn't help but look. A scar on his right shoulder, still red as if the wound were recent, was the only blemish on his strong body. Even his stomach was molded into ridges of muscle, his skin tawny, smooth. Stretched out on the bed, rippling muscle beneath sun-browned skin, he made her think of a lion—beautiful to behold and dangerous. Her pulse quickened. "I was never afraid of you, *Sasanach*."

"I'm not one to call a beautiful woman a liar, but if you were to say that again, that's what I'd have to do." His expression was grave. "And call me Jamie. This *Sasanach* business is getting old. What does it mean, anyway?"

"Englishman."

He shrugged. "That's not so bad."

"A dog does not mind being called a dog."

"Do you hate us all, Brighid?"

She had grown up hating the English. The English had killed Aidan's father, starved her mother, sold her father into slavery, stolen her family's land. The English had taken away the churches, killed or exiled priests, slaughtered countless Irish. Just today, an English lord had tried to rape her, had stolen her from her family and given her away as a prize. Did she hate them all? She looked into Jamie's green eyes. "I want to get dressed now."

"You should sleep while you can. We'll need to leave in a few hours if we're going to get you away from here."

"I can't be sleepin' under his roof with you here and both of us ... naked!"

"I see." He rolled out of bed, an irritating grin on his face.

Brighid got a glimpse of his backside, tight and muscular, before she averted her gaze. She heard the rustle of cloth, felt something soft land on the bed beside her. It was her chemise. She grabbed it, pulled it beneath the sheets and tried to find the sleeves.

Jamie stepped into his drawers, tied them fast. He was still hard, near to bursting. He didn't suppose he'd ever been so aroused without enjoying sexual release, and he ached from lack of it. God, how he wanted her. It had taken every ounce of decency and will he possessed not to press her further, not to seduce her. The sight of her beautiful body—her full breasts with their dusky nipples, her softly rounded belly, the creamy curve of her hips—had been more than he could take.

He tried to pull his mind away from his aching cock. He'd never had trouble finding women eager to spread their legs for him. Brighid didn't want to be here to start with, and she certainly didn't want him. There was no reason for him to waste time burning for a woman who hated him when there was willing flesh to be had elsewhere. When he returned to England, he could call upon any number of women who would welcome him into their beds. But they were not like Bríghid.

He watched, genuinely amused, as Bríghid struggled to dress beneath the covers. "It might be easier if you got out of bed. I'll turn my back."

She ceased struggling, looked at him doubtfully from beneath impossibly long, sooty lashes. "If you would, please."

"Let me know if you need help." Jamie picked up his breeches, turned away. He could hear her soft footfalls on the lush carpet, the rustle of petticoats and silk. The sound and the thought of her putting on clothing he had removed only a short time ago did nothing to cool the heat in his blood. He tried to shut out thoughts of her—the feel of her breasts against his skin, the scent of her, the taste of her lips. Pretending to deflower her had cost him—exactly what it had cost him he wasn't certain, but it had cost him.

He hadn't been lying when he'd told Sheff he'd been thinking of her all day. Since this morning when he'd first seen her, she hadn't left his thoughts. It had been years since he'd reacted like this to a woman. Then again, he wasn't sure he'd ever reacted this way to a woman.

Aye, he'd made a fool of himself a few times as a young man. There was Peg, the pretty bondswoman who'd seduced him in her cabin when he was sixteen. She was a good ten years older than he and over a period of weeks had taught him things no boy of sixteen should know. He'd mistaken his own animal lust for love until it became clear to him Peg was bedding him in hopes of gaining some kind of advantage.

He was, after all, her master.

At seventeen, he'd fallen in love with the daughter of a neighbor only to watch her marry a man three times his age. She'd said she loved him, too, but when faced with her father's wrath, she'd turned away from Jamie and meekly done as her father had commanded. Jamie had said some impertinent things, and Alec had put him on the next ship bound for England.

Then there was Sarah. The daughter of a landed English gentleman, she was beautiful, educated and witty—everything a young man could desire. She and Jamie had become lovers during his third year at Oxford. Jamie had fallen and fallen hard. He'd shared his dreams with Sarah, had loved her until they both lay sated and panting as the sun rose outside her bedroom window. He'd even asked her to marry him. She hadn't answered him, only smiled and slid her hand inside his breeches.

Then one day, she'd told him she was pregnant.

He had immediately repeated his offer of marriage, but she'd laughed. "You're so sweet, Jamie," she'd said, her hand on his cheek, "but the child is not yours."

She'd claimed the father of her child was her fiancé, about whom Jamie had known nothing. Jamie had been nothing more than a sexual diversion for Sarah, one last thrill before entering the confines of an arranged marriage. Whether the child was truly his or belonged to the man she quickly married, Jamie would never know.

Since then, his relationships with women had not gone beyond the unadorned exchange of sexual pleasure. He preferred it that way — simple, clear-cut, uncomplicated. Women seemed to want only one thing from him. Widows, rebellious daughters, bored wives with elderly husbands, the occasional courtesan — they were eager for the pleasure he could bring them with his hands, his lips, his tongue, his cock. But they were loath to promise more. He gave them what they wanted, took what he wanted.

In all the years that had passed, he had yet to meet a woman he could trust or love. In fact, he wasn't sure he was still capable of love. He certainly had no desire to marry. The fact that he was almost thirty and without an heir might distress his sister, but it concerned him little.

But he did have a problem.

What the hell was he going to do with Bríghid? She couldn't go home, that much was certain. Sheff would surely send his men after her again, and she'd find herself on her back while Sheff did as he pleased. The idea sickened Jamie.

Nor could she stay with him. He would be sailing for home soon and had important business to conclude in the meantime, business that demanded both his time and his wits. The last thing he needed was a woman to distract him.

Jamie reached for his shirt, yanked it over his head.

There was only one answer. He'd take her to England and leave her with Elizabeth, Alec's sister. She and her husband, Lt. Matthew Hasting, lived on the Kenleigh estate outside London. They would surely take Bríghid in and give her a place in their household. She'd be safe there until her family could move to another county far from Skreen parish and Sheff. They could see her safely home again when the time was right, and she could go about her life as if none of this had ever happened.

But Bríghid wasn't his only problem. His decision to protect her—made without hesitation—could have dire consequences to his mission here. Jamie had been counting on Sheff's support and his influence in the House of Lords. Lives depended on it. Perhaps if Sheff thought Jamie's wits addled by lust, he'd forgive Jamie for stealing Bríghid from under his roof. If not …

Jamie would have to succeed without his help. He could not abandon her to a life of shame and torment. Nor could he forget the frontier families who daily faced the threat of the French and their Indian allies. There was a way out of this, and he would find it.

Sheff was a changed man. He was cruel, arrogant, and more than a little depraved if tonight were any indication. He'd left his pretty wife behind in London and openly bedded servant women. Had he always been this way? Had youth and inexperience caused Jamie to misjudge him so badly years ago?

Careful to keep his back to her, Jamie searched among the covers until he found what he was looking for. He grasped the knife, nicked his thumb, dabbed his blood on the sheets.

"No!" Wearing only her chemise and petty coats, she rushed to the side of the bed and stared at the bloodstains, an expression of horror on her face. Her palm connected with his cheek with a loud smack. "Now no man will believe me!"

The knife fell to the floor.

Jamie stood, hauled her roughly up against him, and was gratified by her gasp of surprise. "*Don't* do that again. Your reputation was ruined from the moment the earl's men took you. Or hadn't you realized that yet?"

She glared at him defiantly, but he could see the fear in her eyes—and the hate.

"I'm risking far more than you can imagine helping you tonight, so you might try to find some room in your heart for gratitude." He wanted to kiss her, wanted to make the hate vanish from her eyes.

"'Tis because of you I'm here in the first place!"

The truth of her words made his anger sharper. "That's *my* blood on those sheets and not yours only because you were lucky enough to be given to a man who finds rape repugnant. Do you think many other men would have turned down a gift as appealing and helpless as you, my sweet?"

She looked away, but not before Jamie saw the tears well up in her eyes. "Let go of me."

"You must understand the earl will try to find you again unless he thinks me so besotted it seems not worth the effort. Those bloodstains may make it hard for you to prove your virtue, but they could make the difference in preserving it. Do you understand?"

She refused to meet his gaze, said nothing.

He released her, stuck his thumb in his mouth, tasted blood. Furious, he searched the floor for his stockings, slipped them on. He didn't need this. He didn't need any of this.

He heard the rustle of silk. "I'm dressed, *Sasanach*."

Still angry, Jamie shot her a glance, felt his gut clench. She'd left the corset off and pulled her chemise up to cover her breasts and shoulders. It didn't matter. The soft swell of her breasts was more than evident behind the lace and linen, and he found her attempt at modesty more appealing than Sheff's effort to turn her into a whore.

She stood by the fireplace, combing her hair with her fingers, her head tilted slightly to the side to reveal the slender column of her throat.

"You have beautiful hair." The words came out as if he'd meant to say them.

"My father often said 'tis the image of my mother's." She didn't look at him.

"You never knew her?"

"I don't remember her. She died when I was three, starved by the English during the famine." She spat the words at him as if he were personally to blame.

Jamie refused to take the bait. "She must have been lovely."

Bríghid said nothing.

Jamie sat on the bed, pulled on his stockings. "My mother died the day after I was born."

She began to weave her hair into a braid, turned her back to him.

So she thought to ignore him. He wasn't going to make it easy for her. If they were to fight a battle of wills, he would be the victor. He would force her to see him as a man, not merely a hated *Sasanach*.

"My father lost his wits after she died. He couldn't even remember his own children. He died when I was six. I barely remember him." Jamie fastened the buckles at his knees, aware she was looking at him again. He'd gotten her attention. "My sister, Cassie, and her husband,

Alec, raised me, took care of my estate until I was old enough to manage myself."

"Do you own lands in Ireland?" Her words were a challenge. He could hear the malice in her voice. She began to tie off her braid with a blue ribbon that Jamie recognized from her stockings.

It distracted him to think of her slender legs left bare beneath her skirts. "No. My estate is in Lancaster County, Virginia."

Her eyes widened in surprise, and she gaped at him. "You're from the colonies?"

"Aye. I was born there."

"I knew you were different."

Jamie met her gaze, oddly gratified, raised an eyebrow. "Oh?"

Even in the dark, he could see her cheeks turn pink.

She looked away, changed the subject. "Do you own slaves?"

"No, not any more. My brother-in-law did away with that when I was still a boy. For years, we've been bringing over our own bondsmen. Our slaves have been freed, though it is against the law. Those who remain are free but have no place to go. They farm the land in return for a share of the crop and a place to live."

She was staring openly at him now. "Have you other brothers or sisters?"

Jamie hid his satisfaction at having found a window through the wall of hatred she'd put up around herself. "No. Just Cassie. My mother bore six of us in all, but the others were stillborn or died in infancy. And you? You said you have brothers."

"Aye. There would be seven of us, but four died, God rest their souls. Padraíg died of fever when he was two. He was the firstborn. Then came Finn. Dear Conall died when I was ten after a horse kicked him in the head. Tadgh and Aoife both died of a sickness when they were little. I never knew them. I was born later. Then came Ruaidhrí."

"Who was the red-haired boy I saw today?" Jamie didn't know why he'd asked. It was no concern of his.

She eyed at him suspiciously, turned to face the fire. The braid hung, long and thick, down her back. "Aidan. His mother died givin' birth to him, and his father was shot in the back — by the English."

The window slammed shut.

"And your father?"

"My father is … was a teacher. You English outlawed schooling for Catholics. You forced him to teach in secret in barns and along hedgerows. When he was caught… he was transported to Barbados and sold as a slave." There was a knife's edge to her voice as it wavered between rage and tears.

So her father had been transported. No doubt he'd used teaching as a means to incite young Irishmen to rebel against the Crown. Only a serious crime could provoke the English courts to pass such a sentence. No wonder she and her brother hated everything English. They'd been bred to it. "I'm sorry."

She ignored him.

Jamie felt his temper rise. Beautiful she was—aye, and as sweet as a copperhead. "I mean to leave before dawn. You should get some sleep."

"I cannot. I must find my things."

"What things?"

"My clothes, my cross, my grandmother's brooch. I can't go home dressed like—"

"Your grandmother's what?" Jamie ran his fingers through his hair in frustration. God, how he needed a drink. And a woman.

"Brooch. It has been in my family for generations, and I —"

"Can live without it." He cut her off, gestured toward the hallway. "He's probably still awake, looking for someone to take to his bed, Bríghid. Would you risk everything?"

"It's all I have of my grandmother." Her chin was held high, but he could see the warring emotions in her eyes—uncertainty, fear, anger.

But it was her grief that pricked him, made him speak sharply. "I'm certain she'd not want you to risk your very life to find it. Sleep, Bríghid, before I decide rescuing you is too much trouble and let you fend for yourself."

For a moment, she looked as if she might defy him and go off in search of her trinkets. Then, her eyes spitting anger, she walked to the bed and slipped beneath the covers.

Jamie crossed the room to the bureau, poured himself a brandy. By the time he turned around, she was asleep.

"*B*ríghid, wake up."

She was too sleepy. She turned over, ignored the voice. She was asleep on a cloud. It was soft and fluffy, and she was nice and warm. No straw scratched her skin. No mice tried to share her blankets. No cold earth pressed into her back.

"Bríghid, you must wake." A hand caressed her cheek.

"*Lig uaim, a athair.*" *Leave me alone, Father.*

But it wasn't her father's voice. Her father would never speak English to his children. Her father was gone.

With a gasp, Bríghid opened her eyes. The events of the night came flooding back, detail by terrible detail. She sat, struggled to clear the sleep from her mind.

The Englishman stood beside the bed fully dressed, his greatcoat on. "It's time to go."

Disoriented, she pushed herself into a sitting position, marveling at the softness of the bed. It was the softest thing she'd ever lain on. No wonder she'd been dreaming of clouds.

Her hand touched something cold and metal. She looked, gasped. *The brooch. Her cross.* They lay on the pillow beside her. Her own clothes lay draped across the foot of the bed. A lump rose in her throat.

She clutched the brooch and cross to her breast, gaped at the Englishman in surprise. "How —"

"They were tossed in a heap in the servants hallway."

She hesitated, unsure of what to say. "Thank you. I —"

He dismissed her gratitude, his eyes cold. "Hurry, and dress. We must go."

She swallowed the lump, slipped the leather cord that held the cross over her head, and reached for her old woolen gown. She started to ask him to turn his back to give her privacy, but he was already facing the fireplace.

She got out of bed, slipped off the blue gown, the petticoats and the chemise. As new and soft as they were, they belonged not to her, but to the accursed *iarla*. She wanted nothing to remind her of this night. She'd wear her own tattered chemise, her worn petticoats, her old red woolen gown, and her threadbare cloak, and she'd wear them with pride.

"I'm ready." She slipped her feet into the worn leather of her brogues.

In silence, he helped her don her cloak. Then he left her to fasten it and went to fetch his travel bag, which he had packed while she'd slept. The two of them started toward the door, his hand on her waist.

They stepped quietly into the darkness of the hallway.

He shut the door behind them, and she felt his warm fingers close around hers. She tried not to think about how reassuring it felt and pulled her hand from his grasp.

"This way."

He moved with the silent grace of a cat. She followed as quietly as she could, every creaking floorboard causing her heart to skitter. Down the stairs they went, through the long hallway where she'd sat, terrified, around the corner, and down more stairs.

Once she'd thought them undone when her cloak had caught on the edge of a table and unbalanced a vase of flowers, but he'd caught it in time. The only damage, other than what her heart endured, was water on the floor.

In the hallway outside the kitchens, Jamie stopped, put a finger to her lips. A dim light came from the room and cast flickering orange shapes on the walls. Leaving her for a moment, Jamie crept silently forward and peeked into the room.

She held her breath, marveled that a man of his size could move without making a sound. He motioned for her to join him. In the kitchen, a fire had burned low in the hearth. A servant, likely the cook, snored on a pallet nearby.

Slowly, quietly, they crept through the room, its stone floor offering a quieter path than wooden floorboards.

They reached the back door, which stood locked.

She held her breath as Jamie carefully lifted the bolt, slid it back. It squeaked, shuddered, then gave way.

Relief surged through her as fresh, cold air filled her lungs. She hurried through the doorway, welcomed the feeling of chill rain on her face.

Silently, Jamie shut the door behind them. He took her arm in his, guided her through the dark. "We must make haste. We'll have to ride two to my horse. I brought no other. But once we reach Dunsany, I'll hire a carriage."

"Dunsany?" Bríghid stopped, pulled her arm free. "I'm not going to Dunsany. My home is the other way, toward Lismullen."

He dropped his travel bag, took her shoulders. "Listen, Bríghid. Now is not the time to argue. If you go home, Sheff will find you and bring you back. Everything I didn't do to you tonight, he will."

"There's only one thing you *didn't* do, *Sasanach*! For all you spared me, you might as well have done the deed!"

Rather than apologizing or looking contrite, he chuckled, his gaze devoid of laughter. "You silly, naïve girl." But his fingers dug deeper into her shoulders. "If Sheff gets hold of you, you'll spend every night until he tires of you on your back. Do you understand that?"

"But—"

"Listen! I can give you a safe home in England, where Sheff can't —"

"You lied! You said you were taking me home!"

"I never said where I was taking you. I only said I would help you get away from here."

Enraged at this trickery, afraid she might never see home again, Bríghid began to fight in earnest, pummeling his chest. "*Stríapach fir! Bréagach, thú!*" Whoreson. Liar.

He deserved to be called worse.

He clapped one hand over her mouth, pulled her hard against him. "Believe me, this wasn't in my plans either. I have no wish to suffer your company any longer than necessary. As soon as your family is able to move to another county far from here, you'll be returned. There your reputation will be intact, and you and your brothers will be beyond Sheff's reach."

He took her arm, picked up his bag, pulled her along.

"No!" She tried to pull her arm free. "My family can't afford that! We've a lease—"

"I'll take care of it."

"I will not—"

"Quiet, woman! Or maybe you'd like his grooms to hear you and send up the alarm?"

She glanced warily about, fell silent.

They rounded the corner of the stables.

Before them stood two men, dark, faceless.

Jamie heard Bríghid gasp, felt something strike him in the chest. He wanted to protect her, to put himself between her and these men but found he could not move. He looked down and saw the blade of a sword buried in the left side of his chest.

The blade was jerked free, and Jamie heard himself moan as searing pain shot through him. Something wet and hot ran down his skin—his own blood.

"Oh, sweet Mary, no!" It was Bríghid. She was kneeling beside him.

How had he come to be on the ground? Icy rain spattered his face. Bríghid was speaking, but he couldn't understand her. She was talking to the two men. Their words made no sense. Gaelic.

"Cad tá déanta agat, a Rhuaidhrí?"

Ruaidhrí. He'd heard that name before. Her brother. Her brothers had come to save her. The irony of the situation would have made him laugh had he the strength for it. Had she known they were here, waiting?

"Tar liom, a Bhríghid! Caithfimid bheith ag imeacht! Fág an Sasanach mar atá sé!"

"Ní rachaidh mé! Faighfidh sé bás má imeóimid!" She touched his face. She sounded angry. "Jamie, can you hear me? Ruaidhrí, Finn, help me!"

A cold such as he had never known crept over him.

This must be what it is to die.

He felt no fear of death, no sadness that his life was over, only a sense of regret at having failed to complete his mission.

Forgive me.

Whom was he asking to forgive him?

Alec and Cassie. This would hit them hard.

Nicholas.

He felt Bríghid search beneath his coat, felt her press something against the wound. She was trying to staunch the bleeding.

"Bríghid ... " Pain engulfed him. He heard himself moan.

Then there was only darkness.

Chapter Six

Bríghid laid a cool cloth across Jamie's forehead. He was burning up.

For three days, she'd fought to save his life. For three days, she'd wondered if she would be the death of him.

She'd known right away he was grievously hurt and had feared he would die from blood loss before she could treat him. She could have awoken the *iarla*, who surely would have called a real doctor to heal his friend. It would have been the best thing for Jamie. A wealthy man like the *iarla* would have precious laudanum to ease his friend's pain and all manner of powders for fever and medicines to draw the sickness from the wound.

But revealing themselves would have meant certain death for her brothers and servitude in the *iarla's* bed for her. They'd had no choice but to run. She'd tried to staunch the bleeding first, then had her brothers tie him to his horse. They'd traveled through the cold of night to an old, abandoned cabin not far from the ancient hill of Teagh-mor, where Bríghid and Ruaidhrí could hide.

At first, she'd worried he'd lost too much blood. He'd lain so cold and still on the bed, like a man already dead. Her brothers had argued over how to dispose of his body, until Bríghid had shouted at them to shut up before they invited Death into the cabin with careless words. She'd had Finn bring every herb and poultice she owned to the hideout, had sent Ruaidhrí outdoors to gather bog moss and bring fresh water from a spring. She'd cleaned the wound with whiskey and bound it with clean linen and poultice made of sweet violet leaves.

Then fever had set in, and the wound had become angry and red. While she considered herself skilled with herbs and poultices for everyday ailments—coughs, scrapes, the flux—she'd never before cared for a wound like this. She'd tried a draught of mayweed at first for the fever, for it was safest, but the fire in his body had raged on. Then she'd switched to *seamsóg*, fairy bells, which was stronger. It seemed to help, but it couldn't cure the wound itself.

For that, she'd need a miracle. The wound was deep but narrow, and the whiskey clearly had not gone deep enough. None of her silly poultices could make their way so deeply into him. To reach the sickness, she'd need to cut him, make the wound wider somehow. But he'd bled so much already. And she had nothing, nothing at all, to ease his pain.

If he weren't so strong, he'd likely have died already. And strong he was. Once the fever had set in, he'd become delirious, rambling and thrashing about. It had taken both Ruaidhrí and Finn to bind him to the bed so she could care for him.

He moaned in his sleep, turned his head from side to side. His brow was furrowed, his blonde hair wet with sweat, and she knew he hurt. She dipped the cloth in cool water again, wrung it out, and bathed his face.

She wanted to hate him, wanted to feel indifferent to his pain. He was English, and the English had never cared about the suffering they caused her people. If she was now in the odd position of trying to save an Englishman's life, it was only out of obligation, the repayment of a debt. Besides, if he died, she and her brothers would be guilty of murder under English law. She'd be a fool to let that happen.

But try as she might to harden her heart, she could not ignore his suffering. These past three days, she'd relived every moment of that awful, terrible night. It haunted her, left her feeling confused, mixed up inside. Fear and rage, disgust and humiliation.

Shame. Desire.

Her feelings about the Englishman were the most confusing of all. Her cheeks flamed with fury and embarrassment when she thought of the things he'd done to her. He'd undressed her, kissed her again and again, thrust his tongue inside her mouth. He'd allowed her to see him naked, climbed on top of her, forced her legs apart, and pretended to ...

Dear God, Mary and Joseph!

And if her brothers hadn't come along, he'd have spirited her off to England, perhaps never to see home again. He wasn't all that different from the *iarla*.

Even as the words formed in her mind, a rebellious voice answered. He *was* different. Hadn't Jamie, though a *Sasanach*, tried to protect her? Hadn't he been gentle when he could have been rough? Hadn't he taken only kisses and caresses when he could have taken everything? Hadn't he found her cross and brooch and returned them to her? Hadn't he kept the *iarla* from laying his hands on both her and Ruaidhrí?

And if he had also kindled an unwanted, unwelcome yearning within her?

That sin was hers, not his.

Now he was fighting to stay alive. She didn't want to care, but she did.

He strained against the ropes that bound his wrists to bed's wooden frame, cried out. "Nicholas!"

"Rest, Jamie."

She lifted the flannel from his wound. Ruaidhrí's blade had struck closer to the Englishman's shoulder than his heart, and for that she was grateful. She'd given up on violet leaves and had soaked the flannel in garlic juice instead, but redness from the wound was beginning to spread. If she didn't stop it, the poison would reach his blood.

And he would die.

She knew what she needed to do, but she was afraid to do it.

The door to the cabin opened. Cold night air rushed in.

"God in heaven, what is that stench?"

"I hope you've brought more peat." She was still too angry with her brother to look at him. "What we've got won't keep the fire going through the night, and we must keep him warm."

Ruaidhrí dropped blocks of dried peat by the hearth, walked over to the bed. "I once heard an old woman say you can save a man's life if he's on the brink by bindin' him with a rope that was used to hang a man who survived the hangin'."

She glared at him. "If you come by just such a rope, Ruaidhrí, I suggest you go hang yourself with it. For if he dies, you'll have murdered a man, and God have mercy on your soul!"

She ignored the stricken look on her brother's face, walked to the table, and began to sort through her herbs and ointments. Powder of horseradish she had, and lavender oil. She had oil of thyme, as well, and powdered holly berries. The bog moss was almost dried and ready for use. If only she had turpentine.

"How was I to know? He's a *Sasanach*—"

She spun about, faced him. "I know what he is!"

"But—"

"You've hated the English your entire life, Ruaidhrí. Aye, and so have I. But maybe they're not all evil. Besides, how much will your life be worth if he dies? Not a farthing!"

Ruaidhrí looked at her, his expression one of astonishment—and doubt. "What does he mean to you?"

"I already told you. He spared me. He helped me escape." Bríghid turned back to the bed, ignored the probing tone in her brother's voice. She had already told her brothers how Jamie had protected her, but she hadn't told them everything. She hadn't told them how Jamie's kisses had ignited a fever in her blood or how his touch had made her skin tingle. She hadn't told them how the feel of his tongue entwined with hers had made her knees weak, or how the briefest glimpse of his naked male body had made it hard for her to breathe.

"Are you sure that's all he did?"

"If you don't believe me, bring the midwife!"

Finn stepped in, shoulders hunched against the cold, his blonde hair hidden beneath a blue knitted cap. "What's the shoutin'?"

"Ruaidhrí seems to think the midwife ought to examine me." She turned her back on them both, tucked the blanket under Jamie's chin.

"I didn't say—"

"Don't dishonor your sister, little brother, or you'll have me to deal with." Finn moved to the fire, warmed his hands. "If you hadn't opened your bloody gob, Bríghid would never have been in danger in the first place. Now come and help me unload the cart."

Finn and Ruaidhrí carried in what supplies Finn had been able to bring from home—the old oatmeal chest filled halfway, cheese, *bainne clábair*, butter, a few eggs, bacon, more potatoes, a jar of barm for bread should Bríghid get the time to make any, a large pile of peat for the fire.

Aidan had sent Bríghid a little straw cross he'd made. The innocent sweetness of his gift made her smile. She hung it over the doorway, an ache in her heart. Sweet Mary, how she missed him. He was staying with Muirín, who'd sworn to Finn that caring for the boy would help to ease her grief. A childless mother and a motherless child.

"There's plenty of feed for his horse." Finn stood beside her, held out a tattered book. "I brought this, too."

"Oh, Finn." It was her favorite—the story of Don Bellianis of Greece. Her brothers, Finn especially, teased her about reading chivalric romances—silly girl stories Finn called them—but she loved them. She'd read this one dozens of times and had been lured from dreariness and drudgery by the magic of its worn pages. She reached over, set it on the table. There was no time for reading now.

She dipped the cloth in the bucket of cold water, wrung it out, placed it back on Jamie's forehead. She voiced the fear that had haunted her all day. "I'm afraid he's dying."

She felt Finn's reassuring hand on her shoulder. "You've done everything you can."

"No, not everything." Her mind was made up. She stood, crossed the tiny room to where her cloak hung on a nail by the door. She hesitated, then unfastened her brooch. The dragon's red eyes gleamed at her, candlelight glinting off the stones like tears.

It was all she had.

She turned to Finn, held out her hand. "Take this to Baronstown. There's a doctor there who lives there just down the street from the cheeser. Trade it for turpentine and the sharpest knife he'll give you."

Her brother's blue eyes opened wide. "Oh, Bríghid. You would sacrifice this?"

"For him?" Ruaidhrí indignant voice intruded.

"Do you know how afraid I was when the *iarla* started to undress me right there in front of his servants? My legs shook. I felt sick. I wished myself dead rather than have his hands on me. I thought he was going to rape me right there. But I didn't fight, and I didn't run because I thought I was protectin' my brothers." She heard her voice quaver, fought the tears that pricked her eyes. "That man stopped the *iarla*. He protected me. He saved you, too, Ruaidhrí. We both owe him a life debt."

Ruaidhrí's gaze dropped to the floor.

"Take it, and go." She took Finn's hand, placed the brooch in his calloused palm.

"I'll do it." Ruaidhrí took the brooch. "Finn has already ridden half the night to get here."

Bríghid shook her head. "But if anyone sees you—"

"It's dark. No one's going to be lookin' for me in bloody Baronstown."

"All right, but stay out of trouble, and hurry. Take his horse."

His gaze met hers. "I'm doing this for you, not for him."

"Ask the doctor if he's got laudanum or anything special to fight a fever."

"Aye." Ruaidhrí walked toward the door, opened it, and was gone.

While Finn slept, exhausted, on a pallet of straw near the hearth, Bríghid tended Jamie. She bathed his forehead and chest with cold cloths, changed the flannel on his wound, coaxed another draught of *seamsóg* down his throat. All the while, she listened for the sound of hooves. But it wasn't until just before dawn that Ruaidhrí returned. His cheeks and ears were red with cold, his fingers, too. Without speaking, he handed her a linen bag, then went back out to tend the horse.

Eagerly, she opened the bag. Inside was a small knife with a thin, sharp blade, a bottle of turpentine, a packet of some strange powder, and a smaller bottle that smelled of spirits.

Laudanum.

Relief, gratitude and feelings of guilt washed through her. She'd spoken harshly to Ruaidhrí, more harshly than she'd intended. She'd apologize when he came in, but now she needed to boil water.

By the time the water had begun to bubble, Finn had awoken, and Ruaidhrí had returned. He came to the hearth, warmed his red, cracked fingers over the fire.

"I'll need you to hold him for me."

They nodded.

Ruaidhrí peeled off his coat. "I told the doctor you'd cut yourself and the cut had festered. He said turpentine would likely do the trick if you mixed it with mustard flower. He wrote down his recipe for using the powder. It's some kind of tree bark."

She nodded, dropped the knife into the boiling water. She'd once heard a midwife say some doctors boiled their knives and was willing to try anything if it might help, though what it could accomplish she knew not.

"What in God's name did you do that for?" Ruaidhrí gaped at the knife in disbelief. "Is that breakfast?"

She ignored him. The first thing she needed to do was give Jamie the tincture of poppy. It would dull his pain. She uncorked the little bottle, poured some in a spoon. Setting the bottle aside, she lifted his head gently with her free hand.

"Drink, Jamie." She held the spoon to his lips, trickled the precious liquid into his mouth and sighed with relief when he swallowed. Just to be certain, she gave him a second, smaller spoonful.

Almost immediately, he seemed to fall into a deep sleep. His brow was no longer furrowed, and his breathing was deep and even.

She closed the bottle and went back to work. Despite what the doctor said, she'd always found horseradish to stop a creeping redness faster than mustard flower. She set powdered root of horseradish aside, and opened her little vial of lavender oil. The pungent aroma filled the air. She changed her mind, opened the thyme oil instead. Its heady scent tickled her nose, nearly made her dizzy.

She wasn't sure how long doctors boiled their knives. She hadn't thought to ask the midwife. If it were porridge, she'd know when it was done, but a knife? She waited a few more minutes, growing more anxious with each breath.

Could she do this?

She had no choice. She owed the Englishman a life debt, and she would see it repaid.

She reached for her cross, muttered a prayer to St. Bríghid, to the Virgin Mother and to God. Then she lifted the cross from around her throat and walked to the bed.

"Oh, good God." Ruaidhrí groaned.

"Don't blaspheme." Finn elbowed his brother.

She lifted Jamie's head, slipped the thong over it and laid the iron cross against the tanned skin of his throat.

"Puttin' that cross on a Protestant—that's blasphemy!" Ruaidhrí protested.

"I wouldn't have the cross if it weren't for him. 'Tis only right I use its power to heal him."

Jamie stirred as if he knew they were speaking of him, but continued to sleep.

She walked to the hearth and, using a wooden ladle, lifted the knife from the steaming water. The knife's handle burnt her when she tried to hold it. She gripped it with the folds of her skirt, handed the ladle to Ruaidhrí. "Fill this with water, and carry it to the table."

She walked to the bed and looked down at the man who now slept so peacefully.

She didn't want to cause him pain.

She didn't want to make him suffer.

She didn't want him to die.

Ruaidhrí placed the ladle carefully on the table and joined her at the bedside. "What are you doing, Bríghid? You're no surgeon. If he dies—"

"We shall both be to blame."

Her brothers held Jamie's shoulders fast to straw mattress. The ropes beneath creaked at the added weight.

Bríghid took the knife from the folds of her skirts and held it above the wound. Her hand trembled. She fought to steady it. He was just a *Sasanach*.

She pressed the knife slowly into the wound.

Jamie moaned.

Flesh parted. Foul, yellow liquid oozed forth as she pressed the knife deeper, made the wound wider. Blood spilled onto his skin, made it hard for her to see. But she had planned for this. When the wound was as wide as she dared make it and the blood flowed freely, she dashed to the hearth, removed a red-hot skewer from the ashes, dashed back. She hesitated only for a moment, then pressed it into the cut she had just made.

A searing sound filled the air, along with the stench of burning flesh.

Jamie arched, cried out.

Her brothers struggled to hold him still.

Ruaidhrí's eyes were wide. "Jesus, Bríghid!"

Jamie's eyes flew open. His fevered gaze met hers. "Bitch!"

Bríghid ignored the stabbing sensation in her heart, removed the skewer.

The bleeding had all but stopped.

Almost at once, Jamie's eyes closed, and he lay silent again, his face pale.

Ruaidhrí shook his head, watched her. "I can't believe you just did that."

"She's doin' what needs doin', and let that be a lesson to you."

She ignored her brothers' bickering, returned the skewer to the hearth and took up the ladle. She carried it carefully so as not to spill the water, which had now cooled considerably. She poured it into the wound to wash the blood away and followed that with a draught of whiskey. Then she dried his chest, soaking up blood, water and whiskey with clean cloths.

Jamie groaned, mouthed unintelligible words.

Using the knife to hold the wound open, she dribbled in the turpentine and thyme oil and followed that up with a hearty sprinkling of powdered horseradish. She knew she ought to stitch him, but she was afraid to close the wound yet.

"Are you tryin' to kill him?" Ruaidhrí wrinkled his nose.

She was almost done. She walked back to the table, took a handful of cleaned bog moss and soaked it with garlic juice.

Ruaidhrí coughed. "God save us! I'm sleepin' in the barn."

"Good." Finn smiled. "That means I can hog the fire."

The powerful smell made Bríghid's eyes water, but she paid it no mind. She carried the compress to the bedside and pressed it against the wound. Then she bound it in place with a length of clean linen torn from her petticoats.

She was finished.

Trembling, she sat on the bed, closed her eyes, drew a deep breath.

She felt Finn's strong hands on her shoulders and was grateful for his comforting presence.

It was up to God now.

Chapter Seven

The girl lay on her back across his writing table, small breasts bared. A week ago, she'd been a maid, but a few compliments, a comb for her flaxen hair, and the promise of extra food from the kitchens for her elderly parents had persuaded her to yield her innocence.

It was almost too easy.

Sheff pushed her skirts above her waist, grasped her slender calves and spread her legs wide. He liked it this way. The position allowed him to explore her with his fingers, to look his fill between her thighs, to watch as his cock drove into her.

She was rosy and smelled of woman. She was no match for the beauty Jamie had enjoyed—and stolen—but she would do. She had already done quite nicely.

He loosed his breeches, positioned himself between her thighs. He didn't feel like wasting time with meaningless preliminaries. With one thrust, he was inside her. She was deliciously tight and pleasingly wet as he moved inside her.

She moaned, lifted her hips to meet him.

"I told you you'd learn to enjoy it. All women do."

A knock came at the study door.

He groaned. "What is it?"

"I'm reportin' in as you asked, my lord."

Edward.

Sheff maintained his rhythm. "Come in."

The girl made to sit up, cover herself, but he pressed her back onto the desk.

"Stay as you are." He continued to drive into her, the interruption making his arousal sweeter. He liked an audience.

Edward opened the door, entered cap in hand. He was Sheff's most trusted servant and was used to his master's ways. His gaze barely even lighted on the girl.

"What news?"

Edward bowed lightly. "He ain't there."

"What do you mean he isn't there?"

"Word from London is he ain't been home. His family thinks he's still here."

Sheff felt his testicles tighten as his climax approached. His gaze dropped to where his body joined hers, watched himself enter her again and again, spilling his seed inside her with a groan.

So Jamie was nowhere to be found. Sheff pondered this fact as he withdrew, wiped himself on her skirts, buttoned his breeches. "You may go."

Blushing furiously, the girl leapt to her feet, curtsied, and hurried from the room.

Sheff had already forgotten her, his mind on Jamie. They'd checked every wayside inn from here to Dublin and found nothing. They'd checked ships' records and found nothing. Now London had turned up nothing, as well. Had Jamie boarded one of his brother-in-law's ships in secret and sailed for Virginia? No, he would have at least bid his family farewell or sent them word. Besides, Parliament was about to open. He wouldn't jeopardize his entire reason for coming to Britain. No, Jamie was nothing if not persistent and dedicated.

There was only one explanation: Jamie hadn't just taken her. He thought to hide her, to keep Sheff from finding her. "The game is afoot."

"So it seems, my lord."

"You may go." Sheff needed to think.

"By your leave, my lord."

Sheff poured himself a brandy, swirled it in the snifter, savored the aroma. He liked the smell of it more than the scent of woman that lingered on his fingers. Brandy raised his spirits, dulled his pain, made it possible for him to sleep at night.

Damn Jamie Blakewell!

Sheff had gone out of his way for Jamie, offered him unrivaled hospitality, treated him as an equal. He'd listened to Jamie's interminable lectures on colonial politics with good humor. He'd even tolerated Jamie's challenge to his authority—something he'd not have endured from anyone else. And Jamie had repaid his generosity by stealing the very woman Sheff had offered him as a symbol of friendship.

Sheff chuckled, shook his head, torn between amusement and anger. Jamie had always been given to ridiculous demonstrations of passion when it came to women. He'd treated the whores of Turlington's like ladies and had fallen in love with a woman who'd obviously been using him. And now he'd insulted Sheff's hospitality over a pretty bit of skirt.

Sheff would forgive him, of course. He'd always had a soft spot where Jamie was concerned. But first Sheff would find him. Jamie presumed too much, and it was time he learned a lesson about humility.

Wealthy though he might be, Jamie was but a commoner, the son of a colonist. His sister had gotten lucky and married into the English gentry. Even so, Jamie could not insult one of His Majesty's peers without consequences. Sheff would find him, feign outrage, snub him in Parliament. He would force Jamie to apologize for sneaking out of his house in the dead of night like a thief. He would show Jamie that it was he who had the power.

Of course, what Sheff really wanted was the girl. A rare beauty she was, even if she was Irish, and he would not allow Jamie to keep her to himself. His men were still looking. Like a pack of hounds, they'd flush Jamie out, and her with him. If not, Parliament was about to open, and Jamie would be forced to surface—

Like a pack of hounds.

You call this hunting?

Jamie's words from the day of the hunt came back to him. And Sheff knew.

Jamie had gone to ground. He hadn't gone to England at all. It made no sense. How could he hope to persuade Parliament to send a fleet to the Colonies if he were hiding here? Still, Sheff knew in his gut it was true.

Jamie thought to hide in Ireland for a time, to throw Sheff off the scent.

Sheff let out a triumphant whoop, swallowed his brandy.

"Edward!"

*J*amie was thirsty, so very thirsty.

He struggled to open his eyes, recognized the bitter aftertaste of laudanum.

The left side of his chest hurt like hell. What had happened? He tried to remember, fought to clear his mind. The Wyandot had attacked the encampment, taken Nicholas. Had Jamie been shot? Yes, in the arm. But it was only a flesh wound. Why did he feel so weak?

Nicholas!

Where was Nicholas? Jamie had to find him, had to save him.

He opened his eyes. The world was a blur. Above him, smoked hovered beneath a ceiling of thatch. Orange light from a fire bobbed and flickered against crumbling, soot-darkened walls. Where was he?

He tried to lift his head, wrinkled his nose. Something smelled strongly of turpentine and garlic.

Then he saw her. He remembered her name.

Brighid.

She was sound asleep. Her head rested on the bed beside him, though she sat on the dirt floor. The wooden beads of a rosary were draped over her fingers, now relaxed in sleep. Her long, dark hair had come out of its braid and lay across her face, across the bed, across his right arm. Had she been praying for him?

She stirred, opened her eyes, gasped. "Saints be praised, you're awake!"

"Wat—" He struggled to form the word.

"Shh. Don't try to speak." She sat on the bed beside him, touched his forehead with one cool, soft hand. "You've been feverish for a week. You need rest."

"Wa-ter."

She stood, walked across the room and dipped a wooden ladle into a bucket. Jamie felt his eyes close. It seemed an eternity before she returned, lifted his head and held the ladle to his lips.

"Slowly."

Jamie opened his eyes again, drank every sweet, cool drop. "More."

She disappeared in a swish of skirts, returned, and satisfied his thirst.

Even befuddled by laudanum, he could tell she hadn't slept well for days. Dark circles made shadows beneath her eyes.

What had happened? He struggled to remember. "Where ... am I?"

"You're in an abandoned cabin not far from Teagh-mor. We've been hiding here for more than a week. You've been very sick."

"Hiding?" He tried to sit up. Pain sliced through him. He heard himself groan, sank back against the bed.

Her hand rested softly on his right shoulder. "Don't try to move. Just rest."

A blast of cold air filled the tiny room.

A young man looked down at him — the Irish hothead — spoke words he didn't understand. "*A, tá sé ina dhúiseacht.*"

And Jamie remembered. "You ... bastard!"

The hothead's face turned red.

"It was a mistake, Jamie. Ruaidhrí didn't know." Brighid stood beside her brother, a hand on his arm.

"He ... tried to kill me. And you ... didn't stop him."

"I didn't see—"

"You don't have to listen to this, Brighid. This *Sasanach* doesn't know when to be grateful."

Jamie would have laughed if he'd been able. "That's what I was going to say about you."

"We should put him on his fine horse and send him back to his friend, the killer *iarla*."

Killer *ear-la*? Jamie didn't know who that was.

It was so hard to think.

"Why, Ruaidhrí? So that the *iarla* can send his men here and finish both of us, too? Foolish boy!" Brighid sat down on the bed beside Jamie, adjusted the woolen blanket that covered him. "Besides, he can't sit a horse. He can't even sit."

Eer-la. Earl? Did they mean Sheff?

"We can tie him on like we did before."

"Ruaidhrí!" Brighid stood, faced her brother. She sounded angry. "*Amach leat!*"

Jamie couldn't understand her words, felt himself begin to drift away.

Later — how much later he couldn't say — he heard a woman's soft voice speak to him. She supported his head, held something warm to his lips. "Drink."

He didn't feel like drinking. He wanted to sleep.

"Please, Jamie. You must regain your strength." Her voice was sweet, lilting.

He swallowed. It was some kind of tea. Though it was bitter, it soothed his throat. He hadn't realized it, but he was desperately thirsty again. He opened his eyes to find Bríghid holding a cup in her hand. His head lay cradled in her lap.

"How do you feel?"

"Like hell." His entire body hurt, remnants of the fever. He didn't need a doctor to tell him he'd come very close to dying. Every inch of him felt as if he'd been pulled back from the very brink—with grappling hooks.

"This will help." She slowly gave him the contents of the cup. "It's got mayweed and nettles."

"You've sent your brother away." His head began to clear some. "Good. I'm liable to kill him … next time I see him."

"You're in no shape to be killin' anyone." The corners of her lips lifted in a smile. "Besides, that was yesterday."

"Yesterday?" Jamie found it hard to believe he'd been asleep for a full day.

"Aye, yesterday. The poppy makes you sleepy." She placed the cup on a nearby table, then lifted his head, laid it back on the pillow, and stood. Her skirts swishing, she walked back to the hearth and stirred something in a pot that hung over the fire. "Ruaidhrí is off cuttin' peat for the fire."

She wore the same red, woolen gown she'd had on the night they'd fled. Frayed green ribbons decorated its hem. Over it, she wore a green apron. Tattered white lace hung from her sleeves. A gray knitted shawl covered her shoulders. She looked warm and soft and womanly.

Jamie was surprised to feel the faint stirrings of appreciation. In his current state, he wouldn't have expected even to notice such things. But he did. It only added to his growing sense of frustration. He couldn't remember having been so weak, not since he was a child and had come down with the dreaded ague. "How long has it been?"

She turned, wiped her hands on her apron. "Eight days."

"Eight days. Parliament! The state opening." He struggled to sit, groaned as white-hot pain seemed to split his chest and shoulder.

She hurried back to his side, put her hands on his shoulders to still him. "You're in no position to be worrying about silly Parliament. Lie down." She spoke as if he were a child.

"Damn it, woman! You don't understand! I'm trying to save lives!"

"So am I! Yours!"

Jamie could tell she was angry. Good. So was he. He reached for the edge of the bed to pull himself up only to discover his wrists were bound to the frame. Frustrated, furious, he glared at her. "So I'm a prisoner?"

She glared back. "Of course not! We had to keep you from harmin' yourself. It took both Ruaidhrí and Finn to hold you down."

She sat beside him, started to unbind his right arm. Her brow furrowed in concentration as she bent over her work, and Jamie was struck again by the delicate beauty of her face, the creamy smoothness of her skin, the claret fullness of her lips. He remembered tasting those lips, touching that skin, holding her trembling body in his arms.

What a fool he'd been.

After a moment, she shook her head. "You've pulled the knots tight. Maybe I should just leave you this way, as you're threatenin' to kill my brother."

"For your sake, I hope you don't." This wasn't funny. He'd come to Britain on a mission vital to the colonies. People were dying. Now, thanks largely to his lust for a dark-haired Irish wench and his desire to play the hero, his mission was compromised. There was no way he could make the opening of Parliament now.

Damn it to hell!

How was he going to explain this to Alec and the other members of Virginia's House of Burgesses? How was he going to explain it to the husbands of wives raped and mutilated along the frontier or the mothers of children who'd been scalped alive and left to die in the cold forest? What of the families of the men killed at Fort Necessity? What of Nicholas?

"For God's sake, wench, untie me!"

She placed her hands on her hips, looked down at him as if he were a naughty child about to receive a scolding. "And what will you do to me if I don't?"

His gaze met hers, held it. He said nothing.

Her eyes grew round. Her lips formed a rosy "o." Her cheeks turned a damnably pretty shade of pink, and he found himself wondering what she'd interpreted his gaze to mean.

She took up a knife from the table, walked back to him, and began to cut at the rope. "I stitched the wound while you slept, and I think you'll heal now, but not if you thrash about like a fish in a net."

The rope gave way.

Jamie lifted his right arm, bent it to ease the stiffness. "Does your brother often do this?"

"Do what?" She moved to the other side of the bed and began cutting the rope that bound his left arm.

"Impale Englishmen who are trying to rescue his sister."

Her gaze met his, and he could see the fire in her eyes. "He thought—"

"I know what he thought. That doesn't change the fact he almost killed me in cold blood." It galled him that she could defend her brother.

"I'm sor—"

"Why didn't you tell me they'd be coming for you?"

The rope that held his left wrist fell away.

"I wasn't sure."

"Is that why you had the knife? Had you planned to slice my throat while I slept, then meet your brothers outside?"

She stood abruptly, glared at him. "If I had wanted you to die, *Sasanach*, do you think I'd have spent the past week trying desperately to save your accursed life?"

He hadn't thought of that. She could have left him to die on the cold ground. "Why did you help me?"

She turned, stamped over to the table and began to hack potatoes into slices. "I owed you a debt."

"I see. It was a simple matter of obligation then?"

"What else would it be?"

Jamie felt his irritation grow at her answer, though he couldn't say why. "Now that the debt has been satisfied, I must get back to England."

"You're in no fit state to travel."

"Be that as it may, I must get back." He tried to move his left arm. Sharp pain shot through his chest and shoulder. He bit back a moan.

"I thought I told you to be still." She looked over at him. "Now your dressing has come loose."

Jamie bent his neck, tried to look at his chest. He could see what looked like moss held loosely in place by linen bandages. He reached with his good arm to move the moss, but she slapped his hand away.

"I'll not have you spoilin' all my hard work." She sat down beside him on the bed, carefully unbound the linen that held the moss in place, her hands sliding beneath his back to pull the strip of cloth through. Her hair, still unbound, pooled on his abdomen as she worked.

Despite his anger, Jamie found his gaze drawn to the fullness of her breasts hidden modestly beneath her gown, to her slender throat, then to her eyes, concealed by long, dark lashes. She seemed to be avoiding his gaze.

"Hold this." She put the ball of linen in his right hand. She stood, walked to the table, and retrieved a wooden bowl, which she filled with water. Taking a clean cloth from the table, she returned, sat beside him. "It might hurt, but I must clean the wound."

Was that genuine concern he saw in her eyes?

The roughest edges of his anger were smoothed way. "Do your worst."

She sat beside him again. Holding the bowl of water in one hand, she lifted the moss from his chest with the other and discarded it.

Jamie bent his neck and was shocked by what he saw. An incision ran from below his collarbone almost to his breast as if he'd been cleaved with an ax. Small, neat stitches of green thread held the flesh together. Though the edges were still an angry red color, the flesh surrounding the cut was not inflamed. It was a wonder he hadn't bled to death or died of infection.

"It festered badly." She took the cloth, dipped it in the water, and gently wiped the incision. "I had to cut you."

The water was warm, pressure on the incision quite painful, but Jamie found himself distracted by the graceful movements of her hands, the occasional fleeting touch of her fingers against his skin.

Her words finally hit him. "You cut me?"

"Aye." Her gaze met his for a moment, flitted nervously away. "The wound was deep but very narrow. I could not get medicine deep enough."

Jamie was amazed. This slip of a woman had performed surgery on him. "Did I not bleed all the more?"

"Aye, but I cauterized it."

He had no memory of it, and for that he was grateful.

Her gaze met his. "I'm not a doctor, but you'd have died else. I had no choice."

"Sure you did. And you chose to help me." He watched the way his words made her cheeks turn pink, then made her frown. "You're a healer."

"Not like some. I know but a little." She reached for a wooden bowl.

Jamie didn't have to ask what was in it. The smell of garlic was overpowering. "You remind me of Takotah. She could cure a toad of warts, but she never takes credit for her skills."

"Who is Ta-ko-ta?" She stumbled over the pronunciation, and her brow turned down in a frown. Her gaze was fixed on a clump of moss, which she soaked with garlic juice.

If Jamie didn't know better, he'd swear she was jealous. He couldn't resist. "A beautiful Indian woman."

"An Indian?" Her surprise was quickly masked by indifference. She placed the damp moss over the wound.

Jamie couldn't stop the hiss of breath that passed between his teeth. It stung like hell. "Aye. Her people, the Tuscarora, were all but destroyed by settlers. She found refuge on my estate." Because the irritation on her face amused him, he didn't tell her Takotah was as ancient as the hills and had come to live at Blakewell's Neck long before he'd been born.

She snatched the ball of linen from his hand and began to bind the dressing in place. As she slid her hand beneath him to pull the cloth through, he was treated to a whiff of lavender and a glimpse of her creamy breasts.

There had to be some silver lining to being half dead.

"There." She tucked in the end of the linen strip and stood. "I think you'll live."

"Help me sit." It galled him to realize he truly needed her aid.

"Stubborn man." She reached behind his head with her arm and lifted. "If it will keep you from hurtin' yourself, I'll help."

He gritted his teeth against razor-sharp pain.

She tucked a pillow behind his head, supported him as he eased back onto it. "Is that so much better?" Not waiting for an answer, she walked to the table and began slicing potatoes.

It was then Jamie noticed the weight of the cross around his neck. He recognized it as hers, remembered finding it in the servants' hallway while she slept. He reached up with his right hand, felt the pewter between his fingers. Warm from contact with his body, it was the oddest shaped cross he'd ever seen. Its four arms jutted out from a shared center and reminded him more of a windmill than a cross. It stirred him some way he couldn't describe that she had shared with him the power of this charm, which obviously meant so much to her.

He heard her gasp.

He looked up to find her gaping at the cross. Then her gaze met his.

Jamie had seen that look in her eyes before. She was afraid.

"I won't apologize." She lifted her chin, dared him to insist otherwise.

"For what?"

She looked at him in surprise. "Are you not angry?"

"Aye." He was angry about a great many things.

"Well, as I said. I won't apologize." She wiped her hands on a cloth, walked toward him. "I meant only to save your life, not to offend you."

She stood for a moment beside the bed, her hand out, and Jamie realized she was waiting for the cross.

With his right hand, he lifted the leather thong over his head. "Just what have you done to offend me?"

She stared at him, confusion on her lovely face. "St. Bríghid's cross. It—"

"You think it offends me?" He handed it to her.

She took it from him, slipped it over her head. "You are Protestant, are you not?"

Jamie tried not to notice that the cross had come to rest in the cleft between her breasts. "I'm supposed to be angry because you dared hang a Catholic symbol around my neck when you, a Catholic, were trying to save my Protestant life?"

"Then you're not angry?"

"No, Bríghid." He stifled a crazy urge to take her hand. "Where I come from, there are more religions than days in a month. I decided long ago such things aren't worth fighting about. I doubt God cares one way or another how we pray, as long as we make time for it once in a while."

She gaped at him as if shocked by his words. Then she turned, walked back to the table, continued slicing. "If you had died, we'd be guilty of murder. I had to do everything I could to keep you alive."

Whatever warmth Jamie had been feeling for her vanished. He almost laughed at himself. She'd gone to extreme measures to save his life not out of concern or affection for him, but to save her own skin and that of her brothers. In her eyes, he was nothing more than a hated

Sasanach. Hadn't he learned long ago that women, with few exceptions, acted for their own selfish reasons? "What makes you think I won't turn your brothers in once I'm gone from this place?"

She turned to face him, her face pale. "You would do that?"

Because he was angry, because he was in pain, he made her wait for an answer, forced her to meet his gaze. "No."

She went back to her work without a word, but he could see her hands shook.

Jamie felt like an ass, but couldn't bring himself to apologize. Instead, he took in his surroundings. From this vantage point, he could see the entire cabin. It was tiny, with whitewashed clay walls that had begun to crumble. Daylight shone through cracks here and there. There were no windows. The floor was hard-packed dirt. Other than the bed, which was big enough for only one person, the room held only two rickety chairs and the rough-hewn table. Smoke from the hearth floated to the ceiling, hovered.

"Your chimney is stopped up."

She continued to slice potatoes, didn't look up from her work. "There is no chimney."

Jamie found this astonishing. Then he noticed everything—the walls, the door, the legs of the table—were covered with a thin layer of soot. The thatched ceiling was black with it.

The cabin was more primitive in some ways that the clapboard slave shanties of Virginia.

"Who owns this place?"

She continued to slice. "We're not sure. It's been empty for a long time. We do know it's off the *iarla's* lands. But barely."

"*Ear-la*. I've heard that word before. Earl? Is that what it means?"

"Aye, I suppose so."

"The killer earl. What did your brother mean by that?"

"I'm surprised you remember." There was something about the tone of her voice. "Are all Englishmen so full of questions after wakin' from the dead?"

"Bríghid, tell me."

She dropped the potatoes into the pot. Liquid splashed into the fire with a hiss. "Father Padraíg is dead, God rest his soul."

"The old priest?"

Bríghid nodded, crossed herself, her back still turned to him.

"How do you know Sheff ... the Earl had anything to do with it?"

"The good Father was found hanged not far from the Old Oak eight days ago. Someone had put a sign around neck that read 'Traitor.'"

That must have meant Sheff's men had hanged the priest shortly after the crowd had dispersed. They'd walked some distance away, then killed the old man. But was it Sheff's bidding or their own doing?

Even as he asked the question, Jamie knew the answer. He'd seen the rage on Sheff's face, had known in his gut Sheff was not going to back down. But he'd let himself be deceived, and an innocent old man had died.

"Good God." He lifted his right hand to his temple. His head had begun to ache. "I'm sorry, Bríghid. I thought—"

"I don't blame you. I know you tried to stop him."

Then it dawned on him. Why hadn't he thought of it immediately? "Bríghid, I must get a letter to London, or you and your family could be in grave danger."

Chapter Eight

Ruaidhrí sat by the hearth, watched as his sister helped the *Sasanach* get out of bed.

"Put your arm around my shoulder." She bent down, lifted his right arm, put it behind her neck.

The *Sasanach* pulled his arm away. "Let me be, woman!" His voice was strained, his face pinched with pain as he turned, put his bare feet on the floor, tried to stand.

"Don't be foolish! You'll crack your noggin, and you'll be back to keepin' me up nights." She put her arm around his waist. "Ruaidhrí, get his other side."

"No! I don't need his help."

Ruaidhrí shrugged. "That's fine by me, *Sasanach*."

Pushing off the bed with his right arm, the Englishman fought to stand. A groan escaped him as he came to his feet. His face went pale. His weight sagged against Bríghid, and for a moment Ruaidhrí thought the two of them would end up on the floor in a heap. But the *Sasanach* seemed to regain his balance and, with Bríghid to steady him, took first one, then another step toward the table.

On the table sat ink, pen and paper. It had taken another ride into Baronstown—this time with coin the Englishman had provided—to fetch it.

"That's it. We're almost there." Bríghid crooned to the Englishman as if he were a child.

It didn't sit right with Ruaidhrí, his sister standing so close to a man who was wearing only his drawers. It didn't sit right with him, his sister breaking her back like this to care for a stranger. Ruaidhrí had told Finn what he thought of it all, and Finn had called him an idiot, boxed his ears, reminded him of the debt he owed this particular Englishman. That didn't sit right with Ruaidhrí either, even if it were true.

His sister was still angry with him for nearly killing the man, but how was Ruaidhrí to have known? He'd been on his way to rescue her, planning to kill the *iarla* if he got the chance. Then he'd come upon the Englishman holding possessively onto Bríghid's arm, and he'd reacted as any brother would. When he'd understood what he'd done, he'd felt a wee bit sorry for himself. If his sister was telling the truth, he'd taken one step closer to eternal damnation, a step he could ill afford. He'd thought he'd been acting the part of a hero.

In the days that followed, Ruaidhrí had watched Blakewell fight for his life and hadn't cared if the man lived or died. Blakewell was nothing but a wealthy *Sasanach*.

But then he'd seen the shadows in Bríghid's eyes when she'd told them what the *iarla* had meant to do with her. The miserable bollocks! It had torn him apart, made him want to rip the *iarla* devil's head off. Ruaidhrí had been forced to admit to himself that Blakewell had spared her from a terrible fate. Now he was torn between unwelcome gratitude and the familiar comfort of hate. If given a choice, he'd stick with what he knew.

The Englishman sank into the chair, bit back a moan.

Bríghid took the blanket from the bed, wrapped it around his bare shoulders. She was different somehow. Ruaidhrí wasn't the fine thinker Finn was, but he knew it just the same. He could see it in her eyes, the way she looked at the *Sasanach* when she thought no one was watching. He could see it in the way she moved, the womanly sway of her hips that hadn't been there before. He could even hear it in her voice, the soft way she spoke to the *Sasanach*—when she wasn't yelling at him.

Not that the Englishman wasn't handsome. Ruaidhrí supposed from a female point of view this Jamie Blakewell was very pretty. But he was English and a Protestant. Nothing he'd done, no matter how noble, could clean the heretic blood from his veins. Such blood was meant to be spilled. His kind were responsible for the rape of Ireland and for the death of the true religion among so many Irish, who sought to evade the penal laws by turning their spineless backs on the Church. Wasn't this *Sasanach* himself a close friend of the accursed *iarla*? How decent and honorable could he be? Besides, he could never marry Bríghid. English law and common decency forbade it. Her feelings for him could only bring her pain and dishonor.

Ruaidhrí knew Finn and Bríghid thought him hotheaded, with more temper than good sense. But he was certain about this. If Finn was right that this situation was Ruaidhrí's fault, then Ruaidhrí had a duty to make certain Bríghid was not made to suffer more than she already had. He'd keep a close eye on Blakewell, do everything he could to keep Bríghid from making a terrible mistake. The sooner the *Sasanach* left, the better it would be for all of them.

When he was gone, and Bríghid was safe, Ruaidhrí would make the *iarla* pay.

*B*ríghid draped the blanket over Jamie's shoulders, retreated to the hearth. What was wrong with her? She had helped a sick man, a *Sasanach*, get out of bed, nothing more. Yet her pulse was racing, and her belly fluttered. From the moment his arm had gone around her shoulder and he'd leaned against her for support, she'd been unable to think. Sparks had coursed through her where their bodies had touched. The few steps to the chair had seemed to last forever.

Perhaps touching him brought back bad memories from what had been the worst night of her life. But what she felt wasn't revulsion or fear. It was more akin to surprise or excitement, as if some part of her had been shocked into awareness. She'd felt it before. She'd felt it when he'd kissed her. Only then she'd been afraid, confused.

She was still confused.

During the long days and nights when he'd lain near death, she'd convinced herself that strange feeling hadn't been real. She'd been so bent on saving his life she'd been able to keep her mind off the carved planes of his chest, his broad shoulders, his strong arms. But now he was awake again and growing stronger. He seemed to fill the small cabin, dominating the room with his presence. Even weakened, the masculine power of his body was undeniable. It called to her, and to her horror, some primal part of her answered.

She tried to clear her thoughts, busied herself making more mayweed and nettle tea.

"Busy hands make for a clean conscience," her father had always said.

It was near to dinnertime. There were fresh oatcakes she'd cooked to be eaten with butter. She had a stew on the boil. Ruaidhrí had managed to snare a couple of conies this morning, and their meat would add flavor to the onions and potatoes and make a strengthening broth for Jamie. It would also help to stretch their food supply. Finn couldn't be traveling here with a cart full of bread and bacon every other day, not if they wanted their whereabouts to remain secret. And while Jamie had given Ruaidhrí coin to stock up on supplies like flour, salt pork, and oatmeal when Ruaidhrí had gone to buy paper and ink, someone would have to travel to Baronstown again and risk being seen when their stores were gone.

She carried the cup to the table, placed it far from the precious paper. "I've made more tea."

He didn't look up, didn't speak, but wrote with deft strokes, quill scratching noisily as it moved. His thought was obviously bent on his words, not the cup of tea she'd made.

What did she expect? He'd nearly lost his life, had been cut off from his family, his affairs. He'd said he had important business to attend to with Parliament, and if people like the *iarla* were his friends, he must be a man of some consequence among the English. He had better things to do than make idle chatter with a poor Irish girl.

Brighid stirred the stew, her eyes taking stock of the cabin. If Jamie had come from a home like that of the *iarla*, as his speech, horse, and clothing suggested he did, he was used to big rooms with shiny wooden floors and thick carpets, hallways that held nothing but empty chairs. He was used to sleeping in beds that sat high off the floor and thick feather mattresses, downy pillows, and sheets made of the softest linen.

How primitive this cabin must seem to him. His mattress was of threadbare homespun stuffed with straw. It rested on a web of ropes strung across a pinewood frame a mere foot off the ground. There were no carpets, just a dirt floor. Cracks in the crumbling walls let in cold air, rain, mice. There was only one room, and it didn't have enough chairs for them all to sit on. Smoke filled the air, stung the eyes, left dark smudges on the skin.

While this cabin didn't belong to her, it wasn't all that different from the one she called home. There were no cracks in the walls at home, to be sure, and they did have both a window and a chimney. But its floor was made of dirt, and it was tiny, with one main room, a pantry, and a small side room where she slept on a straw pallet with Aidan.

And what about the women in his life? What of his sister and this beautiful Indian woman, Takotah? Did they dress in worn woolen gowns trimmed in frayed ribbons? Were their hands reddened from work, her faces smudged with smoke? Or did they dress as Brighid had been dressed that night, in silks so soft they felt like warm butter, stockings made of gossamer threads, new ribbons and pure white lace?

She put the lid on the stew none too gently and jabbed the fire with the poker.

Foolish girl! What did she care what he thought of her? It was no sin to be poor. She could not change who and what she was, nor would she want to. She was a Ní Maelsechnaill, and that alone was enough. Her ancestors had been high kings and queens of Ireland at a time when England was lost in darkness. Let him scorn her poverty. She owed him a debt, and she would repay it as best she could, whether he said thank you for the tea or not.

Jamie heard her put down the tea, forced himself to focus. He needed to think, to concentrate, but her very presence made that nearly impossible. He couldn't remember ever having been so aware of a woman. He heard every word she spoke, whether he understood her or not. He knew every step she took. The soft swish of her skirts, the gentle motions of her hands, the play of emotions in her eyes, even the scent of her skin—he noticed it all. And it was playing havoc with his senses, as battered as they were. He knew this obsession was nothing more than the pent up sexual frustration of having touched and tasted—but not taken. That didn't make it any easier to bear. As soon as he was back in London and had enjoyed a woman in his bed, he'd be able to put Bríghid and her sapphire blue eyes, soft curves and long, dark hair behind him.

He heard the lid clank into place on the stew pot, felt her gaze on him, forced himself to concentrate. He'd left Sheff's early on November 11, and today was already November 21. If Sheff were looking for him, he might have had time to discover by now Jamie hadn't yet returned to London. For certain he'd have had time to scout inns and check ships' records.

But would Sheff pursue them, or would he let it go? Jamie had no way of knowing.

If only he had gotten this letter off sooner. He'd have asked Matthew to create a diversion, to send a servant to inns along the road to Dublin to reserve rooms in his name. He'd have asked Matthew to instruct the servants to tell anyone who asked that he was home but not to be disturbed. He'd have done something to draw Sheff's eye to England and hold it there. He could still do these things, of course, but it might already be too late, especially by the time his letter reached London and Matthew'd had time to act.

He wasn't concerned for himself. This was 1754, after all, not 1054. Bríghid was not a serf, so Jamie had stolen nothing. The worst that could befall him was public ribbing and animosity from Sheff's allies in the House of Lords. Given his crucial mission, that was bad enough, for if he failed, it could well mean the end of British claims along the Ohio frontier and the deaths of more British families. Alec had trusted him to carry out this mission. The Virginia House of Burgesses had trusted him. Washington had trusted him. He could not fail. Not this time.

But Bríghid and her brothers stood to lose just as much as any frontier family—their home, their freedom, their lives—and Jamie could not abandon them. He could not abandon *her*. Sheff had shown himself capable of malice Jamie couldn't have imagined, and it wouldn't surprise him if he had planned to kill Ruaidhrí all along. He'd gone back on his word about the priest. Why not Ruaidhrí?

Not that the boy hadn't worked hard to earn it. It was his sword that, with no warning and no challenge, had nearly put Jamie in his grave. Hatred flowed in Ruaidhrí young veins like water in a stream. If he didn't come to his senses, he'd find himself at the end of a hangman's noose some day. Jamie could only hope Bríghid and the rest of her family didn't get caught in the middle.

Meanwhile, Jamie had to keep her safe until he was back on his feet, then he needed to get Bríghid far from County Meath. But how? He considered the possibilities, mulled over the possible consequences. There was only one option that made sense, but there would be hell to pay. Bríghid would hate him even more than she already did, to say nothing of her brothers.

Ruaidhrí stood, walked to the hearth, bent over the stew pot, sniffed. "Just what are you writin' in that letter, *Sasanach*?"

Bríghid shooed him away. "You ought to be mindin' your own business, Ruaidhrí. For shame!"

"This is my business." Ruaidhrí glared at Bríghid. "Did it not occur to you, sister, that he might be writin' to turn us all in to the English?"

Bríghid looked searchingly at Jamie, and he saw the fear and doubt in her eyes.

He checked his temper. "I said I wouldn't turn you in, Bríghid, and I won't."

No, he wouldn't turn her or her brothers in. But he would betray them.

Bríghid and Ruaidhrí began to argue in Gaelic. After a moment, Ruaidhrí stomped out the door in a rush of cold air.

Jamie had already turned back to his letter. He dipped the nib of his quill into the ink bottle, tapped it on the glass, wrote. By the time the letter was finished, he felt as if he could sleep for a year. His chest hurt like hell, and he was more than a little dizzy. He folded the letter, removed his signet ring—a gift from Alec and Cassie for completing his studies at Oxford—then dripped a bit of plain white wax from the candle onto the envelope and sealed it with his mark.

"I've made a stew." Bríghid placed a steaming bowl before him. She sounded vexed. "If you're up to it, you can have some oatcakes, too."

Jamie forced himself to raise his head and accept the spoon she handed him. He hadn't the strength to fathom her changing moods. Instead, he concentrated on lifting the spoon to his mouth.

The stew was warm and more flavorful than he'd imagined. Though he hadn't felt hungry, he was suddenly ravenous. He consumed the entire bowl, together with a few oatcakes, before succumbing to exhaustion and pain. Dismissing Bríghid's offer of help, he made his way shakily back to the bed—the matter of a yard or two—and sank onto the straw mattress.

"God's balls!" He cursed the pain in his chest, his weakness.

"Sure and that's a fine thing to say." She pulled the wool blanket over him, felt his forehead with one soft hand. "Are you sure you won't take some poppy? It will help you sleep more deeply and—"

"No!" Pain made him speak more harshly than he'd intended, and he saw the hurt in her eyes. "Laudanum will only dull my wits."

The door burst opened. Cold air poured in, and with it came Ruaidhrí. He carried an armload of straw and a blanket. His face was red with cold, but his blue eyes held fire. He glared at his sister.

"If he's strong enough to get out of bed, it's time I quit sleepin' in the cowshed and started keepin' an eye on him."

Ruaidhrí dropped the straw in a pile on the floor in the corner near the hearth, lay down and covered himself with the blanket. With one last angry look at Jamie, he curled up to sleep.

Then it dawned on Jamie. Where did Bríghid sleep? There was no other bed, no other room. He turned his head, spied a pile of straw in the corner behind the table and a blanket folded over the chair.

Hell!

It wasn't right for her to be sleeping on the floor on nothing but straw. The cabin was cold, drafty. As the only woman, she ought to take the bed. He started to object, to insist they trade places, but he couldn't keep his eyes open, couldn't ...

Before he could finish the thought, he was asleep.

Chapter Nine

*M*uirín watched Aidan eat, couldn't help but smile. The child gobbled his food as if he'd never been fed before. "Will you be wantin' more?"

"Aye." He smiled, his blue eyes wide with anticipation, then grew serious. "If there is more. Finn says I'm not to be eatin' your last potato."

"Don't worry. I haven't yet cooked my last potato." Muirín took his bowl to the hearth, refilled it with beef soup, trying to ignore the flutter in her belly. "What else does Finn say?" She felt wicked asking the child, but the question was out before she could stop herself.

"He says I'm to mind my manners."

"And so you have." She carried the bowl back to the table, placed it before him, and knelt until her gaze was level with his. "When he comes today, I'll tell him you've been a perfect Irish gentleman."

"Finn is right. You *are* pretty." Aidan beamed at her, then attacked his soup.

Muirín sat, felt heat rise to her cheeks, felt her pulse quicken. Finn thought her pretty?

She dared not think too much about that.

It would be hard to think about anything but that.

"I take it you like my cookin', young Aidan."

Aidan nodded, looked up at her with bright eyes from beneath eyelashes almost as red as his hair.

She smiled again, surprised at how easy it had become. When Domhnall had died in the spring, she'd felt she might never smile again. Then his babe had grown strong inside her, and life had mattered again. But the babe had strangled in her womb, going to its grave without having taken a single breath. She'd wished God had taken her, too, with her wee son still inside her. But she had lived. She had lived, though each day seemed a burden, though laughter was intolerable, smiles insufferable. She had lived, though she felt dead inside.

The kind women of the parish had tried to comfort her. Most of them had lost a child and knew her pain. Though she was grateful for their sympathy and understanding, Muirín had felt cut off, alone. Life in the parish had gone on as it had before, seeming to her a cruel parody of the world she'd known before. Even her body had mocked her. Milk had made her breasts ache, pearling creamy white on her nipples, but there had been no babe to suckle. The weight of her grief had seemed enough to keep the sun from rising.

The pain was still there. It hadn't gone away. Muirín feared it would never go completely away. But in these past few days, she'd felt something she hadn't felt since she'd held her son's lifeless body—hope.

Like light from darkness, it began when life seemed it could not get worse. It began early in the morning the day after the babe's funeral, the day after Father Padraíg—God rest his soul—was martyred. Finn had come to her early in the morning and asked her to watch Aidan. While Aidan sat sleepily in the horse cart, bundled in a blanket, Finn told her the Englishman who'd persuaded the *iarla* to give her baby's body back had been horribly wounded while trying to help Bríghid escape the *iarla's* clutches. Bríghid was doing all she could to save his life while in hiding, and Finn was needed to get supplies to their hideout. He was afraid Aidan might be punished with the lot of them if they were caught. Finn's handsome face had been lined with worry—for Bríghid, for Ruaidhrí, for Aidan, for her and even for the injured *Sasanach*.

"I know you're deep in mournin', Mistress Ó Congalaig, but I've no where else to turn, no one I can trust with the truth. He's a good boy. He'll be no trouble to you. Can you take him?"

It was as if she'd awoken from a dark sleep. "Aye, Master Uí Maelsechnaill," she'd said. "It would be an honor."

She, too, owed this mysterious *Sasanach* a debt. If not for him, her son would have been laid to rest in a nameless grave in a heretical graveyard. She owed Finn Uí Maelsechnaill, as well. From the day Domhnall died, he had taken on the chores of a husband. He'd cut and stacked peat out of the rain where it could dry. He'd tended the enormous bull that was supposed to have secured a future for her and Domhnall. He'd taken this year's cattle to market and gotten a fair price. When her belly had become so swollen with child that milking the cows was an ordeal, he'd taken on that task as well. She'd never asked him to help, and he'd never asked for anything in return.

Each night when the work was done, he'd knock on her door. "Is there anything you need, Mistress Ó Congalaig?" He would stand, cap in hand, sweat on his brow, his blue eyes filled with concern.

Finn had been steadfast, undemanding, polite. Though her heart still sorrowed for Domhnall, Muirín wasn't blind. Finn was tall, vigorous, more handsome than most. Like most Maelsechnaill men, he had deep blue eyes and blonde hair, but his hair was shot through with darker tones. In his face, he resembled his sister, but where Bríghid's features were delicate, his were manly, aristocratic. When Muirín looked at him, she fancied she could see the royal Uí Naill blood still strong in his veins.

She'd been in awe of him as a little girl. Like other families, her family had shared whatever harvest they had—honey from the hive, cheese, a cut of beef—with the Uí Maelsechnaill, descendants of the High Kings and rightful heirs of the land. Master Uí Maelsechnaill, Finn's father, had been a hedgerow teacher and had risked his life to teach parish children—boys and girls—to read and do math. He'd taught them ancient Irish history, shared the stories of the Tuatha De Danaan and the unlucky children of Lir, of Oisín and Tír na nÓg, of mighty Cuchulainn and Queen Meadhbh, of brave Finn Mac Cumhaill and lovely Gráinne. He'd taught them to walk proud and not to bow down under the weight of the *Sasanach*. And when he'd been caught and dragged off like a common criminal to be sold as a slave... Muirín had wept for him and his family.

"To be Irish is to remember," he'd said.

She would remember him.

As a little girl, Muirín had revered her teacher, thought his son a true prince of Eire, perhaps Finn Mac Cumhaill reborn. She'd thought him as far beyond her reach as the sea from the stars. But now...

Handsome and kind though he was, she tried to ignore the way her heart beat faster when he was around. Domhnall—God rest his soul— had been dead only seven months, and she had no business caring for another man. Not yet. But she could help Finn, return the kindness he had showed her by caring for little Aidan.

Finn had brought Aidan to her, and with Aidan had come the sunshine. He chattered all the time, asked lots of questions. He worked as hard as a boy of nine could. He kept the hearth piled high with peat, fed the chickens and cows, collected the day's eggs without cracking a single shell, carried water from the well. She suspected he was trying to be the man about the house, and she would indulge him and praise him for his efforts as long as he didn't do something that might get him hurt.

Muirín watched, charmed, as he scraped the bottom of the bowl for the last bit of broth, wiped his mouth on his sleeve. "Have you eaten your fill, or would you like a third helping? I can't have you doin' a man's work on a child's portion."

"I'm full now, thank you." He belched, and his hand flew to his lips in surprise. His cheeks flamed crimson. "Excuse me."

Muirín smiled, touched a finger to his nose. "What fine manners you have, Aidan. And you're welcome."

He hopped up from the table, scattering crumbs on the floor. "You know what?"

"No, what?"

"Finn says I'm going to be taller than him someday."

"And well you might. I remember your da', and he was a tall man. You take after him."

Aidan's chin lifted, and his little chest visibly swelled with pride at her words. "You know what?"

"No, what?"

"Finn says—"

But his words were cut off by the sound of approaching hooves.

Muirín felt a surge of panic. "Aidan, quick! Hide in the corner under the bed. Don't come out, no matter what! Do you understand?"

The boy's face paled, but he lifted his chin. "I'm not afraid! I can fight—"

"I know you're not afraid, Aidan. You're a brave boy, but now is not the time to fight. Do as I say. And don't come out until I call you, no matter what you see or hear! Go!"

Aidan moved reluctantly at first, but as the hooves neared the cabin, he ran to the small bed and disappeared beneath it.

Muirín smoothed her apron, took a deep breath, tried to calm herself. Her mind exploded with unanswered questions. Had the *iarla* found the hideout? Did he know she was helping Bríghid and Finn? Had he sent his men for Aidan?

She pushed the questions aside, opened the door, stepped out, tried not to gasp.

The *iarla* himself.

She closed the door behind her, prayed Aidan would do as he was told. The day was cold and overcast, but in her fear she barely felt the chill.

The *iarla* jerked his mount to a stop. Behind sat half a dozen men on horseback.

"My lord." She curtsied, buried her trembling hands in her apron. "I am honored."

"You are O'Connelly's widow, are you not?"

"Aye."

"You live here alone since your husband's death."

Muirín hesitated. "Aye, my lord."

"Do you hear, gentlemen? This good woman is out here all alone without male protection."

His men shouted, their voices tinged with lust.

"We shall do our best to keep an eye on you. I'd hate for anything to happen."

She heard the threat in his voice, kept her silence. *Please let him ride on.*

"I'm told that the eldest of the old hedgerow teacher's sons often visits you."

More lustful shouts from his men.

Her heart raced. Her mouth went dry. "Master Uí Maelsechnaill has been kind enough to do the man's work here since my husband passed on."

Lascivious laughter rose from the men, and some made crude gestures with their hands to show exactly what they thought men's work entailed.

She felt her face flame, forced her gaze to the pebbles at her feet.

"You wish to see me, my lord?"

She gasped, spun about. 'Twas Finn. He'd come up behind her and stood, sweat on his brow, hayfork in hand. Relief flooded through her. But where had he come from?

His eyes told her not to ask, then his gaze shifted from her to the *iarla*. Though he held the hayfork with its tongs pointing into the earth, she felt the tension in his body, sensed the masculine power coiled within him.

He came forward, put himself between her and the *iarla*.

Finn looked into the eyes of the soulless bastard who had kidnapped his sister, threatened his brother, murdered Father Padraíg—and felt deadly calm steal over him. He'd come over the crest of the hill to see the *iarla* riding straight for Muirín's cabin. At once, he'd abandoned his cart of freshly cut peat on the road and run, only one thought on his mind. Muirín and Aidan were in danger.

He'd kept to the ravine that ran behind her fields, where no one would be able to see him and had approached the cabin from behind. He'd heard the *iarla's* voice, heard the filthy laughter of his men, slipped into the barn. Though they outnumbered him seven to one, he would not face the whoreson without some kind of weapon.

No one would touch her or the boy.

"Speak of the devil." The *iarla* shifted in the saddle, smiled arrogantly down at Finn. "I understand you've been helping the good widow with her chores since her husband's death. How charitable."

"I can't take all the credit, my lord. The men and older boys in the parish stop by when they can to lend a hand." Let him think Irishmen were popping in and out all day long. Let him think she was rarely alone. "Mistress Ó Congalaig has suffered great loss, and we all want see she's cared for. Might I inquire about my sister, my lord?"

The *iarla's* eyebrows rose, nearly touched his white wig. "It's on your sister's behalf that I've sought you out. I'm afraid a guest of mine has spirited her away from under my very roof, and I don't know what's become of her."

Finn did his best to look shocked, angry. It wasn't hard. "But, my lord—"

The *iarla* raised a gloved hand, cut him off. "I have men looking for him both here and in England. I trust we'll find him soon. I thought perhaps she might have contacted you in some way or that you might have heard something. A rumor of her whereabouts?"

Finn allowed his voice to take on an edge. "I've heard nothing of my sister since your men took her, my lord."

"And what of your brother, the young rapparee?"

"I sent him away, my lord. I'll not be havin' him stirrin' up trouble for the rest of us."

"Quite sensible." Disappointment tinged the *iarla's* words. "Where did you send him?"

"Dún na nGall, my lord. County Donegal. We've relations there."

"You Irish seem to have relations everywhere. You breed like rats." The *iarla* sighed, motioned one of the riders forward.

Finn tightened his grip on the hayfork, held his ground.

The rider approached, drew a white bundle from under his coat handed it to the *iarla*. The *iarla* shook it out, unfurled it like a sail, dropped it at Finn's feet. His men laughed.

Finn realized it was linen, a bed sheet. And it was stained with blood.

Careful to keep his grip on the hayfork and his eye on the *iarla*, he bent, retrieved it, stared at the brownish patches of old, dried blood.

"I was hoping I could prevail upon you to keep eye out for this Englishman. As you can see, he was quite taken with your sister. He enjoyed her quite thoroughly before stealing away with her."

Rage was a drum beat in Finn's ears. His hand balled into a fist, clenched the linen, crushed it. He forced his arm down to his side, drew cold air deeply into his lungs. But nothing could remove the expression of anger from his face. He met the *iarla's* gaze unwavering. "Aye, my lord. My sister is an honorable woman. Whatever this Englishman did to her, it was not of her desiring. I will keep my eyes open. If I find him, I will — "

"You will send for me. I will take care of him myself. " The *iarla's* voice was heavy with arrogance. "Any Irishman who raises a hand to him will pay with his life. He is an Englishman and therefore my problem. Is that clear?"

The Sasanach was a lying, deceiving bastard. "Aye, my lord."

The *iarla* kicked his horse with his heels, turned its head. "Keep the sheet. Let it be a souvenir to remind your sister of her lost innocence."

Finn watched them disappear, sent silent curses winging after them. "God's blood!"

He heard Muirín's sigh of relief, felt her hand rest tentatively on his shoulder. Her touch helped calm the fury, sent sparks skittering through him.

"They're gone." Her voice was almost a whisper.

He let the hayfork fall to the ground, turned to her. Her face was still pale with fear, and he could see she was trembling. "Aye, they're gone. But for how long? I heard how he threatened you."

Then he did something he should not have done. He dropped the sheet, pulled her into his arms, held her close. Fragile she was, soft, and she shook from head to toe. He felt her shudder, felt her wet, warm tears through the linen of his shirt. He rocked her back and forth, his lips on her hair, as she wept. "I'll not let him hurt you, Mistress Ó Congalaig."

She sniffed, stepped back, looked up at him. "Please, Finn. Call me Muirín. Once a woman has soaked your shirt with her tears it's permitted." A small smile crept over her lips.

Her beauty assaulted him. Lovely she was, like a wildflower. Her small nose was kissed with tiny freckles, her skin clear and soft. Her hair was tucked demurely beneath a white *ciarsúr* as was customary for married women, but he remembered it was thick and long, the color of wild honey. Her eyes, though shadowed by grief, were green like a meadow in springtime. Her lips... He had no business thinking about her lips or how much he longed to kiss them, taste them.

"Aye, Muirín." He raised a hand to her cheek, wiped her tears away. It felt so good to speak her name, to hear her speak his.

"What are you going to do?" She looked down at the sheet.

Finn felt the edges of his anger return. "I don't know. Bríghid says the *Sasanach* didn't defile her, and I don't think she'd lie to me, unless ... "

Unless she had feelings for the *Sasanach* and wanted to protect him. Ruaidhrí suspected as much. Perhaps Finn should have paid more attention to what his little brother had to say.

"It could be anyone's blood, Finn. The *iarla* wants your help, and that's why he showed you this. He meant to provoke you."

"Aye, you're right. I need to talk to Bríghid. But if I find out she lied, the *Sasanach* will wish he'd died the first time."

Chapter Ten

*M*uirín gasped. "Aidan!"

Finn grabbed the sheet, followed her through the door. It was the first time he'd come inside since Domhnall had died. He'd not wished to intrude on Muirín's grief, had kept his distance. Domhnall was a good man. He'd been a good friend.

"You can come out now, sweet." Her gaze fixed on the bed in the corner. "Finn has come."

Aidan emerged face-first, eyes wide with fear. When he saw them, he scooted quickly out, rushed to Muirín, buried his head in her apron.

She stroked his red hair, murmured reassurances to him. "You did exactly as I told you, and I'm right proud of you, Aidan."

Something twisted in Finn's chest. If only her child had lived. She'd have been a wonderful mother.

The boy turned his head, looked up at Finn. "I was afraid. I heard the horses, and I was afraid the bad man would take Muirín, too, just like he took Bríghid."

"I'm not going to let that happen, *a phráitín*." He hadn't been able to stop it when they'd taken Bríghid. Or Father. He hadn't been there.

Aidan stepped back from Muirín, as if suddenly embarrassed to be hiding in a woman's skirts. He lifted his chin. "I didn't mean to be afraid, Finn. I want to be brave like you and Ruaidhrí."

Finn knelt before him, put a hand on Aidan's shoulder. "I was afraid, too. I saw those horses ride up to the door, and I was afraid."

Aidan looked stunned at this news, regarded Finn through solemn eyes.

"Bein' brave doesn't mean you're not afraid, son. It means you do what you must despite bein' afraid. Muirín says you did exactly what you were told, and that means you were very brave." Finn stood, tousled the boy's hair.

Aidan smiled up at him as if relieved of a burden.

"Now run outside and fetch us some water from the well. Talkin' to that vile *Sasanach* has left a bad taste in my mouth, so it has."

The boy flew out the door, wooden bucket in hand.

Finn turned to Muirín. He'd made up his mind. He hadn't even had to think it over. "Muirín, I—"

She held up her hand to quiet him and gave him a sad smile. "Thank you."

Finn felt his thoughts scatter like leaves in the wind. How could her smile affect him so? "For what?"

"For standin' up to the *iarla*. For protectin' me. For protectin' us." A blush rose into her cheeks.

"I did nothin' but stand there with a hayfork and listen while he insulted you, while he insulted my sister and all of Ireland."

"I think the proper response, Finn, is, 'You're welcome.'" This time her smile wasn't sad. It was almost … teasing.

He felt as if the breath had been knocked out of him. "You're welcome."

She walked to the hearth, stirred something that smelled delicious. "Have you had anything since breakfast?"

He watched her hips sway as she walked, felt the lure of her femininity even from across the room. "No."

"Sit." She motioned to the rough-hewn table at the center of the room.

Muirín fought not to smile. He was a big man and graceful out of doors. But inside the tiny cabin, he moved awkwardly as if he felt out of place or nervous.

He sat, placed his big, work-roughened hands on his knees. "Muirín, I've something to say, and you might not like it."

She ladled soup into a bowl, placed it before him with a spoon, sat. She had a feeling she knew what was coming. "Speak your piece, Finn."

She saw his gaze fall to the soup, but he held back. "I know you don't want to move back with your family, but I think you ought to reconsider. The *iarla* might come back."

It was as she suspected. She felt a spark of irritation. "I'll not leave my home."

"Muir—"

"I'll hear no more of it." She crossed her arms. She'd left for a reason, and nothing would make her go back. She'd take the accursed *iarla* and his threats over the drunken lust of her own father any day.

"So be it." He dug into the soup, chewed as if the conversation were over.

"So be what?"

"If you won't leave, then I'll have to stay here. In the cowshed."

She stood, hands on her hips. "Now wait just a minute, Master Uí Maelsechnaill!"

"Finn." He took another bite, smiled.

"If you think you're moving into my cowshed, *Finn*, you're dead wrong." She couldn't stand to think of him out there in the cold and wet. He'd done so much for her already.

Finn stood, forcing her to look up at him. "You know what that man is capable of. He has no soul, no conscience. I heard what he said to you."

"And so did I. But I won't have you stayin' in the cowshed."

"Confound it, Muir—"

"Not another word! If you want to play the hero and watch over us, you'll have to sleep by the hearth. I can't have you shiverin' all night and scarin' my cows with your chatterin' teeth!"

It was his turn to look surprised.

She met his gaze, defied him to argue with her.

He gaze softened. He looked at her as if she were something precious, his blue eyes brimming with concern. "People will tittle."

"Let them tittle away. You and I will know the truth."

The warmth in his blue eyes made her pulse race. "I would never do anything to dishonor you, Muirín."

"I know. That's why you're welcome to sleep inside, Finn." She turned from him, her heart aflutter. She grabbed some oatcakes, placed them on the table next to the butter urn. "Sit and eat before your soup gets cold."

*J*amie slipped his shirt over his head, grimaced at the pain in his chest and shoulder as he moved his left arm into the sleeve. *Damn*!

He cursed his weakness, cursed the entire situation. He'd have been in London for a fortnight by now. He'd already have met with Alec's contacts and would likely have a strategy in place for seeing a bill through Parliament.

Instead, he'd allowed himself to be pulled off course by a bit of skirt with long, dark hair and big blue eyes. He'd nearly lost his life and had gravely imperiled his mission. He'd have been smarter simply to leave her to her fate. She was not his problem.

Even as the thought formed in his mind, he rejected it.

It was at least partly his fault she was in this predicament, which made her his problem. Even had that not been the case, he would not have been able to walk way, to turn his back and leave her at Sheff's mercy. He remembered the look of panic on her face as she'd entered the dining room—and the look of anticipation and excitement on Sheff's. She was an innocent, Sheff a predator.

No, he could not have turned his back on her, mission or no mission.

He pulled the shirt down, shook out the lace cuffs. It felt good to be clean again. He'd made good use of the basin of warm water Bríghid had left for him. She had removed his stitches this morning, and he'd finally had the chance to shave, to wash his hair, to wipe the remnants of illness from his body with soap and water.

He smiled despite himself as he remembered the way she had fretted as she'd pulled the stitches out, afraid she was hurting him. But he had scarce noticed the discomfort. Instead, he'd had to fight the urge to touch her, to lift her chin and taste those lips of hers again.

When she had finished, she had poured his water, told him to take his time, left him in privacy. Where had she gone? Perhaps she was outside reading that book of hers.

What did it matter? He cared not.

He tucked the shirt into his breeches and buttoned them. She had obviously done her best to wash the bloodstains out of the linen, but a faint beige tinge showed where blood had soaked through, thread stitching the cut made by Ruaidhrí's sword.

He reached for his stock, decided to forego that silly bit of stiff cloth, donned his waistcoat instead. It was likewise stained, the embroidered damask in far worse condition than the simple linen of his shirt. He could see she had tried to launder it and had stitched the tear, but the garment would never be the same. He removed it, tossed it carelessly onto the straw that was now his bed. His frock was likewise in terrible shape. It might be abysmal manners, but he'd be wearing nothing but his shirtsleeves until he got back to London. Though he had other clothing in his travel bag, it was far too formal to wear under these circumstances. He'd look like a fop.

He sat in a chair, slipped into his stockings, began to work the buckles at his knees. It had taken some effort, but last night he'd managed to persuade Bríghid to take the bed and leave the corner behind the table to him. She had refused to yield until he was able to get out of bed without help, as getting up from the floor would be a great deal more difficult.

Bríghid was damnably stubborn. He hadn't seen that side of her the first night he'd met her. But she had been terrified, fearing—and barely escaping—the worst. He supposed that, under the circumstances, she had shown a great deal of pluck. Most women would likely have dissolved into tearful hysterics, and understandably so, but she hadn't wept at all. He had to admire her for that. And for the resolve with which she'd tended him during his illness. He wasn't quite sure how he'd survived, but he knew it had everything to do with her determination to keep him alive—and help her brother avoid a murder charge.

He supposed he should be satisfied that she wanted him alive, regardless of the reason. Did he truly expect her to feel gratitude? She'd been angry with him that night. Moments before he'd been run through with a sword, she'd accused him of having done everything but violate her. Such evil intent had not been there—he'd been as unhappy to be thrust into that situation as she—but she couldn't know that. Certainly he'd enjoyed parts of it, but how could he not? What red-blooded man could hold her in his arms and not feel pleasure?

His blood stirred at the memory. For days now, he'd watched as she went about her work in the cabin—cooking, baking, cleaning. He'd remembered how soft her skin was, how it seemed to glow in candlelight. He'd remembered the lush fullness of her breasts, how they had pressed against his chest, their rosy peaks taut despite her fear, revealing the passion he was certain lay just beneath her cool and modest façade. He'd remembered the taste of her lips, the feel of her smooth, shapely legs, the tantalizing triangle of dark curls that hid her sex, the way she trembled at his touch. He'd remembered all these things, though he'd tried to put them from his mind. More than once he'd found himself fighting painful arousal and had done his best to hide the evidence. He'd no doubt Ruaidhrí would run him through again if he knew what Jamie was thinking.

Aye, even weakened by fever, he'd been attracted to her. The pull of her femininity was undeniable and as strong as the tide. Three weeks had passed since he'd been injured. As his strength slowly returned, so did the blatant sexual desire he'd felt for her from the moment he'd first seen her.

He'd made it his business not to care for women, so he was unwilling to admit, even to himself, that there might be more to his feelings for her than basic lust. And if he felt a strong urge to protect her? He supposed her vulnerability had aroused some last vestige of gallantry in him, first in the clearing when she'd been cornered with other Irish, then again in Sheff's dining room when she'd walked out of the dim hallway dressed like a whore and obviously terrified. But wanting to keep her safe was a long way from falling in love with her—something he would not allow.

It's not that he didn't believe in love. Alec and Cassie loved one another, had risked their lives for their love. But he'd found love to be nothing more than an invitation for betrayal. A man who handed a woman his heart shouldn't complain when she threw it in the dirt and stomped on it. Jamie had no intention of handing any woman his heart again.

No, he would not allow himself to care for Bríghid. He hadn't the time for such foolishness. She certainly didn't care for him. He was nothing more than a *Sasanach* in her eyes, an enemy with whom she'd made a temporary truce. She was likely looking forward to the day he was well enough to return to England. Then she would do her best to forget him.

But things weren't going to go quite the way she imagined.

He would leave her life soon enough, but first he had to know she was beyond Sheff's reach. Then he could focus on his real reason for being here. He'd come to persuade Parliament to move decisively against France in America. The future of British colonies might depend upon him, and he would not fail. As soon as he was strong enough to travel, he would resume his mission—and solve the Bríghid problem.

He reached for his greatcoat and gloves, slipped them on, then opened the door and stepped outside for the first time. He wanted to see to Hermes. The stallion needed regular care and had likely grown restless and unkempt from loneliness and neglect. Though Ruaidhrí insisted he was taking good care of the horse, Jamie was certain the hotheaded boy knew little about such things.

The day was chill and overcast, the clouds a heavy blanket that held no warmth. A cold wind blew through his damp hair. It was exhilarating. He'd been cooped up far too long in the smoke-filled cabin. Though he still felt a bit dizzy, he was strong enough to walk around a bit and breathe fresh air again.

He had expected to find Bríghid out here, her nose in the book she read when her work was done and she thought no one was watching. But she was nowhere to be seen.

He took in his surroundings. The cabin looked as small from the outside as it did from within and just as rundown. Its whitewashed clay walls were crumbling back into earth. Overgrown rosebushes grew up the front on either side of the door, their nude branches a tangle of thorns. The roof of thatch grew green with moss so thick it had become a fertile loam and sprouted grass. The ground around the cabin was dotted with dark clumps of moss that had lost their hold on the slanted roof and fallen.

A few steps from the door rose a grey stone wall—no doubt some kind of windbreak—that stretched the length of the front of the house and wrapped around a knoll covered in gorse. Beside it ran the rutted, grassy remains of a road. A thick copse of trees rose on either side of the road and behind the cowshed. Ash and birch, their bare branches in lacy silhouette against the gray sky, mixed with what had once been part of an orchard, gnarled apple trees heavy with withered fruit.

A short distance from the cabin stood a ramshackle cowshed. Eager to see how Hermes fared, he walked to the shed, entered—the door had long since fallen from its hinges—and allowed his eyes to adjust. Fresh straw covered the ground, a good sign the stallion had received at least some attention. In front of Jamie were three empty stalls, likely built for milk cows, as their gates were relatively low. A partition divided the shed into two halves. He could make out Hermes' sleek form against the far wall on the other side of the partition and started toward the stallion.

He took two steps, froze.

In the straw before Hermes' stall sat a wooden tub. In the tub sat Bríghid as naked as the day she'd been born. Her clothes lay in a heap in the straw. Her eyes closed as she massaged soap into her locks, her breasts half out of the water. He could smell the soap's lavender scent from where he stood. Her legs were bent, two pink knees poking up above the water. Steam rose into the air around her, a shimmering, translucent curtain.

Jamie watched, transfixed. Some part of him was dimly aware it was wrong for him to stand there, but his feet had grown roots. Her wet shoulders glistened in the weak light that leaked through cracks between the stones. The rosy peaks of her breasts stood like tight buds in the cold air. He longed to feel them, to cup them, to mold them with his hands.

Heat rushed to his loins. In an instant, he was hard, painfully rigid.

Suddenly she disappeared below the water, then rose up again, her neck arched, her breasts thrust upward, water sliding down her skin, over the dark river of her hair. She wiped her eyes.

As if awakened from a dream, Jamie cleared his throat.

Her head snapped around. She gasped, sank deeper into the tub, peered at him through eyes wide with surprise.

"Had I known the delights to be had out here, I'd not have done my ablutions alone inside." He didn't know why he said it. It wasn't the apology she deserved.

Bríghid felt heat rising in her cheeks, and with it, anger. "Wh-what are you doing here?"

"I came to check on Hermes. I can see he's had a better time of it than I." But he wasn't looking at the horse, which stamped and snorted a greeting in its stall. He was looking at her, devouring her with his eyes. His gaze scorched her, soaked through her wet skin, to the blood that surged beneath.

She stared back, her breathing strangely rapid. He had shaved, the smooth planes of his face scandalously handsome. His hair, tied with a black ribbon at his nape, was still wet. No longer a man fighting for his life, he looked healthy, strong, alive. She struggled to find her tongue, to form words, strangely bereft of speech. "Go. Now."

"Aye." But he didn't move. His gaze captured hers, and his eyes, usually hard and cold, had warmed to the deep green of the summer.

He'd already stolen her tongue. The heat of his gaze stole her breath.

"Isn't this is cozy?"

For the second time, she gasped, ducked. "Finn!"

Jamie muttered something under his breath and faced her brother.

"I'm not surprised to find you together. I've a question that needs an answer." He took a white bundle out from under his arm, shook it out.

She felt the blood drain from her face.

The bloodstained sheet.

Chapter Eleven

"I can see by your face you recognize this." Finn threw the sheet in the straw. "Oh, Bríghid!"

Bríghid heard the suppressed rage in her brother's voice. His gaze held hers, his eyes brimming with anger and, worse, grief. He thought she'd lied to him. "It's not what you think!"

"No? Tell me then!"

She was so eager to allay Finn's fears, to assure him she hadn't lied, her words came out in a jumble. "I ... that is ... Jamie—"

She stopped, cut off by a chuckle.

Jamie was laughing. He was laughing! How could he laugh? There was nothing at all funny about this. Did he not realize how angry her brother was, how much shame she felt?

"Oh, Sheff, you bastard. What scheme have you devised?" His gaze met Finn's. He didn't look the least bit worried. "I assume this came from the earl?"

"Aye, dropped in the dirt at my feet by the earl himself." Finn's jaw was tense, his body rigid with anger. "He said things I won't repeat here, things I bloody well hope are not true for your sake, *Sasanach*."

Jamie leaned against one of the support beams, crossed his arms over his chest as if he hadn't a worry in the world. "I did not steal your sister's innocence. Presuming that really is the sheet from my bed, it's my blood."

Finn's brows shot up. "Your blood?"

"Aye, mine. I had hoped to fool the earl into believing your sister had been ... taken. I had hoped he would think me so besotted, he would lose interest in her and not pursue us."

Finn's face darkened with rage. "Did you not think how that might blemish her name?"

"Aye. She spoke quite eloquently on that subject herself." He smiled ruefully. "I felt preserving her reputation was less important than preserving her virtue ... and her life."

The air was heavy with uncomfortable silence, and Bríghid could feel the tension that stretched between the two men. Finn was the first to break eye contact. He shifted his gaze to hers, his eyes revealing both doubt and hope.

"Bríghid, look me in the eyes, and tell me whether this man speaks truly."

She met her brother's gaze unflinching. "I am a maid still, Finn. That is his blood."

Her brother's blue eyes searched hers for truth. She watched his doubt fade to regret, watched the anger drain from him.

"'Tis sorry I am for doubtin' you, Bríghid. I've never known you to lie." He shifted uncomfortably. His gaze fell to the straw. "Forgive me."

"What else could you have done, Finn? There is naught to forgive." Bríghid wanted to throw her arms around her brother, to comfort him, then suddenly remembered she was naked in her bath. "Now if the two of you would please *get out*!"

Finn looked mortified, nodded. "Aye."

"Sorry for the intrusion." Jamie bowed slightly, but he didn't look one bit sorry. A suppressed smile tugged at his lips. His gaze met hers once more. Then he turned on his heels and was gone, Finn behind him.

She sighed with relief, laid back in the water, her head against the back of the tub, her eyes closed. Her arms crossed protectively over her breasts. *Sweet Mary and Joseph*!

"*I*'ll not berate you, Englishman. You spared my sister a terrible ordeal, and, as I was not there, I cannot judge you for how you did it. Sometimes fate deals a strange hand."

"Aye." Jamie knew this was Finn's way of apologizing, but he didn't need an apology. He opened the cabin door, entered the smoky warmth, Finn behind him. "Tell me what happened—exactly what happened."

He sat at the table and listened as Finn retold the story of his encounter with Sheff. Jamie felt anger build inside him as Finn recounted Sheff's thinly veiled threats against the woman whose baby had died.

Muirín was her name, and Finn said she was a widow, too. By the time Finn related Sheff's words about Bríghid, anger had become a dark and deadly calm coiled like a viper in Jamie's gut.

"He wanted my help in trackin' you down."

"He's not really looking for me."

Finn's brows knitted in puzzlement. "What do you mean?"

"I've broken no laws. For a variety of reasons, he can do nothing to harm me. Oh, yes, he can create difficulties for me in the House of Lords, and I expect he will." Jamie waived his hand dismissively. "He wants that which was taken from him. He wants Bríghid. And I suspect he wants Ruaidhrí, too."

He let Finn think on this for a moment, was surprised to see the younger man smile.

"You say our names very well—for a *Sasanach*. Are you certain one of your parents wasn't from our island?" A broad smile split Finn's face.

Jamie chuckled, wished for a moment he and Finn could be friends rather than enemies who'd temporarily found common ground. "Pure *Sasanach*, I'm afraid." Then he grew serious. "The earl wants them, Finn. He wants Ruaidhrí dead or worse, and he wants Bríghid to serve his basest needs. He will get what he wants unless we are very careful."

Finn's face darkened, all signs of laughter gone. "Aye. I should have sent them away that night, but … "

The unspoken words hung in the air between them.

"But you were saddled with a dying Englishman."

"Aye. Now that the *iarla* and his men are scouring the countryside, I'm not sure I can get them to our kin in County Clare safely. Then there's Muirín. I cannot leave her alone."

Jamie chose his words carefully. "I could arrange passage for all of you to the colonies. In Maryland, you'd be beyond the earl's reach and free to live your lives as Catholics, untouched by the laws that oppress you here."

Finn gaped at him. "Leave Ireland? We could no more leave Ireland than a fish could leave the sea. It's in our blood. Besides, we could never repay you."

"Consider it a fair return on the debt I owe all of you for saving my life. You could just as easily have left me to die."

Finn's brow furrowed, and he appeared to consider the idea. "We can't just leave all we have behind."

"Yet you risk your very lives by staying. Bríghid and Ruaidhrí are in grave danger. On the other side of the Atlantic they'd be safe."

"Are you thinkin' I should send them away with you, send them over the ocean?" Finn met Jamie's gaze, and Jamie could see doubt, fear, anger.

"It may be the only way to ensure their safety." Jamie said no more, letting Finn think on his words.

Finn looked troubled, shook his head. "It likely makes no sense to a *sasan* … an outsider, but Ireland is in our blood, in the beating of our hearts. The Uí Naill are an ancient clan. For centuries beyond count, our ancestors have lived and died here. If we were to leave, we would be turning our backs on a thousand years of dreams and prayers. We'd be turning our backs on everything we are, everything our da' taught us to be."

"It takes courage to leave everything you know and sail to an unknown land."

"Aye, I see that." Finn took a deep breath. "But I'd like to think it takes as much courage to stay, to face hopelessness and yet hope."

Jamie could hear the strain in Finn's voice, and he knew it wasn't easy for this proud man to speak so openly of something so personal. "The offer stands should you change your mind. You need only contact Kenleigh Shipping in London, and arrangements will be made."

Finn nodded. "That's right and kind of you. But it's an offer I cannot accept."

It had been Jamie's last option, his only way out. Now he had no choice but to betray them all.

He stood, his mind made up. He walked around his chair to the corner where he'd slept and reached for his travel bag. He unbuckled it, felt inside for the wooden case. He grasped the case, walked back to the table, and sat. He lifted the lid, withdrew one of two pistols, turned the handle toward Finn.

Finn's eyes were round with amazement as he took the weapon in hand, got a feel for its weight. "Bloody lovely." He laid it across his palms, stared with open admiration at the intricate silver designs on the polished wooden handle. "French?"

"Aye." Jamie took up the other pistol in one hand, the black velvet cleaning cloth and ramrod in the other. "My brother-in-law had them made as a birthday gift last year."

"Such a gift!" Finn turned the pistol over in his hand.

Jamie wrapped the cloth around the ramrod and began to clean the inside of the barrel. "Do you know how to use it?"

Finn gaze rose to meet Jamie's, his eyes full of wariness. "I've never even held such a weapon. Catholics are forbidden to own firearms."

"I want you to keep it. I'll teach you what you need to know."

Finn's eyes widened in surprise. "I cannot accept this. It must be worth—"

"It is nothing I cannot easily replace."

Finn shook his head, but did not relinquish the pistol. "Did you not hear me? 'Tis against the law."

"I heard you." Jamie wiped the pan and lockplate clean, tested the cock. He looked up, met Finn's gaze. "And now you must hear me. I will do whatever I must to make certain Bríghid is safe."

"What is my sister to you?"

What was Bríghid to him? He'd asked himself the same question and found no clear answer. He felt Finn's measuring gaze upon him, feigned a calm he did not feel. "An innocent in need of protection."

"And I suppose you're a knight on a white horse come to save her." Finn shook his head. "You've been readin' Bríghid's books. Don bloody Bellianis."

Jamie chuckled, and then grew serious. "I'm no knight. It's partly my fault she's in danger to begin with. That day at the oak, in the midst of the chaos, I ... noticed her. Sheff ... The earl saw, made a gift of her to try to win back my friendship. It's my responsibility to keep her safe."

"I heard this story from Bríghid. And to hear you speak it now— well, you're an honest man. I see that. But answer me this. Can you keep her safe from yourself?"

The question hit Jamie like a fist. Could he keep from touching Bríghid when his desire for her grew with each passing day? Could he turn away from her when his thoughts ran heavy with the memory of her softness, her scent, her luscious body? Could he ignore his mounting hunger to kiss her, to taste her, to feel her beneath him?

He must. They had no chance of a future together, and a woman like Bríghid deserved a man who could give her more than a few nights of physical passion. "I've no intention of touching your sister."

"But you will break the laws of your own country to help her?"

Jamie met Finn's gaze. "Sometimes fate deals a strange hand."

The door flew open. Instead of Bríghid, it was Ruaidhrí, his brow wet with sweat, his hands grimy from hours of cutting and loading peat. He gaped at the two of them, at the pistols in their hands. Then a smile spread across his face. "Bloody grand! Who are we shootin'?"

*B*ríghid pulled her cloak tighter about her to stop the chill. As angry as she was, she was surprised smoke wasn't coming out of her ears. She'd come in from emptying the tub to find Jamie teaching her brothers how a pistol works. At first she'd been too shocked to speak. Then she'd demanded to know what was going on, for it was clear something was afoot. First, the hated *iarla* pays her brother a visit, then Jamie gives Finn a pistol and offers to teach her brothers to shoot. Chance perhaps?

She was no child, though they treated her as one.

She'd hollered a fair bit, but they'd paid her no mind until Finn lost his temper, told her it was men's business, and demanded she get on with her chores. He'd never spoken to her that way before. It had taken every bit of willpower she'd possessed not to cry.

A hundred terrible possibilities had crossed her mind. The *iarla* putting out a reward for her brothers for some fictitious crime. The *iarla* showing the bloody sheet throughout the parish. The *iarla* threatening Finn, demanding to know where she, Jamie, and Ruaidhrí were hiding. Since this morning, her imagination had run wild, and fear had filled her belly with butterflies.

But the men seemed unaffected. They stood behind the cowshed taking aim at a row of apples Jamie had set up along the low stone wall. Had they lost their senses? If they were caught, they'd be hanged. What had driven them to this?

"At half-cock, it cannot be fired. You must pull it back to full-cock like this before you pull the trigger." Jamie demonstrated by aiming the pistol at an apple and pulling the trigger. Nothing happened. "Now let's see you cock it, aim, and fire."

Jamie pointed the barrel at the ground and handed the pistol to Finn, who took it awkwardly in hand. He raised it, cocked it, hesitated.

"Align the sight top of the barrel with the bottom your target, and gently squeeze the trigger. Don't jerk it. Keep your arm steady."

The crack of gunfire made Bríghid jump. The sound seemed to echo forever. Sweet Mary, what if someone heard them?

Finn shook his head, began to reload. The apples sat unmolested where Jamie had placed them.

"You pulled up a bit at the last second, a common mistake. It takes hours of regular practice to shoot well. Try it again."

Again Finn tried, as Jamie coached him and Ruaidhrí offered unsolicited advice.

Bríghid watched, envious of the easy camaraderie Jamie seemed to have built with Finn and even Ruaidhrí. He was never this unguarded when speaking with her, but reserved, distant. Never had they had a simple conversation. Never had he given her a glimpse of the thoughts that hid behind those green eyes of his.

He'd shed his greatcoat and stood in his shirtsleeves, seemingly oblivious to the cold. With his fine leather boots and breeches and the soft linen of his shirt, he looked every bit the refined country gentleman. He moved with the easy grace of a man confident in himself and his abilities.

Again and again Finn fired. A few times he hit the stones, sent up a spray of mortar, but the apples remained untouched.

"One more, and we'll give Ruaidhrí a try. He's been giving you advice for a while. Let's put him to the test and see if it's as easy as he says it is."

Finn stood sideways, took aim, fired. An apple seemed to explode.

Finn let out a whoop, got a smack on the back from Ruaidhrí.

Bríghid forgot herself, cheered with them.

"Did you see that, Bríghid? He got it!"

"Aye, Ruaidhrí, I saw."

Her brothers hastened to the fence to inspect Finn's damaged apple. Beside them stood Jamie, his face made impossibly handsome by a wide grin. The ties of his shirt had come loose, and Bríghid could see the crisp golden curls that nestled there. She remembered the feel of them against her cheek.

She'd been afraid that night, afraid and angry. But now she had so many questions, questions she dared not ask. What would it be like to lie in his arms willingly, to lie against his chest each night as she slept?

What would it be like to be kissed each day the way she'd been kissed that night? What would it feel like to have him look at her the way he'd looked at her when he'd lain above her, his strong body stretched, vigorous and naked, over hers?

Something clenched deep in her belly at the memory.

As if he knew she was thinking of him, Jamie turned toward her. He met her gaze, held it, his eyes the unfathomable green of the sea.

Her breath caught in her throat.

For a moment, neither of them moved nor spoke. Bríghid wondered if he really had read her mind, if he knew that even now she was remembering the feel of his lips against hers. Inadvertently, her gaze was drawn to the full curve of his mouth.

Jamie felt he'd slipped into a dream. He'd looked at her and every rational thought had fled his mind. She stood huddled in her thin cloak, her cheeks red from cold, her gaze fixed on … his mouth. Her fingers rested lightly on her lips, traced their outline in an unconscious gesture both innocent and deeply sensual. He knew without knowing she was thinking of kissing him.

His blood ran hot. Her gaze rose to meet his again, her sapphire eyes full of innocent longing. She shivered.

Jamie forced himself to turn away, strode to the workbench where he'd tossed his greatcoat. He retrieved it, walked quickly back to where Bríghid stood, her gaze now fixed shyly on her feet.

"You're cold." He wrapped the heavy woolen coat around her shoulders, fastened a button beneath her chin. His fingers inadvertently touched the skin of her throat. The contact sent sparks through him. "That ought to keep the chill out."

"What about you? You've only just shed a fever. You shouldn't even be out here." She gazed up at him, her face the picture of womanly sweetness.

"I'm fine." He brushed away her worries, tried not to notice how her concern touched him. Then something gave him pause. "What happened to your grandmother's brooch?"

Bríghid's gaze dropped to her feet. "I—"

"Hey, *Sasanach*, I'm ready." Ruaidhrí's voice intruded.

"Aye, I'll be right there." He glanced over his shoulder to where Ruaidhrí stood expectantly, then turned back to Bríghid. "Did you lose it?"

She looked up at him, and he could see the sadness she tried to conceal. "I sold it."

"You sold it?"

"Aye. I had no poppy, no turpentine. I—"

"You sold it to buy medicine for me?" Jamie felt strangely pleased. He knew what that brooch meant to her.

She nodded, looked away. "It was my duty to see you well cared for, and my brooch was the only thing at hand."

Her *duty*.

Jamie's ardor began to cool. His voice hardened. "If you had but told me, Bríghid, I'd have given Ruaidhrí coin to buy it back."

"That's very kind, but—"

"But you'd rather lose it than ask for my help?"

"Your *help* might well get my brothers killed, *Sasanach*. If they are caught with your pistol, there will be no mercy." She unbuttoned his coat, let it fall to the ground. "If it weren't for you, we wouldn't need anyone's help!"

With one last withering look, she turned and disappeared inside the cabin.

His anger barely in check, Jamie turned back to Ruaidhrí, who bounced on his heels, eager for his turn at the trigger. Jamie repeated the same lesson he'd given to Finn, barely aware of his own words.

Damn her! How like a woman to twist the situation! How like her to blame their predicament on him! He had tolerated their insults. For God's sake, he had even excused her brother's attempt to murder him. Now he was giving them the ability to protect themselves, and she *blamed* him for it? She had no idea what he risked by tarrying here, what was at stake for him. Hadn't he almost lost his life trying to save her? Did she not realize that in teaching them to shoot, he, too, could be branded a traitor and executed?

"Like this?" Ruaidhrí turned toward him, his attention on the pistol, which he absentmindedly aimed at Jamie's chest.

In one move, Jamie stepped out of the line of fire and wrenched the weapon from the boy's hand. He looked Ruaidhrí gravely in the eyes. "Never point a loaded weapon at another man. Your carelessness could get someone killed."

His anger with Bríghid gave his voice a harsh tone he hadn't intended.

Ruaidhrí flushed to the roots of his blonde hair, looked at the ground, mumbled something that sounded suspiciously profane.

Jamie pointed the barrel at the ground and held it out again. "A loaded pistol must never be handled lightly."

Ruaidhrí's gaze met his, and Jamie realized the boy was embarrassed as much as angry. Ruaidhrí took the weapon carefully and listened to the remainder of Jamie's instruction. By the time he was ready to fire the pistol, Ruaidhrí's enthusiasm was restored. But enthusiasm quickly turned to frustration as he failed to hit a target, and Jamie found himself grateful for the reprieve that arrived with cups of steaming liquid.

"I've made broth." Bríghid handed them each a mug. She did not meet Jamie's gaze.

She was still angry. Fine. So was he.

"Ah, Bríghid, my sweet, you're an angel." Finn drank his in several hearty gulps. "It warms a man to his toes, so it does."

Finn was right. Jamie swallowed his broth, grateful for its warmth.

Ruaidhrí glowered into his mug.

"Oh, don't take it so hard, Ruaidhrí, my lad." Finn laughed, clearly enjoying his revenge for all of Ruaidhrí's unsolicited advice. "Not every man can shoot an apple at twenty paces."

"Let's see you do it, *Sasanach*." Ruaidhrí stood before him, pointed the barrel at the ground and thrust the pistol at Jamie, an unmistakable look of challenge on his young face.

"Very well." Jamie handed Bríghid his empty mug, then reloaded the pistol. He motioned for the three of them to stand behind him. "I'm aiming for that apple."

"The one on the end?"

"No, Ruaidhrí, the one hanging on the tree."

"Hanging on the tree? Bloody hell! That must be at least —"

"I'd say it's a good thirty paces." Jamie turned, raised his right arm. "Let's see if I can shoot it out of the tree without hitting it."

"He's daft! Hit it in the stem at thirty paces?"

"Shh, Ruaidhrí, let him concentrate."

But Jamie didn't need Finn's help. He quickly focused on the apple, lifted his arm so that the tip of the barrel pointed a hair's breadth above the fruit, squeezed.

A crack. A burst of smoke. The tang of gunpowder.

Jamie lowered the pistol.

The apple had vanished.

Finn and Ruaidhrí ran forward, leapt the fence.

"I'll be buggered." Finn held the apple up for all to see.

It was whole.

"I can't believe it! How did you do that?" Ruaidhrí began to talk in excited Gaelic with his brother.

Brighid gaped in astonishment, unable to hide her surprise as Jamie turned to face her. "You're quite the marksman."

"My brother-in-law saw to it I was trained in the gentlemanly arts from a young age."

"Is killin' a gentlemanly art? Or breakin' the law?"

"Yes, Brighid, when the occasion calls for it. Finn is only doing what he must as a man and the head of this household."

Fear clutched at her belly. "What aren't you telling' me? Can you not see it's worse to let me imagine a thousand horrible things than to tell me the truth?"

Unshed tears pooled in her eyes. She hastily blinked them away, ashamed to reveal her turmoil to a man who already saw far too much of what was inside her.

Jamie looked down at her, his brow furrowed. Then his gaze softened. He seemed to hesitate for a moment. "The earl is searching for you, Brighid. He's scouring the countryside, and he aims to find you."

She felt the color drain from her face, dread settling in her belly like lead. "I feared so."

His hands cupped her shoulders through her cloak, steadied her. "There's more. He threatened Muirín this morning."

Brighid gasped. "Muirín! What about Aidan?"

"He's fine. Finn has moved in with the two of them to keep them both safe."

"And you've given Finn the pistol in case … "

"Aye, Brighid, just in case."

"I see. Thank you for tellin' me the truth." She turned, walked with a calm she did not feel back inside the cabin, closing the door behind her.

Then she let the tears come.

Chapter Twelve

*B*ríghid lay flat in the tall grass, panic like ice in her veins. A scream was trapped in her throat. Her mouth had gone dry. Her pulse was a hammer in her ears.

If she didn't move, he might not see her.

She held her breath, forced herself to lie completely still. She could hear the soft clop of hooves against the hard-packed dirt road.

Keep moving! Keep moving!

Even as the words echoed through her mind, the hooves slowed, stopped.

Sweet Mary, no!

She pressed herself flatter against the cold earth, prayed. She could hear the creak of his saddle, the horse's breathing, the impatient stamp of hooves.

Then came the predatory hiss of laughter.

He'd seen her.

Hooves tore into the grassy ground, headed toward her.

Her heart nearly exploded from fear. She leapt up, lifted her skirts, fled toward the nearby forest.

Pounding hooves approached from behind, drawing nearer and nearer.

Into the trees she ran. Branches tore at her skirts, scratched her face. Undergrowth blocked her path, tripped her. She dodged the thorny branch of a hawthorn, felt her ankle twist on a stone. The muscles in her legs burned. Her lungs ached for air.

She didn't stop, couldn't stop.

He was gaining.

She tried to run faster, heard horse and rider coming up behind her. But no matter how hard she tried, her legs could move no faster. She felt like she was running through deep water, legs churning uselessly.

Dear God, no!

Then he was upon her, one terrible hand clutching at her. She whirled about, gaped in horror at the sneering face of the *iarla's* man, the one who had groped her.

She screamed, but no sound came from her throat.

*J*amie rolled over, pulled from sleep. Something warm and fuzzy was running up his leg beneath his blanket. He didn't need to look to know it was a mouse. They were the real residents of this cabin. Still half asleep, he reached beneath the blanket, grabbed the little rodent, flung it aside.

But the mouse wasn't what had awoken him. There was something else.

Now fully alert, he listened.

A soft whimper came from across the room.

Bríghid.

She was having another nightmare. It was the third night in a row.

He understood nightmares, understood what it was like to be afraid to close your eyes. In the weeks and months that had followed the Wyandot attack and seeing Nicholas's charred body, he'd dreaded sleep. He sat, looked across to the other corner. Ruaidhrí appeared to be fast asleep, his breathing slow and even, his eyes closed.

Bríghid thrashed in her bed, small frantic whimpers coming from her throat.

Jamie glanced back at Ruaidhrí's sleeping form, threw off his blanket, and quickly crossed the room to the bed, the earthen floor cold against his bare feet. He sat beside her, stroked her cheek. "Bríghid, wake up."

Her head twisted from side to side, and she pushed his hand away. "*Éirigh as!*"

Jamie lifted her into his arms, held her tight, whispered in her ear. "Wake up, Bríghid, my sweet."

She struggled against him, trapped in her nightmare. Her lids fluttered open, and for one moment she gazed at him through eyes dark with dreams. Then she blinked. "J-Jamie?"

"You're safe, Bríghid. It was a dream, nothing more."

She pressed her face into his chest, clung to him. Her entire body trembled, and Jamie felt renewed fury at the man who had caused this. He didn't have to ask what she had dreamed to know Sheff was the source. Though she tried to hide it, he knew she was terrified that Sheff was looking for her.

Her fear and helplessness tore at him. He wanted to comfort her, to assure her no harm would befall her. His need to protect her, to make her feel safe, was so strong it startled him. In the light of day, he might have questioned it, fought it, dismissed it. But here in the dark with Bríghid so afraid she trembled and wept, he surrendered. He held her and ignored the heat she kindled in his blood. He demanded nothing, questioned nothing, offered her only his strength, his reassurance.

Grateful for Jamie's presence, Bríghid held onto him, her body shaking uncontrollably. She felt sick to her stomach, tears flowing down her cheeks. She fought to quell the fear that made her heart pound.

"Shhh, love, it's going to be all right. I won't let him touch you. I won't let him near you." His voice was deep, soothing. He felt warm, strong, his hand caressing her hair.

The icy fingers that clutched her heart began to melt. She lifted her gaze to meet his, feeling awkward. He hadn't touched her this way since ... "I'm sorry. I woke you."

"You don't need to apologize." He gently wiped the tears from her cheeks with his thumbs. "Shall I make you a cup of tea?"

His concern, his thoughtfulness surprised her. "There's no need ... "

But he had already released her and was walking toward the hearth, where the fire had burned down to glowing embers.

She hugged the blanket closer. The cabin seemed chilly and dark now that he had stepped away. She heard peat land with a muffled thud on the embers, and soon a blazing fire filled the cabin with warmth and golden light.

Bríghid watched as Jamie hung the kettle over the fire. Dressed only in his shirt and drawers, he opened the tea canister, filled the linen tea sock with dried leaves and set it in the waiting pot.

No man besides her father had ever made her a cup of tea. It felt intimate in a way she couldn't explain and left her feeling flustered. But

Jamie Blakewell confused her in so many ways. She was too tired and
shaken to figure him out tonight—or to think about the way he made her
feel. She accepted the cup of steaming tea from his hands.

"Drink. It will help to banish your dreams."

Curious, Ruaidhrí watched through half-closed eyes as the *Sasanach*
comforted his sister, made her tea, sat on a chair beside her bed, spoke
softly to her.

The bastard *Sasanach* cared for Bríghid. A blind man could see it.

Worse, Bríghid cared for the bastard *Sasanach*. Ruaidhrí was
certain, even if she herself refused to admit it.

The hell of it was that the bastard *Sasanach* wasn't such a bastard.
Ruaidhrí had watched the man closely these past weeks, and the
Sasanach was always surprising him. He was English and a Protestant,
but he had broken English law to help a family of Catholics. He was
deadly with a gentleman's pistol, but knew how to wield a hammer and a
hayfork, too. His clothes were as soft and pretty as a lady's, but his
tanned skin and muscles proved he'd done his share of manly work.
Yesterday Ruaidhrí had returned from cutting peat to find Blakewell
covered to his elbows in clay from patching the cracks in the cabin walls.
Loathe as he was to admit it, Ruaidhrí was finding it harder and harder to
hate the man.

But something wasn't right. Time and again Ruaidhrí had asked
Blakewell when he was planning on leaving, but the man had yet to give
him a clear answer. The *Sasanach* was clearly strong enough to make the
journey. What was keeping him here?

Ruaidhrí didn't like the only answer that came to him: Bríghid.

But his sister and the *Sasanach* had no business caring for one
another. Their nations were dire enemies. Their churches condemned
each the other, forbade marriage. They came from different worlds,
Blakewell having grown up in comfort, Bríghid in poverty. They could
no more build a life together than a sparrow and a salmon.

Even if by some miracle they managed to find a way—to elude the
British crown, the law, the Church—Ruaidhrí would not allow a
Sasanach into the family. It was unthinkable.

Ruaidhrí pondered the situation, listened to his sister and the
Sasanach whisper together.

"You've nothing to fear, Bríghid. I will do everything I can to keep
you and your brothers safe. Don't let the earl steal your sleep."

"It's not him, it's … "

For a moment, there was silence.

"Maybe it would help to talk about it."

"It's one of his men, the one who took me away. He … "

Something in his sister's voice made Ruaidhrí's muscles tense.

"What about him, Bríghid?" The *Sasanach's* voice was still gentle but had taken on an edge. "What did he do?"

"It doesn't matter now."

"If it gives you nightmares, it does matter."

Ruaidhrí couldn't agree more.

For what seemed an eternity, there was only the soft crackle of the fire.

Then Bríghid spoke, her voice barely a whisper. "He touched me."

Ruaidhrí felt anger kindle and burn within him. He knew which man Bríghid feared. The bastard would die alongside his devil of a master.

The *Sasanach* took her into his arms again, held her. "He won't touch you again. Ever. I promise."

Why had Bríghid shared this awful fact with the *Sasanach* and not her brothers? Ruaidhrí pondered this, didn't like the answer.

The *Sasanach* stood, bid Bríghid to sleep well, pushed his chair back to the table.

Ruaidhrí closed his eyes and feigned deep sleep as Blakewell walked back to his pallet.

He'd have to think more on this tomorrow. But one thing was certain. It was time for the *Sasanach* to go.

*J*amie lifted the saddle onto Hermes's back, ignored the twinge of pain in his shoulder.

The stallion stomped, jerked his head. He was restless and needed a good run to soothe him after weeks of inactivity.

"Settle down, boy. In a few minutes, you'll be free to run your fill."

Jamie tightened the girth, checked the stirrups, slipped his pistol with powder and shot into one of the saddlebags. Since the day he'd taught Finn and Ruaidhrí to shoot, he'd kept his pistol loaded and with him at all times.

He understood the stallion's restlessness all too well. He, too, felt impatient, on edge, troubled. It was time to leave. For Bríghid's safety, for the sake of his mission, it was time he returned to London. He would have departed days ago had he been certain everything was in place. But even if all had gone according to plan, he'd need a few more days. He couldn't risk leaving before then.

Still, that was a long time. He could only hope Sheff had given up the hunt or lost interest, though neither seemed likely, knowing Sheff. As it was, Jamie was surprised Sheff hadn't found them yet. Perhaps Matthew's efforts in London had distracted him. Or perhaps this cabin was so old that Sheff was unaware of it.

But Sheff wasn't the only problem. Ruaidhrí was becoming suspicious. Every day, he asked when Jamie would be leaving. Every day, Jamie found another excuse to stay. Yesterday, it had been to finish repairing cracks in the cabin walls. Today, it was the need to make certain Hermes was in good condition. And tomorrow?

Jamie sensed her a moment before she spoke.

"He's lovely." Bríghid walked up beside him, held her palm out for the stallion to sniff. Her braid hung like a thick, sable rope over her shoulder. Her face brightened as the stallion nuzzled her hand, lipped her hair.

Jamie could see dark circles beneath her eyes, bruised half-moons that marred the porcelain perfection of her skin. Sleepless nights and nightmares were taking their toll.

Damn Sheff and his thugs to Hell!

"Did you hear that, Hermes? The lady called you 'lovely.'"

Hermes snorted, jerked on the reins as if nodding in accord.

"What's that you say, old boy?" Jamie pretended to listen to the stallion, smiled at Bríghid. "I quite agree."

She laughed, touched her cheek to the velvety softness of the stallion's smoky-grey muzzle. "Do you mean me to believe you speak with horses?"

Jamie knew he was being ridiculous, but he wanted to wipe the fear from her eyes, replace it with some measure of happiness. "Only intelligent ones like Hermes. Some horses, like some men, waste a man's time."

She laughed and smiled. "Then tell me—what did he say?"

"He said he agrees that he is lovely, but he thinks you're even lovelier."

Pink rose into her cheeks, and she smiled. "You're daft!"

He'd give anything to hear her laugh again. "Did you hear that, Hermes? She thinks you're daft!"

Hermes snorted.

"Not the horse!" She laughed, shook her head. "You, Jamie Blakewell. You're daft."

Jamie turned back to the horse. "Now she's calling me mad, as well. What? You're absolutely right, old boy."

"Now what did he say?"

Jamie looked at her, feigned an expression of severity. "Hermes says you need to watch that sharp Irish tongue of yours if you plan to ride with us."

She gaped up at him. "Ride with you? I'm not goin' to ride with you."

Jamie took Hermes' reins, led the stallion past her out of the cowshed. "Hermes says you are."

Hermes began to stamp and shift, eager to run.

"Hermes says nothin'. He's a horse." She followed, looking at Jamie as if he were a mischievous child.

Jamie stepped into the stirrup, lifted himself into the saddle, held firmly to the reins to still the restless animal. "Come. I'll lift you up."

She stepped backward, her sapphire eyes round with a mix of excitement and doubt. "I can't go riding! I'm strainin' barm for bread!"

"Strain your barm later." He nudged Hermes into a walk, moved toward her, gestured at the overcast sky. "It is the perfect day for ride."

"'Tis cloudy and cold and looks like rain." She backed away, but not far or fast enough.

In one movement, Jamie reached down, caught her around the waist and pulled her sideways into the saddle before him. "Enough of this."

"Ooh!" She shrieked, grabbed onto the front of his coat, stared up at him with wide eyes.

"What in the bloody hell are you doin'?" Ruaidhrí had stepped outside and glared up at Jamie, his face an angry frown.

"I'm takin' your sister for a bloody ride on my bloody horse!" Jamie answered in his best Irish brogue. He loosed his grip on the reins.

Hermes needed no urging. He broke into a prancing trot and headed down the lane.

"Bríghid!" Ruaidhrí shouted after them. "Bring her back, *Sasanach*, or I'll rip your bloody head off, so I will!"

Jamie adjusted Bríghid's insubstantial weight evenly in the saddle, painfully aware of the soft curves of her bottom where it touched his thighs.

Evidently frightened by the movement, she gasped, gripped his coat tighter.

Jamie chuckled, held her closer. "Don't be afraid. I won't let you fall."

She adjusted her skirts, moved deeper into his lap. "I'm not afraid, *Sasanach.*"

"*Bréagach, thú.*" He smiled at her shocked reaction.

"You just called me a liar!"

"I know." He'd picked up a few words of Gaelic here and there. Most were words he'd learned from Ruaidhrí and wouldn't use in the company of a woman.

"Well, your accent needs work." A smile tugged at her lips.

"Does it now?" Jamie raised an eyebrow, gave Hermes his head.

The stallion broke into a gallop.

Bríghid gasped, her eyes wide, her hands fisted in the wool of his coat.

"I've got you." He held her tighter, felt the tension ease from her body.

Soon a smile had spread across her face, and her cheeks were flushed with excitement. Her laughter rang through the air like the tinkling of bells. Her eyes glittered with pleasure. Her hair, loosed from its ribbons, flew out behind her like a dark, silken mantle, caressed Jamie's face, tickled his nostrils with the scent of lavender.

Her waist felt so tiny in the crook of his arm, her body soft and lusciously curved. Suddenly, he wondered if taking her with him was such a good idea. He'd done it to lift her spirits—and, if he were honest, to spend some time with her away from Ruaidhrí's disapproving gaze. He hadn't expected a simple horseback ride to add fuel to the fire in his blood. But how his blood burned.

While she was plagued by nightmares, he'd lost sleep to dreams of touching her, tasting her, taking her, dreams that stayed with him all day, no matter how hard he tried to drive them from his mind. His body yearned for the pleasures of a woman, but he could not, would not seek his release with Bríghid. She was untouched, as innocent as a daisy, not the sort of woman he could dally with, then leave behind. He'd be in London soon, and he'd find plenty of women happy to give him relief.

As for today, he had made his bed, so to speak, and now he'd have to lie in it. He'd wanted to brighten her day, and from the smile on her face, he knew he'd achieved his goal. And if his blood ran a little too thick, a little too hot? If holding her like this made him think of holding her in an even more intimate manner? Well, this wasn't the first time in his life he'd had to practice discipline. It was nothing he couldn't manage.

Bríghid watched the ground disappear in a blur beneath them as the stallion released its pent-up vigor. She'd been on horseback before, but she'd never experienced anything like this. The nag her father had owned was old and weary and probably wouldn't have galloped if a burning brand had been tied to its tail.

But Hermes flew over the land as if on wings. She could feel the powerful animal surge beneath her, muscle and sinew. She could feel the power of the man, as well. The hard muscles of his legs shifted ever so slightly, controlling the stallion, as if the two were one.

She turned herself to face forward, held her arms out like wings, closed her eyes and savored the feeling of cold wind rushing over her face. Laughter bubbled up from somewhere inside her, and she felt the shadows lift from her heart. "I'm flyin'!"

She couldn't remember the last time she'd done something so fun or carefree. There was always so much work to be done, so many responsibilities and obligations. The best she could hope for most days was a little free time to read, and often she didn't get that.

She felt Jamie shift in the saddle and opened her eyes just as the stallion leapt over a low stone fence. She gasped, grabbed the horse's mane as the stallion sailed through the air.

"I've got you." His hold on her waist tightened.

Hermes' hooves hit the soft earth. She was rocked forward at the impact, then back against Jamie's hard chest.

Startled at the contact, she struggled to sit up straight. But seated before him, one leg crooked over the pommel of the saddle, the other pressed close to his left leg, she had nowhere to go. Her senses were heightened from the excitement of the ride, and she was suddenly very aware of him, of the way his arm was wrapped intimately around her waist, the way she pressed into his chest, the way his breath caressed her cheek.

She wanted to pull away, to end the disturbing contact between them. If only it didn't feel so ... right. She'd spent weeks mulling over that terrible November night. She'd tasted something that night, something she didn't understand. Overwhelming fear and mistrust had tainted the experience. What would it feel like to kiss him when she wasn't afraid? What would it feel like if he were to encircle her with his strong arms and hold her close? Last night, his embrace had chased away her nightmares, his tenderness so unexpected. How would it feel if he held her just to hold her?

What she needed was a husband, a man to make her forget Jamie Blakewell. She should ask Finn to help her find a husband. She would be eighteen in two months' time, more than ready for marriage. It was only natural for a woman her age to have questions, wasn't it?

And what of desires? Was it natural for her to have those, as well?

With the wind in her face, her hair unbound and flying in the breeze, his arm around her waist, her questions didn't seem so improper. Before she could admit to herself what she was doing, she slowly began to relax until even her head rested against him. Even through his great coat, through her cloak, his warmth made her skin tingle. Something stirred inside her, and when her heart beat faster still, she knew it more than the excitement of riding.

The stallion began to slow its pace. In the distance ahead of them to the northeast, she could see the gentle rise of the broad hill that marked the heart and soul of Éire.

"Teagh-mor." She didn't realize she'd spoken until she heard her own voice.

"Teagh-mor?" His voice was deep, resonant in his chest.

"The Hill of Taragh."

Chapter Thirteen

She felt the muscles of Jamie's arms shift as he reined the stallion to a walk, turned its head to the northeast, heading straight for the hill.

"Taragh? Is it an old castle?"

"No, Taragh is a place. We call it Teagh-mor in *Gaeilge*. 'Tis the ancient home of my ancestors, the heart of this land."

"I should like to see it. Can you tell me its history?"

"'Twould take all day!"

"Since we won't go back until I decide to turn around, I'm certain we have the time."

She met his gaze, saw the teasing look in his eyes, and couldn't help but smile. She had no idea what had caused him to let his guard down, but his smile and his laughter were like sunshine. "Perhaps you have the time, lazy *Sasanach*, but I've bread to bake and food to cook to fill your English belly."

The ground beneath them started to rise, and they quickly reached the crest of the hill. Wide it was, not high or rounded. Beyond, most of Ireland was visible, field and forest, stream and strand.

Jamie dismounted, grasped her waist and lifted her to the ground as if she weighed nothing.

"Oooh!" As her feet touched earth, she stepped on the hem of her skirts, tripped and would have fallen had strong arms not shot out to steady her.

"Careful." His hands rested intimately on her waist.

"Aye." She looked up at him, and the breath left her body in a rush.

He gazed down at her, his eyes dark with an emotion that made her heart beat faster. Some primal part of her recognized it as desire, delighted in it, and she felt the wild urged to stand on her toes and press her lips against his.

She turned away, took several hurried steps, tried to breathe. She stopped a few feet away from the grassy double ring that once had been the ramparts of a mighty fort, hugged her cloak tightly around her. "This is Rath Laoghaire, or what remains of it."

When he did not answer, she looked back.

He stood where she had left him, the stallion's bridle in one hand, the other affectionately stroking the stallion's muzzle. He did not look in her direction. "What does that mean?"

Bríghid searched for the right word. "Ring… or Fort of Laoghaire. He was a pagan king. 'Tis said he's buried here, standing on his feet in full armor, ready to fight his enemies."

Her eyes swept across the broad stretch of hill. Sheep grazed among the standing stones. The grey sky weighed heavily upon the landscape, the smell of winter in the air.

The last time she'd been here, she'd been a girl of nine. Her father had strayed with her through the earthen ramparts, told her stories, tested her memory. It had been a warm summer's day with the bright sun overhead and wildflowers at her feet. She'd been so excited to see Teagh-Mor with her own eyes.

A shard of unexpected pain stabbed her heart. *Oh, Da'!*

Bríghid lifted her skirts and walked around the outer ring until she stood between it and the even greater set of rings beyond. A feeling of hushed reverence came over her. Before her was the place her ancestors had called home. Here they had watched the sun rise and set. Here they had planned marriages, given birth, raised children, held the hands of loved ones as they died of age, disease, the wounds of battle. Here they had made decisions that determined the fate of all Ireland.

She closed her eyes, breathed in the history of the place. If only she could see it as it had been a thousand years ago. Standing here, she could almost hear the echoes of voices—the laughter of children at play, the cheerful hum of women working, the clang of a blacksmith's hammer. In the distance, there would be the clash of sword against sword as men tested their strength in mock battle …

Jamie took a deep breath, certain now his emotions were again under control. The slow ride up the hill hadn't been easy. She had leaned against him, let herself sink into him, and he'd found himself struggling to conquer his body's response. It had been pure delight. It had been sheer torment. And when she'd tripped it had taken every ounce of will he possessed not to take advantage of the situation and crush her against him in a brutish kiss. But she was innocent—untouched and untouchable.

He wanted her, more than any woman he'd known. But he could not give in to his want. He would not bind himself to her or any other woman, and a woman like Bríghid deserved more than a quick tumble in the grass by a man who would lift her skirts one day and leave her the next. Besides, he'd made great sacrifices to preserve her virginity. He'd almost died, for God's sake. What kind of man would he be if after all that he stole her virtue himself?

He tied Hermes's reins to a nearby tree, left the horse to graze. Then he walked to where she stood atop the outer ring of a much larger set of rings. Her eyes were closed, lashes dark against her cheeks. Her ebony hair, grey cloak and red skirts billowed gracefully in the wind behind her. She looked like a pagan princess from some distant past or a heathen priestess lost in an incantation. Before her stretched the broad hilltop— rings within rings, mounds, and standing stones.

Jamie felt the deep stillness around him, thought of Indian sacred sites Takotah had shown him, and knew he stood on hallowed ground. "What is this place?"

Her eyes flew open, and she seemed startled, as if she'd forgotten he was there. "It is Teagh-mor. It was once the seat of a great kingdom."

"This one is much bigger." He came to stand beside her, gestured to the giant rings before them.

"Aye. It should be. It is the Rath Righ, Fort of the High Kings. For more than six centuries, it was the home of the Ard Righ, the High King of Ireland." She lifted her skirts, walked toward the center where there were yet more rings. "'Twas the home of my forbears."

"Your forbears?" Jamie stopped, looked at her through new eyes. "So you are—"

"A many-times great-granddaughter of Niall Noígiallag, one of our greatest kings."

Sheff had told him that most Irishmen believed themselves descended from ancient heroes and kings, even mythological creatures. At the time, Jamie had been amused and laughed with Sheff at the absurd imaginings of illiterate, ignorant peasants. But after what he'd witnessed, Jamie knew Sheff had a twisted view of this land and saw only what he wanted to see. And while Jamie had so far had but a taste of Ireland, he had never known Bríghid to lie or tell fanciful stories. Perhaps she'd been fed false tales of royal lineage by her father. Or perhaps it was the truth.

He saw her hand lift to her throat where her brooch should have been, then slide away, disappointed. "What do you know about King Niall?" he asked.

"I know he subdued the Picts in what you call Scotland." She tilted her face towards him, smiled sweetly. "I know he harried the Romans when they had made a slave of your country. His descendants ruled Ireland for six hundred years."

"He must have been a fierce warrior."

"Aye, but he was wise, too." She slipped into a tale about King Niall's youth as she wandered through the grass, stopping to name this set of rings or that standing stone.

Jamie followed, lost in her story, lost in the beauty of her voice, the sweet lilt of her accent, the grace of her movements. He felt he could listen to her speak forever and never weary of it. The burdens he'd carried these past months seemed to lift from his shoulders.

"But while his brothers saved from the fire only things that could be remade and forged anew, Niall saved the forge itself from destruction. When his father saw the deep wisdom of Niall's actions, he called his court together and said, 'It is Niall and no other who shall succeed me as Ard Righ of Eirinn.'" She stopped before a tall standing stone that jutted from the ground like a giant phallus. "This is the Lia Fáil, the Stone of Destiny. 'Twas said it roared when touched by the rightful king of Taragh." She reached out as if to caress the stone, pulled her hand back.

"What's this?" Jamie looked with fascination on a low, grassy mound with a base built of piled stones. An opening led to a low stone passageway inside. He crouched and looked within.

"Don't!" Bríghid grabbed his coat sleeve. There was genuine fear on her face. "Do not go in there! The Sidhe! Such mounds are said to be the gateway to the world of the Faery, the Otherworld."

Jamie might have laughed, as he didn't believe in such things. But there was power here. He could feel it. This was sacred in some way or had been at one time. He could just make out designs carved into the rock—concentric circles, cup shapes, lines. The hands that had made them had long since turned to dust, and their meaning was now lost. What did they signify? Jamie would have loved to take a closer looked, but some ancestral memory told the Irish to stay out, and he would respect that just as he respected Indian burial grounds in Virginia.

"It is called the *Dumha na nGiall*—The Mound of Hostages." She then told a story of King Naill and the hostages he brought back with him to ensure the cooperation of conquered enemies and vassal kings. "'Tis said he kept hostages from as far away as Gaul here at Teagh-mor."

"You tell the stories well. Your father must have brought you here many times."

Her step faltered. "Only once, and that was long ago."

Jamie heard the pain in her voice, regretted his ill-chosen words. He had wanted to make her smile, had instead stirred her grief. He fought his urge to comfort her, to hold her. He did not trust himself to be near her.

They strayed in silence for a time, Bríghid interrupting the stillness to name a mound or set of rings — *Teach Chormaic*, *Rath na Seanad*, *Rath Gráinne*. The names were foreign and exotic to Jamie and conjured up images of some magical past beyond the reaches of history. Yet, it was all real and alive to Bríghid. What must it be like to know your family's history back to its dawning? What must it be like to be tied by your very blood and the crumbled bones of your ancestors to the landscape? While Jamie loved Blakewell's Neck with its forests, fertile fields, and the rushing of the nearby Rappahannock River, he was but the second generation of his family to live on that land, by comparison little more than a newcomer.

She stopped before a long, rectangular indentation, perhaps the foundation of a great, long hall. "This is the *Midh-chuarta*, the Banqueting Hall. Some say the king held the great *Feis* here every third year. The kings, chiefs, nobles and the *seancaithe* — the lore-keepers — met to settle disputes, pass laws and hear the entire history of Ireland recited."

"No doubt the stories grew taller with each retelling."

She gaped at him with wide eyes. "Oh, no! Any *seanchaí* who dared to change the history or weave lies into his tale would have been condemned by the others and risked becoming an outcast."

"Do you mean to tell me the Irish storytellers never embellish the truth?" Jamie didn't believe that for one second.

A smile played at the corners of her mouth. "Well, perhaps when they've had a bit too much *poitín*."

"What other stories do you know?"

"No *Sasanach* truly wants to listen to the tales of old Ireland." Bríghid met Jamie's gaze, felt as if she herself were on the drink. He looked so handsome in his woolen coat with its brass buttons. His shoulders were so broad, his jaw strong, and the way he looked at her...

He cupped her cheek in his hand, traced a circle on her skin with his thumb. "Ah, Bríghid, then I am not like other *Sasanach*."

His touch left a trail of fire on her cheek, drove away all thoughts but one. She wanted to know. She needed to know. "Kiss me. I want … "

She looked away, shocked and mortified at her own boldness. But the words were out. She could not take them back.

He lifted her chin, forced her to look into his eyes. "What do you want?"

The warmth of his gaze left her weak, spellbound. "I want to know what it feels like … to be kissed when … when I'm not afraid."

His eyes closed, his brow furrowed. A low sound like a moan came from his throat, as if the idea brought him pain.

And she understood. Shame made her cheeks flame. He didn't want to kiss her. She was naught but a poor Irish maid in his eyes, a destitute girl dressed in tatters. "I-I'm sorry. You don't want to. I understand. I was wrong to—"

His eyes opened. He chuckled, and then his voice softened. "I'm afraid you don't understand, Bríghid, my sweet. I want very much to kiss you. I want it so much it hurts. But be sure it's what you want."

Sure and this was not what she had expected him to say. His words made her heart beat faster, made it hard to speak. "That night, I felt … But I was so scared, and … I need to know. Just a kiss."

His gaze locked with hers. "Aye. Just a kiss."

She closed her eyes, fisted her hands in the folds of her cloak, unable to breathe. Just standing near him she could feel the enticing masculine strength of his body. She tilted her chin up to him, felt his arms enfold her, the hard press of his body against hers. At the first tentative brush of his lips against hers, she thought she would melt.

He kissed first her upper lip, then her lower. Then his mouth gently took hers, his lips warm and soft, and she *did* melt, sinking against him with a whimper, her palms flat against his chest. But the kiss wasn't over.

She felt his tongue trace the outline of her lips and found her lips parting of their own accord. Heat flared in her belly as he tasted her, penetrated her. This was much better than what she remembered, much more potent, more thrilling.

"*Bríghid*." When his lips took hers again, all gentleness was gone, replaced by an intensity that almost frightened her. She could not breathe. She could not think. Rather than pulling away, she found herself clinging to him, returning his passion with a fervor of her own. Their tongues twined, caressed, parried.

It was like nothing she could have imagined. She was on fire as he held her, consumed her, ravished her mouth.

He twined his fingers in her hair, pulled her head back and trailed kisses along the sensitive skin of her throat. She gasped at the delicious new sensation. When his tongue traced the whorl of her ear, her knees gave way. "Jamie!"

Gently he lowered her to the ground, the thick grass a blanket beneath them. He cradled her head in the crook of his arm, continued to kiss her throat. His body stretched, hard and strong, beside hers.

Through a haze of pleasure, she felt a hint of alarm. "Just a kiss. You said—"

He lifted his lips from her quivering skin, looked down at her, his eyes dark with passion. "Bríghid, my sweet, this is just a kiss."

Then his lips took hers again, and she forgot her fear. He filled her senses, the taste of him, the manly smell, the feel of his masculine body so close to hers. Her lips tingled, pulsed as he plundered her mouth, kissed her cheeks, nibbled the skin of her throat. Other parts of her tingled, too. She felt wet, hot with longing.

She heard herself moan, felt herself arch against him. Her fingers laced themselves through his blond hair, sought the planes of his back through the frustrating thickness of his coat. What was wrong with her? Her body burned as if with fever, alive and wanting.

"Ah, Bríghid." His voice was strained. "We must stop."

But she didn't want to stop. Not yet.

When he at last broke the kiss, she felt bereft, forlorn, desperate. Her breathing was as rapid as if she'd just run up a hill. Her lips ached for his attention, her body for his touch. A maid though she was, she knew what she felt was nothing less than a woman's full desire. She felt overwhelmed by it, both afraid and enthralled.

Just a kiss.

He gazed down at her, the look in his eyes one of undisguised male hunger. He trailed a finger along her cheek. "You have now been good and thoroughly kissed, Bríghid Ní Maelsechnaill. Do you have your answer?"

Bríghid could scarcely remember the question. "Aye."

"And how was it?"

How could she answer that question? She searched for the words, felt suddenly awkward. What would he think of her if she admitted how he had made her feel? She didn't want to admit it to herself, much less to him. Yet, how could she deny it? She'd reacted like a wanton. "I didn't hate it this time."

In truth, his kiss had shaken her to her soul.

He smiled, and she knew he'd seen through her feigned indifference. "Ah, Bríghid, you do know how to humble a man."

The reality of what she'd done began to sink in as her passion cooled. She had brazenly kissed a *Sasanach*, and it had touched her to her core.

She tried to rise, suddenly eager to be far away from him.

His weight held her fast.

"Which part did you not hate the most? This?" He gently brushed her lips with his.

She heard her breath catch, as the fire he'd stoked within her leapt to life again.

"Or this?" He deepened the kiss, tasted her with his tongue.

She whimpered, opened her mouth to his lingering, lazy intrusion.

"Or perhaps this?" His lips found the sensitive spot just beneath her ear and teased it.

She moaned, a low earthy sound of pleasure.

Abruptly, he pulled away.

Through a mist, she realized he was waiting for an answer. A blush crept into her cheeks. "I-I don't know. It was all much better than ... " She let her words trail away. She had not meant to stir those memories.

His brow furrowed. "Bríghid, about that night ... I said things, did things I would normally never say or do—"

"Please!" She held her fingers to his lips. "I don't want to talk about it."

"It frightens you." It was a declaration, not a question.

She nodded. "Aye."

"Yet you wish to know the truth. Why ask me to kiss you else?" His voice was deep, husky with desire.

She had no response. He saw too much, understood her too well.

"The truth is, Bríghid, I'm sorry for what you endured that night. I wanted only to protect you from something far worse. If I were truly to make love to you, it would be so much different than it was that night. When I make love to a woman, I take my time, and I make certain she enjoys it as much as I. Her pleasure comes first."

His lips lingered a mere inch from hers. His words made her belly do a flip. They also reminded her he'd been with other women, perhaps many.

She sat abruptly, pushed him away. "I wonder if you're after pleasin' them for their sake or just to satisfy your male pride."

He stood, helped her to her feet, a smirk on his damnably handsome face. "Why, Bríghid, don't tell me you're jealous."

"Jealous?" She brushed grass from her cloak. "I don't care—"

She heard it the same instant he did and froze, heart in her throat.

Men's voices and the frantic neighing of a horse.

Chapter Fourteen

"*H*ermes!" Jamie took Br#ghid by the hand, bent low, and began to run back in the direction they'd come.

The gentle curve of the hilltop blocked their view of the stallion. It also prevented whoever harried the animal from seeing them—for the moment.

Bríghid held her skirts with her free hand, struggled to keep up with him. He seemed to move without making a sound, as he had that night when they'd fled tfhe *iarla's* house. His pistol had somehow appeared in his hand, and a shiver ran through her when saw it was already cocked.

Back across the hilltop they ran, until they came to the *Dumha na nGiall*, the Mound of Hostages. They took shelter behind it.

The stallion's shrill screams filled the air.

The men's voices were clear now.

"It's going to kill me!"

"Hold tight! Don't let it pull free!"

A chill ran down her spine as she recognized the second voice. It was the man who'd kidnapped her, who'd groped her, fondled her breasts. *The man in her nightmares.*

"You recognize that voice?"

She nodded, feeling sick. "The *iarla's* man."

His jaw line grew rigid. His gaze hardened to jade.

She closed her eyes, sank back against the mound, fought to quell a wave of panic.

"Take this."

She glanced down at the object he'd pressed into her hands, closed trembling fingers over the polished wooden handle of a dagger.

"Don't hesitate to use it."

The memory of that long ride, of that awful man's hands on her body, flashed through her mind. Rage mixed with fear. "I won't."

"Stay here no matter what, do you understand? Hide inside if you must, legends be damned."

"Aye, but—"

"But what?"

Don't leave me alone! The words were on her tongue, but she swallowed them. She looked into his eyes, subdued her fear. "Be careful."

He gave her a teasing, lopsided grin. "Why, Bríghid, I didn't know you cared."

With that, he was gone.

*J*amie crept around the side of the mound, considered his options. He doubted Sheff's servants would have orders that permitted them to harm him. Still, he could not be certain. Sheff was not the man he remembered. If it became necessary to defend himself, he'd have only one shot. There might not be time to reload.

Ordinarily, his dagger would serve as a backup in that situation. Takotah had taught him to throw knives as a boy, and he was almost as accurate with a dagger as with lead balls. But he couldn't leave Bríghid without some means of protecting herself. If anything happened to him, she would be helpless. They would find her, and …

He brushed the thought aside, focused on his quarry. Bent low, he ran toward the largest set of rings, crept along their outer edge. As he came round the circle, he could see two men struggling to restrain Hermes, who bucked and reared, deadly hooves slicing the air. They were not far now.

Hermes whinnied in panic and rage, the whites of his eyes flashing.

"For God's sake, shoot it! It's broken my arm!"

"Grab the bridle! Hold its damned head!"

"My arm!"

Jamie chose his moment. "Let him go!"

The two men whirled about, gasped, dropped the reins.

The stallion reared and galloped away.

Jamie did not recognize one of them. The stranger cradled his limp arm, his face pale and covered with a sheen of sweat. But the other, the man with the dark, bushy hair and the pimple-scarred face, Jamie recognized as Sheff's lackey. Edward was his name. Jamie knew instinctively which man Bríghid feared, which man haunted her dreams. He felt an overwhelming urge to smash his fist into the Edward's ugly face.

Edward smiled, gave a nervous laugh, spoke in an oily voice. "There you are. I knew it was your horse. Didn't I?" He looked at the other man.

The man nodded, his gaze fixed on Jamie's pistol.

"Such a fine animal. We thought it had run off, escaped, didn't we?"

The other man nodded forcefully, hugged his forearm to his chest. "We saw the horse and ... Oh, damn, it hurts!"

"Stop your bleating! You frightened that poor stallion, and because of that we're looking down the barrel of a pistol." Edward hunched his shoulders submissively, gave an unctuous grin. "You don't really mean to shoot us, do you, Sir? We weren't trying to steal the beast."

Jamie could see the fear in both men's eyes, caught their nervous glances. "Get back on your horses, and ride out of here, and I'll let you live. This time."

"Oh, now, Sir!" Edward looked at Jamie imploringly. "We've done nothing to earn your ire. We're two simple servants riding out on our master's business when we noticed your horse all by itself."

Jamie was not fooled. "Move your hand one inch closer to your pocket, and I'll put a bullet through your forehead."

Edward's face paled, and he slowly raised his hands.

"You remember what I can do with a gun, don't you, Edward? You were there that day on the hunt when I brought down the stag."

Edward nodded, licked his lips. "A fine shot you are, Sir, but there's no need—"

"You were there when we rode into the crowd of Irish peasants. You helped murder the priest, didn't you? And when you were done, you went after her."

Edward had begun to sweat. Droplets pearled amid the stubble on his upper lip. "I-I don't know what you're gettin' on about. I didn't—"

"Oh, but you did, Edward. I know Sheff had the priest murdered. And I know you kidnapped her, took her from her family, abused her, and delivered her to the Earl." Jamie took a menacing step forward. "Are you always such an obedient toady?"

"There's no reason for insults." Edward took a step backwards. "I didn't harm the girl. I was sent to fetch her for you. You must be pleased with His Lordship's gift, since you took her with you. You might say I did you a favor."

"Did me a favor?" Jamie laughed, a harsh sound even to his own ears, but his aim did not waiver. "Two servants out on their master's business, you say? Pray tell, what is that business?"

"Just lowly errands, Sir." Edward smiled again, shrugged. "Nothing as would interest a gentleman such as yourself."

"Is that so?"

Both men nodded.

"Is she here, Sir?" Edward glanced about. "Or have you tired of her and put her aside?"

Jamie did not answer, let the silence stretch. His rage grew. He didn't want this man thinking of Bríghid, let alone speaking of her.

Edward squirmed, hands still in the air. "His Lordship has no quarrel with you, Sir. But the girl's family is lookin' for her, and it was his job to look after her and all. It's a matter of honor, if you take my meanin', Sir. The Earl won't do nothin' to her you ain't already—"

Jamie moved so quickly he had Edward by the throat before either man could react. He pressed the pistol hard against Edward's temple. "You know nothing about honor! Listen carefully, toady. I've a message for your master. You tell Sheff I know he's hunting for her. But if he so much as touches her, or anyone dear to her, I'll be hunting *him*—with a knife between my teeth! And I won't fail. Have you got that?"

Edward nodded, eyes bulging, clawing desperately at the hand that cut off his breath.

Jamie's nostrils were assailed by the stench of Edward's unwashed flesh and rotting teeth. The thought of this man touching Bríghid was utterly revolting, filled him with blind rage. It was all he could do to keep himself from breaking the bastard's neck. "As for you ... If I so much as see you again, if you come anywhere near her, I *will* kill you."

He took the poorly concealed pistol from Edward's pocket, thrust the man from him.

Edward rubbed his bruised throat, staggered backwards. "I'll just be goin' then."

"You do that."

Edward turned and hurried downhill toward the two horses tethered below. The other man followed, cradling his broken arm.

Jamie watched them ride off, certain they would carry his message to their master, but equally sure he had not seen the last of them.

When they had vanished round the bend, he turned to find Brighid standing nearby, Hermes' reins in one hand, the dagger in the other.

"I thought I told you to stay where you were!" Anger with Sheff and fear for her safety made his voice sharp. He snatched the dagger from her hand, slipped it back into his boot.

"What if you'd been hurt?"

He lifted her none too gently into the saddle, put his foot in the stirrup and mounted behind her. "You'd have managed only to get yourself captured again. Is that what you want?"

"Of course not!"

"Then do as you're told!"

She muttered something in Gaelic under her breath, cast him a furious glance.

He urged Hermes to a canter, turned the stallion's head to the west, away from Ruaidhrí and the cabin.

"Where—"

"They might try to track us. I'm going to put them off the scent."

In silence, they rode west until they came to a small, half-frozen creek. Jamie guided the stallion into the shallow water and let Hermes pick his course southward through water, ice and slippery stone. Brighid sat stiffly in his lap and seemed to be trying to avoid touching him. 'Twas just as well.

Jamie had nearly come undone today. When she'd asked him to kiss her, it had been on the tip of his tongue to refuse. But his tongue had proved a traitor. It had wanted to taste her sweet lips, to slide inside her warm mouth, to mate itself to hers, consequences be damned. He'd known he was taking a risk touching her. But he'd understood her need and wanted for the world to replace the memories of that night with something better, something real. It was, after all, just a kiss.

He hadn't expected to find himself pushed to the brink by her sensual response. Untouched though she was, there was passion in her blood, passion that craved only a man's touch to rouse it. It was a good thing he'd been dressed in his greatcoat and she in her cloak. He'd been able to hide his body's reaction, but it had taken every bit of self-control he possessed to part his lips from hers.

God curse him, but he needed her. He needed her to put out the fire she'd ignited inside him. Yet she was the one woman he could not have. If the situation weren't so painful, he'd be tempted to laugh at the absurdity of it all. He was consumed by desire for a beautiful woman who considered him her enemy and whose innocence he had all but sworn to protect. What was it he'd said to Finn?

I've no intention of touching your sister.

He'd be lucky if he could think of anything but touching Bríghid after today's folly. When he got back to London, he would head straight for Turlington's and bed five of the prettiest women there. Five? Hell, he'd bed ten—one after the other. Ten lusty women should do it. Ten lusty women and a few hearty pints. Then he'd be himself again.

The stallion tripped on a stone, stumbled.

Bríghid gasped.

Jamie tightened his grip round her waist, but Hermes had already regained his footing. "He's surefooted. I'll not let you fall."

She pulled away from him, as far away as she could.

'Twas obvious she was angry with him. But she wasn't being sensible. He'd done his best to keep her safe, and she'd defied him. Did she truly believe she could have helped him had the situation with those two thugs turned ugly? She'd have found herself overpowered in an instant and on her way to Sheff's bed—or worse, on her back in the grass. Jamie hadn't missed the gleam of lust in Edward's soulless eyes when he'd spoken of her.

Jamie made the mistake of looking down at her face and felt an instant pang of regret. Her cheeks were reddened from the chill, her lips set in a gentle frown, her brow knitted with worry. He had taken her riding to bring a smile to her face and chase her fears away. She was not smiling now, and he knew it was more than her anger with him. Seeing those men had terrified her. Her face had gone white as a snow when she'd heard that bastard's voice.

But why should Jamie feel any remorse? 'Twas not his fault.

Still, his conscience assailed him. Hadn't it been his idea to take her riding in the first place? Hadn't he exposed her to danger for no better reason than to make her smile? Or had his real motivation been the desire to spend time alone with her?

By the time he'd answered his own questions, he was mad as hell—at himself.

*I*t seemed to Bríghid they had been riding forever. The day had lengthened into late afternoon. Her fingers were stiff from cold, her entire body chilled. Her stomach rumbled with hunger. Her back ached from sitting like this. Her bottom wasn't too comfortable either. She'd never spent so much time on a horse.

They'd left the creek behind where it bent to the west and now were headed northeast through forest and open field. It could not be too far now—unless Jamie had gotten them hopelessly lost. She did not know this country well. It lay far south of her home.

The temperature had fallen, the sky grown dim. Shadows stretched into darkness. A few fat flakes of snow were drifting down from the darkened sky.

Another gust of wind buffeted Bríghid with icy-cold air. She shivered, fought to keep her teeth from chattering. She would not show the *Sasanach* any weakness.

He'd treated her like a child or a servant to be ordered about and scolded. She hadn't done anything to deserve his wrath. She'd been careful. Even he hadn't known she was hiding nearby. She had only wanted to help, and he'd raised his voice to her like a parent to a wayward child.

But she was a woman, not a little girl, though Jamie and her brothers persisted in treating her like one. Wasn't she grown up enough to heal their sicknesses, cook their meals, keep their clothes mended and their home in order? Was she not strong enough to share their worries? Did they not depend on her as much as she relied on them?

Another gust of icy wind seemed to blow straight through her cloak.

Her teeth chattered violently.

"Oh, for God's sake, Bríghid, let me warm you."

"I d-don't n-need your h-help, *Sasanach*!"

"You might not need it, but you're going to get it."

She felt him shift in the saddle, realized he was unbuttoning his coat.

"No!"

But he ignored her protests and struggles, and she soon found herself hauled up against his hard chest and enfolded in the thick warmth of his coat. It was a battle she was grateful to lose, though she'd never admit it. The heat of his body chased away her chills, and her shivering soon subsided.

The next thing she knew, Jamie was speaking to her.

"Bríghid, love, wake up."

Her head lay against his shoulder, and she was toasty warm, except for the tip of her nose. Had she fallen asleep?

The sun had set, and a thin blanket of snow lay on the ground. The cabin stood before them, ghostly white in the darkness. The warm smell of peat smoke was in the air.

No sooner had they dismounted, than the door opened, spilling light into the gloom.

"Where in the bloody hell have you been? I've a notion to bust your head wide open, *Sasanach*! Miserable bollocks!"

Jamie led Hermes toward the cowshed. "Wait until I've had a bite to eat, would you?"

Bríghid saw genuine anguish on her brother's face, felt a stab of regret for the worry she had caused him. "Everything is all right, Ruaidhrí. We're home."

"It's about bloody time! Mother of God, I'm hungry!"

S heff stared out the window at the falling snow, swirled his cognac, tried to ignore the shooting pain in his arms and legs.

A log settled in the fireplace, breaking the silence.

"Are you certain that's what he said?"

"Aye, my lord. I'm not likely to forget words spoken by a man pointin' a pistol at me head."

Sheff turned, glanced at Edward, took a sip. "I should think rather the opposite. Perhaps, overwhelmed by fear, you misunderstood him."

"Oh, no, my lord!" The servant shook his head. "He said, 'You tell your master I know he's huntin' for her. But if he harms her or any of her family, I'll be huntin' him with a knife in my teeth, and I won't fail.' Pardon me, my lord, but those were his words, not mine."

"I realize that, Edward. I'm not so stupid or heartless as to blame the messenger for the message." Sheff looked back toward the darkened window and the fat flakes falling outside. "Damn this bloody snow! If not for this infernal weather, we could have set out early tomorrow with the dogs and perhaps picked up their trail. When the snow lets up, you will take me to the exact spot where you spoke with him."

"Aye, my lord." Edward paused, shifted. "He called me a toady, my lord."

"Yes, well, you are a toady, Edward. It is your job to be obsequious and obedient to my commands, is it not?"

Edward looked confused, but nodded. "Aye, my lord."

"You may go."

"Aye, my lord." Edward bowed and turned to leave.

"Oh, Edward, one last thing." Sheff rubbed a hand over the stubble on his chin. "Did it not occur to you to lie in wait for him and to follow him rather than trying to seize his horse?"

Edward shifted nervously. "We thought if we had his horse, he'd come to us."

"Indeed, he did." Sheff smiled at his servant's stupidity. "I rather think you underestimate him."

Edward bowed his head. "It won't happen again, my lord."

"Go." Sheff sank into his favorite chair in front of the fireplace, let the rage come. Beneath it lay an emotion he loathed, one he refused to name or acknowledge.

How could Jamie say such things? How could Jamie threaten him over a woman? How could Jamie treat him with such disdain and cast aside his friendship with such finality? A swell of anguish rose up from inside him, strong enough to eclipse the pain in his limbs.

Damn Jamie Blakewell! And damn the Irish bitch who ruined him!

Sheff tossed back the rest of his cognac, hurled the crystal *tulipe* snifter into the fireplace, the shatter of glass giving expression to his tangled emotions. Before he had been torn between amusement and irritation. But he was no longer amused.

Jamie had crossed the line. There could be no forgiveness now.

Sheff rose, poured himself another drink, and began to pace the room.

You tell your master I know he's hunting for her. But if he harms her or any of her family, I'll be hunting him with a knife in my teeth, and I won't fail.

Sheff mulled over Jamie's message to him.

I know he's hunting for her.

How could Jamie know that? Perhaps it was a lucky guess. They knew each other very well, he and Jamie.

But if he harms her or any of her family...

Her family. Why should Jamie give a damn about her family? He'd never even met them.

Or had he?

An impossible idea occurred to Sheff. Had Jamie been colluding with the Irish against him? Had Jamie somehow won over the girl's brothers and persuaded them to hide him among them? Had they agreed despite the dishonor Jamie had done to their sister?

Such a thing seemed too ridiculous to be true. Jamie was every bit as English as Sheff, and the girl's family had a history of rebellion against the English. Worse, Jamie had stolen her virtue. Then Sheff remembered the morning in the clearing. Jamie had argued for leniency toward the Irish traitors that morning. No doubt some in the crowd had heard. Did they perhaps view him as some kind of champion for defying an English lord?

Sheff swirled his amber drink, held it to his lips, swallowed. Questions ran in circles through his mind until his head hurt. He sank into his chair, held fingers to his temple.

This was intolerable. Already he'd tarried in Ireland far longer than he'd intended. If not for Jamie, he'd have been in London for a fortnight by now. As it was, he'd been forced to plead illness and had missed the state opening of Parliament. Not that he truly regretted that. In truth, he found sitting through sessions in the House of Lords to be quite dull. Still, it was his duty as Lord Byerly to maintain a presence in London politics. He needed to leave for London—and soon.

"Jamie, what I am to do with you?"

Snow fell outside the window, a thick curtain of drifting white.

You tell your master I know he's hunting for her. But if he harms her or any of her family, I'll be hunting him with a knife in my teeth, and I won't fail.

Her family.

Perhaps it was time to pay another visit to her brother—and the pretty young widow he was trying to protect.

Chapter Fifteen

*I*t continued to snow for four days without stopping.

Each day, Jamie grew more restless. Certainly part of it was his body's aching, unfulfilled need. He hadn't been inside a woman for almost two months, though he'd been tortured with desire for one particular woman. He reminded himself this particular woman was the kind who both wanted and deserved a loving husband and was not for him. But his cock refused to listen and grew erect at the slightest provocation.

Like when Bríghid smiled at him with those sweet lips. Or when she walked past him, hips swaying and smelling faintly of lavender. Or when she ladled him a bowl of stew with her small, soft hands.

Being in the cabin with her was hell.

But the tension he felt was more than sexual. His sense of unease was growing stronger by the hour, and he'd found himself searching for ways to occupy both mind and hands. He'd risen this morning unable to hide his misgivings and had immediately left the confinement of the cabin. First he'd gone for a short ride—to condition Hermes, he'd said. In truth, he was scouting, looking for any sign that Sheff and his men might have set out despite the frigid weather. All he'd found were rabbit tracks.

Then he'd cleaned Hermes's stall, groomed the horse as best he could, hauled water from the spring. When that was done, he'd cleaned his pistol. He'd performed this task in the dim light of the cowshed because the sight of the weapon frightened Bríghid, reminded her of their peril. A peril that was growing.

Jamie could feel it.

He looked out of the cowshed at the falling snow, slid his pistol into the waistline of his breeches. Sheff would have gotten Jamie's message days ago and would be using this time to think, to plan. Sheff now knew they were somewhere nearby. When the snow let up, he'd saddle his horses, arm his men, and release the hounds. It was just a matter of time before he found them.

Jamie wanted to leave now. His every instinct told him not to delay. But was he doing the right thing?

Aye, he was. It was the only option open to him. He'd considered other possibilities, mulled them over in the dark hours of the night, but there was only one way to be certain Bríghid was safe.

And what of Ruaidhrí?

Jamie cursed under his breath, took up a makeshift hoof pick and walked over to Hermes's stall. Keeping busy was the answer to the endless stream of questions in his mind, the constant uneasiness.

He patted the stallion's withers, slid a hand down its left foreleg.

Compliantly, Hermes lifted his hoof.

Jamie held the horse's pastern between his knees and gently dug out the dirt that had become lodged inside the horseshoe.

What of Ruaidhrí?

Ruaidhrí was reckless and governed by his temper. He was a danger to himself and his family. Had he kept his mouth shut, likely none of this would have happened. But he was barely more than a boy, and Jamie understood at least some of the young man's rage. Would Jamie have kept his mouth shut at sixteen if the French had invaded Virginia and taken his land? Not bloody likely.

Ruaidhrí was not a bad sort, but he was young and inexperienced. Jamie felt the need to keep Ruaidhrí safe, not only for the boy's sake, but for Bríghid, who clearly loved her brothers and who had already lost so much.

But how?

He pondered this as he checked around the frog for stones, then released the hoof, sliding his hands reassuringly up the stallion's leg to its flank. Then he moved to Hermes's left hind leg.

What about Finn? As soon as Jamie returned to England, Finn would become an easy target for Sheff's wrath. Somehow, he needed to warn Finn about the encounter at Taragh, let him know of the danger. Finn needed to take Ruaidhrí, Muirín, and the boy Aidan and flee the county before Sheff had time to move against them.

Jamie brushed the remaining dirt from the left hind hoof and moved round the horse's rump to its right hind leg. Then it occurred to him. It was so simple.

He took the horse's right hind hoof, scraped it clean, a new urgency in his actions.

He would have to be careful. Ruaidhrí had been furious with him since the day he'd taken Bríghid riding, furious and spoiling for a fight. He wasn't likely to take direction from Jamie. But Jamie had been sixteen once. He remembered how he'd felt when Alec had tried to tell him what to do. Poor Alec. The man had shown the patience of a saint.

Jamie brushed the hoof clean, moved to the next one, giving the horse a pat on its flank as he passed. Hermes' coat had grown thick during the five weeks he'd been stabled here. With no proper curry comb, no way to clip his coat, he was beginning to look shaggy and unkempt.

"I'll give you a thorough grooming when we get back to London, old boy."

"And when will that bloody be?" As if conjured by Jamie's thoughts, Ruaidhrí stood just inside the cowshed doorway, arms across his chest, legs spread in a stance clearly meant to convey defiance.

"I leave as soon as the snow lets up." Jamie brushed the remaining dirt from the hoof, released it. He brushed the dirt from his breeches. "I'm glad you're here, Ruaidhrí. I need to take a message to Finn."

*B*ríghid lifted the last two potatoes out of the basket, turned them over in her hands. They were covered with eyes and had gone a bit soft, but they would do. She had cooked with worse many times and had been grateful for the meal.

Food was running low. There was a fair amount of oatmeal left, a bit of butter, a few onions, and some old, wrinkled apples she'd plucked from the trees outside, but little else. If not for the brace of conies Jamie had somehow managed to catch this morning, they'd have no meat. After this meal, the potatoes would be gone. She'd have to make this stew stretch.

There was no way around it. They'd have to go for supplies soon, either to Baronstown or home. And that would mean risking discovery.

Bríghid took up her knife, began to cut the eyes away, tried to ignore the fear that knotted in her belly. Fear of hunger. Fear of being caught. Fear of nightmares that might come true.

That afternoon at Teagh-mor had made her realize just how much danger she and Ruaidhrí were in. The *iarla* now knew they were not far from his lands. It was only a matter of time before they found this place—perhaps weeks or days or maybe even hours.

They ought to flee, take the wagon, take Muirín and Aidan and make the journey to the home of their cousins in County Clare. But it was such a long road, even during the warm days of summer, and they had little coin to spare for room or board. They'd wind up sleeping among the trees, poorer than a band of tinkers, who at least had their wagons for shelter. It was a journey she dreaded.

She was grateful the snow had prevented Jamie from leaving. For four days it had snowed, fat flakes driven by the chill north wind. As long as the snow continued to fall, he would stay. And while he was here, she knew she was protected. She'd seen what he'd done near Rath Laoghaire. She'd watched him take the *iarla's* man fiercely by the throat, press his pistol to the man's head. She heard the threat he'd made.

If he so much as touches her, or anyone dear to her, I'll be hunting him—with a knife between my teeth. And I won't fail.

And she'd known without a doubt he'd meant what he said.

Certainly, there was nothing more to her reason for wanting him to stay. He was a source of protection, and these were dangerous times. It had nothing to do with the way her heart skittered every time he looked at her, or smiled, or accidentally touched her. It had nothing to do with the way his kisses had made her weak and breathless. It certainly had nothing to do with how wonderful, needy, and frantic she'd felt as his tongue had possessed her mouth and his body had pressed against hers.

You have now been good and thoroughly kissed, Bríghid Ní Maelsechnaill.

Aye, she had. Kissed by a *Sasanach*. And she had liked it.

Was it always that way between men and women? Is that how her mother had felt when she'd kissed her father? Or was Bríghid unusually lustful? She'd felt lustful.

No, she'd felt free. He had kissed her, held her, and, lying in his arms, she had felt like the dawn—new, radiant, completely alive.

Was she starting to have feelings for him?

She dismissed that question without bothering to wait for the answer. She, Bríghid Ní Maelsechnaill, have feelings for an Englishman and a Protestant? Not likely! Not even one as decent and handsome and strapping as Jamie Blakewell.

A pesky voice in her head laughed at this answer. Why, the voice asked, was she thinking about him in her bed every night? Why did she imagine what it would be like to lie with him? Why did she do her best to recall in vivid detail the taste of his lips, the feel of his strong hands on her skin, the planes and angles of his strong body?

With a start, Bríghid realized it had happened again. She'd become so distracted she'd forgotten what she was doing. In her left hand, she still held a potato, but the knife had somehow slipped from her right hand.

She muttered an oath, took up the knife and resumed cutting.

She heard shouting outdoors, sighed. Jamie and Ruaidhrí were arguing again.

The door opened with a rush of chill air.

"I'm telling you it's too dangerous." Jamie bowed his head and ducked through the doorway. "I can't let you do it."

Ruaidhrí followed, his face red. "I don't recall anyone puttin' you in charge, *Sasanach*."

"It's a long distance, and the earl's men are looking for you. Just draw me a map, and I'll be on my way." Jamie walked over to his travel bag and reached for something.

Bríghid put down both knife and potatoes. "What—"

Ruaidhrí ignored her. "You'll just get yourself lost. It should be me goin'."

"Goin' where?"

Jamie tossed her an annoyed look, pulled out ink and paper. "I need to get a message to Finn. I've asked Ruaidhrí for directions, but he seems to think he should be the one to go."

"I know the land, *Sasanach*. You don't."

"I'm a fast learner. Besides, this will require both speed and stealth. I'll leave Hermes here so that if you need to get away quickly, you'll be able to ride."

"Tell me—" Bríghid felt her fear swell.

"I'm swift and quiet as a fox." Ruaidhrí puffed up his chest.

Bríghid stomped her foot, shouted. "Someone had best be tellin' me what the bloody hell is goin' on!"

Jamie and Ruaidhrí gaped at her, astonished at her outburst.

Ruaidhrí spoke first. "The *Sasanach* has decided he needs to let Finn know what happened at Taragh in case the *iarla* tries to take his anger out on Finn."

Bríghid hadn't thought of that. But Jamie was right. Now that he knew they were nearby, the *iarla* wasn't likely to believe that Finn knew nothing. Her brother would be an easy mark, a target, a hostage to be used against them. Someone needed to warn him.

Ruaidhrí went on. "I should go, bein' as I already know the way."

"I don't like the idea of either of you out in this cold." She didn't like the idea of Finn going unwarned, either.

"There are still a few hours of daylight left. A strong man ought to be able to make it there and back before dawn." Jamie placed paper and ink on the table. "Draw me a map."

"What if you get lost and spend the night in the wild?" Ruaidhrí glared at him.

"It wouldn't be the first time. The American wilderness is much more dangerous than anything you have here."

Bríghid didn't know what to think. She didn't want either her brother or Jamie out in the snow. She knew Jamie was strong and fast and had learned tricks from the Indians that enabled him to track, fight, move graceful and quiet as a cat. She'd seen that for herself. But Ruaidhrí knew the way and was strong and capable enough to make the trip himself. He'd done it before. "Perhaps you should both go."

Both men shouted in unison. "No!"

Jamie glanced at her. "Someone needs to stay here to protect you."

She tried not to look relieved. She hadn't liked the thought of being alone at night.

"Aye, he's right, Bríghid. We cannot leave you alone." Ruaidhrí pointed at Jamie. "You've got the pistol, *Sasanach*. You should stay with her. I can take care of myself."

Jamie's brow furrowed with disapproval. "I can't let you take that risk."

"You don't have the right to be tellin' us what to do. This is a matter for Bríghid and me to decide as it involves the fate of our family."

Jamie crossed his arms over his chest, met Ruaidhrí's gaze. "Very well."

At a truce, both men looked at her expectantly.

She hesitated. A dozen "what ifs" raced through her mind, none of them reassuring. She looked at her brother, who was impatient and fair bursting with vinegar, and Jamie, who returned her measuring gaze with an inscrutable gaze of his own. "Let Ruaidhrí take it, Jamie. He knows the way. He won't get lost, and he knows how to hide and keep warm."

Jamie stood, hands on his hips, his expression grave. "If they should catch him or he should fail—"

"That won't happen, *Sasanach*."

"Let's hope it doesn't." Jamie sat at the table, quickly wrote a letter, folded it. He dripped wax from the candle onto the paper to seal it, marked it with his ring.

Bríghid took a deep breath, worried for her brother's sake. "Let me pack you some food to take along. Meanwhile, sit down and have some stew. There's nothing in it yet but rabbit, but it'll warm and nourish you."

She dished Ruaidhrí a bowl of broth and cooked meat, then took the cloth bag that had held potatoes and dropped in several oatcakes, a few bites of cheese and an apple.

"Take this." Jamie rummaged through is travel bag and pulled out a leather pouch. "Pemmican."

Bríghid took the pouch, unsure she'd heard him correctly. "Pem … What?"

"It's a kind of travel food used by the Indians—dried meat and fruit set in animal fat. It tastes like hell, but it will fill your stomach and give you strength."

Ruaidhrí wrinkled his nose. "I've heard they eat dogs."

A broad smile spread over Jamie's face. "Not if young Irishmen are available."

Bríghid smiled despite herself, dropped the pemmi—whatever it was—in the bag. "Any Indian silly enough to eat my brother would end up with a devil of a bellyache."

In no time, Ruaidhrí had filled his stomach and stuffed his coat with straw for extra warmth.

"Remember to ask Finn for bacon, eggs, potatoes, cheese— everything you can carry." Bríghid wrapped his scarf around his neck, pulled his hat down over his tousled blonde hair. "There's a blanket in the bag if you get too cold."

Jamie shook his head. "It should be me going."

"Oh, shut your gob." Ruaidhrí rolled his eyes, tucked the letter in his coat. "You'd just get lost, and then I'd have to go find you. This saves me time."

"Be careful, Ruaidhrí." Bríghid gave her brother a hug.

"I'll be fine." Ruaidhrí kissed her on the cheek. "Don't worry."

"I'm your sister. It's my job to worry."

Ruaidhrí stepped to the door, opened it, looked back. Doubt clouded his eyes. "*An mbeidh tú sabháilte anseo leis an Sasanach úd?*"

Was she going to be safe alone with the *Sasanach*?

She glanced over her shoulder at Jamie. He stood, arms crossed over his chest, leaning against the wall by the hearth. She would never be safe around him, not when her own desires betrayed her. She nodded. "Aye."

"See you in the morning, sister." Ruaidhrí nodded, slung the bag over his shoulder. "Take care of her, *Sasanach*, or—"

"She'll be safe."

Bríghid felt a stab of sadness. Her little brother looked so young and vulnerable walking into the snowy afternoon alone.

"He'll be fine." Jamie came to stand beside her, looked out the door at the sky. "The snow is letting up."

"So it is." Her feeling of sadness darkened to gloom.

*B*ríghid cleaned the last of the dishes, dried her hands on her apron, looked toward the door for what must have been the tenth time.

Jamie had gone out to the cowshed as soon as he'd finished wolfing down his supper. He'd said he needed to settle the stallion for the night. Did he usually spend all bleedin' day with his horse?

Not that it mattered to her. She had her book to keep her company until bedtime. She didn't need him around.

If she'd thought he'd take advantage of being alone with her, she'd been wrong. Quiet he'd been during dinner—pensive. There'd been tension in every line of his body from his furrowed brow to the grim line of his lips to the fist he'd kept clenched on the table while he ate. She'd tried to make conversation, and though he'd listened to her, he hadn't had much to say himself. Something was worrying him, and that made Bríghid afraid. When he'd noticed her looking at him, he'd said his mind was on political matters in London and he needed to be leaving as soon as Ruaidhrí returned.

Her heart had fallen at these words. "So soon?"

She had tried to imagine going about her life without him, never seeing him again. She didn't like the way it made her feel.

Then he'd said something that had shocked her utterly.

"You should come with me. Let me take you to my brother-in-law's estate outside London where you'll be safe. The earl won't be able to come near you there."

She'd gaped at him, speechless at first. "I am not leavin' Ireland. I am not leavin' my brothers."

"By staying, you place them in danger. If Sheff—the Earl—knew you were on our estate under my protection, he would have no choice but leave all of you alone."

She'd dropped her spoon, unable to eat more, said nothing.

It was true her presence here brought greater danger to her brothers. As men, they'd be able to move more freely without her to protect and feed. But what would she do without them so far from home? How would she be able to stand living among *Sasanach*, sharing their meals, speaking their language, while their countrymen continued to enslave her beloved Ireland?

"You hate the English that much?"

His question had startled her. Had he read her thoughts? "When you're gone, my brothers and I will leave for County Clare. We'll be safe there."

He'd looked at her long and hard. "As you wish."

Then he'd excused himself and gone back to his horse.

Bríghid walked to the bed, lifted her pillow, pulled out the tattered book, determined to fight off the sadness that had gripped her. Though she knew the story of Don Bellianis by heart, it was still her favorite. She carried it to a chair by the hearth, sat where the light could hit the pages, carefully opened it to where she'd left off.

"Don Bellianis did propose to the Sultan, his father-in-law, the finishing of the War with the Emperor of Trebizone, and offered his service to go in person about it. But the Sultan would not by any means consent to that. Neither would the Princess Florisbella bear any such proposition, telling them that she had rather lose ten such Empires than permit him to make such a journey."

Bríghid realized with a start it wasn't Don Bellianis she had pictured in her mind, but Jamie—golden hair instead of dark curls, green eyes instead of brown.

She didn't want Jamie to leave. She didn't want him to go.

Sweet Mary, what was wrong with her!

She tried to force her attention back on the page, focused on each word.

"*As low as the Emperor was in his present misfortunes, yet he was high in his own opinion and so in his reply. For having lost that which he chiefly sought—the Princess Florisbella—he cared not what he did.*"

The door flew open, and Jamie stormed in. Without bothering to shut the door, he strode to his corner, picked up his travel bag and walked quickly back outside.

Bríghid tucked the piece of straw she used to mark her page back in the book, dropped the book on the table, ran to the door.

The stallion stood outside fully saddled.

Her heart gave a sickening thud. "They found us?"

"No, and they're not going to find us." Jamie tied his travel bag behind the saddle. "We're leaving."

Bríghid's mind reeled. "What?"

He looked over his shoulder at her, his gaze grim. "Gather your things, or we'll leave without them."

For a moment, she was too confused, too astonished to speak. Even as her mind rejected it, she realized the truth. He was leaving. He was leaving tonight, and he was forcing her to go with him.

A surge of fury helped her find her tongue. "I'm goin' nowhere, *Sasanach*! Leave if you want, but I'm stayin'."

He checked the cinch, then turned and strode toward her.

The look in his eyes—hard, unyielding—made her turn on her heels and run.

But there was nowhere to go in the tiny cabin.

She darted behind the table, turned to face him, her back to the hearth, heart thudding.

He stepped inside, closed the door behind him, cut off her only escape. He took one step, two in her direction, his gaze never leaving hers. "Don't fight me, Bríghid."

"Go to hell, *Sasanach*!" She looked around for some weapon to hold him at bay, saw the knife on the worktable to her left.

Spurred by pure panic, she lunged for it, grabbed the handle.

Strong arms imprisoned her from behind, held her motionless.

"I know you don't really want to hurt me." His breath was hot on her cheek.

"I wouldn't wager on it." She tried to twist free, could not.

"Drop it, Bríghid!" His voice was silky but dark with warning. "You haven't the strength to fight me, so don't try."

Desperate, she struggled, thrashed. "Let me go, you bastard!"

"I've no wish to bind you, but I will if you force me."

She screamed, kicked, felt the wooden heel of her brogues connect with his shin.

"Ouch, damn it!" He shifted his hold on her and clamped one hand around her wrist. "Drop it!"

His grip was iron, made her fingers weak.

"You're hurtin' me!"

"I'm trying to keep you from hurting yourself!"

The knife slipped from her numb fingers to the earthen floor with a thud.

In a blink, he lifted her off her feet as if she were a child, turned her to face the wall, pinned her against it with his body. Through the fire of her rage she felt his hard thighs press against her bottom, his hips against her back. Some traitorous part of her reveled in his physical power, in the masculine feel of him. The realization only made her anger sharper. "Curse you, Jamie Blakewell!"

"If you had any sense, there'd be no need for this." He pulled her arms behind her, held her wrists firmly together.

She felt soft cloth against her skin as he bound her hands behind her back. Fury gave way to fear. "Ruaidhrí will be back in a few hours! Please, Jamie, I can't abandon him! He's just a boy! He'll be so afraid!"

"Your brother isn't coming back." He turned her around, marched her over toward the door, strong hands on her shoulders.

"Wh-what?"

He grabbed her scarf and cloak from the wall and quickly put them on her. "I explained to Finn what I'm doing in my letter. He'll know there's no reason for Ruaidhrí to return. If he has any sense, they'll be on their way out of the county by dawn."

The weight of what he'd said took a moment to sink in. *The lying bastard!* "You tricked us! You wanted Ruaidhrí to take that message all along!"

She shrieked in rage, tried to kick him, but only succeeded in pitching herself off balance. She fell toward the floor face first, no hands to break her fall.

He caught her round the waist before she hit, hauled her backwards up against him, turned her abruptly to face him. His eyes were dark, his gaze tinged with anger. "You can't get away from me, Bríghid, but you might well hurt yourself trying."

He took her elbow, steered her toward the door, which he kicked open with his foot.

"My book!" Bríghid craned her head back toward the table where her beloved *Don Bellianis* lay. "Please, my book! My medicines!"

He ignored her, forced her over to where Hermes stood, lifted her into his arms as if she were nothing more than a child.

"Please, Jamie! Let me fetch it!"

He said nothing, lifted her into the saddle, put his foot in the stirrup to mount.

"Jamie, please! The book—it's all I have!"

The catch in her voice made him look. Tears were streaming down her lovely face. She might as well have stabbed him in the gut with the knife.

He paused, took his foot out of the stirrup. "Where is it?"

"O-on the t-table." She sniffed.

The knife in his gut twisted.

He walked quickly back through the open door, grabbed the book, looked over the tiny cabin one last time. Little jars of oils and herbs lined the worktable. Two bars of soap sat wrapped in white linen in the back corner. He knew without checking that one smelled of lavender. He tucked the book beneath one arm, gathered both jars and soaps, walked back outside.

She sat as he'd left her, but she was no longer crying. She held her chin high, refused to look at him, and he was reminded of how she'd looked standing on the great ring at Taragh—like an ancient princess. But, though her dignity suited her well and was one of the things that drew Jamie to her, her pride was going to be the death of him.

He opened the pockets on his travel bag and carefully placed the bottles and soaps inside. In another, he placed the tattered book. Then he quickly mounted, adjusted Bríghid's weight in the saddle in front of him, took the reins and urged Hermes to a slow trot.

It was time to get his life back in order. They were going to London.

Chapter Sixteen

*M*uirín stirred the stew, scooped it into three wooden bowls, careful to give the biggest chunks of beef to Finn. The dear man had risen before dawn and had worked without ceasing all day, Aidan in tow. For four days it had snowed, the cold and wet making for more work. They'd be back any minute, hungry and chilled to the bone.

She turned back to the hearth, lifted the teakettle from its hook, poured steaming water into the teapot. The oatcakes would be done in a moment, and supper would be ready.

It had almost been two weeks since Finn had moved in with her. Over a period of several days, he'd brought his chickens and cattle, along with his stores of hay and grain, and housed them with hers. He'd also brought the food from his own cupboards and the pallet that Aidan had once shared with Bríghid. It now sat in one corner, where Finn and Aidan slept each night.

Finn had taken the *iarla*'s stained sheet—after she'd boiled it clean—and had put up a curtain for her. It hung it from one of the ceiling beams and sheltered her pallet from view. 'Twas to protect her privacy, he'd said. His gesture had touched her deeply.

Strange that she should already have grown so accustomed to his company.

She watched each day as Finn went quietly about his work, showing Aidan how best to prepare tar to cure an infection in a cow's foot, how to strip a turf-bank, how to clean the stall of an impatient and angry bull. There seemed to be nothing he could not do, no farm work beyond the skill of his hands. In this, he was very unlike Domhnall, God rest his soul. Domhnall had been more a daydreamer than a farmer, full of big plans, but out of sorts when an animal fell sick or the blade of a saw broke.

Muirín tried not to compare the two men. She did not want to dishonor Domhnall's memory. Yet, it was difficult not to notice the differences. Where Domhnall had been lanky, Finn was solid, his body muscular from years of physical labor. Where Domhnall loved to dance a jig and sing, Finn was quiet, almost shy. Where Domhnall could tell a pretty story or recite a poem, Finn knew the deep history of Ireland and how to read and write.

God forgive her, but as the days wore on, she found herself wondering what it would be like to lie with Finn, to feel his large, work-callused hands on her skin, his lips on hers as he moved deep inside her. Such thoughts left her sleepless, tormented, made her ache. She could no longer deny it. She wanted him. More than that, she feared she'd fallen in love with him.

But how did he feel about her? She knew he cared for her. He'd worked hard for her after Domhnall's death, asking nothing in return. He'd given up his own home to protect her from the *iarla* and his men. He'd treated her with respect, always the perfect gentleman. Was he just showing uncommon kindness to a widow or did he have feelings for her?

She placed the butter crock on the table, eager to shift her thoughts before Finn returned and read them in her eyes.

The door opened, and he entered, Aidan at his heels.

"Sure and it's a cold one. I'd say we got another couple of inches today." He strode toward the hearth, held his hands out to warm them. "Supper smells like a slice of heaven."

Muirín scraped oatcakes onto the plates, avoided his gaze, fought to keep her voice light. "Sit and eat. The tea will chase away the chill."

Finn and Aidan hastily removed and hung their coats and scarves, sat at the table. Aidan reached for his spoon, but Finn stopped him.

"Mind your manners, son."

Muirín sat, folded her hands, said grace. She tried not to laugh as Aidan crossed himself and tore into his food almost at the same moment.

"It's been years since I've seen a snow like this one." Finn took a gulp of tea. "A good foot, and it's still comin' down."

From his tone of voice, she knew he was worried about Bríghid and Ruaidhrí and their *Sasanach* visitor. Not once since the *iarla* had ridden to her doorstep had he dared to make the journey to the squatter's cabin. He was afraid the *iarla* had set a watch on the house and would follow him or take advantage of his absence to harm her or little Aidan. But they would not speak about it in front of Aidan for fear of frightening the boy.

"How is Neasa?" Muirín's favorite milk cow was about to bear another calf, this one by the enormous bull Domhnall had purchased to increase the herd.

"She's cranky and didn't like it when I touched her belly."

Aidan giggled. "She tried to kick him."

Muirín laughed, met Finn's gaze, felt her heart trip. "Did she now?"

"Aye, she did." Aidan was clearly delighted. "But Finn was too quick for her."

Finn's smile lit up his handsome face like sunshine. His blue eyes twinkled. "It took a few tries, but I finally felt her calf moving. I expect she's got a couple weeks left before she'll be ready to drop."

Muirín looked away, reached for the butter crock. Her hand met his. Her breath caught in her throat. Frissons of awareness skittered up her arm. She would have pulled her hand away, but her fingers lingered on his skin, until his hand closed over hers and held it.

Their gazes collided, and Muirín found her answer.

Domhnall had never looked at her that way.

The door burst open, made Muirín jump.

Finn leapt up, whirled about, knife in hand.

Ruaidhrí stood just outside the doorway, shaking straw from inside his coat. His cheeks were red from the cold. He smiled. "Is that any way to greet your brother?"

"Oh, for the love of … Come in! Warm yourself." Finn pulled his brother through the door, shut out the cold night. "When your teeth have quit chattering, you can tell me what in God's name you're doin' out on a night such as this."

Ruaidhrí shivered, pulled the cap from his head, shook off the snow. "I've brought a message from the *Sasanach*." He reached inside his coat, pulled out a letter.

Finn took it, opened it, read in silence. When he finished, he folded it, set it on the table, fought to keep the violence of his temper from his face.

But he didn't fool Muirín. "What does it say?"

Finn glanced at Muirín, at Aidan, then at Ruaidhrí. "We'll talk about it later. For now, let's hear Aidan tell about what he did today."

*J*amie and Bríghid rode in tense silence deep into the night, through forest and over hills, past hayshed and byre. The snow had stopped but for a stray flake or two, and the sky had cleared. A silvery half moon shone down on a landscape draped in sparkling white.

Brighid watched in silent anguish as the world she knew disappeared behind her. She was too angry for tears. She was cold and so very tired. When she had refused to share Jamie's coat, he had wrapped a blanket around her, but it was not enough to ward off the chill and did nothing to warm her feet. Her struggles had tightened the bonds on her wrists, and her hands had long since lost feeling. Her shoulders ached.

Why had she trusted him? Why had she believed he was any different from any other *Sasanach*? Why had she allowed herself to lose herself in daydreams about him?

He had deceived her. He had deceived her brothers. He had deceived them, and he had betrayed them. And now, as like as not, she'd never see her brothers again. He'd told her he intended to send her back to Ireland when the whole affair with the *iarla* was settled and her brothers had made a safe home for her in County Clare.

Brighid didn't believe him. Why should she? He hadn't been truthful with her so far.

He'd lulled her into a false sense of safety, let her think she could trust him, only to take up where he'd left off that terrible night. He'd wanted to take her to England then. Only Ruaidhri's blade had stopped him.

She gritted her teeth against the ache in her shoulders, tried to wiggle her fingers. Shards of pain shot into her fingertips. She bit back a moan, determined to show no weakness.

"Brighid?"

If she opened her mouth to speak, she would cry out, so she said nothing.

He reined the stallion to a halt and started to adjust the blanket. As he drew her nearer, his thighs pressed against her hands, sending white-hot pain through her fingers.

She cried out.

"Bloody hell!" He cursed, ripped the blanket from her shoulders.

She felt his fingers work to unbind her wrists, felt the cloth slip away. The pain intensified as blood rushed back into her fingertips. She moaned, bit her lip.

"You should have said something." His voice was harsh, but his hands were gentle as he massaged hers back to life.

His fingers were strong and warm, and gradually the pain left her hands. But when he began to massage the ache from her arms, she jerked away from him, nearly unseating herself. Strong arms steadied her, pulled her close, held her fast.

"Enough of this stubbornness! Do you think by harming yourself, you can hurt me? Let me warm you and take what care of you I may."

She started to tell him exactly what she thought of his care, but the truth of his words stopped her. She might salvage some of her pride by refusing to let him help her, but she would suffer for it.

He wrapped her cloak tightly around her, pulled her inside his coat, then draped the blanket over her skirts. "We'll soon be in Baronstown."

Before long, she was reasonably warm everywhere except her toes, and she had just begun to fight sleep when they reached the edge of town. Houses, their windows darkened, loomed out of the snow like shadows. A single street stretched into the distance, looking eerie in the glow of moonlit snow.

Jamie guided the stallion down the road, turned into the courtyard of a darkened two-story building. A sign hanging above the door read, "The White Stag."

His voice startled the silence. "Whatever you're thinking, whatever scheme you have in mind, I'm warning you now, Bríghid, don't try it."

"Go to hell, Jamie Blakewell." Never mind that she had no plans for escape—yet. She was too tired, too cold for that. Now was not the time.

He dismounted, lifted her to the ground, held her to steady her.

Her feet were numb with cold, her limbs stiff and sore. "Let go of me."

"Not quite yet." Jamie tried the door, found it locked, knocked with a gloved fist.

"They're asleep. They'll not hear—"

The bolt turned. The door opened.

Without a word, a short and sturdy fellow gestured them indoors, shut out the night behind them. "You made it, Sir."

"It's good to see you, Travis." Jamie shook the man's hand. "When did you get here?"

"Three days ago, Sir."

"Is everything ready?"

"Aye, Sir. She's ready to sail at a moment's notice. We've got your room and carriage booked under the name George Washington, just like you asked."

Jamie grinned. "Rouse the innkeeper. I've a lady in need of a hot bath and some tea."

"My pleasure, Sir. Good evening, Miss." Travis gave a slight bow of his head, smiled at her. "Your room is upstairs, last door on the right."

Bríghid listened in disbelief to their exchange, gaped at Jamie as Travis hurried off to do Jamie's bidding. "You planned this all along!"

"Keep your voice down." He took her arm, led her up the stairs, down the hall.

She tried to jerk her arm from his grasp, failed. Then it dawned on her. "The letter. You arranged this when you sent that letter to London weeks ago."

"Aye." Jamie opened the door to the room, pulled her inside with him, closed it behind them. "Hate me if you wish, Bríghid, but this is the only sure way to spare you a life of misery as the earl's whore. Of course, if that's what you want, let me know. I'll release you right now and spare myself the headache."

She was tired, chilled, and his words hurt. She spoke the first thing that came to her. "I do hate you, *Sasanach*! I thought you were different, but you're just another Englishman who thinks he knows what's best for the Irish! You're just like the *iarla*!"

Before she could react, he pulled her roughly against him, forced her head back so she had no choice but to meet his gaze. His voice was harsh, his eyes hard. "If I were *anything* like the Earl, I'd have spent the past six weeks enjoying myself between your legs and you would likely be breeding a half-English bastard by now."

A knock came at the door.

Jamie released her, opened it, his jaw tense, his lips drawn into a grim line.

"My man is seeing to your horse, Master Washington." A plump older woman, obviously roused from sleep and clad in her dressing gown, entered carrying a tray. "It's just tea and bread, Sir, but it's the best I could do in the middle of the night with no warning."

Bríghid could hear by the woman's speech she was English and dropped the idea of asking her for help. No doubt Jamie had planned this part of it, too.

"It will do nicely, Madam. Thank you." Jamie turned to Travis, who stood in the hallway. "I have business to attend to. Watch the door. No one but the innkeeper's wife may go in—or out. I'll be back as soon as I can."

With that, Jamie strode from the room and was gone.

In what seemed like no time, Bríghid found herself stepping into a copper tub of steaming water set before a blazing fire. Who could imagine a bath could feel so good? As she soaked and washed with the soap Jamie had brought from the cabin, the cold and the tension melted away, and she found herself all but falling asleep in the water.

She knew she should be plotting ways to escape, but she could hardly summon the strength to get out of the tub. Struggling to keep her eyes open, she dried, dressed, pulled down the blankets and crawled beneath the covers. She thought of Jamie and wondered vaguely what business he could possibly have in Baronstown in the middle of the night. She wondered when he would return and whether he would try to join her in bed. She started to curse him, started to plot her escape, but by the time her head touched the pillow, sleep had claimed her.

Jamie sat in front of the fire, watched Bríghid sleep. Her dark hair spread like a sable blanket over her pillow. Her face was almost impossibly beautiful in the half-light of the fire, her sooty lashes a contrast to the creamy white of her skin. Her breathing was slow and even, and he knew no nightmares would disturb her tonight. She was exhausted.

They needed to leave soon. They needed to be on the road before first light, but he hated to wake her. *Just one more hour.*

Jamie knew he needed sleep, too, but there'd be time for that later. She wouldn't be safe until they'd reached the ship and gotten under sail. They still had a long journey ahead of them.

Guilt stabbed at him, nagged him.

He thought he'd taken care not to make her bonds too tight. He'd meant only to subdue her, not cause her pain. When he'd realized he'd hurt her, he'd called himself every foul name he knew. He had hoped she would come along without a fight. But he should have known better. She'd lunged for the knife, and he'd feared one of them would end up bleeding if he didn't do something. He'd warned her, and she had defied him. What choice had she given him?

I do hate you, Sasanach! *I thought you were different, but you're just like the* iarla!

Her words were sharper than any knife. While his mind rejected them, their meaning rolled around in his stomach like bile. But hadn't he anticipated this? He'd known what this course of action would do to the fragile trust he'd built with Bríghid and her brothers.

Why should her hatred bother him? It was of no consequence. They'd soon be in London. She'd be safe at the Kenleigh estate, and he'd be busy meeting with MPs and other men of influence as he tried to salvage his mission. Once her brothers sent word from County Clare, he'd see to it she was safely brought back to Ireland and be done with her for good.

Why the idea of finally being free of her should leave him feeling so desolate he knew not. Perhaps he needed sleep more than he realized.

*B*y the time the sun was up, Sheff and his men had already reached Taragh. A faint scent trail led the hounds to a small frozen creek before vanishing. And although they checked on both sides of the creek for some distance in both directions, the hounds were not able to pick up the scent again.

Sheff wasn't surprised. Jamie was more skilled than most men at tracking and had learned things few Englishmen knew, like tricks for concealing himself and evading hounds. Clearly, he didn't want to be found.

But Sheff had another option.

Chapter Seventeen

*F*inn drove his ax blade into the ice that covered the trough, cracking it with a single blow. Water gurgled up from beneath—a drink for thirsty livestock. He led the animals one by one from their stalls to drink, his mind far from the task at hand.

He hoped Ruaidhrí would find a warm inn where he could take shelter before dark. It was a long journey to Clare, but Ruaidhrí was not without coin to buy comfort. The *Sasanach*—Finn didn't know whether to thank or curse the bastard—had hidden a fortune in pounds in the leather pouch of Indian food he'd given Ruaidhrí to carry. In his letter, Blakewell had explained he was taking Bríghid to England, where he'd be better able to protect her.

Aye, the bastard had kidnapped their sister.

Blakewell had then warned them the *iarla* might vent his wrath on Finn if he didn't find Bríghid. He had urged Finn to accept the coin as payment for their care of him and use it to take Muirín, Aidan, and Ruaidhrí to County Clare immediately.

Finn had kept the contents of the letter to himself until he and Ruaidhrí had gone out to check on the animals. Ruaidhrí had gone into a rage, and Finn couldn't blame him. Finn felt just as betrayed, just as angry. But over the past weeks, he had watched the *Sasanach* carefully, and his gut told him Blakewell cared for Bríghid and would never intentionally harm her. Finn's gut was rarely wrong.

So he had done his best to calm Ruaidhrí, had tried to work past his own blinding anger to make Ruaidhrí see sense. Then he'd ordered Ruaidhrí to get a good night's sleep and to set out for County Clare in the morning. Red in the face, Ruaidhrí had finally settled down. At dawn, a portion of Blakewell's coin in his pockets, Ruaidhrí had started for their cousin's home, where he'd be safe—provided he kept out of trouble.

Finn couldn't leave, at least not yet. The livestock would not be able to make such a long journey and would have to be sold. In the dead of winter, that was no small task. There was no fair to attract interested buyers, so Finn would have to trek about the countryside make inquiries, get the word out. It could take weeks.

Once the livestock were sold, he'd use the money to buy horses and a wagon. They'd pack up their goods, join Ruaidhrí in Clare, and start a new life. As soon as they were settled, he'd send for Bríghid. And if the Englishman were not a man of his word and did not send her, Finn would be free to go after her himself, knowing Muirín, Ruaidhrí, and Aidan were safe and settled.

There was only one catch to all of this. Muirín didn't want to go to Clare. She didn't want to sell her livestock. She didn't want to leave her home. When he had suggested she move back home with her parents, she had lost her temper, forbidden him to speak of it again. As she wasn't his wife or sister, Finn could not command her.

It made him want to take a page from Blakewell's book. Aye, Finn felt he understood a thing or two about this Englishman.

When the animals were watered, Finn set to work repairing an old fence. Though the sun shone, the air was bitterly cold. His hands grew stiff, his fingers numb. He was almost finished when he heard the thunder of hooves.

He looked up to see the *iarla* himself riding toward him.

Blakewell had been right.

Finn deliberately turned his eyes back to his work, as if such a visit from the *iarla* were nothing. His mind leapt to the pistol, which was safely concealed in Muirín's wooden coin box hidden in the thatch of the cabin ceiling, but he dismissed that idea. There was one of him and six or seven of them. What good was a pistol against those odds? He'd get one shot and go down before he could reload. No, he'd best save that for a time when there was no other choice.

He forced his thoughts back on his work. Only when the *iarla* and his men had reached the cabin and reined in their horses did he stop working and turn to greet them.

"My lord." He removed his cap, bowed his head slightly.

The *iarla* dismounted, gestured to his men. "Seize him!"

Finn didn't resist as three strong men took hold of him, wrenched his arms behind his back. A fist connected with his gut, drove the breath from this lungs.

"Filthy Irish dog!"

Another slammed into his jaw, and he tasted blood.

Something hit the back of his neck, made him see stars. He sank to his knees, felt a boot drive into his belly, found himself facedown in the snow.

"This is what happens to Irish troublemakers!"

A boot connected with his chest, and he felt ribs break.

Through a haze of pain, he heard the sound of splintering wood and knew the *iarla*, or one of his men, had kicked down the cabin door.

Crockery shattered and wood cracked as the *iarla* and a few of his men tore the inside of the cabin apart. Finn heard the *iarla* curse, felt a swell of satisfaction that lessened his pain. Destroy the cabin they might, but they would not touch that which was dearest to him.

Muirín. She had wanted to build a life here, but, thanks to him, she was about to lose everything.

"Check the cowshed and the fields behind the house. She must be here someplace." The *iarla's* boots crunched in the snow. "Get him up."

Finn was yanked to his feet.

The *iarla* glared at him. "You've been lying to me, haven't you?"

Finn bit back the words he longed to say, gave the necessary reply. "No, my lord."

"Your father was a traitor. Your brother is a traitor. And you're a traitor." The *iarla* stepped closer, his brown eyes cold with malice.

"I've never raised a hand against you, my lord."

"You lied to me about your sister's whereabouts! You know where she is!"

Rot in hell. "I didn't lie to you, my lord."

"I don't believe you."

A fist drove into his gut, and Finn doubled over, sucked air into his aching lungs. "Believe it ... or not ... as you wish, my lord. But I've some notion where they are now."

"What are you saying?"

A hand pulled Finn's hair, jerked him upright. "Get your thugs off me, and we can talk."

"You'll talk whether my *thugs* release you or not." The *iarla* stood so close Finn could smell the liquor on his breath. Then the *iarla* gave a wave of his hand, and his men withdrew.

Finn was surprised to find it hard to keep his balance. The blow to his head had left him dizzy. But he lifted his chin, met the *iarla's* gaze. "Just before the snows set in, a friend of mine saw the Englishman in Baronstown. The forest south of there shelters a few abandoned cabins. He must be hidin' in one of them."

"How do I know you're not lying, Irishman?"

"I guess you don't." Finn met the *iarla's* gaze, unwavering despite his dizziness. "'Tis a shame the snows set in. I'd have gone after him myself else."

"That would have been a mistake." The *iarla* stepped back, turned to his men. "Well?"

"She isn't here. We've checked everywhere."

The *iarla* faced Finn again, and Finn could see he was disappointed. "Where's O'Connelly's widow?"

"She's helpin' the midwife down at the Uí Faelain place." There were no Uí Faelain in Skreen, but Finn was certain the *iarla* didn't know that. Irish clans were beneath his notice.

"That's just what the world needs—another Irish brat." He turned to his men, shouted to them to mount up. Then he turned to face Finn again. "If I discover you've lied to me, you and everyone dear to you will pay the price. Have I made myself clear?"

Fuck yourself. "Aye, my lord."

The *iarla* strode to his horse, mounted.

"My lord," Finn called after him. "If you find I'm tellin' the truth, what's my reward?"

The *iarla* gazed down at him as if he were a pile of dung, and for a moment, Finn was certain he wouldn't answer. "What do you want, Irishman?"

"Your promise that neither you nor any of your men will lay hands on Mistress O'Connelly."

The *iarla* smiled. "Granted. But since I think you're lying, you can imagine how much I am looking forward to doing exactly that."

The *iarla's* men laughed heartily, turned their horses, and rode off.

Finn watched while the *iarla* and his men disappeared over the hill headed south, mouthed curses the likes of which he'd never uttered before. He had no doubt the *iarla* would find the cabin. But it would be empty, Blakewell and Bríghid long gone.

Finn hoped the game he had just played would buy him a bit more time. He had persuaded Muirín to take Aidan and spend the day at the midwife's cabin a short distance away. But as soon as she returned, she'd be in danger again. Finn needed time to convince her that her safety — and Aidan's — depended on leaving the parish. After today, how could she deny it?

Finn took a step forward, intending to repair the damage done inside the cabin, but his legs buckled. The world around him faded, and he pitched forward in the snow.

The day had stretched into evening by the time Sheff and his men found the tiny cabin sheltered by a sliver of forest. They approached cautiously, weapons drawn, hoping to take Jamie by surprise, but found it abandoned.

Sheff peered into the decrepit structure, it's walls and ceiling black with smoke. "I wouldn't house a sow in here. Filthy Irish."

He stepped inside, noticed the stack of unused peat beside the hearth. A pot hung on its hook above a fire long since grown cold. Something foul lay congealed within. A crock of butter was overturned on the table, a basket of oatcakes and a brick of cheese abandoned on a nearby worktable. A knife lay on the earthen floor.

Someone had fled this hovel in a hurry.

Jamie had been here. Sheff could feel it. But somehow Jamie had known Sheff was coming, had again fled like a thief in the night. There was no way the brother could have warned them. There hadn't been time. Yet somehow Jamie had known.

Sheff let his eyes roam over the contents of the cabin. A table. Two chairs. A tiny pallet sat against one wall. He wrinkled his nose in disgust.

A shadow darkened the doorway. "My lord, we've searched the cowshed. There's been a horse kept in there, all right."

"Ride ahead, Edward. Prepare the household for my departure. We leave for England."

"Aye, my lord."

"And, Edward, set a watch on this place just in case."

"Aye."

Sheff glanced around the cabin one last time. "You've won this round, but the game is not over, old friend. I shall find you, and I shall take her from you. And you shall watch as I enjoy her, just as I watched you."

Chapter Eighteen

London

Bríghid sat up, looked around her gilded cage.

She sat in the middle of a great bed with four delicately carved posts that rose almost to the ceiling. Above her stretched a canopy of beautiful rose-colored cloth. The mattress beneath her was fluffy like a cloud, its ticking made of softest linen. The blankets were thick, woven of finest wool. On top was a coverlet made of the same shimmering rose cloth as the canopy. Her pillows—four of them!—were stuffed with downy feathers. She pulled one out from behind her, plopped it in her lap, patted it.

A wood fire crackled in a fireplace set in one wall. Two plush chairs with ornate carved arms sat before the fireplace, a small round table of polished wood between them. Beside the bed was another little table, trimmed with tiny gilt roses. On top was a carved comb made of some kind of ivory-colored wood. Or was it made of ivory?

She stood, felt her feet touch thick carpet. Strange it was to stand on something so pretty, soft, and warm. She walked first to an ornately carved chest. Four drawers it had—each with two brass handles—and feet in the shape of a great beast's paws. The top was inlaid with different colors of wood in the shapes of vines and flowers. She traced her fingers across the polished surface. On top, a white porcelain vase held a bouquet of dried roses, their pinks and yellows faded with age.

She walked to the opposite side of the room, ran her hands over the plush cushions of some kind of couch. Nearby, stood a desk of polished wood with ink and pen. Behind the couch and desk, there were three windows, each as tall as a man and as wide as a door and covered by curtains made of the same rose-colored cloth as the canopy and coverlet.

She searched for ties, then drew them back, flooding the room in daylight.

The room itself was easily twice as large as the cabin she'd shared with her brothers, larger still than the squatter's cabin. The floor was made of polished wood, but was mostly hidden under carpets with ornate flower designs in hues of dark blue, ivory, rose, deep green and black. Jamie was accustomed to such lavishness. And a feeling akin to embarrassment welled up inside her. Or was it shame?

Jamie must have found her and her brothers the most wretched of peasants. Yet he'd never said a word, never looked down his nose at them, never complained. He'd thanked her for his supper, demanded to sleep on the floor, done his share of the men's work as soon as he'd been able. Oh, how he bewildered her!

With a frustrated moan, she pushed all thoughts of him from her mind. She was thinking about him again, and she didn't want to think about him at all.

Not now. Not later. Not ever.

She turned back toward the bed, gasped.

She hesitated, took a step forward, then another. She was looking at her own reflection. She'd never seen a real mirror before. She'd seen her face in pools of water and on the lids of finely burnished cook pots. But this was different. The mirror was taller than she, framed by ornately carved wood, and her reflection seemed ... real.

Who was this young woman staring back at her? She had dark blue eyes fringed by long, sooty lashes. Her long, dark hair hung, tousled and unbound, to her hips. So dark it was that her skin seemed palest white by comparison, except for the faint pink blush on her cheeks. Her lips curved into a smile, revealing white teeth.

She reached out a hand.

The woman in the mirror did the same.

Their fingers touched.

She's got her mother's look about her. There isn't a prettier young lady in the county, nor all of Ireland I'd wager.

Her father's words from so long ago came back to her. And for a moment, she caught a glimpse in her mind's eye of another woman—pale, too thin, with dark hair bound in braids, sad blue eyes, and a lovely face. The woman cradled her, sang sweetly, smiled at her. Longing, sharp and bittersweet, shot through her, the almost forgotten memory suddenly as bright as sunlight.

Mamaí.

Tears welled up in Bríghid's eyes, spilled down her cheeks.

But as the longing passed, she decided—if it wasn't vain to think such a thing—that she *was* pretty. She let here eyes travel down her reflection. She wore only her chemise, threadbare and more grey than white. The cloth was so thin she could see the dusky roundness of her nipples, the shadow of her belly button, the dark triangle of curls that marked her most private flesh.

Her breath caught in her throat as she remembered that Jamie had seen what she was now seeing. He had seen it, touched and kissed much of it. He had called her beautiful.

Curse Jamie Blakewell!

She turned away from the mirror, turned away from her thoughts. She refused to think about him, to spare a single thought for him.

She walked back to the bedside table, reached for the comb, began to pull it gently through the snarls in her hair.

Where were Finn, Ruaidhrí and little Aidan? Had they fled to Clare? Had they taken Muirín with them? How angry had they become when they'd read Jamie's letter?

Jamie Blakewell had kidnapped her—for that's what it was, kidnapping. He had dragged her out in the dark of night and taken her from her family, from the only world she'd ever known.

He'd awoken her just before dawn her last morning in Ireland, and when she'd refused to cooperate, he'd lifted her out of bed, slung her over his shoulder like a bag of grain, and carried her down the hall, down the stairs, and out into the cold.

A covered carriage had awaited them, Jamie's stallion tethered to the back. Jamie had opened the door, plopped her unceremoniously down on the seat of claret cushions, then spoken a word to his man Travis. "Is everything understood, Travis?"

"Aye, Sir, perfectly."

"You've managed quite well so far. Notify me immediately should ought occur."

"Aye, Sir."

Jamie had climbed in behind her. Then the innkeeper's wife had passed a basketful of food through the door, and they'd been off, Travis waving them on their way.

It had been a cold morning, but Jamie had been prepared for that. In one corner there had been a pile of furs. He'd tucked one around her, a thick fur of deep brown, then sank back on the seat opposite her and glared out the window.

Through a small window in the door, she'd watched the sun rise over the frigid landscape, first rosy pink, then orange, then bright yellow. She hadn't spoken a word to him, nor he to her, and more than once she'd dozed off, snug in her fur.

They stopped only twice—once just after midday to hitch up fresh horses and once when she'd needed desperately to spend a penny. They'd arrived in Dublin in the dark, had gone straight to the docks. She'd gotten only a small glimpse of the town. When the carriage stopped, Jamie'd taken her by the arm, lifted her from the carriage, hurried her toward a small ship.

But as they'd neared the gangway, panic and grief had overwhelmed her. She'd torn her arm from his grasp, turned to run, slipped on ice and fallen hard to the ground. Though the breath had been knocked out of her, she'd managed to dig beneath the cold snow and tear a handful of grass from the ground before he'd grabbed her and lifted her into his arms. Her last glimpse of her homeland had come through the small, round window of the cabin Jamie had locked her in.

Sweet Éire.

As the last of the shoreline had been swallowed by darkness and distance, she'd collapsed on the bunk and wept until she'd fallen into a fitful sleep.

The rest of the journey had been a blur. She'd seen little of Jamie during the sea voyage. A young sea apprentice had delivered her meals and the odd cup of tea. Jamie had looked in on her once or twice, asked her if she was feeling seasick. She had ignored him, staring in silence out her window at the vast expanse of the Irish Sea. She'd ignored him during the final carriage ride, too, though he'd hardly seemed to notice, his nose buried in a newspaper.

They'd arrived at this place in the dead of night. Jamie had awoken her, helped her from the carriage, guided her up a darkened stairway to this room, bidding her a good night and shutting the door behind him. From the fire in the hearth and the downturned covers, she'd known someone had been expecting her. Too tired to think more on it, she'd undressed, crawled beneath the covers, and fallen into a dreamless sleep.

She glanced about the room for her clothes. She'd taken them off, draped them over the chair by the fireplace, and ...

They were gone! Her cloak, her gown, her petticoats, even her shoes.

She reached reflexively for the cross at her throat, closed her fingers over its familiar shape. At least she still had it. But someone had entered while she'd slept and had taken her clothes. Come to think of it, how had the fire been kept burning all night? Aye, someone had entered. But who?

A knock came at the door, and she dived beneath the covers.

The handle turned, and a young woman's freckled face peeked inside. "Pardon me, Miss, but I thought I heard you up and about. I was wondering if you'd be liking your breakfast soon."

Bríghid was so taken aback she sat for a moment, mouth agape, unsure what to say. She hadn't expected to be waited on by English servants. And though a sharp retort was the first thing to come into her head, she had no grudge against this girl, who was about her age. "What is your name?"

The servant girl looked surprised, stepped further into the room, curtsied. "Heddy, if you please, Miss. I'm to serve you as your lady's maid, though I ain't never been a lady's maid before."

A lady's maid? The very idea almost made Bríghid laugh.

"Heddy, do you know what's become of my clothes?"

"Aye, Miss. Master Blakewell had me fetch them and take them to be laundered and mended. He said you'd made a frightful long journey and I wasn't to wake you."

Bríghid felt her temper rise, but fought not to take it out on Heddy. So, he thought her gown dirty and tattered. "Is his *Lordship* after makin' me walk around naked?"

"Oh, no, Miss! If you please, there be a trunk of gowns for you sitting in the hallway. I ain't brought it in yet, as they told me not to wake you. I thought you might want to eat first."

Bríghid *was* hungry. "That's thoughtful of you, Heddy."

"Shall I bring your breakfast tray, then, Miss? And will you be having tea?"

"Aye, thank you, Heddy. Oh, and Heddy, what day is it?"

"'Tis December the twenty-third, of course—the day before Christmas Eve." The servant curtsied, closed the door behind her.

Christmas.

Bríghid had completely forgotten about Christmas.

*J*amie swallowed the last of his tea, set the cup down on the dining table. He'd just spent the past two hours telling Matthew and Elizabeth what had happened over the course of the past six weeks. They sat in silence now, finishing their breakfasts and digesting his tale.

Jamie had risen early this morning. He'd immediately sent two dispatches, one to Sheff's London residence and one to Ireland, informing Sheff that Bríghid was with him in London and that she and her family were under his protection. He'd hoped it would divert Sheff's attention from Finn and the others to England, where Jamie could meet him on more equal footing.

Then he'd made certain the servants understood they were to treat Bríghid as an honored guest. He'd also explained that under no circumstances were they to permit her to leave the manor or to receive visitors without him. This had caused a few raised eyebrows, but no one had questioned his instructions. Elizabeth ran a well-disciplined household.

He'd then found a servant girl to act as Bríghid's maid and sent the young woman off to find suitable clothing for Bríghid. The servant had managed to locate a trunk of gowns once worn by Anne, Matthew and Elizabeth's youngest daughter. Meanwhile, he'd sent Bríghid's old gown away to be repaired and laundered.

Bríghid would never forgive him. Of that Jamie was certain. She'd kept up an icy silence for the length of their journey to London.

Except when they'd set sail.

He'd seen the panic hit her as he'd been about to lead her up the gangway. She'd torn herself from his grasp, had tried to run, but had slipped on the icy ground and fallen. When he'd lifted her out of the snow, she'd been clutching a handful of withered grass as if it were a treasure. The sound of her sobs as they'd weighed anchor had left him feeling like the cruelest bastard ever to walk the Earth.

He did not wish to cause her grief. Quite the contrary. Why could she not see that? Why could she not see he was trying to take responsibility for a situation he had helped create? Did she truly believe she'd be better off back in Meath without his protection?

Finally, Matthew spoke, drawing Jamie out of his meaningless musings. "This does complicate matters. He can make things hell for you in Lords. Though far from being the most influential nobleman in England, he is not without friends."

Jamie nodded. He'd known this. "I expect he could do even worse."

Matthew's silver brows furrowed. "Are you saying you think he'll go so far as to try to steal her away now that she's under our protection?"

Jamie turned this over in his mind for a moment, met Matthew's concerned gaze. "I believe him capable of almost anything."

"The filthy goat!" Elizabeth frowned. "I never did like him."

Jamie laughed. "You just didn't approve of my coming home legless drunk every time I went out on the town with him."

Elizabeth had been like a second mother to him growing up. He'd been placed under Matthew's supervision during his college years. More than once she'd scolded him, warned him that Sheffield Tate might be the son of an earl but he was also an ill-mannered brat.

"That was part of it." She leveled a stern gaze at him. "I also felt he was cruel to the young women he pretended to court in hopes of lifting their skirts."

For a moment, no one spoke.

"I'll increase the watch immediately, of course." Matthew rubbed his thigh absentmindedly. He'd lost his leg in the battle of Malplaquet more than forty years ago, and Jamie knew it still pained him.

Jamie pushed his chair away from the table, stood. "I've thought through it a thousand times, and I just don't see what else I could have done."

Matthew shook his head. "Nor I. You took the only honorable course available to you—and at great risk to yourself."

"Good heavens, Jamie! What if they had left you to die?" Elizabeth rose from her chair, walked to Jamie's side, and began to untie his jabot. "I still think we should have the physician take a good look at you."

"I'm fine." Jamie gave Matthew a pleading look.

"For God's sake, Elizabeth! He's a grown man!"

"I'm just going to see for myself." The tone of her voice brooked no interference.

"Very well, but let me do it." Jamie took over the task of undressing himself and bared his chest to Elizabeth's perusal.

Both she and Matthew gasped.

"Oh, God!" Elizabeth gaped at him, ran cool fingers over the scar.

Matthew frowned. "'Tis much larger than I'd imagined."

Jamie tied his shirt, met Matthew's gaze. "We've both seen worse on the battlefield, Matthew."

"Aye, but few men with a wound like that would have survived."

"To think how close we came to losing you." Elizabeth covered her mouth with one elegant hand. Though the years were telling on her face, she was still a beautiful woman. "My dear boy, I'm so glad you're home. We couldn't ask for a better Christmas gift."

"We owe this young woman of yours a debt of thanks. How do you say her name?"

Jamie pronounced Bríghid's full name slowly and carefully until both Matthew and Elizabeth could say it reasonably well. "But she's not *my* young woman."

Matthew and Elizabeth exchanged a guarded glance.

"What did that mean?" Jamie glared at them.

"What, dear?" Elizabeth looked at him with wide, innocent eyes.

"You know—that glance the two of you just shared."

"It meant nothing." Elizabeth smoothed her skirts. "Oh, my, look at the time. It's half past nine already, and there's so much to do with Christmas upon us."

"When do we get to meet Bríghid?" Matthew took up his cane, stood, his wooden leg tapping the floor.

"Well, I for one intend to meet her right now." Elizabeth turned in a swish of skirts and walked away from the dining table.

"Be careful." Jamie's mood had suddenly grown sour. "She can be a hellion."

*B*ríghid didn't know when she'd had a better breakfast.

Heddy had arrived with a tray laden with eggs, bacon, toast, strawberry jam, and tea, and it had been all Bríghid could do not to gobble it down all at once. She'd felt so lonely she'd asked Heddy to stay while she ate, and soon the two of them had fallen into a conversation about their brothers, Heddy sitting next to her on the giant bed.

Heddy had four brothers, and from her tales of them, each was more ill-behaved than Ruaidhrí. "So, not to be outdone, John tied a dead fish to the underside of Father's chair!"

Bríghid laughed.

"Every time Father sat in it, he'd say, 'Oh, Lord, what is that stench? What in God's—'"

The door opened.

A tall, elegant older woman entered. "Heddy, can you excuse us, please?"

Heddy, eyes round, leapt from the bed, picked up the empty breakfast tray, curtsied, and fled the room.

The woman shut the door behind her.

Suddenly self-conscious, Bríghid pulled the coverlet up over her breasts. It took all her determination to meet the woman's measuring gaze.

"You must be Miss Ní Maelsechnaill." Though her dark hair had turned mostly silver and her face now bore the lines of age, the woman had obviously been quite beautiful once. Her blue eyes sparkled with kindness.

Bríghid nodded, more than a little astonished to hear a strange English woman pronounce her name correctly. "Please, Ma'am, call me Bríghid."

"I'm Elizabeth Kenleigh Hasting. I am Jamie's sister-by-marriage, but I think of myself more as his aunt—or a second mother. I am so pleased to make your acquaintance, Bríghid. We have so much to talk about. But first why don't we make you comfortable?"

In no time, a large copper tub had been placed before the fire and filled with steaming water. Bríghid had been left to bathe in private, though Heddy had been sent in to wrap her in a blue velvet dressing gown and help her style her hair. While Bríghid would have been content just to braid it, Heddy insisted on coiling it and twisting it into a style the likes of which Bríghid had never seen before.

"Oh, you've got lovely tresses, Miss. Why, if I had hair like yours, I'd wear it fancy every day."

At first, the whole experience reminded her of the night at the *iarla's* house. But with Heddy's cheerful chatter and bright winter sunshine streaming through the windows, the sick feeling in Bríghid's stomach had quickly faded away.

It was a new experience for her to be waited on hand and foot. She felt silly and kept expecting someone to realize she was just a poor Irish girl and send her to work in the kitchens peeling potatoes.

Just as Heddy finished applying a small amount of rouge to her cheeks, Elizabeth returned carrying a pile of folded, white undergarments. "Why, Bríghid, you are breathtaking!"

Bríghid didn't know what to say.

Heddy helped Bríghid dawn a fresh chemise, clean petticoats and, to Bríghid's dismay, a corset, while Elizabeth removed the gowns one by one from the trunk and draped them across the bed. There were so many gowns in so many colors, Brighid felt bedazzled—soft green, lavender, light blue, deep blue, white with embroidered rosebuds, rosy pink, deep claret, bold red, soft gray.

"You'd look captivating in all of them, my dear. Which would you like to try?"

Brighid stood, ran her hands over the soft material of her petticoats. "I don't know. They're all so lovely." She reached out, touched the lavender cloth. Soft it was, like butter. "Is this silk?"

"Aye, it is. If I might make a suggestion, I think the sapphire blue would look lovely on you—a compliment to your eyes."

Brighid nodded.

Heddy helped Brighid lift the gown over her head and lowered it into place.

When Elizabeth was satisfied, she took Brighid by the hand and walked her over to the mirror. "You're such a tiny thing. We'll need to take in the waist and raise the hems."

But Brighid hadn't heard. She gaped in astonishment at her own reflection. Who was this woman in the mirror? Certainly, this was no poor Irish girl. The same eyes stared back at her, the same features she'd seen earlier this morning. But something had changed. This woman was elegant, graceful, even beautiful.

Smiling, Elizabeth watched Brighid stare in wonder at her own reflection.

The girl was simply stunning. Elizabeth could easily understand why Jamie had been drawn to her in the crowd. Not only was she beautiful, she had a sense of innocence and vulnerability about her, a feminine sweetness that tugged at the heartstrings. Those qualities, combined with her charming Irish accent, were enough to intoxicate any man.

Yet there was a sadness about Brighid, shadows that never left her eyes. Jamie had told them over breakfast about the girl's parents, how her mother had died in a famine and her father had been sold into slavery. He'd also told them what had happened the night he'd met her, how Sheff had tried to give the girl to Jamie as chattel to warm his bed.

The very thought made Elizabeth's blood steam.

And now the poor child had been taken from her family, from the only home she'd ever known. From what Jamie had told them—and Elizabeth was certain he'd omitted certain details—his acquaintance with Brighid hadn't been an easy one.

It was a rough road that lay ahead of Jamie, but he had chosen well. Elizabeth had watched him grow from a boy of four years into a man and thought of him as a son. The past year had been hard on him, hard on all of them. They had all loved Nicholas—Elizabeth had been present at his birth and could still remember his first cries—and they had all lost him. She knew Jamie blamed himself for Nicholas's death, though Alec and Cassie had done their best to reassure him it was not his fault.

War did strange things to a man. Hadn't she seen that in Matthew when they'd first met—the pain, the wariness, the state of constant alertness? Once a man set foot on a battlefield, there was a part of him that never came home again.

What Jamie needed was a wife, someone to help him heal, someone to soften his rough edges. Nothing would please her more than to see him happily settled with a woman who loved him—and a handful of children to keep him busy.

Jamie might not realize it yet, but he was besotted with Bríghid. And from the way Bríghid went out of her way not to mention Jamie or even acknowledge his existence, Elizabeth was pretty certain Bríghid was besotted with him, as well.

Chapter Nineteen

*J*amie stared out the window of Matthew's study, listening while Matthew spoke.

"Unfortunately, Newcastle is as ineffectual a prime minister as his late brother. His only ambition seems to be to maintain the status quo on behalf of the elite Whig families. He won't do anything they don't want him to do."

Jamie turned his face toward the man he considered an uncle. "What of Lord Shelburne?"

Matthew frowned, shook his head. "I know Alec thinks highly of him, but he's more interested in affairs on the Continent than in the Colonies."

"I'd say that's true for the lot of them." Jamie walked back to where Matthew sat in a stuffed leather armchair before the fire and sank into the empty armchair across from him. "What think you of William Pitt?"

"He's a fine orator." Matthew's brow furrowed as he considered Jamie's question. "He was re-elected to Commons this year, and he just married Hester Grenville—an excellent match for a gentleman of his prospects."

"I'm told he's sympathetic to colonial problems."

"Aye, he is—some say too sympathetic."

"Then I must make his acquaintance. I shall arrange a meeting as soon as the blasted holidays have passed." Jamie stood again. Restlessness thrummed in his veins.

Matthew chuckled. "Patience, Jamie! You needn't worry that you've missed your window of opportunity. Parliament got off to a late start, and thanks to Newcastle's incompetence—"

There came a knock on the study door.

"Come."

Elizabeth stuck her head in. "I'm sorry to disturb you, gentlemen, but I need a quick word with you, Matthew."

"Yes, love?"

Elizabeth shot Jamie a pleading glance. "It's a private matter."

"I shall leave you two alone. Thank you for your insights, Matthew. They've been most illuminating." Jamie started toward the door.

"Jamie, dear," Elizabeth called as he passed, "could you please do me a favor?"

"Of course." He needed something to distract him, to keep his mind off his mission—and Bríghid.

"I promised Bríghid a tour of the manor and the grounds, but I find myself caught up in other matters. She's waiting for me in the drawing room. Could you see to it she learns her way around?"

Jamie stopped abruptly, cast Elizabeth a withering look. It was on the tip of his tongue to refuse.

Elizabeth smiled sympathetically. "You can't avoid her forever, Jamie."

"I can bloody well try." Jamie turned on his heel and strode down the hall, his restlessness becoming temper.

*E*lizabeth watched Jamie disappear and knew he was vexed with her. She smiled.

"I can see, wife, that you have something to say." Matthew rose with the help of his cane and walked to her side.

"She is the sweetest, most exquisite creature, Matthew." Elizabeth reached out a hand, stroked her husband's whisker-rough cheek. "Jamie is miserable with desire for her, I'm certain. And she for him."

"And this pleases you." Matthew traced a finger intimately down Elizabeth's throat to the cleft between her breasts.

"Immensely. She is just what Jamie needs." She pondered for a moment, distracted by the pleasure of his touch. After all these years, he still had the ability to drive her wild. "I've been thinking— "

"I'm certain you have." Matthew's blue eyes twinkled with amusement.

"—that perhaps we should accept Anne's invitation to spend the holidays with her and the children in Kent instead of having the family here this year."

"And leave the two of them alone?" He arched an eyebrow in feigned surprise.

She whispered. "Alone *together*."

"Very well, wife. I shall make the arrangements."

Jamie didn't like being manipulated. He knew Elizabeth meant well, but her meddling infuriated him. He didn't need a mediator. He didn't need a matchmaker. He certainly didn't need to spend more time with Bríghid. The less he saw of her ...

He rounded the corner into the drawing room, stopped still.

She stood looking out the window, her face cast in delicate profile. Her long hair had been fashioned into an elegant twist, baring the slender grace of her neck to his view. She wore a gown the color of sapphire, ivory lace tumbling gracefully from the sleeves. Cut after the French fashion of several years before, it enhanced the curve of her hip, the slender hollow of her waist, the creamy swell of her breasts.

Her loveliness cut him to the quick, made it hard for him to think or breathe. Her deep femininity enticed him, ensnared him. The sexual need he'd tried for weeks to ignore roared to life in his veins.

Why had he wanted to avoid her? Clearly, he'd been a fool.

She glanced toward the door, and Jamie heard her quick intake of breath when she saw him. She turned to face him, a look of surprise or dismay on her face, one hand raised protectively to the tiny cross at her throat.

Clearly, she had wanted to avoid him, as well.

Jamie took a step toward her, felt oddly like a schoolboy. "Elizabeth asked me to show you the manor and grounds. I trust she has treated you well."

Bríghid stared in amazement at the man who stood before her. His long hair had been washed, combed and pulled back into a black velvet ribbon. Over his broad shoulders he wore a frock of deep forest-green velvet. An embroidered waistcoat of forest-green silk covered his muscular chest, cream-colored lace at his throat and wrists. Breeches of forest-green velvet sheathed his corded thighs, cream-colored stockings his well-built calves. Brass buckles decorated his polished black shoes.

She'd gotten used to seeing him dressed in his shirtsleeves and breeches—and dirty up to his elbows in peat like any Irish farmer. Standing there, he looked so fine, every inch the landed gentleman. Yet she could feel his physical power, the vigor beneath his well-dressed surface. "Aye." She struggled to remember his question. "Elizabeth has been most kind."

"You look lovely."

The way he said it—slowly and with the emphasis on the word "lovely"—made her insides go warm and soft. She met his gaze, felt her heart trip. There was appreciation in his eyes, proof he meant what he said. "Thank you."

He turned, offered her his arm. "Shall we?"

She hesitated, reminded herself she hated this man. He had lied to her, betrayed her, kidnapped her. But he'd also risked his life more than once to protect her from the *iarla*.

She accepted his arm. "Don't think this means I've forgiven you, *Sasanach*."

His rich baritone laughter filled the room like sunshine. "I shall try to remember how very much you despise me."

He led her out into the long, spacious hallway, with its polished wooden floors, ornate sideboards, and many paintings, sharing with her the history of Kenleigh Manor. He showed her the Great Room with its twin fireplaces and dozens of gilt chairs set against the red walls. 'Twas used mostly for political meetings, he told her. Then he led her around the corner to the Walpole Room. It was, he said, a formal dining room named in honor of a prime minister who had so often dined there.

Bríghid stood inside the doorway, mouth agape as she stared at the ornate ceiling. It was plastered with symmetrical patterns and designs, some of which were painted gold. Around the edges of the room, where the ceiling met the blue walls, she could see the carved shapes of deer and hounds. On the walls hung dozens of paintings of men and women, some with children, dressed in their finery.

One portrait was larger and stood out among the others. A tall man, dark and strikingly handsome, stood behind a woman with curly rose-gold hair. She had lovely green eyes that seemed familiar, and on her lap sat a dark-haired baby. Beside her stood a young boy, his head crowned with shining blonde hair.

"Who are they?"

"That is Alec Kenleigh, my brother-by-marriage, and Cassie, my sister."

"And this is Mr. Kenleigh's home?"

"Aye. One of them. He has lands in Virginia, as well."

Bríghid looked at the woman in the painting, and the man beside her. "Your sister is quite lovely. You have the same eyes. Those must be her children."

"The one on her lap is my nephew Nicholas. He ... was killed this past July." His voice was thick with pain, and she saw the shadows clearly now in his eyes, watched as he fought them into submission. "Indians. The war with the French."

Nicholas.

Bríghid remembered that name. Jamie had cried it out when he'd been fitful with fever. She touched a hand to his arm, tried to offer comfort. "I'm sorry. Was he their only child?"

A faint smile tugged at his lips. "Heavens, no. There are five others—two boys, three girls—and one due any time now."

"Your sister is with child?"

"Aye, though Alec swears it will be their last. He says that every time. He cannot bear knowing that she must suffer."

"Yet he cannot keep himself from her. He must love her very much." The idea seemed terribly romantic to Bríghid.

"He does." The tone in Jamie's voice was one of deep respect. "And he loves his children."

"Who is the other child? He has her eyes."

"It is I."

"You?" She took a step closer, gazed up at the painting. The hair was lighter, the features softer, but she thought she could make out the strength of his jaw, the fullness of his lips on the sweet face of the little boy he'd once been.

She glanced up at him to compare, found he was watching her. The warmth in his eyes made her feel almost dizzy. "Aye, it is you."

Next, he led her to the Billiard Room. Smaller than the others, it held several round tables—for playing cards, Jamie said—and one very large table, the surface of which was covered in cloth and sunken in. When she looked up at him, confused, he released her arm and crossed to the far side of the room, where he picked up a long stick and three ivory balls, two white and one red.

"The goal is to use the cue to hit your ball off the banks so that it hits the other two balls." He placed a few little balls on the table, bent down, aimed, and jabbed at one with the stick. It sped across the table, hit one bank, collided first with the other white ball, then another bank before bumping the red ball. "It's based on geometrical concepts and has become quite the popular diversion among the upper crust."

"Do ladies play?"

"Aye, some with great skill." He smiled, cocked an eyebrow. "Would you like to try it?"

Bríghid couldn't help herself. She took the cue from Jamie and tried to do what she'd seen him do. But the cue felt so large and awkward in her hands, and when she went to jab at the ball, she got the cloth on the table instead.

"Try again." He came up behind her, bent over her, one arm behind her back to grip the wide end of the cue, the other stretched alongside hers where she held the narrow end. He adjusted the angle of the cue, his face so near hers she could smell the pine of his shaving soap. "Here."

Flustered by his nearness, unable to concentrate, she jabbed at the ball.

It rolled across the cloth, bumped into the far bank, then sped back toward her, and collided with the other white ball.

"I hit it!" She spun about, almost in his arms, smiled.

He steadied her, his hands on her shoulders. "So you did."

"Am I interrupting?"

Bríghid gasped, whirled toward the sound of the voice. An older man with a wooden leg stood at the door. He had white hair that was pulled back and worked into a beribboned braid. His square jaw was softened by a friendly smile that lit up his light blue eyes. He wore dark brown breeches and a deep blue waistcoat. In his right hand, he held a cane of carved and polished black wood with a golden knob at the top.

"Matthew, allow me to introduce Miss Bríghid Ní Maelsechnaill." Jamie smiled at her reassuringly. "Bríghid, this is Lt. Matthew Hasting, Elizabeth's husband."

Bríghid was amazed at Matthew's grace as he walked forward, took her hand, kissed it. "We owe you a debt of deepest gratitude, Miss Ní Maelsechnaill. Jamie is as a son to us. If there is anything we can do to repay you for your care of him, you have only to ask."

She felt her face grow warm at Matthew's gracious greeting. "Thank you, Sir."

"I wouldn't have interrupted, Jamie, but this just arrived, and I knew you'd want to see immediately." Matthew retrieved what looked like a letter from inside his waistcoat and handed it to Jamie. "If I were to be entirely truthful, I must admit I wanted to meet you, Miss Ní Maelsechnaill."

Bríghid didn't know what to say. "Thank you, Sir. 'Tis a pleasure meetin' you, too, Sir." She felt so silly, so out of place. She glanced over at Jamie, hoped to see some sign on his face she wasn't making a fool of herself.

But his gaze was focused on the letter, his brow furrowed, the line of his mouth hard. He handed it to Matthew, who quickly read it, handed it back.

She could feel the tension in the two men, but neither said anything about the letter's contents. A tendril of fear snaked through her belly.

"Thank you, Matthew." Jamie slipped his arm through hers again as if nothing had happened. "Shall we continue our tour?"

After the Billiard Room, he showed her the two-story Salon, lined with chairs and boasting a balcony for musicians. They used the room for large parties and dancing, he said.

Then he led her down a side hallway to a set of large double doors.

"I think this will be your favorite room." An enigmatic smile on his face, he grasped the brass door handles, pushed the doors open.

A shaft of daylight spilled into the hall, and she peered within.

She gasped, clutched his arm. "Oh, Jamie!"

The walls of the room were lined floor to ceiling with bookcases. Rows and rows of books stretched out before her. How many she could not even guess.

Jamie watched delight spread across her lovely face. He'd deliberately saved this room for last. God, how he loved her smile, the sound of her laughter. He would have to tell her what was in the letter, but he didn't want to do it now.

She left his side, took several steps into the library, an expression of wonder in her eyes. She hurried to the nearest shelf, reached out her hand, stopped. "May I touch them?"

"They are yours to read as you like."

She met his gaze, her eyes round. "All of them? Truly?"

"Aye, truly."

Jamie leaned against the wall, watching as Bríghid explored the library's offerings. She drew out first one book, then another and soon had a small pile of tomes sitting on one of the sideboards. He smiled to himself, lost in the grace of her movements, enthralled by her enjoyment of so simple a pleasure. There had been far too little happiness in her life.

He watched her run her slender fingers over the spines of one book after another, found himself wondering how those fingers would feel running over his skin. His thoughts had taken a decidedly erotic turn, when she squealed and pulled a book from the shelf.

She held it up for him to see, then read from the binding. "*The Lives and Actions of the Most Notorious Irish Highwaymen.*" She thumbed carefully through it. "Well, 'tis written in your tongue, but I can manage that."

"I'd say you can."

She met his gaze, flashed him an unguarded smile. Then her gaze focused on something to his right, and her brow furrowed. "What is that?"

"A globe."

She put the book down, walked over to the orb, which was suspended on a stand that rose nearly to her waist. She reached out a hand, hesitated. "May I—"

"Yes, of course."

She touched the surface, turned it slowly, frowned. "Where are we?"

Jamie walked over to stand beside her, turned the globe until England lay beneath his fingertips. "We are here. Outside London."

"Then this is Éire." She stood so close that he could smell the lavender soap she'd used in her bath, feel the warmth of her body.

"Aye. Dublin is here, which means Meath must be ... here."

"It's so tiny! See how small Ireland is compared to the rest of the world?" She looked up at him, amazement in her eyes.

"The world is a vast place." He wanted to touch her, run his fingers across the satin of her cheek.

"Where is Barbados?"

She was thinking of her father.

"Here." Jamie turned the globe, pointed.

"So far away." She reached down, touched the green shape, a speck in a vast blue sea. And for a moment, she fell silent. "Show me where you come from."

Jamie traced his finger up the orb's curve, until it found its way to the familiar coastline of Virginia and the Tidewater lands of Chesapeake Bay. "My estate is in Lancaster County, on the banks of the Rappahannock River. I was born there."

She looked up at him again, rested a hand on his arm. "'Tis such a vast land."

Her touch, so innocently given, was like a brand. Jamie could feel its heat through his clothing, through every part of his body. Suddenly, it all became so simple: He needed to kiss her, to taste her. Nothing—not even the voice in his mind that told him he was a fool—could stop him.

His gaze captured hers. He saw her pupils dilate, heard the breath catch in her throat, and knew she understood what he meant to do. He tucked finger beneath her chin, bent over her, and took her lips with his.

Chapter Twenty

*B*ríghid knew he was going to kiss her, did nothing to stop it. She felt the first tentative brush of his lips on hers, like the lick of flames. The raw pleasure of it made her whimper. What spell had he cast over her? She hated him, didn't she?

Aye, she hated him. Despised him. Wanted him. Needed him.

Moved by a longing too strong to deny, she wrapped her arms around his neck, and lifted herself to meet him. His response was immediate. He pulled her hard against him, took her lips in a fierce kiss. And when his tongue sought entry, she gave it willingly, eager for that sweet invasion.

On the grass at Teagh-Mor, his mouth had tempted her, but now it possessed her, consumed her. She lost herself in the hot, wet slide of tongue over tongue, in the taste of him, in the feel of his hard body pressed against hers.

And hard he was. She could feel the rigid length of his sex against her belly. An image of his body, naked and powerful, leapt into her memory, and something deep inside her clenched. Not in fear, but in desire.

He broke the kiss, but not to free her. His eyes told her he would not free her. Not yet. "I like your hair down."

She felt the fingers of one hand slide into her hair, remove the pins that bound it, felt the heavy mass tumble free.

He made a low, feral sound like a growl, fisted a hand in her tresses, pulled her head back. "You taste *so* good."

She gasped, felt teeth and tongue rake her skin, a cascade of pleasure as he sucked, nipped, licked his way down the sensitive column of her throat. She clung to him, almost afraid of the way he made her feel, stunned by her own passion. This was so much better than being angry with him, so much better than not speaking to him.

Then his mouth strayed from her throat to the exposed mounds of her breasts where they rose above her gown, his lips hot against her surprised flesh as he kissed first one, then the other. She felt her insides quiver, her knees grow weak. "Jamie!"

Before she could object, he had borne her to the plush carpet and stretched himself out above her. She knew she should tell him to stop. She shouldn't be doing this. Instead, she found herself twining her fingers in his hair, pressing his head closer, urging him on.

"Oh, God, Bríghid." He cupped one breast, ran his thumb over her nipple through the silk of her gown, once, twice, again.

A shaft of pure pleasure shot from her where he had touched her to the heated flesh between her legs. Her nipple drew taut, tingled. She moaned, pressed her breast more fully against his hand. "Jamie, aye!"

"You are a banquet to a starving man." His voice was rough with desire, his breath steamy against her skin. "I would taste more of you."

Then he did something she never could have anticipated. His mouth closed over the sensitive peak of her nipple and suckled it through her gown.

She cried out, a wild, erotic sound. Ragged sensation tore through her, made her entire body tremble. The cleft between her thighs ached, grew wet, and for the first time in her life, she yearned to be filled. Her hips lifted of their own accord, pressed against him. He pressed back, his rigid length thrusting against her just there, just where she needed it most.

She knew she should put a stop to this. Why then was she moaning with pleasure as he grabbed her skirts in great fistfuls, lifted them, and caressed the bare flesh above her stockings? Why did she arch toward him when his mouth closed over the cloth covering her other nipple? Why was she running her hands beneath his shirt over the bare skin of his powerful shoulders?

Then his hand cupped the mound of her sex. No one had ever touched her there.

She drew her thighs together with a surprised squeak, but that didn't stop him.

He began to move his hand in slow, agonizing circles, and she could no longer think or question. The shock of it, the delicious heat of it, made her body quake. A desperate yearning overcame her, part pleasure, part ache, as the heat between her legs became a raging blaze.

And that wild whimpering, that soft keening sound—could that possibly be coming from her?

"Let me bring you pleasure. Let me give you release, *a Bhrìghid*. I'll go no further. I promise."

A Bhrìghid. The Irish form of direct address. Where had he learned that? He'd heard Ruaidhrì say it, of course. Ruaidhrì. Her brothers.

Guilt slammed into her like an icy wave. Her brothers were in Ireland enduring God only knew what, while she lay on the floor practically making love with the *Sasanach* who had taken her from them.

"S-stop!" She pushed his hand away, twisted away from him, sat up, her skirts askew. "I can't!"

Breath hissed from between his clenched teeth, a strained expression on his face as he fought to bring himself under control. He stood, helped her to her feet. His gaze met hers, his eyes dark with the same need that ran thick in her veins. "Cannot, or will not, Brìghid?"

She looked at the results of their ardor—rumpled clothing, his long hair loose about his shoulders, the darkened patches of silk where his kisses had made her gown wet. "With you, they are one and the same, *Sasanach*."

For the briefest second, his eyes filled with pain before growing hard and cold as jade.

She turned toward the door and fled.

*F*inn lifted the oat bag over the gelding's head, gave it a pat on the withers.

He knew he had to tell her. She deserved honesty at least. But how? He'd never been good at courting women—not that he'd had much practice at it. While other young men had chased girls like satyrs, he'd stayed home to help his father. He'd been eleven when his mother had died, had almost starved to death himself. The others had been so little, Brìghid and Ruaidhrì just babies. He'd been determined never to go hungry again, to help his father provide for their family, and had learned all he could about farming and raising livestock.

He could cure a cow of almost any sickness, geld an aggressive bull calf, help a ewe through a difficult birth. He knew when best to plant, when to harvest, when to leave the ground fallow. But speaking tender words to a woman—that was as far beyond him as the moon from the sea.

He wished for a moment he had Brighid's book. What would Don Bellianis say? Something flowery and poetic and pretty to female ears.

Finn took up another oat bag, hung it over the second gelding's head. The two animals, purchased this morning, would haul them all the way to County Clare. Though Finn couldn't say he was happy the *iarla's* men had beat him senseless, two good things had come of it. Muirín had fussed over him, treating him with such tenderness that he'd found himself wishing he hadn't recovered so quickly. But most of all, it convinced her of the need to flee. She hadn't objected once since then— not when he'd sold the livestock, not when he'd bought the wagon, and not when he'd bought the team of bay geldings.

He'd gotten considerable help from Travis, the strange *Sasanach* man Blakewell had left behind to spy on them. Travis had found him unconscious in the snow and had dragged him indoors. Travis had done the heavy chores for the few days Finn remained abed and had then helped Finn track down buyers for the animals. He suppose he owed Travis—and Blakewell—his life, as he'd likely have frozen to death on the cold ground before Muirín had returned home.

She'd come home early to find her cabin torn apart and a strange *Sasanach* hovering over him. Her English was not as good as Finn's, and it had taken Travis some time to convince her he didn't work for the *iarla* and that he was not responsible for attacking Finn or destroying her home.

Poor Muirín. Finn knew the past weeks had taken a toll on her. Now she was faced with a long journey to a faraway place where she had no kin. But Finn wanted to change that. If she married him, she'd be part of his family with kin aplenty.

But how could he explain his feelings?

He could tell her the green of her eyes was like the blades of fresh browse that cattle fed on in springtime. But what woman wanted her eyes compared to grass? He could tell her that her face was as beautiful and delicate as a snowflake or a rainbow or the web of a spider covered with dew. But that sounded stupid, even to his ears. He could tell her that her breasts—

He'd better not say anything about her breasts.

Or her lips. Or the gentle curve of her hips. Or the fact that he hungered to kiss her, to touch her, to make her his. He felt himself grow hard at the very thought.

God, he was a bastard. She was a widow, a woman who had recently birthed and lost her only child, and all he could think of was bedding her. Every night he lay on his pallet aching for her, imagining everything he would do if he held her in his arms. Who was the satyr now?

He would not dishonor her. He'd made her a promise, and he would not break it.

There was only one thing to do.

Tonight, he would tell her the truth. He would make his intentions clear, and God willing, Muirín Ó Congalaig would soon be his wife.

Resolved, Finn finished his work in the dark, closed the door to the cowshed.

He walked back to the cabin, his brogues crunching against the snow. A few stars shone weakly in the darkened sky. Perhaps the sun would shine tomorrow.

Assailed by doubts, palms sweating, Finn opened the door to the cabin, entered its welcoming warmth. Travis had gone to Baronstown to post another letter to Blakewell and would likely not return until the morrow. Aidan was already asleep in the pallet, a blanket tucked under his chin.

Muirín stood by the table pouring a cup of tea. "You must be chilled to the bone."

Finn was on fire, but didn't say so. He hung his coat on its nail, accepted the mug, took a sip. "Thank you." He sat at the table, tried to collect his courage, tried to find the words.

But just as he opened his mouth to speak, she disappeared behind her curtain. He was too late. Curse his slow tongue!

He sat in frustrated silence, furious with himself, and listened to the soft swish of clothing as she undressed for bed. He forced his gaze away from her curtain and onto the burning peat in the hearth.

He burned, too. Ached. Never had he wanted a woman the way he wanted Muirín. Aye, he'd felt desire before, but never had it ruled his every thought. He'd always been able to control his response, to turn his mind down other paths. But no longer. His need for Muirín felt reckless, violent, beyond reason.

His pain grew worse at the sound of the brush as she drew it through her long, honey-colored hair, stroke after stroke. He hadn't seen her hair since she'd wed Domhnall, save a stray strand here and there. But he knew it would feel soft in his hands, like the silk of a horse's muzzle. He took another sip of tea, tried to banish the image of himself running his fingers through her long, glistening strands.

"Finn."

He looked up, forgot to breathe.

She stood before him, hair unbound, dressed only in her nightshift. Like an angel she was, a vision of paradise.

"Muirín." He rose to his feet, helpless as his gaze traveled over her, drank her in. Her golden hair hung in waves to her hips, glistened in the firelight. Her bare arms were pale and slender. Her breasts, their crests visible through the worn white linen of her gown, were full and round. Her ankles and bare feet were delicate, tiny.

Blood pounded through his veins, his heart a hammer in his chest. He felt heat rush to his groin, felt his breeches grow tight. God almighty, he wanted her. Now.

Muirín felt the heat of his perusal, saw his eyes darken with the same emotion that burned in her. She knew she was being forward, but she feared unless she did something, Finn would never touch her. He'd promised not to dishonor her, and he'd been irritatingly true to his word. It had only made her love him, want him, all the more. And want him she did. Her body was healed from the travail of childbirth and hungered for his touch.

As his gaze swept her, she found it hard to breathe, and she wondered for a frightful instant if he would find her wanton and reject her.

He took a step toward her. "Muirín, I—"

"Finn—"

They spoke at the same time, stopped.

She gazed into his eyes as a charged silence stretched between them.

"'Tis lovely you are, Muirín, the fairest sight that e'er I've seen. I apologize, for I fear I cannot keep my eyes from you."

"Finn, I—"

"Please, Muirín, forgive me, but I've somethin' to say. Words do not come easily to me. If I don't say it now, I might never get it out." His brow furrowed, he drew one step closer. "I know you've suffered grief. I've no wish to intrude upon your sorrow, but … I'm a simple man, Muirín, so I'll just speak my piece. I've got feelings for you—the kind of feelings a man has for a wife. I would count myself the luckiest and happiest of men if I could but see your face when I rise each mornin' and when I fall asleep at night."

Muirín felt as if her heart had grown wings. She hadn't dared to hope for this. "Are you askin' me to marry you?"

"Aye, I am. And as soon as possible, as I don't know how much longer I can resist my desire for you." The look in his eyes was one of deep sincerity, mingled with pain.

She crossed the distance between them, placed her hand on his broad chest, felt his heart leap beneath her palm. "I have feelings for you, too. I would count myself the luckiest of women if you would take me to wife. And if you don't make love to me tonight, I shall die for want of you."

A low sound like a groan escaped him. "Make love to you? I'm afraid to touch you. You're so ... small. What if I should hurt you in my clumsiness? I've ne'er held a woman before. I've ne'er ... "

Muirín couldn't help but smile. She should have known a man like Finn would approach his marriage bed untouched. "You could never hurt me, Finn." She took his hand, so large and calloused compared to hers, and held it to her cheek.

"Should we not wait for the priest?" His thumb traced her lips.

"There is no priest."

For an instant that seemed to stretch into eternity, he looked into her eyes. Then with a groan, he pulled her against him and lowered his lips to hers.

*R*uaidhrí tossed another brick of peat on the small fire he'd built, warmed his fingers. He'd learned what he needed to know today. By this time tomorrow, he'd be well on his way to Dublin and, from there, London.

Ruaidhrí looked about at the familiar walls of the little squatters cabin. The place seemed terribly lonely without Bríghid. Still, it would be a blessing to sleep on a pallet in the shelter of a real cabin again. He'd spent enough nights in bowers and cowsheds to last him the rest of his life.

He knew the *iarla's* men had been here. He'd seen the dogs' paw prints, the hooves of a dozen horses carved into the icy snow. Blakewell had been right about that—God curse him for a lying bastard otherwise.

But surely the cabin was safe with the *iarla* back in England.

Ruaidhrí sat at the wooden table, pulled food from his knapsack, bit hungrily into a brick of cheese. He hadn't eaten since this morning, and his stomach was fair aching from lack. Fortunately, Blakewell's coin was plentiful and would supply anything he needed—food, shelter, passage to London.

He'd thought about staying at an inn, but he didn't want Finn to hear about it. He was supposed to be on his way to Clare, not sneaking about the countryside in Meath. He knew Finn would be angry with him, but there was no other way.

The *iarla* had threatened their sister, had kidnapped her and given her to a man to be used and defiled. He had threatened them all. He had killed a priest. He didn't deserve to live. If British law couldn't bring him to justice, Ruaidhrí would.

Ruaidhrí would be careful. There were lots of Irish in London to hide among until he had a plan. And then...

He reached down, reassured by the hard outline of the pistol in his coat pocket. He'd felt bad taking it from its hiding place in the wooden box when Finn was supposed to use it to protect Muirín and Aidan. He didn't want to leave them defenseless.

But once the *iarla* was dead, they'd no longer be in danger. They wouldn't need the pistol. Then Ruaidhrí would return it to its rightful owner. If Bríghid were untouched and unharmed, he'd simply return the weapon, take his sister, and go. If not, the *Sasanach* would receive the pistol back, one lead ball at a time.

*L*illian poured Jamie another glass of cognac, carried it over to where he sat bare-chested on her bed, his back against the satin headboard, one powerful leg draped over the side of the bed so that his foot touched the floor. It had been so long since he'd been here. He'd returned to the colonies years ago, and she hadn't thought to see him again. He'd been devastatingly handsome as a young man—tall and broad with muscles that made her ache with desire and thick, fair hair that made her fingers itch to touch it. More than that, he'd been a wonderful lover, leaving her sated every time he slid between her thighs.

When word had come from one of her girls he'd arrived, she'd grown excited, almost breathless, and had decided to see to him personally. She'd been eager to see the kind of man he'd become, eager to feel his lips tugging at her nipples while his thick cock thrust deep inside her as it once so expertly had done. She'd greeted him dressed only in her white silk dressing gown, already wet and ready for him. She hadn't been disappointed—at least at first. He was full-grown now, taller and more muscular than she remembered. His face had lost its boyish charm and taken on the grave lines of maturity. He had a fresh scar on his chest, and one on his shoulder, but that only made him seem a bit rugged, even dangerous.

Lillian ached for him.

But he had been wounded in more than flesh, and it was his wounds that had brought him to her tonight. She had discovered that almost immediately, when she had asked about Nicholas.

In a voice so lacking in emotion that it failed to hide the deep pain beneath, he'd told her of the terrible battle and how he'd lost track of his nephew when the Indians had stormed the encampment. He'd told her how he'd waited until his wound was tended and then had run through the night and most of the next day to free Nicholas. And, voice catching only once, he'd told her of Nicholas's horrible fate.

Lillian had wept.

She'd been fond of Nicholas. She'd met him when he'd come to England to study at Oxford. He and Jamie had been together in London for a summer and spent their fair share of nights at Turlington's. As dark as Jamie was golden, Nicholas was just as powerfully built, just as apt a lover. Lillian had spent one delicious night with both of them—Jamie and Nicholas. A bit drunk, they'd come up to her room together, had caressed her skin, kissed her, licked her, fondled her, suckled her, taken turns thrusting inside her until she lay weak and sated in their arms.

Lillian would never forget that night. She would never forget Nicholas.

She had comforted Jamie as best she could, though he brushed off her concern and condolences. She'd hoped that once he'd taken his pleasure with her, he'd be able to let go of his grief, to explain why he blamed himself.

But in that respect, she *had* been disappointed. He'd been in her rooms all night, and had only stripped down to his breeches. Other than to kiss her cheek and stroke her hair, he hadn't touched her. Instead, he'd stopped talking about the war and poured out his anger and frustration over an Irish girl who had him in a muddle.

Lillian had listened to the story and had been particularly intrigued about Lord Byerly's role. The rotten bastard—she'd never liked that man. He and Jamie used to come to Turlington's together, two randy young men in search of brandy, cards, and pleasure. Byerly still came around from time to time, but Lillian steadfastly avoided him. He had become a cruel man. Some even said he was mad.

She handed Jamie the glass. "Here you go, love."

He accepted it, took a sip, his gaze focused on something far away. "Oh, Lily, you're the only woman who understands me."

Lillian smiled. She'd heard this before. It's what all the men said—before they paid her, buttoned their breeches and headed back to their wives. She crawled into the bed beside him, draped her arm across his heavy chest, stroked his mat of curls. A part of her still hoped he'd turn his mind away from this woman and toward bedding her instead.

It occurred to her to take advantage of his anger, to tell him this Irish chit was beneath him and not worth this much effort or anguish, to whip his frustration into contempt. Certainly, the girl must be crazy to lie beneath a man such as this, to feel his hands and lips work their magic, and turn him away.

Not every woman is a whore.

What could it gain her to speak against this woman when it was obvious to Lillian that Jamie was in love with her? Oh, he certainly didn't realize it, but men were not as clever as women about such matters and often took a long time to figure out what they felt about anything. "Do you think perhaps you've moved too fast for her? She is a virgin, after all, and raised in a family of men who've sheltered her. Maybe she needs time."

He groaned, sat up, buried his face in one hand. "Aye. I was a fool. It's just … "

Lillian waited for him to find his words, and when he didn't, she finished for him. "You want her and find it hard to wait."

"Worse. I told her brother I wouldn't touch her, and now all I can think of is how badly I want to make love to her. Now. Tonight. In her bed. On the floor. Anywhere. And the hell of it is, I know she wants it, too. I can feel it."

Make love to her.

In an establishment where much cruder expressions were used for the sex act, those words seemed sweet and precious to Lillian. She doubted any man had used them when thinking of or speaking about her. She'd been a whore since she was thirteen, had lost her maidenhead to an old baron who'd wheezed and grunted in her ear, his member thrusting painfully inside her. It had been one man after another after that, and only a few—Jamie and Nicholas among them—had ever brought her pleasure.

Lily decided to return that gift with one of her own. She chose her words carefully. "Have you considered the possibility you're in love with her?"

"Bloody hell!" Jamie bolted to his feet, drink in hand, paced the length of the room like a caged lion. "I cannot be in love with her! I refuse to be in love with her! Love is for the lucky few, and I have never had luck with women. You of all people know that."

Lillian said nothing, let her eyes feast on the ridges and planes of his back, the sculpted perfection of his abdomen, the grace of his movements.

"Besides. She hates me."

"I wouldn't be so sure of that. There's a perilous thin line between love and hate, Jamie dear." Lillian stretched, covered the breast that slipped from beneath her robe. She would not expose herself to him. It would feel like begging.

His gaze met hers, and she saw in his eyes the torment of a man who'd been hurt one too many times to trust his own feelings. He tossed the last of his drink, set the glass on her dressing table. For a moment, he said nothing, just looked at her.

Then he ran a hand through his wonderful, golden mane, took a deep breath. "I've been dreadful company, Lily. I'm sorry."

Beyond her curtains, the first tendrils of dawn curled across the sky.

She forced a warm smile, stood. "It's good to see you again."

"How much—"

She held up her hands, palms facing outward. "Not one farthing. Tonight was my pleasure."

"Are you certain?"

She nodded, pulled her robe tightly around herself to cover the emptiness she felt. "Aye, love. Head home to your Irish girl, and be patient. She's a long way from home and has been through a terrible time."

He drew on his shirt, tucked it into his breeches, then reached for his waistcoat. "Aye, you're right."

"And Jamie, one other thing."

"Aye, Lily, my sweet?" He slipped into his jacket, reached for his stockings.

"Your Irish girl is not Sarah."

Chapter Twenty-one

"It's too much work, this is. I'll never remember." Bríghid folded her hands in her lap, stared in dismay at the array of silver, crystal, and porcelain on the tray before her.

Heddy had brought an entire place setting to her room on a tray and set it on the little polished table to teach Bríghid what to do so that she need not be embarrassed should she dine the family. Table manners had always been a simple thing. Don't eat with your hands. Hold your chin over your plate. Don't talk while you chew. And don't slurp your broth. Now there were napkins and wine glasses and far too many forks.

"It ain't so hard. Let's give it another go." Heddy repeated the name of each utensil, glass, and dish and described the use of each. "This glass is for dessert wine. You'll drink it last."

The maid's instructions passed by Bríghid in a blur of words, and Bríghid felt her frustration mount. What was she doing here? Why was she playing at English table manners? Why was she dressed in silks? Why was she sleeping in a feather-soft bed while her brothers slept in straw?

Bríghid was a poor Irish girl, nothing more. She was used to cooking her own supper, baking her own bread, braiding her own hair. She had nothing to her name save a cloak, a worn gown and a tattered book. She felt out of place at Kenleigh Manor, a plain rook in a room full of peacocks. She did not belong here.

"Oh, Heddy, please stop!" She stood, smoothed her hands nervously over the soft lavender silk of her gown, then began to pace in front of the fireplace. "If they're after makin' me into a fine lady, it won't work. It can't."

The maid looked up at her, her big brown eyes sympathetic, her freckled face grave. "I don't blame you for feeling out of sorts. If I had to sit down to dinner with himself and the mistress, I'd be scared out of my wits!"

"I suppose this is *his* idea?" Bríghid gestured to the tray with the place setting. How like Jamie to—

"Oh, no, Miss!" Heddy shook her head. "It was the mistress who sent me up here. Master Blakewell ain't been home since yesterday afternoon."

It was near noon. He'd spent the entire night away.

"Oh. I see." Bríghid tried to feign indifference. After she'd fled the library, she'd locked herself in her room, had refused to come down to dinner. How could she when she knew desire would be written on her face as plainly as letters on the page?

When Elizabeth came to ask her if anything was amiss, Bríghid had told her she simply needed some time alone. She'd eaten dinner in her room, and breakfast this morning. She had imagined Jamie would hear this and understand it had everything to do with him and what had happened in the library. She imagined him feeling a wee bit guilty, searching her out to apologize. But he hadn't even been home to notice her absence.

Heddy got a smile on her face that showed she knew a secret. The maid leaned forward. "Freddy in the stables says Master Blakewell spent the night at Turlington's."

Turlington's.

The name was familiar to Bríghid, though she couldn't recall why.

And then it came to her.

The ladies at Turlington's always had good things to say about your abilities.

Like an echo, the *iarla's* words rang through her mind.

Heddy whispered. "It's a bawdy house, a brothel."

Bríghid felt as if the air had been knocked from her lungs. She took several hurried, unsteady steps, sat on the edge of her bed. *A brothel.*

Jamie had spent the night at a brothel. He'd kissed her by light of day, aroused her with his hands, his tongue. Then he'd slaked his lust with a whore.

A bright stab of pain pierced her heart, nearly made her cry out. The thought of him lying naked with another woman, his mouth and hands on her body, his body pressed against her, inside her, sickened Bríghid. Why would he do such a thing?

She had refused him.

But she'd been right to refuse him, hadn't she? He was English and Protestant. He lived on the other side of the world. He didn't love her. Besides, how much could his kisses and caresses mean if he shared them with prostitutes?

His actions served only to prove how right she had been to flee his embrace. He didn't care for her one whit. He had simply wanted a woman. Any woman.

Through a fog, Bríghid realized Heddy stood before her, a worried look on her face. Bríghid felt wetness on her own cheeks and realized she was crying.

"Pardon me, Miss." Heddy curtsied. "'I didn't know you have feelings for him."

Bríghid wiped the tears from her cheeks with her hands, tried to understand Heddy's words through the empty ache in her chest. "Feelings?" She hopped to her feet, glared at the maid. "I do not have feelings for him! A worthless, lecherous pig he is, nothing more than a vile *Sasanach*! He's a liar and a deceiver and … "

Even as she spoke the words, she knew she didn't mean them. She *did* have feelings for him. Feelings that made no sense. Feelings that forced her to question everything she once held true. Feelings that now lay raw and bleeding.

"Oh, Heddy, I'm sorry. I'm not angry with you."

The maid said nothing, but smiled understandingly.

"I want to go home." It was the truth. Or it felt like the truth until Bríghid spoke the words. She didn't know what she wanted. She felt so bleak inside. "What should I do?"

"My mum always said a smart girl makes the best of her situation, whatever it may be."

Bríghid met Heddy's gaze, considered the maid's advice.

Make the best of her situation.

She took a deep breath. "Why don't you show me that soup spoon one more time?"

Jamie passed through the gates at Kenleigh Manor in the early afternoon. He'd had no sleep and found he wasn't tired in the least.

Instead, he felt he could have fought a cougar barehanded and had vigor to spare.

The carriage drew to a stop in the courtyard, and Jamie alighted at once, gazing up at the sky. It was overcast and grey, a thick blanket of clouds pressing down on the landscape. A chill wind had begun to blow and promised either rain or snow. The scent of wood smoke was in the air.

It was a damned beautiful day.

It was Christmas Eve.

A smile spread over his face. Jamie couldn't remember the last time he'd felt excited about the holiday. He'd spent the morning patronizing some of the finest businesses in London and had the packages to show for it. He'd also made some special arrangements for the evening. He knew Bríghid would be surprised beyond words, and he couldn't wait to see her face.

There's a perilous thin line between love and hate.

He didn't want to think about which side of the line he was walking just now. He suspected that if he were to reflect long and hard on what he'd just done, he'd curse himself for a fool. It was better not to think at all.

After giving the servants explicit instructions about the parcels in the carriage, he strode through the front doors, spied a letter waiting for him on a silver tray on the sideboard.

He recognized the handwriting at once, and some of his good mood vanished. Ripping through the seal with a finger, he opened it, read it, crumpled it in his fist.

Sheff had returned to London.

Jamie had expected this, planned for this. There was nothing to do now except play his cards to the end.

Though he longed for a bath and a shave, he felt compelled to find Bríghid, to see for himself she was safe. He tucked the crumpled letter in the pocket of his waistcoat and went in search of the woman who had occupied his thoughts all night, all morning. He heard her before he saw her. Her melodic, lilting voice came from the drawing room ahead.

"The lame woman bathed her crippled legs in the lake as her doctor had told her, but nothin' happened. They were as crippled as ever. But the great water horse who lived at the bottom had heard her splashin' about."

Jamie stopped in the shadows of the hallway to listen.

"Fierce and angry it was. It rose from the waters, bellowed like a bull at the poor woman and charged. And do you know what she did?"

"Do tell!" Elizabeth sounded just as entranced as Jamie felt.

"She stood up and ran all the way home! So the doctor was right. There was a magic cure in the water."

Both Matthew and Elizabeth laughed at the tale.

Jamie stepped out of the shadows, saw that Bríghid was taking afternoon tea. Dressed in lilac silk, her hair swept up into a knot that spilled soft strands down her nape, laughter in her eyes, she was a vision of feminine loveliness.

She was the first to notice him. She stiffened almost imperceptibly, and the laughter in her eyes died. She shifted her gaze back to Matthew and Elizabeth as if he were not standing in the doorway.

There's a perilous thin line between love and hate.

He walked the razor's edge, strode into the room.

Bríghid felt her pulse quicken the way it did any time he was near. Only this time, her heart felt an unfamiliar twinge of pain. He sported a day's growth of beard on his strong chin, and he was wearing the same clothes he'd worn yesterday in the library. On his face was a look of ... happiness.

The pain in her heart swelled.

"Jamie, dear, I was beginning to worry!"

Jamie kissed Elizabeth's proffered cheek. "There was no cause for that, I assure you."

"Bríghid was just telling us the most delightful tale. You are such a wonderful storyteller, my dear. Isn't she, Matthew?"

"Quite captivating." Matthew smiled.

"Indeed." Jamie walked to where Bríghid sat, forced her hand from her lap to his lips, kissed it. "Our Bríghid is a most charming *seanchaí.*"

His gaze met hers, and he smiled.

Bríghid snatched her hand away, fought the urge to hit him. How dare he prattle in *Gaeilge*! Did he think to charm her? How dare he smile! He flaunted his satisfaction at her, looked every bit like the cat who'd licked the cream. How dare he touch his lips to her skin! Those lips had touched a whore's lips—and who knows what other parts of her body.

That last thought made Bríghid's blood steam. She would have cursed him and walked from the room were it not for Matthew and

Elizabeth. They had been so kind to her, and she had no wish to embarrass them. She sat still, hands clenched in her lap, said nothing.

"Would you like a cup of tea?" Elizabeth reached for the teapot.

Jamie shook. "No, thank you. I think I shall retire to my room for a shave." He ran a hand over the bristles on his chin, grinned.

"You do look a bit rough around the edges." Matthew grew serious. "There was a letter waiting for you in the hall."

"Aye, I found it." He exchanged a look with Matthew that made Bríghid's stomach flip. "We should discuss it when you have a moment."

"Very well." Matthew used his cane to rise. "Shall we discuss it now? Elizabeth and I are preparing to leave for a few weeks and—"

"Leave?" Bríghid found herself on her feet.

"Yes, love." Elizabeth stood, placed a gentle hand on her arm. "We're spending Christmas with our youngest daughter and her husband and children in Kent. Hadn't we told you? We shall be leaving in little more than an hour."

Bríghid struggled to maintain her composure. Matthew and Elizabeth were leaving, and that meant she'd be stuck here in this house with Jamie—alone. "I-I see. A Merry Christmas to you."

She turned and walked from the room as calmly and quickly as she could.

"Does she know?"

"No. I don't want to frighten her." Jamie leaned against the mantle piece in Matthew's study, watched Sheff's letter burn.

Matthew nodded, straightening papers on his desk. "I understand. Still, if she knew, it might lessen her anger and help her realize exactly what you've done for her."

"Don't think I haven't thought of that." Jamie reached for the poker, stirred the embers a bit more forcefully than was necessary. If only it were Sheff's skull. "I don't want to give her nightmares. If you had seen the fear in her eyes ... I doubt she'd sleep at night if she knew he was back in London."

"Still, she ought to know the extent of her peril."

Jamie knew Matthew was right. "Aye. I'll think on it."

Matthew folded his hands on his now immaculate desk, frowned thoughtfully. "And what of Parliament?"

Jamie slid the poker back onto its hook, then faced Matthew. "Sheff is not without enemies. I've sent a few dispatches off to peers who might welcome an opportunity to cause him trouble, enemies he made while at Oxford."

Matthew's eyebrows shot up. "How ruthless are you prepared to be?"

"As ruthless as I must to guarantee Bríghid's safety—and the success of my mission."

*B*ríghid sat on a cushion, stared out her bedroom window into the darkening world beyond. A single candle sat on the sill before her, cast a circle of light against the glass.

Her brothers and little Aidan were out there in the world beyond. Did they miss her as much as she missed them? Were they on their way to County Clare? Were they warm? Were their bellies full? What were they doing now?

Tears slid unheeded down her cheeks.

Nollaig Shona dhaoibh. Merry Christmas, Finn, Ruaidhrí, sweet Aidan.

She sent the wish winging skyward with a prayer for their safety and crossed herself. She'd never been away from them on Christmas. She'd never been away from them at all. Somehow the holiday made the distance seem so much greater. She remembered the globe in the library and how small both England and Ireland had seemed, two tiny islands side by side in a vast, endless world.

Someone knocked on the door.

"Miss Bríghid?" Even Heddy could pronounce her name now.

"Tell him I'm not comin' down."

"Begging your pardon, Miss, but he sent me up with your supper."

A twinge of regret passed through her. He hadn't even asked her to join him. Which was fine, because she would have refused. "Very well, Heddy."

Bríghid didn't bother to look when Heddy entered. Her gaze remained focused on the dark world outside. Tiny snowflakes had begun to fall, driven against the panes of her window by a brisk wind.

"I'll just set it down over here."

"Thank you, Heddy."

She heard the door shut, caught the first scent of her supper, and realized she was hungry. She stood, pulled her gaze from the snow-swirled darkness, turned from the window, and gasped.

He stood leaning against one of her bedposts, arms crossed over his chest. He had shaved, the planes of his face smooth again. He was clad in breeches of deep midnight blue and an ivory linen shirt with lace at its cuffs. No waistcoat. No frock. "No one should dine alone on Christmas Eve."

The rush of joy she felt at seeing him took her completely by surprise. She caught herself about to smile, frowned. "I would rather sup with pigs than dine with you, *Sasanach*."

She started to turn away from him, but he was quicker.

In an instant, he had her wrist in his grasp and had pulled her to him, not roughly, but insistently. With his other hand, he cupped her face. His thumb wiped the tears from her cheek. "My poor Bríghid. Tell me what troubles you."

She tried not to meet his gaze, felt his green eyes pierce her, steal into her thoughts. He was so near, too near. "You. You trouble me."

"I ascertained that much myself." His thumb continued to caress her cheek, her tears long since wiped away. "Tell me why you're angry."

She tried to pull away, tried to end the maddening contact of his hands against her skin.

He held her fast. "Tell me."

She made the mistake of looking up, met the staggering force of his gaze. "Y-you lied to me." It was all she could manage. Her thoughts were scattered, broken into useless fragments.

"I never lied. I told you what I planned to do. You simply forgot."

"You mislead me, mislead my brothers."

"Aye. You refused to be sensible, and I was forced to impose my better judgment."

Her anger gathered strength. "You kidnapped me, took me from my home and kin."

"Aye. Of that, I am guilty."

"You tied me, hurt me." This was not entirely true, as she herself had made the knots tight with her struggling.

An emotion that might have been regret flickered through his eyes. "And for that I am deeply sorry."

Slowly, he lifted the wrist he held to his lips, kissed it where it had once been bound.

Sparks skittered up her skin, ignited her fury. "Stop it! I cannot bear your touch when I know you spent last night with a whore!"

Chapter Twenty-two

*T*he look on Jamie's face was one of complete astonishment. Then he did something she never would have expected. He tossed his head back and laughed. The richness of his voice filled the room like golden light. "How did you hear about that?"

"You don't deny it?" Her heart fell.

"No. I did, indeed, spend all of last night in the company of a whore, though out of respect for her, I prefer to call her a courtesan."

"Respect?" Jamie's words shocked her, fueled her anger. She tried to jerk her wrist from his grasp, failed. "You bastard! You try to seduce me, spend your lust on her, then come to my room seeking company?"

He pinned her arms against his chest with one arm, encircled her waist with the other to stop her struggling. His voice dropped to a husky whisper. "I said I spent the night with her. I didn't say I spent it *inside* her. Would you like the truth, love?"

She glared up at him, fought to suppress the wrenching pain in her heart. "Don't call me that! I am *not* your love!"

He bent closer, until his lips were mere inches from hers. "The truth is I went to Turlington's seeking a bit of bed sport, but once there I found I had no appetite for the ladies, because my mind was filled with thoughts of you, *a Bhríghid*."

What had he said? Bríghid struggled to comprehend his words.

No appetite for the ladies.

My mind was filled with thoughts of you.

"You didn't ... " Her words trailed off. An emotion that could only be relief rushed through her.

"No, I didn't." His gaze held hers for a moment, then fell to her lips.

She tingled in anticipation of his kiss, ached for it.

It never came.

He released her. "Dinner is getting cold."

Still taken aback, she followed him to where their dinner waited before the fire, sat in one of the two chairs. He hadn't lain with another woman because he'd been thinking of her.

Why should this news fill her with such relief?

"I hope you like roast of beef." His voice seemed strained.

"Aye." Bríghid spread her napkin on her lap as Heddy had shown her, stared at the daunting array of forks, knives, spoons, and glasses on the silver tray.

He'd been thinking of her.

He thought of her throughout the dinner. He marveled at the beauty of her face in firelight, the innate sensuality of her movements. He watched, fascinated, as she tried to use the right silverware. He reveled in her childlike joy at the meal as servants brought one course after the next—oysters on the shell, roast beef, puddings, sweetmeats, pastries, jellies, fruits, and nuts. He observed, enchanted, as wine gave her silky skin a rosy glow. He ached with need when a drop of juice from a pear beaded on her upper lip and longed to taste her.

It was but one of many places his tongue longed to taste.

"It is true Cook has a way with food, but she fritters away so much. I saw her toss potato coats in the slop bucket, so I did." She looked at him, sapphire eyes wide at this most shocking transgression. "I thought to speak to Elizabeth, warn her that Cook is wasting food, but I didn't want to cause poor Cook trouble."

Jamie fought back a smile. "That is thoughtful of you, but I'm sure Cook is following Elizabeth's instructions on such matters."

Then it occurred to Jamie that, in her world, potato peels were a meal. Bríghid had never seen such a feast as this. Instead, she'd seen hunger and deprivation, starvation and death.

Never again.

It was a vow, a pledge. She had suffered enough. She would suffer no more.

Jamie knew he had to tell her. He might as well tell her now. "I have word from Ireland."

Her fork clattered as it fell from her hand to her plate. She met his gaze, her eyes filled with fear. "How are—"

"Your brothers are well and on their way to County Clare." He thought he'd tell her the good news first. "Finn sent Ruaidhrí the morning after he got my message. If things have gone as planned, Finn is on his way there now with Muirín and Aidan."

He could see the relief wash over her.

She gave a sigh of relief, then looked at him curiously. "How do you know this?"

Jamie lifted his port, took a sip. "My man Travis, the one you met at the inn in Baronstown, is keeping an eye on them and sent me a letter."

"I see."

It was time for the bad news. "In his letter, Travis also wrote that the Earl came across the cabin the day after I took you away. He had men with him—and dogs."

Her face lost its color, and she clasped her hands together in her lap.

"There's more. Before finding the cabin, the earl paid Finn a visit."

She watched him, warily, like one who has received bad news too many times.

Jamie touched a reassuring hand to her cheek. "Finn is going to be fine, but the Earl's men were rough with him. Travis found him unconscious in the snow and cared for him until Muirín arrived."

Bríghid stood, walked a distance away from the table, a bit dizzy from the wine. The *iarla* had found the cabin. His men had gone after Finn, had beat him. Ruaidhrí was on his way to Clare. Finn was going to be fine. She struggled to grasp all that Jamie had told her. In the muddle of emotion, two things became clear to her.

The first was that her brothers were safe. Saints be praised! How she had worried about them these past days!

The second was that Jamie had once again put himself between her and danger. He had kept the *iarla* from her a second time. Because of Jamie, she was safe. Because of him, her brothers were safe. To think she had cursed him, had fought with him. Had he left her behind as she'd demanded, she'd now be ...

She didn't want to think about that.

She felt Jamie come up behind her and turned to face him, meeting his gaze. "Thank you, Jamie." She wanted to say so much more, couldn't find the words.

His thumb caressed her cheek, his gaze warm. "*Tá fáilte romhat.*" *You're welcome.*

She didn't know if it was the wine or the overwhelming relief, but she suddenly wanted him to touch her. "Kiss me."

Lust, like a hungry wolf, howled inside Jamie. His heart slammed in his chest. His blood grew hot, thick. He wrapped one arm around her tiny waist, cupped her cheek with his other hand, his thumb tracing the outline of her lower lip. She closed her eyes, gave a little sigh of pleasure. Her hands slid up his chest and over his shoulders, igniting his skin. Then she took his thumb into her mouth and sucked.

Her response, utterly innocent and completely seductive, was nearly his undoing. In an instant, his cock was granite, straining against his breeches. The breath rushed from his lungs, the thoughts of his conscious mind nothing more than a distant buzz.

Some predatory part of him knew he could take her now. He could carry her to the bed, strip silk and linen from her delectable body, and bury himself within her. He could touch and taste and take her at his leisure. She would not resist him.

But that's not why he had come to her. "No, Bríghid. We cannot."

Her eyes opened, and she looked up at him, disappointment and longing in her eyes. "But I want you to kiss me."

He groaned, pulled her arms from around his neck, kissed the backs of her hands. She had no idea what she was doing to him. "That's the wine talking, love. Besides, it's time for you to open your first Christmas gift."

"Christmas gift? But—"

"It is Christmas Eve, is it not?" Jamie called for the servants to clear away the dishes, silently cursing his lack of a waistcoat or frock. He was still hard as steel, a fact that would be evident to anyone who glanced at him. He turned toward the fireplace, leaned on outstretched arms against the mantelpiece, pretended to contemplate the blaze, as servants bustled in and left again.

"Now, Master Blakewell?" Heddy stood in the doorway.

"Not quite yet, Heddy." Jamie took a deep breath, willing his troublesome member into a docile state. Then he turned to find Bríghid standing where he'd left her, a look of bewilderment on her lovely face. He guided her into her chair. "Sit, love. And close your eyes until I tell you to open them."

She gazed up at him, a mix of doubt and excitement in her eyes. "Jamie?"

He bent, whispered in her ear. "Trust me."

The last time he'd asked her to trust him, she'd pummeled his chest and cursed him. This time, her lids closed, lashes sweeping shadows across her cheeks.

"No peeking." Jamie strode to the door, took the heavy gift from Heddy.

He turned to find Bríghid, who sat hands fisted in her lap, eyes still closed, her body tense with excitement. "Remember, don't open your eyes until I tell you to."

He walked back to her, lay the gift across her lap. He took one of her hands, placed it on top. "Feel it, love. Tell me what it is."

He watched as her fingers ran timidly at first over the soft fur, then delved into its thickness. Her lips—how he wanted to kiss them!— curved into an uninhibited smile.

"'Tis fur. Oh, 'tis wondrous soft!"

"You may open your eyes, my sweet."

Bríghid opened her eyes, gasped. It was not just fur, but a long, fur-lined cloak of light smoky grey. "Jamie!"

"It is blue fox." He gazed warmly at her, and she was reminded of the portrait of him as a little boy downstairs. There were no shadows in his eyes tonight.

Never had she imagined receiving such a gift. Never had she touched anything so fine. It was too much. She could not accept—

Before she could finish her thought, Jamie held up a fur muff to match the cloak, laid it in her lap.

She shook her head even as she slid her hands inside the muff's comforting warmth. "'Tis most grateful I am, Jamie, but I cannot possibly accept—"

"Why not?"

She thought. Hard. Why not? "I am no fine lady, Jamie. I'm nothin' more than an Irish farm girl and have no business paradin' around in blue foxes."

"Is that your only objection?" He smiled, his lips curving into a damnably handsome smile, cocked an eyebrow. "I'm not impressed. Stand, and let me see it on you."

Her mind whirled with half-formed protests, but it was hard to think with him so near. She stood, her hands still in the muff, her arms pressing the cloak to her breast.

Jamie slipped the cloak from her grasp, wrapped it around her shoulders, fastened the ornate brass toggle at her throat. Then he brushed a finger along her cheek, met her gaze with a look so intense it made her heartbeat trip. "If I have anything to say about it, Bríghid Ní Maelsechnaill, you will never be cold again."

The warmth of his words mingled with the luxurious warmth of the cloak. It was like being wrapped in happiness. She couldn't help but smile.

The cloak fell to just above her ankles. It was both lined and trimmed with thick, blue-grey fur that felt soft against her cheek. The side of the cloak that faced outward was covered with silk the same shade of grey as the fur and embroidered with small, golden lilies of the valley. She didn't realize it had a hood until Jamie pulled it over her head.

It was the most beautiful thing she'd ever worn.

"Let's see you." Jamie motioned for her to turn in a circle.

She'd taken but a few steps when her gaze fell on the single candle burning in the window. She froze, a sick feeling in her belly.

The moment stretched into silence.

"What does the candle mean?" His hands cupped her shoulders reassuringly from behind.

"'Tis a Christmas custom." She tried to swallow the lump that had formed in her throat. "'Tis how we welcome the Holy Family and all lost and traveling souls on Christmas Eve. When someone is away from home ... "

She could not finish her words. Tears pricked behind her eyes.

"You miss your brothers." It wasn't a question. He said the words as if he understood.

But there was more to it than that. How could she explain? "I cannot do this, Jamie."

His hands slid down the cloak over the length of her arms, sought her hands in the folds of fur. He turned her to face him, lifted her chin until she met his gaze. She could see a torrent of emotion in his eyes. "What can't you do, Bríghid? Accept a gift from me?"

"How can I enjoy such comfort when my brothers do not?" She pulled away from him, took several hurried steps toward the bed. "How can I dine on such food while they struggle to fill their bellies? How can I sleep in this soft bed when they sleep in straw?"

Jamie heard the remorse in her voice. He walked over to where she stood, pulled her gently against him, felt her surrender to his embrace. "What good can you do your brothers by denying the comforts I offer? You cannot help Finn and Ruaidhrí by depriving yourself, Bríghid. Do you not think they would rest more easily if they knew you were warm and safe and eating well?"

He pressed his lips against her temple, felt her tears against the linen of his shirt, and wished he could take this sadness away from her. "You are homesick."

She nodded, then looked up at him. "I do not belong here, Jamie."

Her words caused unexpected pain to knife his heart. Had he believed he could bridge the gap between them in one evening? "Then I shall take you someplace you do belong."

*B*ríghid sat wrapped in the warmth of her new cloak and gaped out the windows at the city beyond—or what she could see of it. Tall oil lamps, spaced evenly along streets so long they seemed to go on forever, turned night into twilight. Row after row of houses—some four stories high—stretched into the darkness, their windows lit from within by cheery golden light. Streets of cobbled stone seemed to wind in every direction and were busy with the traffic of horses, carriages, and strolling people.

Never had she seen such a sight.

London.

The name had always seemed threatening to her, ominous. Now here she was, in the heart of the city. But perhaps the heart of the city was rotten.

She wrinkled her nose. "What's that smell?"

"Which smell?" Jamie sat cloaked in shadows across from her, but she could hear the smile in his voice. His long legs were angled so as not to touch hers, a fact Bríghid noted with some frustration. "It might be smoke from coal fires, or it—"

The odor grew particularly strong.

"*That* smell."

"That, my sweet, is the lovely Thames. Be grateful we're not getting any nearer."

"Where is it you're takin' me? Can you tell me now?"

"You'll see when we get there. It won't be long."

Bríghid gave a frustrated moan, ignoring Jamie's chuckle. Someplace she belonged. Where could that be? Since no answer was forthcoming, she snuggled deeper into the fuzzy warmth of her cloak and went back to looking out the window, letting her thoughts drift.

She'd been so relieved to hear her brothers were safe, so happy to know they were on their way out of Meath. Her relief warred with her anguish at learning that Finn had been beaten. She couldn't stand to think of the *iarla's* men hurting him and subjecting him to insults. She realized she owed Jamie far more than she could ever repay. He had saved her from the *iarla's* cruelty twice now. And though Jamie had not answered her when she'd asked where the *iarla* had gone, she knew the answer.

He was here. In London.

She tried to reassure herself nothing could happen to her as long as she was with Jamie and was surprised to find that she had come to trust him. Trust a *Sasanach*? It seemed unbelievable, but it was true.

Her musings were interrupted by the sight of the hulking building that rose out of the ground beside the carriage. The ornately decorated structure reached to the heavens with spires and buttresses so high she could not see where they ended no matter how she craned her neck.

She heard Jamie chuckle again. "Westminster Abbey."

Afraid she was acting like a silly country girl on her first trip to the city—which she was—she willed herself to sit back in her seat and watch as the carriage carried them around corners, past closed shops and offices, and into an alley.

It drew to a stop.

She felt her pulse quicken as Jamie opened the door, alighted, then lifted her to the snowy ground.

His gaze met hers, and he smiled a mysterious smile that heightened her anticipation. Where could they be? Apart from a stray cat, the alley seemed deserted.

"Come." He took her arm in his and guided her to a cobblestone path that ran between two stone buildings.

Ahead in the darkness, an oil lamp cast light on a plain oak door. Jamie led her to the door, opened it, let her inside.

Bríghid gasped, fell to her knees, crossed herself. "*A Mháthair Mhic Dé!*" Mother of God!

Hot tears sprang to her eyes.

An elderly man dressed in black robes looked out of a back room, saw her, smiled. "*Tá fáilte romhat, a leanbh.*"

You are welcome here, child.

"*A* *ufer a nobis, quaesumus, Domine, iniquitates nostras, ut ad Sancta sanctorum puris mereamur mentibus introire.*"

Jamie stood in the back, his gaze never leaving Bríghid, as she joined the congregation in Midnight Mass, her motions graceful and sweetly feminine as she stood, kneeled, bowed her head to pray.

It had taken a few hours of sleuthing early this morning to find a Catholic chapel in London. The city's Catholics, particularly its Irish Catholics, had not been inclined to trust him. A tip had lead him to Lord Benton, one of England's few remaining titled Catholics, which, in turn, had led him here.

Jamie had arrived at the chapel early, having arranged for Bríghid to have an hour with the priest alone. She had emerged with eyes red from crying, but a look of relief on her beautiful face. Jamie knew the old man was a good listener and would help her sort through her feelings. Jamie had met privately with Father Owen this morning and had found himself telling the story of why he'd come to Britain and how he'd met Bríghid. The old man had listened without interruption, without condemnation, and Jamie had found himself admitting the confusing nature of his feelings for Bríghid. But when he came to the desire that burned inside him, his aching need for her, he had paused.

"If you're thinkin' you'll offend me, young man, fear not." The priest smiled. "It's fifty years now I've been a priest. There's nothin' under Heaven that I haven't heard."

Before long, Jamie had told the priest about the women he had loved, or thought he'd loved, including Sarah. And a strange thing happened. By the time he'd finished telling the story, Sarah no longer mattered to him.

There was only Bríghid.

Bríghid with her sapphire eyes. Bríghid with her lilting accent. Bríghid with her silly Don Bellianis and her temper and her loathing for all things English.

He loved her.

And there wasn't a damn thing he could do about it.

"I know you know what to do." The priest had patted him on the shoulder. "When God brings a man and woman together, He helps them find a way."

The trouble was, Bríghid didn't return Jamie's feelings. She'd made that abundantly clear. And the exhilaration he'd felt as he'd bid the priest

farewell early this morning had been replaced this evening by a
bleakness that bordered on desolation.

I do not belong here.

Jamie understood women well enough to know she felt desire for
him. Her responses when she lay beneath him in the library told him that.
But desire wasn't love. He knew that only too well. He would never
again be lulled into thinking that a woman who shared her body was also
sharing her heart.

How could he have been so foolish to let his heart get mixed up in
this? How could he have been so idiotic as to love a woman who did not
care for him? Hadn't he already learned that lesson? Aye, damn it, he
had. And he wouldn't make a fool of himself this time. There was no
reason for Bríghid to know how he felt. He would keep his feelings to
himself. He might have inadvertently let her into his heart, but that didn't
mean he had to give it to her.

"*Suscipe, sancte Pater, omnipotens aeterne Deus, hanc
immaculatam hostiam … *"

Jamie watched Bríghid as she and the others received the old
priest's blessing. Then Bríghid turned toward him. Even from a distance,
Jamie could see that her face glowed.

She walked up to him, smiled shyly. "I don't know how to thank
you, Jamie. This was the best, most thoughtful gift you could have given
me."

Jamie forced a smile. "Shall we go?"

He opened the door, welcoming the blast of cold air on his face.

*F*inn held Muirín in his arms, drowsy with lovemaking. He was still
amazed that anything could feel as good as sex. It was a bloody
miracle. There were no words to describe how he felt when he was deep
inside her, no words to describe that heated union of flesh and mind and
heart—at least none as he could find. And though he might once have
cursed his tongue for its lack of grace, he now knew his tongue had
certain abilities and shouldn't be taken lightly.

Though he might not be able to recite poems or speak fancy words
to Muirín, he knew exactly how to use his tongue to pleasure her. He
knew how to tease her lips, where to stroke inside her mouth. He knew
exactly how to lave her nipples until they were hot, tight peaks that
begged to be suckled. He knew how to kiss her most intimate flesh, how

to drink from her woman's well until she writhed and panted and cried out her pleasure, her fingers twined deeply in his hair.

Aye, his tongue had its uses. Leave poetry to Don Bellianis.

She snuggled against him, one leg tucked intimately between his, and gave a little sigh. Moments ago she'd been beneath him, bucking against his thrusts, her legs wrapped around him. Now she lay like a contented kitten, her body languid, her breathing deep and even.

How perfectly she fit in his arms. How perfectly he fit inside her. The very thought of it set his cock to swelling again, but he would not wake her.

She was everything to him. She was the sun that rose in the morning. She was the deep velvet of the midnight sky. She was music and laughter and the sweetness of honey.

And she was his.

He had used some of the remaining money left by Blakewell to buy Aidan new brogues for Christmas. For Muirín, he'd bought yards of the softest linen and lace for a new shift.

She had run her fingers lovingly over the cloth, tears in her eyes. "It is the finest gift I've e'er been given."

She had knitted him a fine sweater. She'd knitted a matching one for Aidan.

The boy had beamed with pride and put it on immediately. "I look just like Finn!"

Muirín's sweet laughter had been like music. "Aye, that you do!"

What a wonderful mother she was. Finn found himself eager to see her swell with his child and wondered if even now a babe was growing within her.

He reached down to stroke her honey-colored hair.

She shifted in his arms, pressed her face more deeply into his chest in her sleep.

Sweet Mary, but he was a lucky man! He had so much to be grateful for. Muirín loved him, had taken him to be her husband. She and Aidan were safe and on their way with him to Clare. They had food aplenty and a soft bed in a roadside inn. Ruaidhrí would be arriving any day in Clare—provided he hadn't gotten into trouble along the way.

But Bríghid ...

Lord, he missed his little sister. It didn't sit well with him, her being away like this, especially not on Christmas. He didn't much like the fact that the *iarla* had left Ireland in seeming pursuit of her. But he remembered Blakewell's face, the determined glint in his eyes, and the ferocious protectiveness he seemed to exude whenever Bríghid was nearby.

I will do whatever I must to make certain Bríghid is safe.

The man had bloody well keep his word.

As sleep overtook him, he sent a prayer skyward on her behalf and Ruaidhrí's.

Nollaig Shona dhaoibh. Merry Christmas.

*R*uaidhrí struggled back to consciousness, aware only of the pain in his skull and hard, cold stone pressing into his back.

And that sound? It was his own groans.

Where was he? He needed to remember.

He struggled to open his eyes, felt someone press a warm cloth to his face.

"He's comin' 'round." It was a woman's voice, soft and sweet.

"Dirty Irish bastard." A man's voice. A *Sasanach* voice, harsh and hateful.

Something slammed into his ribs, knocked the air from his lungs.

He struggled to breathe.

"Unless you're after killin' him, you'd best leave off!" The woman spoke. It was she who was pressing the cloth to his head. "You've split his skull clean, you have. I'll be forever cleanin' the blood from his face."

Ruaidhrí must have blacked out again, for time seemed to pass. When he next was aware of his surroundings, someone was holding something to his lips.

"Just you be good and swallow, you silly, senseless boy."

He drank, grateful as water soothed his parched throat. He struggled to open his eyes and looked up into the face of an angel.

"Is this Heaven?"

The angel laughed. "Nay. For you, 'tis surely closer to hell."

"Who are you?" He needed to know.

"I'm Alice."

"Alice." Ruaidhrí realized he was lying on a pallet in a dark, windowless room made entirely of brick. His wrists and ankles were shackled. Alarm coursed through him. "Where am I?"

"You're in the earl's cellar. Don't you remember? The earl's men caught you last night. They beat you and brought you here."

Truth penetrated the pain in his skull.

He was a prisoner.

Chapter Twenty-three

*B*ríghid smoothed her skirts, cast one last glance at the mirror.
Heddy had insisted she wear the gown of deep claret silk today in
honor of Christmas. "The color makes your skin seem like
porcelain and looks so pretty with your dark hair."

Bríghid didn't know if any of that was true, but the gown was
beautiful. Ivory lace spilled from her elbows and ruffled the edge of the
bodice. 'Twas a bit lower cut than the other gowns, leaving the tops of
her breasts bared. Would Jamie notice?

She smoothed a strand of hair from her face. She'd brushed it until
it glistened, then pulled it back from her face with a ribbon of black
velvet, leaving most of it to fall freely down her back. Heddy had helped
her put color on her cheeks and lips—just a dab.

"Master Jamie won't be able to take his eyes off you, Miss." Heddy
curtsied and hurried from the room on some errand, leaving Bríghid
alone.

She met her own gaze in the mirror, saw the uncertainty in her eyes.

Something had changed.

She had changed.

Her feelings, always a jumble where Jamie was concerned, were
becoming terrifying clear. She could no longer pretend to hate him. She
could no longer dismiss him as nothing more than a *Sasanach*. She could
no longer hide from herself that she desired him, cared for him, even
loved …

No, she would not say it, not even in the privacy of her own
thoughts. For, although he might desire her, too, no Englishman of his
status would ever bind himself to a poor Irish Catholic woman. It would
be his utter ruination. It was illegal for a Protestant and a Catholic to

marry. Those who defied the law found themselves stripped of social status, their children considered bastards. Unless she gave up her faith and took a heretical oath, the English church would not join them. Unless he converted to her faith—an act of treason in the eyes of English society—no Catholic priest would marry them. There was no way Jamie would choose to burden his life with the consequences of being Catholic, and Bríghid could not renounce her faith.

Yet, even as she tried to accept the truth, her heart defied reason and dared to hope.

"Miracles come to those who believe," Father Owen had told her.

She had been stunned beyond words by Jamie's kindness last night. The fur-lined cloak was a lovely gift, and she treasured it. But nothing could compare to the overwhelming emotion she'd felt when he'd opened that door and she'd realized he'd brought her to a secret Catholic chapel. It astounded her that he would do something so thoughtful, so completely selfless, in order to please her. Surely, what'd he'd done had put him at risk, as it was against the law to attend Catholic Mass. His kindness had shaken her to the core.

She'd spoken privately with Father Owen, a deluge of emotion pouring from her. She'd wept over the murder of Father Padraíg, described her horror at being kidnapped, her shame at nearly being raped. She'd told him how Jamie had spared her a nightmarish fate, had nearly been killed for it. She'd admitted how she'd repaid his kindness by doubting him. She'd even confessed the overwhelming desire she felt for Jamie.

"And though he is a *Sasanach*, my feelings for him are ... "

"You care for him."

"Aye, but surely it is a sin to desire a Protestant, a *Sasanach*, in the way I desire him."

Then the good Father had said something that had sent her mind reeling. "Your blind hatred of the English is your sin, *a Bhríghid*. There is no sin in love."

She had almost laughed out loud. Love? Jamie? How could that be?

But the truth of it was unavoidable.

Her words came out in a rush. "But he is Protestant, and I am Catholic! He is wealthy, and I am naught but a peasant girl!"

"Miracles come to those who believe, child."

Father Owen had offered her absolution from her sins, and then guided her back to the main room of the Chapel, where he'd said Mass for a group of Catholics who, from the sound of them, were both Irish and English. It was a strange experience, to be sure, and not just because she had never before prayed with English.

Bríghid had never once been inside a chapel. The magic of it—sweet incense, a hundred candles, a grand crucifix above the altar—mixed with the sea of emotion in her heart. And, kneeling in prayer, she'd realized without a doubt Father Owen was right: She loved Jamie Blakewell.

But did he love her?

He desired her. He had forsaken the women at Turlington's for thoughts of her. He had protected her with his life. Was that not close to love?

Bolstered by such thoughts, she smoothed her skirts one more time, inspected her reflection, then hurried from the room to join him for breakfast.

O ver a Christmas Day breakfast of eggs, potatoes, ham and strong tea, he surprised her with yet another gift—a beautiful copy of *Gulliver's Travels* by Jonathan Swift.

Bríghid squealed with delight, then gingerly turned the pages, each edged with sparkling gold leaf. "He was Irish."

Jamie smiled, a heart-stopping, handsome smile that made Bríghid's toes curl. "I know."

They spent the morning in the library. She read her new book, while he read correspondence from the Colonies and old newspapers. She found it hard to concentrate on the story with him so near. Dressed only in dark brown breeches and a linen shirt, the ties of which seemed perpetually to have come loose to expose his chest, he seemed every bit the rugged colonial, and not a reserved English gentleman at all. For some reason, it made him all the more irresistible.

When tea arrived, it came with yet another gift—her very own pen, complete with a bottle of ink and clean, bright parchment. Amazement and gratitude at his thoughtfulness rendered her speechless.

"Now you can write to your brothers."

Over a mid-day meal of stuffed partridge, sweetmeats, and pastries, he surprised her yet again—this time with a silver-handled hairbrush and comb. Etchings of rose buds decorated their handles, opened into lovely, cupped blossoms on the broad back of the brush.

"They're beautiful!" She started to brush her own hair, but he took it from her.

"I claim the right as giver of the gift to be the first to use it."

"I wasn't aware of that custom, Master Blakewell." She was surprised by the flirtatious tone of her voice and the teasing smile she gave him.

She was even more shocked by the heat that coursed through her as his fingers lifted the heavy mass of her hair and he began to guide the brush through her tresses. Her breathing unnaturally rapid, she sat with eyes closed as, stroke after stroke, he made her scalp tingle. She longed for his kiss, prayed for the feel of his lips on the exposed skin of her throat. But he did not touch her.

After the mid-day meal, he took her riding around the estate, he on his beautiful grey stallion and she on the loveliest, gentlest white Andalusian mare. It was his turn to tell stories, most of them involving mischief he'd gotten into as a child while visiting from the Colonies. Then he told her about his estate in Virginia, about the mighty rivers, the forests, and the fertile land. Wrapped in her warm cloak with the sun shining on her face, knowing her brothers were safe, with Jamie beside her, she felt sheltered, safe, happy.

Had she ever felt this way before?

A long time ago, perhaps.

When they returned to the stables—immense and holding more than seventy horses by her count—he astonished her by telling her the mare was hers. "A gift from the Kenleigh family."

For a moment, she could not breathe. How could she accept such a gift? Bríghid could not imagine how much such a beautiful animal cost. "Jamie, I cannot —"

"Nonsense. Matthew and Elizabeth will insist, I'm afraid."

Hot tears running down her cheeks, Bríghid leapt into Jamie's arms. "Oh, thank you, Jamie! Thank you!"

She felt his muscles tense in reaction, and his arms moved beneath her cloak to encircle her waist. For a moment, he held her tightly against his hard man's body. Then he gently placed her back on her feet, smiled down at her, his eyes dark again, filled with shadows. "Does that mean you like their gift?"

"Oh, aye!" She turned to the mare, kissed her velvet-soft muzzle, stroked her long, wavy mane. "I shall call you *Niamh*."

The mare lipped her hand, nickered softly.

"I believe tea is waiting for us inside where it's warm."

"But I'm not cold."

"I'm glad to hear that."

He led her back to the house, his arm through hers, told her about Niamh's bloodlines. There were too many sires and dams for Bríghid to keep straight in her mind, but she knew the mare's lineage was impressive just by looking at her. She was the most beautiful horse Bríghid had ever seen.

"Fit for an Irish princess." Jamie opened the door for her, smiled.

And Bríghid saw in his eyes he was not jesting.

*J*amie watched her sleep, entranced. Her eyelashes cast shadows on her cheeks. The lush line of her lips was relaxed, rosy and sweet. The creamy mounds of her breasts, tantalizingly displayed by the delightfully low neckline of her gown, rose and fell softly with each breath.

They had taken tea in the library again, Bríghid speaking excitedly of her mare's smooth lines, fine color, and even temper. "She is the loveliest creature on earth!"

"Far from it. I'm afraid that honor goes to her beautiful mistress."

He'd watched as his words had brought a delicious flush to Bríghid's cheeks. She'd met his gaze, her head tilted shyly to one side, and he'd known without a doubt he was the most besotted of fools.

Rather than doing what he'd wanted to do—pulling her into his arms and making love to her until they both lay weak and sated—he'd picked up her new book and begun to read aloud from the page she had marked. He'd read but a few pages when he'd realized she was asleep, lulled by fresh air, sunshine, and excitement.

Sheer torture. That's what it was. He wanted her. His entire body ached for her. Yet he could not, would not touch her because...

He lined his reasons up like soldiers in a battle line. First, he would not touch her because he'd all but made a promise to her brother. Second, he would not touch her because she deserved marriage, which, by law, he could not offer her. Third, he would not touch her because there was no place for him in her heart.

And so he endured the agony of being near her, because he could not bring himself to be away from her. He suffered the torment of her sweet smiles, because he could not bear to be without them. He bore the lilting sound of her voice, because there was no sound sweeter to his ears. And he gave her gifts because he could not give her his body, his heart, his name.

Jamie had one more gift for her. He knew, as he had known with the others, that she would love it. That was not the same thing as loving him, but perhaps it was the best he could hope for.

*J*amie was troubled. He was holding back. Bríghid could tell, and it made her heart ache. She nibbled at her almond-crusted pastry, listened as he described Christmases of his childhood.

All day, he'd been attentive, warm, charming. He'd given her gifts the likes of which she could never have imagined. And yet something was missing. It was as if a part of him was caged, locked away inside. He seemed distant, restrained.

Had she angered him in some way? Had she hurt his feelings?

"I opened the box to find a set of small dueling pistols, my first firearms." He smiled at the recollection. "I was but eight at the time, and Cassie was furious with Alec for giving me such a gift. But he managed to ... assuage her fears."

"How did he do that?"

"I was too young to understand at the time, of course, but it involved lots of kissing." He smiled.

She all but dropped her dessert fork. Heat suffused her cheeks. "I see."

Lots of kissing.

That's what she wanted, too. Lot's of kissing—and more.

"Is the pastry not to your liking? You've barely touched it."

"Oh, no, it's quite tasty, and I do so love almonds. But I can't be eatin' another bite."

A rich meal it had been—roast goose with mushrooms and seasoned greens, a stew of winter vegetables, sweetmeats and puddings, candied fruits and sugared cakes, pastries and roasted nuts. How had Cook managed it all? Bríghid would have to ask her later.

Jamie called for servants to remove the dishes. As the table was cleared, he stood, crossed the room to an ornately carved sideboard, opened a drawer. When he returned to the table, he held a small silver box in his hands. "*Nollaig Shona dhuit, a Bhríghid.*"

He placed the box on the table, but at first she could only marvel that he had somehow learned to speak the words in her language. Then she knew. She smiled. "Father Owen?"

"Aye, I asked him to teach me a phrase or two." Jamie's gaze dropped to the box.

Hers followed. "Oh, Jamie, it's lovely! Where did you come by such a treasure? I shall have to find something special to put inside it!"

The lid of the box was decorated with gold filigree in the shapes of flowers and vines. The tiny legs were ornately shaped, each ending in a lion's paw. A latch held the lid fast.

Jamie sat in the chair beside her. His eyes met hers, his gaze warm. "Open it."

Feeling breathless with excitement, she lifted the latch, looked inside.

She heard herself cry out, felt the room spin. Overwhelmed by raw emotion, she gaped in disbelief, astonishment.

Staring up at her from a bed of dark blue velvet was her grandmother's dragon brooch, garnet eyes gleaming joy in the candlelight, unaware she was crying until tears blurred her vision. She felt Jamie's hand cup her cheek, felt his thumb wipe her tears away. She lifted her chin to meet his gaze. "H-how? Wh-where?"

"Ruaidhrí told me where to find the doctor in Baronstown. I bought it back from him the night we stayed at the White Stag."

Bríghid struggled to comprehend what Jamie had just said. He'd bought it back for her. While she'd been cursing his very existence, hating him, he'd been walking through the snowy streets of Baronstown in the dead of night in search of her brooch. "Oh, Jamie!"

Jamie saw the warmth in her eyes, felt the pull of his own passion for her. "I showed it to a jeweler in London, a man who deals in antiques."

"What did he say?"

He stood, stepped away from the table, eager to put distance between the two of them. "He said he'd never seen its like before. He said it dates back to the time of the first Norsemen in Ireland."

"To the time when my ancestors still ruled the land." She looked down at the brooch, a note of awe in her voice.

He'd felt the same sense of wonder when the jeweler had shared this information with him. His Irish princess. *No, not his.*

He felt the heat of her touch against his shoulder.

"Jamie?"

He knew he could not trust himself to be near her, not with his blood throbbing in his veins. Despite his better judgment, he turned to face her.

She gazed up at him through guileless eyes, one hand resting on the cloth of his shirt. "I don't know how to thank you. What you have done for me—"

"It was the least I could do. I know how much the brooch means to you."

She shook her head. Her hands moved to rest on his chest. "Not just the brooch, Jamie. Not just your thoughtful gifts. All of it. Were it not for you, were you like most men, I—"

His heart hammered beneath her touch. He held a finger to her lips. "Shh, love. Don't trouble yourself with such thoughts."

She pressed closer, painfully near, her scent an assault on his senses. "I shall never be able to repay your kindness."

"But you already have." He told himself to pull away from her even as he brushed a strand of ebony hair from her cheek. "Were it not for you, I'd have died that night."

"Were it not for me, Jamie, you'd ne'er been stabbed in the first place."

"Were it not for you, *a Bhríghid* ... " He never finished.

With a whimper, she stood on tiptoe, pressed herself against him, and offered him her lips. It was an offer neither his mind nor his body could refuse.

His lips took hers, the restraint he'd imposed on himself snapping to a single thread. He fought to keep the kiss gentle, to taste and not to devour. Her body soft and pliant, she met the teasing of his tongue with her own. In an instant, he was near the edge, his cock hard and aching, the shocking heat of his need for her all but overriding his good sense.

He broke the kiss, gazed down into sapphire eyes. "Bríghid, it wouldn't be right. Push me further, and you'll discover how very much I am like most men."

With that, he set her from him and disappeared in great strides up the stairs.

*B*ríghid lay on her bed, unable to read, unable to sleep, unable to do anything but think of Jamie. Tears streamed from the corners of her eyes down her temples. Beyond her door, the house was silent.

It wouldn't be right.

Aye, it wouldn't. The Church forbade it. England and Ireland frowned upon it. Her brothers would be tempted to kill Jamie for it. And yet ...

She ran her fingers over her lips, conjured the sensation of his kiss from her memory—sweet and scorching. She remembered other things as well—the wild pleasure she'd felt as Jamie had suckled her nipples through the silk of her gown, the heat of his touch between her thighs, the deep, empty sensation that made her yearn for him inside her.

But she wanted more than memories. She wanted him.

It wouldn't be right.

All of her life, she'd tried to do what was right. She'd cared for her brothers and father. She'd cooked and cleaned and mended. She'd cared for them in times of sickness, feigned health when she herself was sick so as not to take them from their work. She'd prayed the Rosary, observed holy days, lived a chaste life.

She had lived to make her father proud, to be the kind of daughter that would have made her mother happy had her mother lived. Never had she let her own desires interfere with her duties to her family. Such a thing had always been unthinkable.

But that was before she'd met Jamie Blakewell, before his handsome smile and intoxicating touch had made her feel alive and free and on fire. Before she'd met him, she hadn't let herself dream. She hadn't let herself want anything. A stolen hour with her book had seemed a luxury and had always been enough to keep her happy. But now ...

She wanted him. She wanted him to make love to her, to teach her the secrets shared by men and women. She wanted him to fill the aching emptiness inside her. Was that so terrible? Could she not decide this one thing for herself, choose her own fate?

It wouldn't be right.

Sure and it was a sin to lie with a man not your husband, and she had always intended to enter the marriage bed untouched. But she'd had no way of knowing she'd fall in love with a man she could never marry. She'd had no way of knowing that circumstances would render her sullied in the eyes of her countrymen, whether she actually slept with him or not.

She sat, wiped the tears from her cheeks.

What if she were to go to him? What if, right now, she were to walk down the hallway to his chamber and give her love to him? What if, just for tonight, she were to claim all the pleasure he could give her?

Would he think her brazen and shameful? Would he grow angry and perhaps cast her out of his room?

Push me further, and you'll discover how very much I am like most other men.

She stood, reached for her new hairbrush, drew it through her tangles with trembling hands. Could she do this? She could. She must.

For amid her doubts and trepidation, she knew one thing for certain: The world might condemn her for loving Jamie Blakewell, but nothing in her life had ever felt so right.

Chapter Twenty-four

*B*ríghid walked quickly, silently down the darkened hallway clad only in her shift, her heart racing. The polished wooden floor felt chilly against her bare feet.

Sweet Mary, was she really doing this?

Aye, she was. Right or wrong, she loved him. She needed him. She wanted to give him the gift that was hers alone to give, the gift that would forever mark her as his—and him as hers—no matter what happened tomorrow.

She stopped before his door, hesitated, hardly able to breathe.

She could do this.

She grasped the handle, pushed the door open, crossed the threshold.

He stood gazing into the fire, one outstretched arm against the marble mantelpiece. His body was bare save for a white linen towel wrapped round his hips. His hair was wet and hung in thick ropes to just below his shoulders. His skin gleamed with moisture in the firelight. Behind him sat a copper tub half full of water, the scent of pine soap in the air.

The sight of him, muscle and wet skin, sent tendrils of heat curling through her belly.

He didn't bother to look up. "You can set the bottle on the table."

On the table near the fire sat an empty brandy decanter and a glass. He'd been drinking.

She closed the door behind her, unsure what to say, what to do. She looked for her voice, found only a whisper. "Jamie?"

His head snapped in her direction, shock and what could only be displeasure written on his face. "What are *you* doing here?"

She felt the heat of his gaze as it raked over her, shivered. "I—"

"You should be in your own room." He turned fully to face her, the broad expanse of his chest and the muscles of his abdomen cast half in shadow, half in golden firelight. He looked like some pagan god or a great mythic warrior, his masculine sensuality enough to make her legs unsteady.

She realized she was trembling, fisted her hands in the linen of her shift. "I couldn't sleep. Jamie, I—"

"Go." His face was a stone mask.

She closed her eyes, swallowed. "No."

"You'll go back to your room if I have to carry you there." He took a step toward her, and she sensed the tension in his body, every muscle taut, ready to spring.

"No." She glanced out of the corner of her eye at his enormous bed, stepped sideways toward it. "I want you, Jamie."

"You don't know what you're saying." His voice was strained.

She took another step sideways toward the bed, her gaze locked with his in a battle of wills. "Aye, I do. I am not a child." She felt her right leg bump up against the bed and sat on the edge.

"No, Bríghid." But regardless of the words that passed his lips, she could see in his eyes the battle that raged within him.

Push me further, and you'll discover how very much I am like most other men.

Amazed at her own daring, she stretched sideways across the coverlet, did her best to look seductive, her gaze never leaving his.

She heard his growl, saw the exact moment when his control broke.

In three strides he reached the bed, and in one fluid motion, he dragged her toward him by her ankle, lifted her, and slung her over his shoulder like a sack of potatoes.

"Jamie, no!" His rejection of her stung, but the indignity of being carried in such a manner infuriated her. "Put me down!"

But he didn't listen. He strode angrily to the door, threw it open, and in a blink he was carrying her back down the hallway toward her room.

"Stop this!"

Jamie ignored her protests, the pounding of her small fists on his back. He didn't know which urge was more powerful at the moment—

the urge to toss her onto her back on the floor, spread her legs and take what she had just offered him or the urge to throttle her. He'd spent the better part of the evening trying to rein in his hammering need for her, only to have her sneak into his chamber and reawaken a hundred unwanted feelings.

It was difficult enough for a man to resist a beautiful woman, doubly so if he loved her and wanted for all the world to claim her. Jamie was trying so hard to do what was best for both of them—and she was doing her best to make certain he failed.

"*A amadáin cruthanta!*"

She was cursing him in Gaelic now. Good. He preferred her anger to the alluring sweetness that had been on her face when he'd looked up to find her standing in his room. If she hated him, it would be so much easier to let her go.

"*A phutaigh raithní!*"

He reached the door to her chamber, threw it open, and tossed her unceremoniously onto her bed. In a flash, she was on her feet, and she would have slapped him across the face had he not caught her wrist.

She glared up at him, reminding him of a hissing kitten. "I am a woman, not a sack of potatoes!"

"I can see that." He could see it all too clearly. That was the problem. Despite his best intentions, his gaze was drawn to the contours of her body beneath the white linen of her shift. Her delicate curves, the pert outline of her nipples, the dark curls of her sex were all too apparent, even in the half-light of the fire. Pure physical need raged through him, shot straight to his groin.

He heard her breath catch in her throat, knew she felt the heat of his perusal. Eyes wide with emotion, her dark hair a wild tangle around her shoulders, her skin satin in the firelight, she was utterly, irresistibly feminine.

Take her.

Jamie felt the call of the brandy in his blood, tried to ignore it. Gathering the last ounce of will he possessed, he turned, strode toward the door.

"Jamie, please!"

It was the catch in her voice that stopped him.

He turned to face her, felt as if someone had knocked the air from his lungs. His heart stopped.

She stood trembling and completely naked, the white linen of her shift pooled at her feet. Her skin glowed ivory in the firelight, her soft curves enhanced by the play of shadows. She met his gaze, her eyes full of uncertainty. She seemed so desperately vulnerable. So beautiful. So intensely alluring.

A virgin seductress.

"*Bríghid.*"

"Don't walk away from me, Jamie. Please!" She seemed to struggle to speak each word. "All I want is tonight—one night out of a lifetime. Is that so much to ask?"

Some primitive male part of him urged him to end the talking and give her—and himself—what they both so desperately needed. But the consequences for both of them would be dire. He stood his ground. "Bríghid, I—"

"I-I know I'm no more than an Irish peasant, and a Catholic at that." She crossed her arms protectively over her breasts, and her gaze fell to the floor, tears on her cheeks. "B-but I thought you at least felt desire for me."

If she had yelled at him or played the coquette, he might have been able to walk away. But he could not bear her tears or the sense of shame he felt welling up inside her. He knew without asking this had taken all her courage. He knew she had never offered herself to a man before, and she never would again. That she should choose him ...

A voice of caution reminded him that lust was not love. But he didn't see lust in her eyes. He saw only longing.

"Bríghid." He lifted her chin, forced her to meet his gaze, ran a thumb lazily over her tear-stained cheek. "Are you certain? What you ask cannot be undone."

"Aye." Her voice was a whisper.

"So be it."

Sexual desire, too long denied, ripped through him, and the battle to refuse her became a battle not to frighten her with the force of his need. She was a virgin. She deserved a first time that was slow and sweet and gentle. He would give her that.

Bríghid looked into the eyes of the man who was about to make love to her. A fleeting feeling of elation was replaced by something that felt very much like fear.

"Don't hide your beauty." He drew her arms away from her breasts, kissed her fingertips. "*Mo Bhríghid álainn.*"

My beautiful Bríghid. Where had he learned such words?

She felt her nipples tighten under the heat of his gaze, closed her eyes, tried to breathe. "I-I don't know what to do."

She heard him chuckle, felt his arms encircle her. "Just kiss me."

His lips were gentle as they brushed over hers, his body warm and strong. He tasted faintly of drink, smelled of pine soap and man. In the eyes of the world, this was wrong, but it felt right, so right.

She gave herself over to the magic of his embrace, to the heady rush of joy she always felt when he kissed her. Her hands found their way up the muscled length of his arms over his shoulders to the sculpted planes of his chest. His skin was soft, the shifting muscles beneath like bands of steel. She found and stroked the ridge of his scar with her fingertips.

He groaned, deepened the kiss, crushed her against him.

She sensed his urgency, felt an answering demand inside. The raw proof of his masculine hunger pressed against her belly, setting off sparks deep within her. She had dreamed of this, wanted this for so long it seemed. Was this what all women felt in the arms of their lovers?

Burning need. Unbearable heat. Sweet desperation.

He scooped her into his arms, carried her to the bed, and placed her gently on the soft, linen sheet. But he didn't join her right away.

Instead, he stood over her for a moment, his heavy chest rising and falling with each breath, his gaze fixed on hers. As she watched, he grasped the edge of the towel—and pulled. It fell to the floor.

He stood before her completely naked now, his sex full and thick against his belly. She'd only gotten a glimpse of him before and couldn't help but stare. She'd heard whisperings of the pain women experienced on their wedding nights.

Now she understood why.

"You have nothing to fear." His voice was a caress.

"I'm not afraid."

"Bréagach thú." Liar.

He stretched out beside her, gathered her in his arms until their bodies were pressed intimately against one another, bare skin against bare skin, the thick length of his arousal touching her belly, one of his legs thrust casually between hers. Then he slanted his mouth over hers, thrust deep with his tongue.

The sensations were almost too much to take in at once—the velvet glide of his tongue, the hardness of his muscled thigh against the soft inner flesh of hers, the sweet rasp of his chest hair against her breasts. She heard herself whisper his name, whimper. When his callused palm caressed her breast, her whimper became a moan.

She pressed her breast deeper into the heat of his hand, eager for more, as his fingers flicked her nipple, teased it, shaped it into a rosy bud. When had she become so greedy, lapping up pleasure the way a cat lapped milk?

But, oh, she wanted more.

When he stopped, she almost cried out in dismay. But soft, hot lips quickly replaced his fingers. Jagged bolts of heat shot through her all the way to her core. She clung to him, almost afraid of the sultry sensations his touch conjured inside her, as his tongue flicked first one sensitive bud, then the other. "Jamie!"

"You have no idea how long I've waited to taste you." He cupped one breast, drew its taut crest into his hot mouth, and suckled.

The wonderful shock of it made her body arch. The soft pull of his lips and the rough caress of his tongue caused liquid heat to pool between her thighs, as he sucked first one nipple, then the other. And soon she was writhing beneath him, her fingers laced through his damp hair.

"Mmm." He scattered kisses across the underside of her breasts, molded them with his hands, his thumbs reaching to tease their wet, sensitive buds. "I can't get enough of you."

When he took her nipple into his mouth again, she felt her insides quiver. Her entire body seemed on fire. The heat between her thighs had become a blaze, and she felt an aching emptiness inside.

"You taste so damned good." His lips continued to tug on her nipples, while one of his hands began to explore her belly.

Fire licked her skin wherever he touched her—the curve of her hip, the hollow of her waist, the rounded flesh of her lower belly. She wanted him to touch her, needed him to touch her as he'd done in the library, his hand between her thighs.

As if to torment her, his hand repeatedly moved nearer to, then further from, the place that burned hottest for him. Slowly, ever so slowly, he caressed her lower belly, tickled the flesh of her inner thighs, brushed lightly over her woman's curls until she cried out, desperate, breathless, reckless with need.

As if through a fog, she realized he was doing this on purpose to tease her, to taunt her, to heighten her arousal. He knew more about her body than she, knew how to unlock its secrets, how and when and where to touch her to fuel her hunger. When at last his hand cupped her sex, she lifted her hips to meet him.

"Oh, aye!" The pressure was sweet as the heel of his hand moved in slow, deep circles, delicious new sensations unfurling in her belly. She writhed beneath his touch, whimpered, whispered his name. "*Jamie!*"

His lips left her breasts, found the sensitive skin of her throat. "I'm going to open you now, but slowly."

He lifted one of her thighs, draped her leg over his, preparing her for his more intimate touch. She fought the impulse to draw her thighs back together. Never had she felt so exposed. Then his fingers slid between her slick woman's folds, parted her, and began to stroke the sensitive nub hidden there, and she felt only delight.

Tremors of pleasure pulsed through her at this exquisite, new feeling. The aching emptiness inside her grew sharper. Her whimpers became breathless moans as he rhythmically flicked a finger over her nub, circling and teasing her. And when she thought she must surely die, he slid a finger deep inside her.

This was what she wanted, what she needed.

His deep groan mingled with her own cry, as he stroked her deeply, caressing a part of her that had never been touched before.

"You are so wet." His teeth nipped her earlobe, her throat. "Soon, I'll be deep inside you, but I want you to feel it first. I want you to know how good it is. Come for me."

His English words made no sense. Come for him?

But her mind was too full of mist, too fogged with desire for her to work it out. And when he slid a second finger inside her, stretching her so sweetly, she could no longer think. There was nothing in the world but Jamie, nothing but the way he made her feel. "Oh, Jamie, it ... feels ... so ... good."

"And it only gets better, love." Gently, persistently, he stroked her, sliding his fingers in and out of her, his thumb pressing relentless circles against her swollen nub. "I've wanted you for so long, *a Bhríghid*, so long."

Something overwhelming began to build inside her, something reckless and hot. She was being washed away, carried to some perilous edge. She tried to draw her thighs together, tried to hold the precipice at bay.

He shifted his leg so that its weight held hers firmly apart. "You can't escape it, Bríghid. Surrender. Give yourself to it."

Her fingers dug into the muscles of his back as she fought to keep her hold on the world she knew. She heard his whispered endearments, her own frantic cries.

"Aye, Bríghid. Take it! Take pleasure from me."

She cried out as the fire within her drew itself into a tense, hot ball in her belly—and then exploded. Waves of ecstasy washed through her, buffeting her with sensations too good to be true. A shower of sparks. Searing bliss.

Jamie moaned with her, trailing gentle bites along her throat, his fingers thrusting deep, until the quivering inside her had ceased and she lay weak and panting in his arms.

"*Mo Bhríghid bhán.*" *My fair Bríghid.* He rained kisses across her brow, her cheeks, her lips, her breasts.

If she hadn't felt him, warm and strong, beside her, she'd have thought she was floating on some calm sea. She opened her eyes, met his gaze, saw the intensity burning in him. And it dawned on her that everything he'd done so far had been intended to give her pleasure. He had yet to sate himself. She was touched by his tenderness, astounded at what she'd just experienced. She'd had no idea it could feel so good for a woman.

She must have spoken that last thought aloud, as he chuckled, smiling at her. "You've had but the merest taste, my sweet. Are you ready for the feast?"

His voice was deep, husky, laden with sexual promise.

She didn't know if she was ready, but his question, the tone of his voice, made her belly lurch. Then she realized with a start his fingers were still inside her. She felt a blush creep over her skin and looked away.

"Look, at me, Bríghid."

She fought to lift her gaze to his.

"You've no reason to feel shame, sweet." He gazed down at her, slowly withdrew from her, and began to caress her sensitive bud with fingers made slick from her own juices. "Everything about you is beautiful, made for a man's touch, my touch."

It felt so good, better than before.

The fire that had burned down to embers burst into eager flames inside her, as his fingers slid quickly, easily over that most sensitive spot.

She ran her hands over his chest, drinking in the manly feel of him. "Kiss me, Jamie. Please."

When he took her lips again, his kiss was savage, relentless. It was a kiss meant to claim her, not seduce her. It left her bruised, breathless, longing for more. It was everything she needed, everything she wanted. And she realized that whatever he'd been holding back had now been let loose.

He had given, and now he would take.

Like a mighty wave, his passion washed over her. Had his weight not anchored her fast to the bed, she'd surely have been swept away by the force of it. His body pressed against hers, flesh against burning flesh, his arousal straining against her belly.

A jolt of answering heat. A taste of fear.

Would it hurt?

She couldn't imagine having him inside her without pain. Even were it so, she wanted him. She needed him, needed to bind herself to him, needed to give him the gift that was hers alone to give. There was no turning back now.

Still kissing her, he stretched his body over hers and settled between her thighs. "Open your eyes. Look at me, Bríghid."

His eyes were dark with passion, his pupils wide. Sweat beaded on his temples, strands of hair clinging to his face, his chest rising and falling with each powerful breath. Every muscle in his body seemed tight, as if he were a drawn bowstring about to snap. And she felt a rush of happiness to know that she was the cause of this.

Then she felt the thick head of his shaft tease her cleft, nudging slowly inside her to press against the taut barrier of her maidenhead. With a groan, he thrust and breeched it.

She cried out, squeezed her eyes shut.

The pain was white hot.

He captured her cry with his mouth, held himself still within her, whispered reassurances, his voice deep, soothing. "From now on, only pleasure, love. I promise."

Slowly, the pain faded. Instead, she felt an erotic sense of fullness. He was inside her, a part of her. And in that moment, it seemed to Bríghid their bodies had been destined to join together in just this fevered way. They were one, she and this strange, wonderful man, this *Sasanach*.

Slowly, he withdrew. When he entered her again, she couldn't help but moan as he stretched her, filled her, made her complete. And just when she thought he'd buried himself totally, he withdrew, then pushed himself deeper still, until she could feel him against her womb. He was deep inside her now, all of him.

"God, Bríghid!" He sounded as if he were in pain. "You are so tight. So hot."

His rhythm began to build, stroke upon stroke, each thrust making her hungrier, more desperate for the next. How had she lived without this? How had she lived without him? Never had she felt anything like this melting ecstasy, this fevered yearning.

"Jamie, oh, Jamie." Her hands impatiently explored the contours of his chest, searching, seeking. "I need ... I need... "

"What do you need, Bríghid, love? This?" He thrust deep, held himself inside her, moved his groin in maddening circles against her aching sex.

"Oh, aye!" She felt the edge of the precipice draw near again and arched against him, not afraid this time. "Jamie!"

All at once he was driving into her hard, drawing helpless, frantic cries from her throat. "Yes, Bríghid! Give yourself to me!"

And then it hit, stronger than before—an explosion, liquid fire, a shower of light. Her inner muscles clenched down on him hard, her body quaking with the force of her release. Maddening pleasure washed through her, heightened by his powerful thrusts.

She heard herself cry his name, felt his body shudder, as with a low groan, he spilled himself deep inside her.

*J*amie gazed at the woman who lay, sated and sleepy, in his arms. Her eyes were closed, her breathing deep and even, her body pliant, soft. He inhaled her scent and the lingering perfume of their lovemaking— lavender, salt, musk.

I didn't know it could feel this good for a woman.

Jamie smiled. Her innocent astonishment at the pleasures of sex both amused him and made him feel fiercely protective.

This was what Sheff had tried to steal from her. But he had failed.

Can you keep her safe from yourself?

Finn's voice echoed, unbidden, through Jamie's mind.

What Sheff had not stolen, Jamie had taken. Her virgin's blood on him and on the sheets beneath them illustrated that only too clearly.

Hadn't he finally done what Sheff had expected him to do that night so long ago?

He supposed he ought to be angry with himself or at least feel some sense of guilt. He'd given into his physical need for her. He'd done what he said he would not do. He'd taken from her that which he'd almost lost his life trying to protect.

Why then did he feel so damned at peace with himself?

Certainly, he'd gotten the sexual release he'd needed for so long. But it was more than physical satisfaction. He'd made love to many women over the years, some whose expertise in bed had driven him to the very brink of masculine control, of madness, but he'd never experienced anything like this.

Bríghid's untried kisses and cries of pleasure had done far more than arouse his body and incite his lust. They had claimed his soul.

Inside her, he'd found his home.

She shifted in his arms, snuggled closer against his chest. Her dark hair streamed like a river of midnight across his abdomen, soft and shimmering.

He pulled the blankets up over her shoulders to ward off the chill, the fire having long since burned to glowing embers.

When God brings a man and woman together, He helps them find the way.

As much as Jamie hoped the priest knew what he was talking about, Jamie wasn't willing to leave it up to any god. He loved Bríghid, loved her as he had never loved any woman, and he would find a way for them to be together, English law be damned.

But first, he had to win her heart.

Chapter Twenty-five

January 15, 1755

"You're talking about starting a war, Master Blakewell." William Pitt grimaced, adjusted his swollen foot where it rested, covered in foul-smelling compresses, on a cushioned footstool. "Damned gout!"

"I'm talking about winning a war, Sir, for the war has already begun."

Pitt seemed to consider this, his forehead bent in a pensive frown beneath his powdered wig. His large, almond eyes, set in a pale oval face, gave him an intelligent, slightly melancholy appearance, and Jamie knew the man's hard-won political successes had come through wit and oratory. Of all the members of Commons, he was Jamie's best hope— and the most influential.

"What do you suggest?"

"A fleet of ships designed to fight in the lakes and rivers of the north—and well-trained sailors to man them. Attack the French where they're most vulnerable—their supply lines, their own towns. Draw them away from English families on the frontier." Jamie returned Pitt's steady gaze, waited.

"That's a bold plan. It would inevitably force them to fight on two fronts or abandon the frontier." Pitt reached for his teacup, took a sip.

"There's more to it than that, Sir."

Pitt raised an eyebrow. "Explain."

"The French have allied themselves with numerous Indian nations—foremost the Huron, Ottawa, Potawatomi and Ojibwa. Most are led by Obwandiyag, whom some call Pontiac. His intelligence and influence should not be underestimated. Not only is he capable of leading his men in battle, but he could easily win more tribes to the side of the

French. He is *metai*, a spiritual leader, and his words carry great meaning for many." Jamie took a sip of tea, let his words sink in, trying not to overwhelm Pitt.

"Go on."

"If we shift the battle to the great lakes and rivers, the French lose whatever advantage they've gained through such alliances. While Pontiac's men are more than capable of defeating British troops on land, they have no means to counter English warships."

Pitt brow furrowed. "What makes you so certain Indians can defeat trained English soldiers?"

"The Indian way of warfare is not the English way. They attack through ambush, not from battle lines drawn up in the open. The French have largely adopted their techniques. At Fort Necessity, they fired at us from high in the surrounding trees. Good Englishmen died, shot down by an enemy they could not see."

Pitt's upper lip curled in disgust. "That's barbaric."

"Perhaps, Sir." Jamie wouldn't bother trying to explain to Pitt the Indian point of view on warfare. What warrior in his right mind stood out in the open in front of enemies who were firing at him? "Still, that's the way it is. An English regiment might easily wander into such an ambush—on a road through the forest or on the banks of a river—and lose every man. To win this war, Britain *must* adapt, Sir, or British claims along the Ohio *will be lost*."

And Nicholas's terrible death will have been for naught.

For a moment, Pitt said nothing but gazed broodingly into the distance.

"Very well, Master Blakewell, I see the point you're trying to make." Pitt wiggled his swollen toes, winced. "But tell me—who would supply such ships?"

"My brother-in-law, Alec Kenleigh, has already drawn up plans for a small fleet of warships specially designed to navigate the northern waterways."

"Of course." Pitt smiled. "War is a bloody profitable business."

Jamie refused to let the comment bait him. "Aye, it can be, Sir. However, Alec is willing to build these ships at no profit to himself."

Both of Pitt's eyebrows shot upward. "At cost? Remarkable."

"My brother-in-law lost his eldest son at Fort Necessity." The pain, the guilt welled up inside Jamie. "He was taken captive and later ... burnt alive."

Pitt's eyebrows shot up, before his face shifted into a scowl of outrage. "I do say—how unfortunate and appalling."

Jamie beat back his grief. "It is war, Sir."

"My condolences on your family's loss." Pitt took another sip of tea. "I've heard nothing but good things about your brother-in-law. I'm sorry he should suffer such tragedy."

"Thank you, Sir." Jamie decided to press his point. "The longer Britain delays in meeting the French threat, the greater that threat becomes. English families are dying on the frontier—men, women and children—and the French are working hard to persuade Britain's Indian allies to switch sides. We dare not dally, Sir."

For a moment, the two men sat, gazes locked.

"Very well, Master Blakewell, I shall represent the Colonial cause in Commons. But I warn you, it won't be easy. Most Englishmen are more concerned with events on the Continent, as the results will have very real consequences here in Britain. Most believe the Crown can force concessions from the French with regard to the American frontier by dominating them in Europe."

"They are blind." Jamie stood abruptly, walked to the nearby window. "They would not tolerate the slaughter of English families on British soil here on this island, but the slaughter of British families—"

"Colonists."

Jamie spun to face him. "—*British families* on the American frontier means nothing to them. For are the colonists not also subjects of His Majesty, equally deserving of his protection and consideration? And what will happen if colonists begin to feel Britain has turned her back on them? It shouldn't surprise me that many would turn their backs on Britain."

"I admire your passion, Master Blakewell, and I agree with you. But it will be an uphill battle, all the more so thanks to your friend." He pinned Jamie with his gaze. "Or should I say erstwhile friend?"

"Lord Byerly."

"He's spreading some rather distressing rumors about you, rumors of collusion with traitorous Irish Catholics. I need to know what truth lies behind these rumors so that I can prepare a proper response."

Jamie had known this would happen. "Of course."

*B*ríghid looked up from her book and gazed out the library window at the tidy grounds beyond. It would be dark soon. Surely, he'd be home any minute. He'd risen early this morning and gone into London to meet with yet another member of Parliament. It had been this way every day this week.

Each morning he woke her with gentle kisses, then shaved, dressed, and bid her farewell. And though she tried hard to keep busy, each day was an agony of waiting. She read books, had tea with Elizabeth, visited Niamh in the stables. She'd even spent an afternoon teaching Elizabeth what she knew about tatting lace.

Still, she missed him.

Each evening when he arrived home, he met privately with Matthew to discuss business. Then he escorted her to dinner with Matthew and Elizabeth, who'd returned from Kent on the first day of the New Year. After dinner, he and Matthew retired to Matthew's study to have a brandy, while she and Elizabeth did needlework, or Elizabeth tried to teach her a tune on the harpsichord. Then the gentlemen joined them for tea and perhaps a game of billiards.

These last hours of the day served only to heighten Bríghid's anticipation for the night to come, as Jamie showed her through covert glances and secret smiles just what he had in mind once they reached the privacy of his chamber. For if her days left her feeling restless and impatient, the nights brought her bliss. Over the past two weeks, Jamie had shown her pleasure she had never imagined, taught her the secrets of her own body—and his. Just when she thought she knew everything there was to know about the union of men and women, he showed her something new. How achingly good it felt if he entered her just so. How much more intense her peak could be if he made her hang at the edge and wait for it. How to drive him wild with her lips, her tongue, her hands, her body.

She'd never known any greater happiness.

And yet there was darkness.

She tried to ignore it, tried to forget. She tried to forget how much she missed her brothers. She tried to forget how poorly she fit in—an Irish peasant among English gentry. She tried to forget about the *iarla*. She tried to forget about the strife between her people and Jamie's, centuries of blood and hatred. She tried to forget about English law and the rules of the Church. She tried to forget, but she couldn't.

For although she loved Jamie Blakewell, she knew this could not last.

Like a story in a book, this fairytale would soon come to an end. One day, word would come from County Clare that her brothers were waiting for her, and her time with Jamie would be over. For even had he desired to marry her—he had never mentioned marriage—by law he could not. And she would not leave her brothers and travel to the Colonies as his mistress, where she would have to watch as he took an Englishwoman—a Protestant—to wife, gave her his name, his children, his love.

Bríghid felt tears prick behind her eyes at the thought, blinked them away.

She didn't want to think that far in the future. She didn't want to think about the way her new silk gowns, her soft leather slippers, her fur cloak, and the other gifts he'd given her would brand her the whore of a *Sasanach* in the eyes of her countrymen. She didn't want to think about how she would have to sell them for food, for rent, for serviceable woolens that wouldn't be ruined by the hard work of running a household in a cabin with no chimney, no floor, no windows. She didn't want to think of the way her brothers would react when they saw her again, for she wouldn't be able to lie.

And if she carried Jamie's child ...

She didn't want to think that far. She had today. She had tonight. Even if it were only a fantasy, she would savor each touch, revel in each moment, knowing full well it could end tomorrow and all happiness with it. She turned her gaze back to her book, *The Seven Wise Masters of Rome*, forced her eyes to the page.

That's where Jamie found her—nose buried in a book. He stood for a moment, savored the sight of her as she read.

She wore one of the new gowns he'd had made for her, a creation of shimmering burgundy-colored silk with ivory lace at her wrists. The color suited her beautifully, as he'd known it would. The cut of the gown complimented her form, her slender waist, her full bosom.

"Jamie!" Bríghid rose, put down the book, her lips curved in a pretty smile.

Jamie drew her into his embrace, kissed her cheek. "My sweet."

Despite her smile, he could see the sadness in her eyes, the unhappiness she tried to hide. He knew she felt out of sorts here. Did she want to leave so badly? Was she so homesick? What was it she'd said?

I don't belong here.

Jamie was looking for a way he and Bríghid could be together, but what if she didn't want to stay with him? He would have no choice but to let her go. The thought was like a blade in his heart. He forced his thoughts down a different path. "Would you care to take Niamh for a ride before the sun sets?"

"Oh, aye!" Her face lit up with a smile that nearly robbed him of his ability to think.

The western sky had begun to turn pink by the time they rode from the stables down the path that led to the eastern edge of the estate, which boasted a small forest of beech trees. Brighid had taken quickly to the sidesaddle and now rode with confidence.

An excited flush on her cheeks, she urged her horse to a canter, then a gallop. "You'll never catch me, *Sasanach!*"

Hermes could, of course, easily outrun the mare, but Jamie reined him in, let Brighid enjoy the thrill of being pursued.

She bent low over her mare, urged her to a gallop, her laughter like the tinkling of bells, her dark hair streaming behind her.

Some ancient male instinct in Jamie's blood reveled in the chase, delighted in knowing he would soon be the victor. He let Hermes close the distance between them. A low rumble of laughter rose from his chest.

Brighid looked back over her shoulder, screamed, her eyes alight with excitement, cheeks flushed. "No!"

The dark edge of the forest drew near, and Jamie gave the stallion his head. Almost immediately he drew even with Brighid. He captured her reins, drew both animals to a stop.

Her breath came in great gasps, her face aglow with anticipation. In her eyes he saw a need to match his own—the need to seize this moment, to join herself with him, to forget all the obstacles that stood between them.

He slid from the saddle, removed a blanket from his saddlebag, strode over to her. "I have won this battle, Princess. To the victor go the spoils."

She squealed as he pulled her down into his arms, pretended to fight him as he carried her in among the trees to the crumbling remains of some ancient hall, her laughter proof it was just a game. Sheltered on three sides by walls almost as tall as Jamie, the ruins provided privacy and a respite from the winter wind.

"I am to be your prisoner?" She ran her hands along his chest as he lowered her to her feet.

"Aye. Mine to do with as I please." Jamie spread the blanket on the snowy ground.

Her eyes held a look of heated female desire, a promise of delight as old as time. "And what pleases you?"

"Only this." He pulled her into his arms, took her lips with his in an urgent, searing kiss. He wanted to forget, needed to forget that time was against them, that state and church stood between them, that an ocean divided them.

She returned his kiss, drew his tongue into her mouth, her desperation matching his.

They landed together on the blanket, rolling and twisting, drunk on the moment.

He felt her fingers struggle with the fall of his breeches, while he lifted her skirts above her thighs. Cold air rushed over the heat of his arousal, as he forced her thighs wide apart with his own. Then he captured her wrists, pinned her arms above her head, and looked down into her eyes.

"You are mine, Princess. Do you yield?"

Brighid looked up at the man she loved, her heart pounding, gave him her haughtiest smile. "Never, *Sasanach*."

"Very well, then." He face took on the lines of false severity. "You leave me no choice but to teach you a lesson."

With one hand, he deftly removed one of the ribbons that held her stockings in place, and before she realized what he was doing, he'd tied one end of it gently around her wrists. The other he bound to the thin trunk of a sapling.

Then he rocked back on his heels, looked down at her, every bit the conqueror. His hands stroked her inner thighs, raised goose bumps on her chilled skin.

She felt deliciously helpless, almost frantic with excitement. She had no way of knowing what he would do next.

When he touched her again it was to bare her breasts. His palms cupped and shaped them, molded them, before he took them in his mouth and suckled her aching nipples.

She writhed beneath him, her hands held fast by her bonds, as the heat of his mouth upon her ignited the fever within her. She let his touch carry her away, far from worries of tomorrow, far from fear and grief. For now, there was only this place, only this man. For now, she could forget.

And then, all at once, he was kissing her exposed thighs, nipping her, teasing her.

"Jamie." She heard herself moan, call his name, felt herself grow damp with desire. But when his lips pressed into the curls of her woman's mound, she stiffened. Surely he wouldn't kiss her there.

Oh, but he did!

His mouth was scorching hot against her aching sex. His tongue swirled delight over her most tender flesh, penetrated her, drew gasps from her surprised lips. Her head rolled from side to side with erotic abandon, as he gave her his deepest, most intimate kiss.

"I've dreamed of tasting you like this—just like this." When he closed his mouth over her again, he began to suck and tug on her tender bud with his lips, his fingers sliding deep inside her.

The pleasure was so intense it was almost unbearable. Could anything truly feel this good? And those wild moans—were they really coming from her?

Then, all at once, it was upon her. She cried out, arching against his mouth as sweet ecstasy rippled through her, making her inner muscles clench, Jamie prolonging her climax with his fingers and deft strokes of his tongue.

When at last she floated down from the heavens, she opened her eyes to find him poised above her, passion still burning in his eyes.

"Do you surrender?"

She smiled, weak from his loving, and whispered. "Never."

He lifted her, turned her until she lay on her belly, her bonds twisting with her.

She gasped, fought not to giggle.

He wadded her skirts, thrust them beneath her, until she lay with her bottom raised at just such an angle. His voice took on the tone of command. "Spread your thighs for me."

"They are spread." Her heart pounded with excitement at the power of his game.

"Spread them wider." His hands, warm and demanding, pressed her inner thighs apart another inch. "Wider still."

Trembling, she complied. She knew she was completely exposed to him now, her most private flesh uncovered, vulnerable.

For a moment he did nothing. He was letting her wait, letting her wonder. The anticipation heightened her excitement, deepened her need.

Then his warm palms caressed the chilled flesh of her bottom, and his thumb lazily slid over her slick, aching cleft. "I ask you again. Do you yield?"

"Never!"

"Very well." He slid into her with one clean thrust, penetrating her completely. His hands grasped her hips, his testicles slapping against her as he reached her very depths with fast, forceful strokes. "Oh, Bríghid. You are so wet and tight. So perfect."

Their sounds of pleasure mingled in the cold air, as he drove himself into her. Her moans quickly became frantic, keening cries as she felt another climax approach.

Then his fingers sought and found her swollen nub, stroked it, caressed it.

"Jamie!" She cried out his name as once again the force of passion claimed her.

Her muscles clenched violently around him, as wave after wave of liquid ecstasy rolled through her. She felt him shudder, heard his deep groan as he thrust hard and deep, spilling himself inside her. Then there was only the sound of their rapid breathing and the feel of him as he gently lowered his weight on top of her, his shaft still hard inside her.

He nuzzled her cheek. "'Tis you who have conquered me, my Irish princess."

*I*t was dark by the time they mounted again and turned their horses back toward the manor. The air had grown colder, but Bríghid felt snug in her fur cloak. Her body felt languid, replete from their loving-making, the telltale wetness between her thighs a sweet reminder that the man she loved had claimed his pleasure inside her.

She was trying to explain the appeal of Cuchulainn to the average Irishman. "He may have been a bit crazy—and he was a wee bit crazy, now, wasn't he?—but he was a mighty warrior and true. If he were alive today—"

She heard a loud popping sound, saw Jamie's head jerk in alarm toward the trees.

Then she felt it—a deep, burning sensation in her side.

She pressed her hand against the pain, felt something warm, sticky. She looked down, saw something dark on her hand. Blood? "Jamie?"

"Oh, Christ! Bríghid!"

She felt his arms surround her as he pulled her off her horse and across his lap. She wanted to ask him what had happened, why she was bleeding, but the world had begun to spin. Or had Hermes broken into a gallop? Pain sliced through her like the blade of a knife, and she felt herself fall into darkness.

Chapter Twenty-six

Jamie pressed the linen tightly against the wound. The bleeding had slowed but had not stopped. "Stay with me, Brighid."

She was unconscious again, and for that he was grateful. They'd given her what laudanum they had, but he knew she was still in great pain.

The bullet had entered her right side at the bottom of her ribcage and had not exited. Jamie knew what this meant. The surgeon would have to remove it.

Like unwelcome echoes, the screams of the men wounded in the Wyandot raid came back to him. The surgeon had treated those he could, removing bullets buried in shoulders, thighs, and bellies, while, in their agony, grown men pleaded for God, pleaded for mercy, pleaded for death.

That is what Brighid would have to endure.

The thought filled Jamie with white-hot rage and desperation. Christ, how he wished the bullet had hit him! If only he could spare her this.

What Jamie wouldn't give for Takotah's healing skill right now. He trusted her, had watched her pull people from the brink of death time and time again. He had more faith in her than any English physician, no matter how exalted his reputation.

What was taking the surgeon so long, anyway? Matthew had gone to fetch him well over two hours ago. *Bloody hell!*

Elizabeth handed Jamie a freshly folded square of clean linen, seeming to read his thoughts. "He'll be here soon."

Jamie quickly switched the clean cloth for the bloody one, pressed it hard against the wound, handed the bloodied cloth to Elizabeth.

Bríghid moaned in her sleep, weakly tried to brush his hand away as if to remove the source of her pain. Her eyes fluttered open, their depths glazed by the effects of the laudanum. "Jamie?"

"Aye, love, I'm here." He reached with his free hand to caress her cheek.

Her brow was furrowed, and she bit her lower lip. "It hurts."

The rage inside him grew. "I know it does, love. The surgeon is on his way."

She shivered, a cold sweat on her brow. "I-I'm so cold."

"We'll build up the fire." He pulled a blanket over her.

Behind him, Elizabeth bid Heddy to put more wood on the fire.

"Jamie?"

"Aye, sweet, I'm here."

"If I die, tell my brothers—"

"You're not going to die." His voice sounded rough even to his ears. "I won't let you."

Bríghid felt herself smile despite the relentless pain. Leave it to her sweet *Sasanach* to think he could tell even death what to do. But she could feel her strength fading. She could feel herself growing weaker, colder. She wanted to tell him just in case. She wanted him to know. She reached for him, ran her hand over the stubble on his handsome face. "Jamie."

He took her hand in his, kissed it. "Just rest, love."

"No, I need to tell you." She felt herself begin to drift, fought the darkness.

"Need to tell me what, love?"

Her lips formed the words she had so longed to say. "*Mo ghrá thú, a Jamie. Mo ghrá go buan, tu.*" *I love you, Jamie. I'll always love you.*

As darkness claimed her again, she didn't realize she had slipped and spoken them in her mother tongue.

*B*ríghid fought to surface from the depth of what seemed a nightmare. She was cold, so cold. And she hurt. Something was jabbing her in the side, something sharp and unbearably painful. Then she remembered.

She had a knife in the waistband of her skirts. A knife to use against the *Sasanach*.

Somehow it was buried just beneath her ribs, buried deep in her side. She tried to pull it out, but she couldn't move.

The knife. Oh, it hurt! She had to get it out.

But why would she still have the knife? She didn't want to hurt Jamie. She loved him.

The *iarla*.

She had taken the knife to protect herself against the *iarla*. Instead, she had managed to cut herself. Hadn't there been blood? Hadn't she looked down and seen her own blood?

Aye, she was bleeding. But where was Jamie?

"Tarrtháil, a Jamie!" Help me, Jamie!

From the hallway outside her room where he was pacing, Jamie heard her cries.

"Damnation!" He lunged toward the door and would have broken it down had Matthew not blocked his path, holding him back, his fingers digging deeply into Jamie's shoulders.

"The doctor has given her plenty of laudanum." Matthew's voice was calm, but Jamie could see the strain on his face. "He must get the ball out. You know that."

Jamie closed his eyes, clenched his fists, his anguish at her suffering far greater than any physical pain. "It should be me in there."

Matthew muttered something about the kind of bastard who would shoot a woman, but Jamie didn't really hear him, his mind on Bríghid and what she must be enduring.

The surgeon, a short, squat man with deep bags under his eyes, had arrived and immediately demanded Jamie leave the room. "The ladies' help will be sufficient to hold her down."

At first, Jamie had refused.

But the doctor had been adamant. "I refuse to expose this young woman to your gaze. Unless you are her husband, Sir, I insist you leave at once!"

Propelled by Matthew's arm in the small of his back, and unwilling to waste time when Bríghid's life was at stake, Jamie had reluctantly complied.

Now he could do nothing but wait.

Bríghid cried out again, and Jamie cursed under his breath.

Though the authorities had written the whole thing off as a stray bullet from a hunter's gun, Jamie knew in his gut that was not the case.

Someone had fired at them deliberately. But firearms were inaccurate at long distances. Had the bullet been meant for Bríghid or for him?

Jamie was willing to bet Sheff knew the answer to that question. As soon as Bríghid recovered, Jamie would rip the truth from Sheff's throat. If Sheff were to blame for Bríghid's suffering, he would live only long enough to regret it.

The door to the bedroom opened, and the surgeon appeared, his face grave.

"How is she?" Jamie struggled to restrain himself.

"She is asleep and resting, but her condition is quite serious." The surgeon fussed at a bright red bloodstain on his linen shirtsleeve. "I managed to recover the ball. It broke one of her ribs, which I removed. Blessedly, it missed her organs. The wound itself is not so terrible, but she has a fever. I fear infection has already set in."

Jamie met Matthew's gaze, saw his own fears echoed in Matthew's eyes. Most men who died during wartime were killed not by balls of lead, but by infection.

"I've left plenty of laudanum, as well as a special draught for her fever. I've instructed Elizabeth to keep the wound clean and apply an antiseptic salve six times a day. There's little else I can do."

"Thank you, doctor." Matthew shook the surgeon's hand.

Jamie nodded his thanks, struggling not to take his anger and fear out on the physician.

"One other thing." The doctor paused. "She is Catholic, is she not?"

Jamie met his gaze without answering, suddenly wary.

"You might wish to send for the priest."

The words were like a boot to Jamie's stomach. "Are you saying you think she'll die?"

"I'm telling you her situation is serious. She might survive, but I've no way to be certain of that. If the infection spreads ... " The doctor shrugged his shoulders, then turned and started toward the stairway. "I really must be going. Lord Worsley's wife is in confinement with her fourteenth child, and the babe is unlikely to wait."

"Allow me to see you out." Matthew turned to follow the doctor.

Jamie took a deep breath, fought to steady his voice. "Matthew, can you please make arrangements for a carriage to pick up the priest? The chapel is in an alley off Michael Street."

Matthew glanced back, met his gaze, his blue eyes grim, nodded.

Jamie was unable to wait longer. He opened the door to Brighid's room, pushed past a wan Heddy, who was on her way out with an armful of bloody linens.

Brighid lay motionless, her face deathly pale. Her skin was covered by a sheen of cold sweat. Her hair was damp, and stray strands clung to her ashen cheeks. She looked small in the enormous bed, small and fragile.

Jamie didn't know when he'd ever felt so powerless. He had promised to keep her safe. He had failed utterly.

Just as he had failed Nicholas.

Elizabeth, also pale, sat next to her on the bed, placed a cool cloth on her forehead. "She has spirit, Jamie. We'll all do everything we can."

Jamie rested a hand on Elizabeth's shoulder. "Get some rest, Elizabeth. It's getting late. I'll stay with her."

"Are you certain?" Elizabeth looked up at him, lines of worry on her face.

"Aye."

Elizabeth rose, wiped her hands on her apron. "I'll send Heddy in to attend you. Send for me if you need anything."

Jamie nodded, sat next to Brighid on the bed. She stirred in her sleep, whimpered, whispered words he couldn't understand.

"I'm here, love." He took the cloth from her forehead, dipped it into a basin of cool water, rung it out, and pressed it against her scorching hot cheeks.

*F*ather Owen arrived just before midnight. His face set with the serenity of one who'd seen death many times, he stood over Brighid, anointed her fevered forehead with oil, and began to speak his Latin words while Jamie watched, feeling wretched, useless.

For the past few hours, Jamie had bathed her with cool cloths to calm her fever. He had stroked her cheek, held her hand, muttered reassurances when the fever gave her nightmares. When Elizabeth had returned to give her another draught of medicine and apply more salve, Jamie had seen how bad the wound truly was—an angry, red incision the length of his thumb carved into her soft, white skin and stitched with sinew.

"*In nomine Patris, et Filii, et Spiritus Sancti. Amen.*" The priest made the sign of the cross, turned to Jamie. "I think I'll be stayin' for a while, if you don't mind. In case she awakes and wishes to make a confession."

Jamie nodded. "Of course, Father."

"While I'm here, you might as well be tellin' me what's on your mind."

*F*ather Owen watched from his chair by the hearth as the Englishman stroked Bríghid's fevered cheek and bathed her forehead.

Jamie obviously loved her. But did he love her enough? That was the question that troubled Owen.

Outside the windows, the rosy fingers of dawn were just reaching across the eastern sky. The world, in all its wretchedness and wonder, would see another day.

"I never meant to bring her dishonor or harm."

"Of course not." Owen fingered the wooden beads of his Psalter absentmindedly. "We rarely mean to hurt those we love. And you do love her, don't you?"

Jamie closed his eyes, took a deep breath. "Aye, Father, with all my heart."

Owen decided to take the risk. "Do you love her enough to marry her?"

Jamie's eyes snapped open. His gaze—angry, fierce—met Owen's. "You know very well our laws forbid it, else I'd have taken her to wife weeks ago!"

Owen had heard this story before. He'd heard it last week from an English squire whose Irish mistress had died in childbed, the child with her. The man had been quite eager to rid himself of guilt, to blame her death on British law, on the Church, on God, on anything or anyone but himself.

Britain seemed to have plenty of Protestant men who loved Irish Catholic women and who'd gladly have married them—if only they could. And because they could not, they took the women they supposedly loved to bed, got them with child, set them up as mistresses, and eventually set them and their bastard children aside.

The tears of Irish women in London easily rivaled the Thames.

Owen prayed Jamie Blakewell would be different from so many of his countrymen.

"When I first spoke with you, you told me that when God brings a man and woman together, he helps them find a way." Jamie's deep voice was smooth, but Owen could feel the barely restrained fury beneath it. "I have yet to find it, Father."

Owen met the intensity of Jamie's gaze and nodded, glad Jamie had come to the point. "There is a way. But it would demand great sacrifice of you, perhaps greater sacrifice than you are willing to make."

"You bloody idiot!" Sheff struck Edward across the face. "You were supposed to shoot his horse, not the girl!"

Edward struggled to keep his footing, flinched as Sheff raised his fist again. "I'm s-sorry, my lord! I didn't mean to, my lord!"

Sheff grabbed him by the collar. "Do you know what you've done, you stupid bastard?"

Edward swallowed. "Shot a woman, m-my lord?"

"You've turned us both into targets, you fool!"

The color visibly drained from Edward's face.

"If she dies, there will be no place for you or me to hide." Sheff shoved Edward away.

He felt shaky, and his head ached. He walked unsteadily to the table and his glass of cognac. He needed something to fortify him, to help him think clearly, to dull the pain. He swallowed the amber liquid, filled the glass again. "The pistol has not yet been delivered, I hope."

"No, my lord, I've got it here." Edward patted his overcoat. "I'm waitin' till tomorrow like you told me."

Sheff sighed with relief. "I'm changing that part of the plan. Give the pistol to me. We'll need to hold onto it now."

He motioned to Edward to set the firearm on the table. As soon as Jamie saw the pistol, he would know Sheff was behind the shooting. And then?

If he harms her or any of her family, I'll hunt him with a knife in my teeth, and I won't fail.

A cold chill ran down Sheff's spine. Then a sneer spread across his face.

Jamie was so confident. Always so sure of himself. But he was nothing more than a commoner. Sheff was an English lord, descended from a long line of English lords. He would double the guard, curtail his social life, hire someone to watch Jamie's every move.

Aye, that's what he would do. Jamie would not be able to touch him.

He took another drink, felt it chase away the pain, felt his apprehension fade.

No, Jamie could not touch him. In the meantime, he needed to know whether the girl still lived. "Do you know what else you may have done, Edward?"

"N-no, my lord."

"You may have spoilt my prize. She was such a pretty little thing." Sheff turned, looked with disgust upon his hireling. "Get out of my sight!"

"Aye, my lord!" Edward fled.

Sheff grabbed the decanter, crossed the room, sank into his chair, his mind heavy with troubles. He needed another drink. He needed to rest. Then he'd be able to think this through, find a way to work Edward's bumbling to his advantage.

It had been a wonderful plan. Edward was supposed to kill the horse, then have the pistol delivered by some hapless messenger the next day. It would have been a glorious blow to Jamie's insufferable superiority about horseflesh to lose his stallion — and a rather shocking way of letting him know that Sheff had captured the young rapparee Jamie had set upon him. It would have been a fitting vengeance for Jamie's betrayal.

Sheff had recognized the pistol the moment it had arrived from Ireland. French flintlock. Matchless quality. If that had not been enough, Jamie's initials were engraved on the lockplate. Sheff had raged for an hour, unable to believe his friend would arm the bloody Irish against him, their noble lord. He wanted to believe the rapparee had stolen it. But the letter from Ireland had been clear. The rapparee had bragged to the little turncoat Alice, who'd been cleverly prying information from him, that Jamie had not only given him the weapon, but taught him to shoot it.

Sheff was tempted to turn the pistol over to the authorities and let them do whatever they desired with Jamie. It was treason to arm an Irish Catholic, treason to incite the Irish to fight. Jamie had done both — out of nothing more than desire for a woman.

But this was a personal matter. There was no reason to get authorities involved — not yet. Sheff would handle it in his own way.

Chapter Twenty-seven

*T*he next several days passed in a blur, Jamie dimly aware of the world beyond Bríghid's room. He allowed no one but himself, Elizabeth, Father Owen, and the surgeon to come near her, though he and the surgeon disagreed mightily over her care.

Drawing on what he'd seen Takotah do, Jamie insisted on giving Bríghid water to drink and sips of strengthening broth, while the surgeon feared it would raise her fever. Jamie had lowered her, naked, teeth chattering, into a bath of tepid water when fever made her delirious, while the surgeon would have left her in bed beneath the blankets. Jamie had begun to use garlic compresses as Bríghid had done with him, a treatment the surgeon called primitive, fit only for superstitious fishwives.

Jamie steadfastly refused to leave her side, not even when Elizabeth had raised her voice and accused him of punishing himself.

"It's not your fault, Jamie. You can't save her by killing yourself!"

He watched the sun rise and set at Bríghid's side and began to lose all sense of time. He took his meals there, though he found it all but impossible to eat. He slept in the chair beside her bed when he slept at all. God, how he loved her. He could not lose her.

That's how Bríghid found him when she awoke—asleep in the chair. His face was covered by several day's growth of beard, haggard from lack of sleep and worry, his mouth set in a grim line even in repose. His hair hung loose about his shoulders. He wore no shirt, no stockings, no shoes.

She struggled to remember what had happened. She'd been hurt. Someone had shot her while they'd been out for their ride. After that she could recall only images—Jamie's worried eyes gazing down at her,

Jamie urging her to drink, Jamie pouring cool water over her fevered body in the tub. Jamie telling her to fight, to stay with him.

Had he been at her side the entire time? And how long had it been?

She reached out to touch him, moaning at the sharp pain that shot through her side.

Jamie's head snapped up, and his eyes opened. "Bríghid, love, you're awake."

He moved to sit beside her on the bed, feeling her forehead for fever.

She tried to push down the blankets. "I'm so hot."

"The fever has finally broken." He closed his eyes, and a look of intense relief washed over his face.

In that instant, he looked so vulnerable and handsome Bríghid wanted to throw her arms around him and kiss him, but she could scarcely move.

He folded down the blankets, giving her relief from the heat. "Heddy, fetch Elizabeth."

"How long?" Bríghid found it hard to speak. Her throat was dry and bitter with the aftertaste of laudanum.

"Eight days, I think." He leaned down, kissed her forehead, his lips light and soft. "Are you in pain?"

"It's not bad." And it wasn't bad—if she held still and didn't breathe deeply.

"Are you thirsty?"

"Aye."

Jamie turned, and Bríghid could hear the sound of pouring water. Then he lifted her head, held a cup to her lips. "Drink, love."

She slaked her thirst, felt herself grow sleepy.

"Rest, love." Jamie's hand stroked her cheek. "I'll be right here."

*M*uirín looked down at Aidan's drowsy face where his head rested against her breast, stroked his red hair. The poor child was exhausted after days in a horse cart. She couldn't blame him. It had been a long trip.

"Are we there yet?" Aidan gazed down the rutted road.

Finn chuckled. "Aye, *a phráitín*, finally we're there."

Aidan sat up, suddenly alert, and looked about with renewed interest.

Muirín, too, was overcome with curiosity and gazed from one cabin to the next. This little village was to be her new home, and she felt more than a little nervous at the thought of meeting Finn's family. "Which one is it?"

Finn pointed. "The one with the rose bushes. There. See?"

A small whitewashed cabin sat at the end of a rutted lane, a row of dormant rose bushes tied neatly to trellises along its front. She smiled, some of her fear dissolving. People who cared so for flowers would care well for their own. "Aye."

In the nearby fields, beside haystacks and from darkened doorways, men, women and children looked up from their work, stared openly, curious about the newcomers.

Muirín found herself secretly grateful the strange Englishman, Travis, had turned back when they'd reached the parish marker, pleading the need to return to London. Arriving with a *Sasanach* in tow would certainly have raised questions and might have soured their welcome. As it was, Muirín wasn't certain how Finn's cousin would feel about the lot of them moving in. It wouldn't be for long—only until Finn could find a safe home nearby. If they were lucky, they'd be settled in time to plant spring crops and a little garden.

Finn steered the horses down a rutted lane toward his cousin's cabin.

"Finn? Finn Uí Maelsechnaill?" A tall, dark-haired man stepped out of a nearby cowshed. Not quite as tall as Finn, he reminded Muirín instantly of Bríghid with his dark good looks. "I'll be buggered!"

Finn reined the team to a halt, gazed grimly down at the man. "You'll be watchin' your tongue 'round my wife."

My wife.

Muirín felt a little rush of joy every time he spoke those words.

The two men stared at one another, their faces grave.

Finn smiled first. "It's good to see you Seanán."

Finn hopped to the ground, and the two men embraced, laughing, hitting, and insulting one another—showing affection in the strange way men do.

"I'd recognize your ugly mug anywhere." Seanán slapped Finn hard on the back, winked up at Muirín. "How did a sod like you end up with a wife, let alone one so pretty?"

She felt herself blush to the roots of her hair.

"'Twas my charm and wit that won her over." Finn gave Seanán a light punch to the arm. "Two qualities you lack, cousin."

"By the saints, it's good to see you again, Finn!" Seanán turned his head toward the cabin, shouted. "Ma, Finn's here, all the way from Meath!"

Muirín saw an older woman—sister to Finn's mother—emerge from the cabin. The family resemblance was strong.

"Well, bless me! Son of my dear sister—may she rest in peace—come all this way?" The woman's gaze fell on Muirín and Aidan, and she gasped. "And with a wife and child!"

Finn turned, lifted Muirín to the ground. "Aunt Bébhinn, Seanán, this is Muirín, my bride."

Muirín curtsied, unsure how to greet them. "'Tis right pleased to meet you I am."

Seanán smiled, took her hand, kissed it. "Welcome to the family, such as it is."

"Such a sweet girl!" Aunt Bébhinn reached out, embraced Muirín. "Welcome, love."

Finn turned, lifted Aidan to the ground. "And this is Aidan. We took him in some years ago."

"Welcome, Aidan." Aunt Bébhinn smiled warmly.

"And a strapping lad he is!" Seanán gave Aidan a light jab to the shoulder.

"He's one of us now." Finn ruffled the boy's hair, and Muirín saw the shine of pride on Aidan's face. The boy cherished Finn.

A girl a few years younger than Aidan poked her head shyly out of the cowshed.

"Who's this charmin' creature?" Finn nodded to the girl, who smiled, a finger in her mouth.

"This is my daughter, Éanna." Seanán reached back, drew the little girl protectively to his side. "It's her mother, my sweet Íonait, you see lookin' out at you from the door. Come, sweetheart, greet my cousin."

Íonait emerged from the cabin, smiled shyly, one hand resting protectively over her swollen belly. "Welcome."

Muirín felt an unexpected shard of pain at the sight of the other woman's rounded body. She thought of the child she'd left behind in the cold ground in Meath, felt an ache in her chest. Finn's hand came to rest reassuringly on her waist. She tried to ignore her sadness, willing herself to smile. "Lovely to meet you, Íonait."

Finn's smiled. "I see you've done well for yourself, Seanán."

"I'd say we both have." Seanán gave Finn another robust slap on the back, chuckled. "What brings you all the way to Clare?"

Finn looked up, puzzled. "Did Ruaidhrí not explain?"

"Ruaidhrí?"

Muirín felt her heart stop, felt a jolt of surprise pass through Finn.

"Don't tell me he isn't here."

Seanán met Finn's gaze, his expression earnest. "I'm sorry, Finn. I haven't seen Ruaidhrí since the summer you all came to visit with your da'."

Finn looked down at her, and she saw deep worry in his eyes. His gaze shifted back to his cousin. "I've come under dire circumstances to ask for shelter for myself and my family. I'll explain everything. But first I need to know where I can find a priest."

*J*amie stood in the shadows against the back wall of Commons, listened. He'd had a few hours sleep before Pitt's missive arrived, informing him that the bill regarding the Colonies would be debated on third and final reading this afternoon. As loathe as Jamie was to leave the house while Bríghid was still so weak, he'd known he had no choice.

He had a mission to complete.

So far, the debate had gone well. Pitt could think on his feet faster than most men and often rendered his opponents speechless with frustration as they struggled to match his wit. Had the stakes not been so high, Jamie would have found it entertaining.

"Is the Honorable Gentleman the only Member unaware—yes, certainly he must be—that the French have seized a British fort and slain British soldiers and colonial troops? Do both deeds not constitute acts of war against the Crown?" Pitts voice filled the chamber.

Several Whigs chortled at his comment, as the MP from Huntingdon turned slowly red in the face. Like a fish, he opened and closed his mouth, but nothing came out.

"Or perhaps the Honorable Gentleman thinks it appropriate to allow the enemy to chip away at lands that belong to our Sovereign. It's certainly a unique approach to maintaining an empire."

More laughter.

On the other side of the room, an older man stood, motioned for quiet.

"My Honorable Friend is right. An act of war has been committed against Britain by the French. Subjects of His Majesty have been killed, shot down by the French and burnt alive by their Indian allies. This demands a response, but what kind of response? My Honorable Friend suggests we heed the advice of the colonists and commission a fleet of specially built ships—an expensive endeavor—and send these ships to the other side of the world. Yet, the last time I looked at a map, France was only a short distance away across the Channel. Would it not be more prudent to take our grievances directly to the French and fight this battle on French soil?"

Cheers arose from the other side of the room.

Pitt stood in silence, his face grave. Jamie realized he was waiting for the cheering to exhaust itself, using silence as a means to enhance the drama of the moment, the power of his next words. Only when the chamber was completely silent did he speak again.

"I wonder, my Honorable Friends, how the Honorable Gentleman from Pembrokeshire would feel should some foreign foe fall upon his family and slay them in the act of seizing his estate. Would he not turn to this body and ask for aid? Would he not expect the Crown to send troops to free his estate and defeat this foe? Would he be content if the Crown instead sent troops into the enemy's country, leaving those who had killed his family free to occupy his estate?"

No one spoke. No one stirred.

"No, I suspect the Honorable Gentleman would demand action from Parliament. I further suspect Parliament would grant him a military response. Do the British whose families have been slaughtered on the frontier merit any less consideration?"

The room erupted into shouting.

Pitt stepped back from the platform, let the tempest run its course, casting Jamie a covert glance. Jamie nodded, particularly pleased with Pitt's last point.

Then one voice rose above the others—the MP from Pembrokeshire. "Is the Honorable Gentleman suggesting that these rustics are sustaining losses comparable to those of a landed gentleman? Most of these colonists are illiterate, descended from convicts, religious fanatics, and malcontents who left England by choice or by force. Many likely own little more than a chamber pot. Should we launch a full-scale war, complete with a specially built navy, to defend malcontents and their chamber pots? Or are we wiser to save coin and fight the French in France?"

Shouts of agreement, calls of outrage echoed through the room.

Jamie felt his temper surge.

Pitt's voice boomed out over the chaos. "Indeed, a chamber pot is a humble object, not of great value—until one finds oneself in need. I suspect that if we tried to relieve the Honorable Gentleman of his many fine chamber pots, we'd be met with fierce resistance."

The room erupted in laughter and applause.

Pitt continued. "The French and their Indian allies don't ask these men, women, and children how much they own, whether they can read, or why they left England before they kill them. They simply see British subjects and slay them. Where shall the dead find justice if not from the Crown, to which they offer fealty?"

The debate raged for another two hours, but Pitt held the mastery throughout. In the end, the bill was approved with minor amendments, but it was only the first stage.

"It must still pass through Lords." Pitt limped out the doors and toward his waiting carriage, the strain on his face betraying the pain in his feet. "I'll do what I can, of course, but my influence is limited there. They could force amendments or bog the bill down in procedure."

"Byerly's foes have promised me they'll press the matter, but whether they'll succeed remains to be seen." Jamie walked beside Pitt, the skin pricking on the back of his neck.

Someone was following them. He stayed just out of sight, hid in the shadows. But Jamie knew he was there. He could hear the man's shuffling gait, his clumsy attempts at silence.

"One can never be sure in politics." Pitt smiled ruefully.

"I know I speak on behalf of the Virginia House of Burgesses when I offer you my sincere thanks for all you've accomplished thus far."

A footman opened the carriage door, helped Pitt up the single step, closed the door behind him.

Pitt smiled. "You might well prevail."

"Thank you. I intend to, Sir."

The carriage surged forward and was gone.

Jamie walked quickly to his own carriage. He had an appointment— and a promise—to keep.

The man in the shadows followed.

*F*inn and Muirín were married late that day in Seanán's cabin with friends and family to witness their vows. Once the priest had bestowed his blessing, Seanán slaughtered one of last spring's calves. Aunt Bébhinn roasted part of it, set the rest to cure. With oatcakes, butter, potatoes boiled with onion, and more than a little *poitín*, it made for a true feast.

Though Muirín's heart had soared as the priest spoke the words that bound her and Finn together, she could not shake the sense of foreboding that had come over her the moment they'd heard Ruaidhrí was missing. Though she'd told herself Ruaidhrí had as likely gotten lost as fallen into trouble, her heart knew better. Something was wrong.

And tomorrow morning Finn would leave her, head back into danger.

She'd lost one husband. She'd lost her son. She could not lose Finn.

*"T*he mistress says you're to stay in bed!"

"I am sick and tired of bed, Heddy, dear." Bríghid placed her feet on the soft carpet, grasped the bedpost, grimacing at the pain in her side. "It will do me some good to stretch my legs and walk a bit. Besides, I'm only goin' down to the library."

Feeling more than a little unsteady, she stood, one hand still on the bedpost.

"You'll faint or catch your death, Miss Bríghid."

"I'll do no such thing." She spoke as much to assure herself as Heddy. Light-headed, weak, she found herself wondering if she could actually make it all the way to the library.

Heddy's hands were twisted in her apron, her eyes wide with concern. "If you tell me what you want, I can fetch the book for you."

"That's sweet of you, Heddy, but I can do this." Bríghid released the bedpost, took one step, another. She wasn't used to having people do things for her and felt silly asking Heddy to do her such a favor. "See, I'm fine."

"They'll have my hide if you fall, Miss."

"I won't fall."

It seemed a long journey to the door, a longer one to the top of the stairs. But soon she was taking the stairs one at a time, both hands gripping the banister, Heddy following nervously beside her.

The maid gave an audible sigh of relief when they reached the bottom of the stairway.

Bríghid found herself wondering if perhaps Heddy wasn't right. She couldn't imagine climbing up those stairs again. It would be hard enough walking the remaining distance to the library. One step at a time, she made her way down the hallway.

The sound of male voices stopped her. They were coming from Matthew's study.

" ... cannot be done ... there is no way ... will be ruined!"

She didn't recognize that voice.

"Must be some alternative..."

That was Matthew.

"Keep her quietly as your mistress ... or set her aside..."

Bríghid felt as if someone had knocked the air from her lungs. They were talking about her—about how to dispose of her.

"... will do whatever I must ..." That was Jamie's voice.

Bríghid could bear to hear no more and walked as quickly as she could on trembling legs to the library, Heddy following behind her. She sank into the nearest chair, heedless of the tears on her cheeks, the pain in her side no match for the ache in her heart.

Keep her quietly as your mistress, or set her aside.

"Oh, Miss Bríghid, now don't you cry!" Heddy wiped the tears from Bríghid's face with her apron. "I ain't seen a man care more for a woman than Master Jamie cares for you. Why, he didn't eat or sleep the whole time you were fighting the fever. He didn't leave your side and wouldn't let anyone else come near you."

Bríghid tried to smile, fought back her tears. "'Tis sweet of you to say so, Heddy."

"My mum says there ain't no shame in a woman being a man's mistress, if she truly loves him." Heddy knelt before her, stroked her hair. "Sometimes it's the only way a poor woman can make her way in this world, and God bless her for it. Or so my mum says."

"Is that what I am, Heddy—his mistress?" Bríghid met Heddy's gaze and read in her blue eyes the unwelcome answer.

But I love him! What else could I have done?

The words exploded in her mind, forced a fresh wave of tears.

"Oh, Miss Bríghid." Heddy wrapped her thin arms around Bríghid, stroking her hair as she wept.

"I must leave here, Heddy. I must get home."

"What are you doing out of bed?"

Bríghid and Heddy gasped in unison, looked to see Jamie standing at the library door, his expression furious.

Jamie saw the tears on her face, the genuine grief in her eyes, felt his gut wrench. He'd overheard her last few words. She wanted to go home. She didn't want to stay with him.

The pain in his chest made him speak harshly. "Heddy, the next time Bríghid attempts something this idiotic you are to get me or your mistress immediately. Is that understood?"

"Aye, Sir."

"You may go."

"Aye, Sir." Heddy curtsied and hurried out the door and down the hall.

"Don't be blamin' her." Bríghid lifted her chin, met his gaze. "She tried to stop me. I was just after fetchin' a book."

Jamie walked to where Bríghid sat, fought the impulse to wipe the tears from her cheek. "Do you realize how foolish you've been? You might have fallen and broken your neck! I'd have gotten the book for you had you but waited."

Sparks danced in her eyes. "I'm not after people waitin' on me hand and foot."

"You'll not get out of bed again until the surgeon says you may. Is that understood?"

She nodded, a stubborn jerk of the chin.

"Which book did you want?"

"The one about Irish history."

Jamie strode to the shelves, glanced over the titles on the bindings, grabbed the desired tome, fought to hide the warring emotions within him. "This one?"

She wants to go home.

"Aye."

He crossed the distance between them, handed her the book. When his gaze again met hers, his anger became concern. Her face was ashen, almost ethereal in its beauty. Her dark hair spilled over one shoulder, a tousled mass. She clutched the arm of the chair as if to keep herself from toppling to the floor.

"You belong in bed." He bent down, gathered the sweet weight of her in his arms, careful not to hurt her.

She gasped in surprised. "It's a long way, Jamie. Are you sure—"

"I could easily carry two of you."

Jamie felt her relax. She rested her head against his shoulder, her slender arms wrapped around his neck. By the time he reached her bedroom, she was all but asleep. He lay her gently on the bed, tucked the blankets under her chin.

She opened her eyes, reached for him. "Stay with me, Jamie. Sleep beside me."

He shook his head. "I don't want to hurt you."

"You won't." Her fingers closed over his. "'I sleep better when you're with me."

And because there was nothing on earth he would rather do than hold her, he removed his waistcoat and slid into bed beside her. "Sleep, love. I'm right here." He kissed her forehead, tried to ignore the pain in his heart.

She wants to go home.

She snuggled against him and almost immediately fell fast asleep, leaving Jamie to wrestle with his demons.

*J*amie kissed Bríghid on the cheek, arose, careful not to wake her. The household was quiet, the clock having long since struck eleven.

It was time for him to act.

He left her room, hurried down the hallway to his chamber. There, he stripped to his breeches, walked over to the hearth, and grabbed handfuls of cold, dark ash. He mixed the ash with water, rubbed the paste over his bare skin, careful to cover every exposed inch. He smeared it through is blonde hair, darkening it to the color of shadows. Then he slipped his knife into the waistband of his breeches.

Without a sound, he moved down the stairs and out into the night.

Chapter Twenty-eight

*J*amie ran through the night, staying off the road, keeping to shadows. While he would have welcomed Hermes' speed, the horse could too easily give him away. This task demanded he go alone—and on foot.

He'd quickly found a comfortable pace, one that allowed him to move swiftly, yet silently. He hadn't used his woodland skills since the night he'd tried to free Nicholas—tried and failed. Still, the challenge was invigorating. His senses heightened by the darkness, he heard the yipping of a solitary fox, the baying of distant hounds, the squeak of rodents in the underbrush. Carriages and riders passed on the road a stone's throw from him, but no one saw or heard him.

The man assigned to trail him certainly hadn't heard him. Jamie had found him lurking in the trees across from the estate's main gate, had walked up behind him and knocked him out with one blow to the back of his neck. The man had never glimpsed his face. Jamie had tied him up in the stables, instructing a startled stable boy to guard him until morning, when Matthew would turn him over to the sheriff. Then Jamie had set out.

The bracing winter air rushed over Jamie's bare skin, felt refreshing as his body began to sweat. He worked his way around the outskirts of the city, heading for Sheff's estate in the country north of London. Clouds drifted across the sky, intermittently covering the pale half moon. But Jamie could find his way without moonlight and, if necessary, without stars. The forest was a good guide—if one knew how to read the signs.

After what must have been about two hours, he neared the gate to Sheff's estate. Concealed among the trees, he consciously slowed his breathing, watched, listened.

Two men guarded the gate, both visibly armed.

"She's got tits like melons and a quim so tight—"

"Shut your bloody mouth! She'd never let the likes of you twang her."

"Twang her I did, and she was happy for it. You should have heard her wail."

They'd be easy enough to take. Jamie could backtrack, cross the road out of sight, come up behind them. But what lay beyond them? Surely, there were more guards.

Jamie backed deeper into the strip of forest, sought one of the higher trees. Carefully, quietly, he climbed until he could see over the estate's wall. There he waited and watched for movement. Slowly, one by one, the men Sheff had set to guard him revealed themselves.

There were the two by the gate. Two patrolled the road that led from the gate to the manor. Two more stood guard at the manor's main entrance. This meant there were probably two more near the back and service entrances. The red glow of a lit pipe and the faint scent of tobacco smoke gave away the man posted by the side gate.

Jamie considered his options and had just begun to climb down, when a movement in the trees on the other side of the road caught his eye. He froze.

"Would you two pipe down?" A man emerged from the forest, holding a flintlock. "I ain't had a woman in weeks, and you're turnin' me bloody rod to bone."

Jamie grinned. Sheff had put a guard on his guards, someone to ambush him when he tried to overcome the watch at the gate.

Silently, he climbed down from the tree and backtracked up the road.

The man in the trees was the first to fall. Jamie approached from behind, dropped him with a blow to the back of the neck, catching him as he sagged, unconscious, to the ground. Just to be safe, Jamie dumped the man's powder onto the moist earth, scattered his shot in the underbrush.

The men at the gate were still discussing who'd tupped whom when Jamie crept up behind them. He fell the first with a quick blow to the head.

The second man saw his friend fall, and his eyes grew round with fear as Jamie emerged from the shadows. Speechless with terror, the man had just enough time to take in Jamie's appearance before he was rendered unconscious by a punch to the jaw.

Jamie dragged both men into the underbrush, considered his next move. The gate was likely locked and would no doubt creak when opened. It was clear Sheff had expected him to try to enter there. The side gate was likely Jamie's best option. Movement there was less likely to attract attention, as it was undoubtedly how the guards themselves entered and left the grounds.

Keeping to the shadows, alert for surprises, he moved along the wall toward the side gate. When he drew near—he could smell the sharp scent of the guard's tobacco smoke—he climbed to the top of the wall. Below him, a lone guard tapped his pipe out onto the ground.

Jamie leapt silently to the grass, struck the man at the base of his skull, and dragged him behind nearby bushes. And for a time, Jamie stayed hidden, contemplating his next move. With the deep shadows cast by the trees, he was certain he could reach the house without being seen. Once there, he'd move round to the back, disable any guards, and enter through the servants' entrance. But he hated to leave armed men at his back. They could too easily be trouble when it came time to make his escape.

In the end, he decided that the risk of taking on men in the open— the two pairs of guards were within sight of one another—was not worth it. Quickly, silently, he moved toward the manor.

S heff lifted his wife's nightgown, exposing her bare bottom. He stroked her rounded buttocks, grasped her hips, then thrust inside her, groaning at the tight feel of her. Giving birth to his son hadn't ruined her at all.

She didn't protest. She never did. But neither did she enjoy it, as some of the servant women did. She simply did her duty, then went to her own chamber to sleep. But she was a lady, of noble birth, not a slut like the others. And so he tupped her rarely, hoped to keep the sickness to himself. The others wanted—and therefore deserved—what he gave them.

He focused on the feeling of being inside her, the hot, slick, tight feel of her. It was good, so good, as he reached his climax and poured himself into her. For a moment, he stayed inside her, savoring the pleasure. Then he withdrew, wiped himself on her gown, and slapped her bottom lightly. "You may go."

Without a word, she crawled out of bed and left the room.

Sheff flung himself back against his pillows, then reached for the half-empty glass of cognac sitting on his bedside table. Some nights, if he mixed enough drink with sex, the pain wasn't so bad. He drained the glass, blew out the candles, and lay down to sleep.

He'd just drifted off when something heavy slammed into him.

Befuddled by sleep, he opened his eyes and found himself staring into a dark face and eyes so angry they seemed to burn.

Jamie!

The cold blade of a knife pressed against his throat.

Panic made Sheff's heart pound, his mouth go dry. The wet warmth of his own urine spread across his thighs.

"It seems you've been expecting me."

Sheff grabbed Jamie's hand, tried to move it, but to no avail.

Jamie kept the knife pressed against Sheff's throat, his voice a feral growl. "I'm going to ask you one question, and I want an answer. If you shout for help, it will be the last sound you make. Is that clear?"

Sheff nodded.

"Who shot her?"

Sheff's thoughts scattered like a flock of frightened birds. This wasn't the Jamie he knew. This man was fearless, brutal, all but naked, his skin painted like that of a heathen. He was savage, a killer. "I-I d-don't know what you're talking about!"

"You forget how well I know you." Jamie's relentless gaze bored into Sheff, his eyes as hard and cold as ice. "You are lying!"

Sheff swallowed convulsively, felt his bowels turn to liquid.

"For the sake of the friendship we once had, I'll give you once last chance."

Sheff tried to steady his voice, failed miserably, cast about for another lie. "Her brother!"

"Her brother?"

"H-he was trying to shoot you!"

"Me?" Jamie laughed, a cruel sound, his white teeth a sharp contrast to the dark of his skin. "Her brothers left Meath a month ago!"

"The rapparee came for her. Then he came for me. Aye, and we had to post guards."

Jamie bent down so that his face was inches from Sheff's. "You lie!"

And Sheff knew. Jamie was going to kill him.

"Bríghid and her family are under my protection. I warned you to stay away from them, but you didn't listen. And now I'm faced with the awkward decision of killing the man I once called friend in his bed, or letting him live, knowing he might again pose a threat."

Then Sheff remembered. The pistol. Jamie's pistol. "I have proof!"

"Proof?"

"Aye, proof! Look! On the table!"

Sheff watched the mistrust in Jamie's eyes, felt the pressure of the blade lift.

"Don't move. Don't make a sound." Jamie stepped off the bed, crossed to the table.

Sheff watched Jamie's face as he picked up his own pistol, turned it over in his hand.

Surprise. Alarm. Rage.

Jamie turned to face Sheff. "How did you get this?"

"I told you! H-her brother! He came for her, then he came for me!" Sheff could see his words were starting to breed doubt in Jamie's mind.

"I don't believe you. Where is the boy? What have you done to him?"

"He's a guest at my hunting lodge, and I've done nothing to him— yet!" Then Sheff had an inspiration. "If you kill me, her brother dies!"

"Don't try to threaten me!"

"My men have their orders."

Jamie stared at the pistol in his hands, scarcely able to believe what he saw. Finn had likely gone on to Clare, thinking Ruaidhrí was ahead of him. But Ruaidhrí must have taken the pistol and, instead of leaving for Clare, he'd gone after ... whom? Was it possible he'd tried to shoot Jamie but had shot Bríghid instead?

No. Sheff was lying about that part of it. Ruaidhrí knew he couldn't hit a target. Why would he take aim with his sister in the line of fire? The boy loved Bríghid.

Yet in Jamie's hands was the pistol. He'd left it in Ireland with Finn. Somehow Ruaidhrí had gotten hold of it, and he'd gone after Sheff, only to be captured. It was the only explanation that made sense.

Jamie saw fear, mingled with triumph, in Sheff's eyes. He slipped the pistol into his breeches. "How do I know you haven't killed him already?"

"I give you my—"

"Your word? And what good is the word of a man who makes promises to his tenants, then breaks them? A man who kidnaps and rapes innocents? A man who murders priests he had agreed to show mercy? Your word is worthless to me!" Jamie's blood was thick with fury.

Sheff had broken into a cold sweat, and the stench in the room told Jamie that Sheff had wet and fouled himself. "It s-seems you have no choice but to believe me."

Jamie knew Sheff was right. If Sheff had Ruaidhrí—and Ruaidhrí was still alive—Sheff still had the power to hurt Bríghid.

Bríghid!

How was Jamie going to tell her about this? It was bad enough that Sheff had her brother, but to tell her Ruaidhrí might have been the one who'd shot her? Jamie couldn't tell her that, especially not while she was still so weak.

With Ruaidhrí captive, the game had changed.

Jamie played his last card. "Know this—it goes both ways. You live as long as he lives. Harm him, and you will pay the price!"

"Then it seems we are at an impasse, you and I."

"For the moment." Jamie could feel Sheff's confidence growing now that the shock had worn off and he knew Jamie wasn't going to kill him. He considered his options. The room was two stories off the ground. If Sheff called for help, Jamie would be lucky to make it out of the house alive. "This is your last warning, Sheff. Harm Bríghid or her brothers, and there won't be enough hired thugs in all of England to keep you safe from me."

With that, Jamie slammed a fist into Sheff's jaw and watched as Sheff fell back, unconscious, onto his pillows.

Then Jamie threw the window open, stuck his legs through and made a leap for the ground.

*T*he heavy wooden door creaked open, letting in a shaft of candlelight, then quickly closed again.

Alice appeared at the top of the stairs, carrying a candle and a basket of food. She'd brought him dinner hours ago. He hadn't expected to see her again until morning.

She'd been his only comfort these past weeks. She'd stitched the gash in his head, brought his meals, shared what little news of the outside world she knew. She had kept him company as often as her *Sasanach* captors had allowed. She'd even brought salve for his wrists and ankles where the irons had chaffed his skin raw.

Ruaidhrí had only ever seen her in candlelight, but that was enough for him to know she was pretty—curly red hair, pale skin, soft dark eyes. It was surely her beauty that had made her a servant of the *iarla*. Though he knew little about her, Ruaidhrí assumed she'd suffered the same fate the *iarla* had intended for Bríghid.

He had not asked her about it. He didn't know how to ask her. And so he treated her as he hoped other Irishmen might have treated his sister had she suffered Alice's plight.

When he escaped, he would take her with him. It wouldn't be easy. The door was always barred from the outside, and at least one man kept watch on it at all hours. There was no other way out, no windows, no loose bricks, no cracks in the wall.

Perhaps she would help him.

"I've brought you some leftovers." She always spoke *Gaeilge* to him with her soft Dublin accent.

"*Go raibh maith agat, Alice.*" He rose to greet her, chains clinking. *Thank you.*

She set the basket of food on the floor beside his feet. "How are you feeling?"

"Happy to see you again."

She frowned as if annoyed, but Ruaidhrí wasn't fooled. He could see in her eyes that his words pleased her. It was the same look she got every time he used his charm on her.

"I thought you might still be hungry, so I snuck some scraps from the kitchens."

"You shouldn't take risks like that. What if someone catches you?"

She smiled. "They won't. I brought the guard a basket of his own."

"You're a clever girl, Alice." He decided to ask her at least one of the questions that had been troubling him. "Why do you let them call you that?"

"Call me what?"

"'Alice.' It's a *Sasanach* name."

She shrugged, looked away from him. "It makes no difference to me."

"But Ailís is so much prettier, gentler on the ear."

At the sound of her real name, her head jerked up, and she met his gaze. Her eyes glittered with temper. "It doesn't matter."

"Don't go gettin' your back up." He fought the urge to touch a hand to her cheek. "It's the name your parents gave you, a good Irish name. You should be proud of it. From now on, I shall call you Ailís."

"Hush, silly boy, and let me check your forehead. I cannot stay long." She took a step toward him, accidentally stepped on his foot, lost her balance.

He reach out to catch her, instinctively pulled her against him, one hand around her waist, the other on the candle.

The contact jarred his senses, made it hard to breath. He was so shocked by the sensation of her body pressed to his that it took him a moment to realize what the nearness had revealed. Then he knew.

"Oh, no, Ailís!"

Her eyes grew wide with dismay, and she pulled away from him, took one step backwards.

Ruaidhrí let his gaze drop to her belly and saw what he had not noticed before.

She was with child.

A torrent of emotion surged through him—disbelief, anger, revulsion.

Then he thought of Bríghid. What if the *iarla* had raped her that night and planted a baby inside her? Would he and Finn have hated her? Would they have been ashamed of her and sent her away?

No. They'd have protected her, and Ruaidhrí would have pummeled any man who dared look down his nose at her.

Ailís saw the disgust on his face. She wanted to be angry with him. But all she could feel was shame, guilt.

For three weeks, the rapparee had been nothing but sweet to her. He'd told her she was pretty. He'd treated her with respect and kindness. He'd thanked her for each seeming comfort she'd brought him—a blanket, salve for his wounds, news from the world beyond.

And she had betrayed him.

She had allowed him to think she, too, was a prisoner, here against her will. She'd done it partly to win his trust and partly because she liked the way he made her feel—as if she were something precious that needed to be protected.

No man had ever treated her that way.

But it was all a lie. She had come to the *iarla's* household on her own after her mother's death. She'd wanted a roof over her head and food in her belly. She'd found both here. And if she'd found it sensible to let the *iarla* use her body in exchange for a better life, that was her affair. She would apologize to no one, least of all a gullible boy who didn't have enough sense to keep himself out of trouble.

She looked into Ruaidhrí's eyes, eyes that had gone soft with pity, and she wanted to yell at him, berate him, hate him. Every kindness he showed her was an unwelcome, grating reminder of the innocence she'd never had.

But she couldn't hate him.

"I'm sorry." He reached out to cup her cheek. "Don't be worryin' that I think less of you. He forced you, didn't he?"

She felt the sweet burn of his touch on her skin, met his question with silence. Let him believe what he wished.

"He tried the same with my sister, God curse him."

"I know." Ailís didn't bother to tell him just what she thought of his sister. Bríghid Ní Maelsechnaill had thought herself too good to be touched by an English lord. She had hit Ailís, cursed her.

"When I get out of here, I'm takin' you with me. I won't be leavin' you behind."

Guilt gnawed at her, sharp teeth against her heart. He was a sweet boy, truly he was. There was something innocent about him, something pure. But he wasn't getting out. When the *iarla* returned, he would be hanged.

If he knew the truth, he would hate her. His eyes, which gazed at her with such compassion, would fill with loathing, and he would know her for what she was.

A part of her wanted to tell him the truth, to see his innocence shredded, to rip away the false image he had of her, force him to see her as she was. But she was too cowardly and selfish for that. He would go to the gallows never knowing the role she'd played in his fate for one simple reason: When she was with him, she felt clean again.

"Well, you're not goin' anywhere tonight." She forced herself to meet his gaze, smiled. "Sit and eat. And let me check your forehead."

Chapter Twenty-nine

"*My* noble and learned Lords, we cannot allow French encroachment on His Majesty's lands to go unchecked. On that much we are agreed." Lord Middleton's deep voice filled the chamber. "The question is not whether we ought to respond, but how we ought to respond. Surely, two regiments of trained British regulars ought to be enough to reclaim the lost fort and cut off the French from the British frontier."

Middleton's words were met with shouts of agreement.

From where he stood in the back corner, Jamie could see the smirk on Sheff's face. Sheff had certainly done his best to derail any chance of the bill's passing. Debate had raged for a week, and the bill had come close to being sent off to some accursed committee, where it surely would have languished.

Sheff and his collaborators had then begun to propose a host of amendments designed to weaken the original bill. One regiment, no ships. Two regiments, no ships.

They might have succeeded had Lord Shelburne, Alec's good friend, not risen from the bench to take up the fight. Though he lacked Pitt's singular wit, he was a valuable ally, a man greatly respected by his fellow Lords.

Lord Shelburne stood. "My Lords, may I express my gratitude for your Lordships' unwavering interest to this issue. For five long days, we have debated. 'Tis seldom one sees such attention paid to a single bill, particularly when the issue demands not debate, but immediate action, as my noble and learned friend, Lord Middleton, has said. If I can have your Lordships' attention for but a short while longer, perhaps this issue can be settled."

Shelburne then described in grisly detail the massacre of a frontier family at the hands of the French and their allies, the burning of British farms and outposts, Nicholas's horrendous death at the hands of the Wyandot.

"Would you, as peers of His Majesty, show less concern for the outrageous and barbaric acts of cruelty committed by our enemies than the honorable gentlemen in Commons?" Shelburne paused, surveyed the chamber, his gaze solemn. "No, my noble Lords, we must act decisively. I move that we recess for an hour and return prepared to vote on the matter."

Shelburne's motion carried.

Jamie threaded his way through the crowd, as bewigged lords began to make their way out the door. He hoped to speak briefly with Shelburne before the vote.

He felt someone slam into his left shoulder, turned to look.

Sheff.

"The game is not over, old friend." His jaw wore a fresh bruise, and his face was a mask of hatred, but Jamie could see the fear beneath.

"No, it's not." Jamie met Sheff's gaze. "Until then, sleep well, *old friend.*"

Sheff turned abruptly and hastened out the door, but not so quickly that Jamie missed the red stain of humiliation on Sheff's face.

*B*ríghid lifted her night shift over her head, dropped it on a nearby chair, and examined her naked reflection in the mirror. Some of the color had returned to her cheeks, though she was still pale. She looked a bit thinner perhaps than the last time she'd seen herself in the glass. The biggest change was the angry red scar on her right side. And the look of deep melancholy in her eyes.

She turned to the tub of steaming water behind her, climbed in. The heat felt delicious against her skin, and, for a moment, she closed her eyes, forgot her troubles, and let herself savor the feeling. Then she took up her bar of lavender soap and began to bathe, her thoughts adrift.

The week was passing so slowly. Jamie had insisted she stay in bed and had enlisted the help of everyone in the household to make certain she did, as he was in London most of the time attending sessions of Parliament. So she'd slept, done needlework with Elizabeth, read countless books, taught Heddy a few letters, grown restless and cross.

She'd been on the brink of losing her temper, when Elizabeth had told her something that made her see things differently.

"He feels responsible for what happened to you, Bríghid. He feels he should have done a better job keeping you safe, just as he feels he should have been able to protect his nephew, Nicholas."

Then Elizabeth had told her about the Indian attack and how Nicholas had been taken captive and burnt alive despite Jamie's efforts to save him. Jamie had blamed himself.

"Let him fret over you for a while. It will make him feel better, and all women deserve to be coddled now and again."

Bríghid hadn't known, hadn't thought about it that way. She'd been aware something was troubling him. She could see it in his eyes, which were never free of shadows now. She could feel it when he touched her, the thrum of tension just beneath his skin. She could sense it in her sleep, when he lay awake through the night beside her, restless.

When she'd asked him what was wrong, he'd told her things weren't going smoothly in the House of Lords. She had believed him, offered him reassurances. But now she knew there was more to it than politics and Parliament.

Bríghid had thanked Elizabeth for her wisdom and good advice.

Elizabeth had smiled. "Once you come to understand men, dear, it's much easier to endure their company."

Then yesterday the surgeon, who said her temper and restlessness were a good sign, had finally pronounced her well enough to get out of bed for short periods of time. Jamie had relented and let her join Matthew and Elizabeth for dinner last night. He'd even allowed her to attend the conversation in the library afterwards. Then he'd scooped her up and carried her back up to her bed. And Elizabeth was right—it was satisfying to be coddled sometimes.

Bríghid rinsed the soap from her body, dunked her head under the water, and began to wash her hair.

How she longed to pour out her heart to Father Owen, to share the pain she tried so desperately to keep secret. Her fairytale was about to come to an end, and she didn't know how she was going to bear saying farewell to the man she loved.

Any day now, Finn would reach Clare and send for her. Then Jamie would put her on his ship and send her back over the Irish Sea to her brothers. Even if he came with her all the long way to Clare, they'd have little more than a month together at most. And then he would bid her farewell.

She remembered the globe in the library, how tiny Ireland was compared to the rest of the world, how far away the shores of Virginia had seemed. Farewell would mean forever. Jamie would go about his life, she about hers. She would never hear of him or see him again. She would never know what became of him. Just like her father, Jamie would be lost to her, swallowed by the sea, by distance, by time.

And so she would take whatever time she had left with him, sin or no sin. She would cherish each moment and hope they were enough to last a lifetime. For no matter how long she waited nor how wide she searched, she would never love a man as she loved Jamie Blakewell.

Tears traced silent paths down her cheeks as she worked the lavender-scented soap through the length of her hair.

She had one other thing on her mind. It probably meant nothing. Still, she couldn't help but wonder. Her monthly flux was late. It wasn't the first time she'd been late, for certain. The spring she'd come down with scarlet fever and she'd been so sick Finn had almost cut off her hair, she'd been late by a week. Two years ago, when crops had failed and food had been scarce, her flux had stopped altogether. Surely this time it was nothing more than the result of having been shot and running a high fever.

She couldn't be carrying Jamie's child—not so soon. Could she?

Her life would be so much more difficult if she were with child. Finn and Ruaidhrí wouldn't send her away, but neither would they take the news well. She'd be scorned by her neighbors, doubly so because the baby's father was a *Sasanach*. She might never find a man willing to take her to wife. People would tittle and call the child names.

Aye, it would make her life—and the child's—more difficult. But a child might also make her life bearable, for she'd have something of Jamie to love.

She dunked her head under the surface to rinse her hair, felt the warm water wash her tears away. Then she leaned back against the side of the tub, let the water soothe her.

*J*amie unbuttoned his greatcoat, tossed it on a nearby chair, checked the sideboard in the foyer for messages. The silver tray held a single letter.

He recognized the handwriting at once, snatched up the letter, broke the seal. A faint smile played on his lips as he read.

It was good news. Cassie had given birth to a baby girl the week before Christmas. Alec wrote that the birth had been mercifully quick, and that mother and child were well. They had named their new daughter Emma Rose.

"She is the very image of her mother, which means, I fear, there will be no end to the trouble she'll cause us when she's older," Alec wrote.

Jamie chuckled to himself as he read, his spirits lifting.

"Emma's birth has helped to ease Cassie's grief over the loss of our dear Nicholas. Your sister is smiling again, and for that, I am most grateful."

And in a breath, Jamie's spirits sank again.

He finished the letter, tucked it in the pocket of his waistcoat.

Rather than seeking out Matthew to discuss the day's affairs, Jamie walked toward the stairs, guided by impulse. He needed to see Bríghid, to see her, to hold her.

It had been a long day. Shelburne had managed to force a vote, but not before Lord Middleton had amended the bill to remove any mention of a fleet of ships. The bill had passed almost unanimously, and immediately the wheels were set in motion. Two regiments—1,400 British regulars—would be on their way to the Colonies by week's end.

"It won't be enough," Jamie had told Lord Shelburne afterwards. "With their allies, the French can muster equal that amount overnight. And if our regulars don't learn to fight as the Indians fight, I fear we are in for a slaughter."

"Don't lose hope." Lord Shelburne had lowered his voice, leaned closer. "A number of us are introducing a new bill next week. Tell Alec he will get his ships. I'll see to it personally."

Jamie supposed it was a victory. British regulars were on their way. Pitt and Shelburne would continue to fight for ships. Still, there was no time to celebrate.

If Sheff weren't lying—and Jamie believed him capable of anything—he still held Ruaidhrí captive in Ireland. Because the boy had tried to attack an English lord with a pistol—Jamie's pistol—he faced a death sentence should Sheff turn him over to the courts.

Jamie couldn't let that happen. Bríghid had warned that the pistol could bring them trouble. She'd been right.

Jamie's plan was simple. His business with Parliament now behind him, he would put the word out that he was returning to Virginia. In a few days time, he would board *The Three Sisters*—named in honor of Alec's and Cassie's daughters prior to little Emma's arrival—and sail down the Thames to await favorable winds at Dover.

As soon as the ship reached the Channel, however, he would round the coastline and make straight for the port at Drogheda. From there, he'd travel over land as quickly as possible until he reached Baronstown. Then, under cover of night, he'd make his way to Sheff's hunting lodge, free Ruaidhrí and head back with him to the ship—that is if Jamie could refrain from killing Ruaidhrí himself.

If Jamie found out Ruaidhrí had, indeed, been behind the bullet that almost killed Brighid, the boy was in trouble.

Of course, the plan had flaws.

What if Ruaidhrí had been moved? There was every possibility Sheff had already turned him over to the authorities.

What would he do with Ruaidhrí afterward? The boy couldn't stay with Matthew and Elizabeth. He was now considered a criminal, his crime a capital offense. Harboring him was itself a crime. Yet, Jamie thought it unlikely that Ruaidhrí would willingly leave Ireland for Virginia.

And what if Jamie were caught? He'd likely be hanged alongside Ruaidhrí. For that reason, Jamie had already made certain changes to his will.

He wished Travis were on hand, as a second set of eyes, ears, and weapons would be helpful. But Jamie didn't expect him back for another two weeks, and he couldn't wait.

He hadn't told Brighid Sheff had her brother. He didn't want to upset her. Nor did he want to make her an accomplice by telling her what he planned to do—or inspire her to try some scheme of her own. The less she knew, the safer she was.

He reached the top of the stairs, made straight for Brighid's closed door. He opened it as quietly as he could, expecting to find her asleep. He heard her gasp, caught a glimpse of rosy flesh as she sank deeper into her bath, her eyes wide with surprise. All the strain and pressure he'd been feeling dissipated. "This is the second time I've interrupted your bath."

Had she been crying?

She sat up, smiled, and leaned back lazily against the tub, until her breasts rose just above the water's surface. "You're just in time to wash my back, *Sasanach*."

"Is that so?" Jamie felt a stirring in his blood, tried to ignore it. She had just recovered from being shot. She ought not to squander her strength on love play.

He doffed his waistcoat, removed his shirt so as not to get it wet, and strode over to the tub. He felt the heat of her gaze as she looked up at him. An answering heat flared in his veins. He knelt beside the tub, reached for her little bar of lavender soap. The scent was irresistibly feminine.

She leaned forward, exposed the delicate curves of her back. "How did the vote go?"

Jamie dipped his hands into the warm water to wet them, lifted the heavy mass of her wet hair aside, rubbed the soap on her soft skin. "The bill passed but we didn't get everything we wanted—not yet."

"Will you be tryin' again?"

Her skin felt like silk beneath his hands, and Jamie found it increasingly difficult to think. "I've played my part. Pitt and Lord Shelburne will handle matters from here on. They might have had an easier time of it had I not been involved at all."

"Because of me."

"No, Bríghid. Because of Byerly." Jamie rinsed the soap away, then leaned down to place a kiss on the wet curve of her shoulder.

Her head tilted to the side, baring the curve of her neck. "Is it soon you'll be leavin'?"

Jamie painted a line of kisses from her shoulder to the spot just beneath her ear, felt her shiver. Was that sadness he heard beneath the feigned indifference in her voice? "I still have some business to complete. I don't imagine I shall be ready to sail for home for perhaps another month. Are you that eager to get rid of me?"

He'd said the words in jest, but the moment he'd heard them, he realized he wanted an answer, needed an answer. In the weeks since they'd become lovers, she had never once told him how she felt about him. He knew she trusted him. He knew she enjoyed spending time with him—riding, playing billiards, discussing history. He knew, too, she enjoyed making love with him. She responded to his touch as if she'd been made just for him, her hunger a perfect match for his. In truth, he'd never met a more passionate woman.

But, as he well knew, passion was not love.

At first, he thought she wasn't going to answer him. Then he felt her body shudder, a quick, ragged intake of breath.

She was crying.

"Bríghid?"

She turned her face toward him, met his gaze. Tears rolled silently down her cheeks. "You silly *Sasanach*. I'm not after gettin' rid of you at all!"

It wasn't a declaration of love, but Jamie's would take it. She was upset at the thought of him leaving—surely a good thing. But if events unfolded as he planned, there would be no reason for tears.

He brushed a strand of wet hair from her cheek, and, without thinking, kissed her tears away. He meant only to comfort her, but at first contact, desire slammed into him, hard and hot. He felt the heat, knew she felt it, too.

"Jamie?"

"Aye, my sweet?"

"Love me."

"I don't want to hurt you."

"You won't."

Bríghid watched as he stood and stripped off his waistcoat, shirt and breeches, and dropped them casually on the floor. She ran her gaze over the lines of his naked body, tried to memorize each ridge, each hollow, the tawny glow of his skin, the power of his erection.

One month. One precious month. She would not waste time on crying, not when the man she loved was right beside her. She would savor every moment, every touch. She would force tomorrow's woes to wait until this day was done.

Jamie stepped into her bath, lowered himself until he sat in front of her, then pulled her gently into his lap. His voice was deep, husky. "Wrap your legs around me."

She did as he asked, felt his arms enfold her and closed her eyes.

"Let me taste you." His mouth found the sensitive skin beneath her ear and nibbled until she shivered with pleasure. Then his lips brushed teasingly over hers, his touch soft and furtive. His full kiss, when it finally came, was hot, deep, slow.

She felt her hunger for him rise, ran her hand over his wet, naked skin, desperate for the hard feel of the man she loved. Then his hands moved to cup her breasts, and she forgot everything but the heat of his touch. "Aye, Jamie. Love me."

Jamie watched the arousal on her face, ignoring his own burning need, her pleasure fueling his own. He wanted to wash her tears away, to bring her pleasure. He caressed her breasts, teasing their tight rosy crests until she whimpered her frustration. And then, when her whimpers became throaty moans, he bent forward, took a taut bud into his mouth, and suckled her.

He felt her fingers clench in his hair, felt her hips shift in the water, a sensual undulation that bespoke her sexual need. She was ripe. She was ready for him.

"Oh, Jamie, I want you now!" She pressed her sex against his.

He groaned, lifted her until his cock was poised at her entrance, their moans mingling as, wet and hot, she slid smoothly down the length of his cock. She felt so good, so tight. She was the only woman he wanted, the only woman he would ever want. She was his beginning, his end. She was the woman he loved. "*Brighid.*"

Brighid clung to him as he rocked his hips, thrusting into her, filling her with each slow stroke. Their bodies, wet and warm, were pressed so closely together that she could scarce tell where she ended and Jamie began. She could feel his heartbeat against her breasts, feel him move deep within her, feel his lips on her skin. It felt so, so good.

"Jamie! Jamie! Jamie!" His name became a sacred litany as bliss claimed her and sent her soaring, her muscles clenching around him in ecstatic rhythm.

One, two, three times he brought her to her peak. Then, as her body quivered with pleasure, he groaned, thrust hard again and again and again, pouring his essence into her.

For a long time afterward, they held each other in silence, Brighid's head against his shoulder, his hands stroking her wet hair. And she found herself wishing she knew some magic, some ancient incantation that could keep them in this moment forever. Sweet Mary, how she loved him! "Jamie?"

"Aye, love?"

She hesitated, but only for a moment. "These weeks with you have been the happiest of my life. No matter what else comes, I want you to know that."

For a moment, he said nothing. Then his lips pressed a kiss against her damp hair. "'Tis the same for me."

S heff hated Jamie Blakewell. As fond of Jamie as he'd once been, that was how much he hated Jamie now. The bastard had managed to find powerful allies in Lords. Lord Shelburne, the pompous ass, had kept Jamie's bill alive, even if he hadn't been able to fend off the last minute amendment by Middleton. The self-satisfied look on Jamie's face had been enough to make Sheff want to knock Jamie's teeth down his accursed throat.

Sleep well, he'd said. The rotten bastard!

Well, Sheff would sleep well soon enough, Jamie's Irish bitch beside him. His new man was keeping a close eye on Jamie, watching his every move. It wouldn't be long now before they'd be able to spring their trap. Then Jamie would see exactly who had the power—and the woman.

Chapter Thirty

*J*amie watched Bríghid, charmed, as she gazed in amazement out the carriage window and spoke happily about the wonders she saw. It was the first time she'd seen London in daylight. For her sake, he'd bid the driver travel by a route that took them over London Bridge and past Tower Hill before looping back over the bridge and heading into the heart of the city.

Along the way, Jamie shared what history he could remember. "Then the assassins entered the tower at night and killed both Prince Edward and his little brother, Richard, Duke of York, in their beds."

"'Tis a fitting name—Bloody Tower." She shook her head sadly. "Those poor boys!"

Jamie found himself wishing he could pull her into his arms, lift her skirts and create some history of their own in the moving carriage. Though they'd made love this morning before rising, he wanted her again. He tried to shift the direction of his thoughts. "Have you no such stories in Irish history?"

"Oh, aye, we do. King Bodbh's daughter turned her own dear sister's children into swans to be rid of them."

Jamie chuckled, amused by her sincerity, her innocence. "I don't think England boasts any *recorded* history quite like that."

All too soon, the carriage rounded the corner into the alleyway and stopped.

Jamie alighted, glanced about to make sure the area safe. Then he lifted Bríghid to the ground, careful not to put pressure on her right side. "Here you are—as promised."

"Thank you, Jamie." She smiled, smoothed her skirts.

Beneath her cloak, she wore a gown of midnight blue silk, one Jamie'd had made to complement her eyes. It was one of the few that she felt was modest enough to wear to church—the gown's only flaw, as far as he could see.

He put his arm through hers, escorted her over the cobblestones down the narrow passage that led to the chapel, his senses attuned to anything unusual. He had to admit he had misgivings about this. He would much rather she remain safely at home and let Father Owen come to her. Jamie had spent a lot of time with the priest lately and had no doubt the good Father would be happy to make the trip himself. Jamie's generous contribution to the church aside, Father Owen seemed to care deeply about Bríghid, as he did all his parishioners, who were scattered around London like lost sheep.

But a promise was a promise, even when exacted by a beautiful temptress who'd just left him senseless and drained from lovemaking.

Bríghid had said she wanted to go to confession and take Communion in a church with the other parishioners. When she'd explained she'd only been inside a chapel once and very much wanted to see it again, Jamie had understood and had quit trying to persuade her to do otherwise.

He open the door for her and followed her inside.

She dipped her finger in the font of Holy Water, crossed herself, then curtsied in the direction of the altar. She turned to him, took his hand, gave it a squeeze. "I'll try not to take too long."

Jamie tried to look serious. "After what we did the other night and this morning—I'm guessing this could take all afternoon."

"Jamie!" Bríghid's tone of voice told him such things ought not to be mentioned in church. But there was laughter in her eyes and a rosy glow on her cheeks. She turned in a swish of silk, walked toward the back rooms where Father Owen waited to hear her confession.

Jamie sat in the back pew, gave his mind over to other thoughts.

He'd had *The Three Sisters* made ready to sail at a moment's notice with provisions enough to last the voyage to Virginia. He'd gone so far as to have most of his belongings packed and stowed away on board. He suspected they'd have to leave quickly once he'd freed Ruaidhrí and wouldn't have time to prepare the ship then. He'd made final changes to his will and dispatched a letter to Alec and Cassie detailing all that had happened since his arrival in late October.

He was ready to leave for Ireland, but for one thing.

Before he left, he intended to marry Brfghid. He had found a way. It meant risking everything. But he had found a way.

Jamie wanted to give her the protection of his name should anything happen to him in Ireland. For all he knew, she might already carry his child. If he should fail to return, or if he should find himself hanging at the end of a rope, he wanted to know she was safe and well provided for. He would not forsake her.

Most of the arrangements for the wedding were made. Jamie'd had a special gown sewn for her as a gift. He'd bought several of the finest bottles of wine in London. He'd bought her a wedding ring—a sapphire set in gold to match her eyes. He'd even given Cook a list of special items he wanted her to purchase for the dinner afterwards. As secrecy was needed, it would have to be a small affair, with Elizabeth and Matthew and perhaps their son and daughters in attendance.

All Jamie needed to do was ask the bride.

In his more rational moments, Jamie wondered how he could face a dozen Wyandot warriors without fear but couldn't find the courage to ask a petite woman one question.

"Brfghid, will you marry me?"

It wasn't that hard. Five words. One sentence. Surely he had face more formidable challenges in his life.

Jamie couldn't think of one.

He should ask her tonight. Aye, tonight. He would ask her tonight.

He surfaced from his thoughts, glanced around him.

What was taking so long? Parishioners would begin arriving for Mass at any moment.

Jamie stood, paced the back of the tiny chapel, restless.

Still, Brfghid did not come out.

As time wore on, his restlessness was replaced by a growing sense of unease. He tried to shake it, told himself he was being foolish. Brfghid was alone with a priest. They were in a chapel in the heart of London. No one had entered since they'd arrived.

Then a terrible possibility occurred to him.

His heart gave a violent lurch, one hard hammer stroke of dread.

"Brfghid!" He turned and ran down the aisle.

He'd gone but a few strides when men in the uniform of the London constabulary flowed out of the back room.

He halted in his tracks, fists clenched. "Where is she? And where is Father Owen?"

One of the constable's men—Jamie counted five—moved toward Jamie, shackles in his hand. "Are you goin' to come wi' us easy like, or am I goin' to have to break your head?"

Then the constable's men parted, made way for someone else.

Sheff.

"You'd do well to cooperate." Sheff smiled, motioned the man with the shackles forward. "It will get you the least number of broken bones by day's end."

The front door of the chapel was kicked open, and several more uniformed men stormed inside. Behind them came clamor of an approaching mob, shouting their hate for Catholics.

Jamie was trapped.

Raged flowed through his veins like molten iron. He met Sheff's gaze. "What's all this, old friend? You couldn't face me yourself? You had to bribe—"

The heavy iron shackles swung through the air into his Jamie's gut, knocked the breath from his lungs.

The man who wielded the shackles kicked him for good measure. "Hold your tongue, you! Here lads—have a go."

The other men rushed forward with cudgels, rained crushing blow after blow on Jamie's skull and back, drove him to his knees.

A boot rammed into his stomach. "Traitor!"

"That's enough!" Sheff's voice pierced the pain in Jamie's head. "Lock him up."

He saw blood on the floor, his blood. The room spun. He felt cold iron close around his left wrist, then his right, felt the bite of fetters round his ankles.

"Get up, bugger!"

Rough hands dragged him to his feet, held him fast.

Jamie struggled to lift his head, white-hot pain pulsing behind his skull. He found Sheff, looked him in the eye, the flow of blood warm on his cheek. "Touch her, and you're a dead man!"

"You do like to make threats, don't you, Jamie?" Sheff turned to one of the men, took the man's cudgel. "But you hear this—I *will* touch her. I will take her before your very eyes, and you will be helpless to stop me!"

With that, Sheff swung and hit Jamie on the temple.

The last sounds Jamie heard as blackness drew him down was that of the angry crowd and breaking glass.

*B*ríghid's stomach rolled and pitched along with the ship. Nauseated, she huddled, terrified, in the dark, damp corner of the little room they'd locked her in. She was belowdecks, somewhere in the hold. It reeked of rotting seaweed, excrement, filth.

Worse, there were rats. She could hear them scurrying about in the inky darkness. She could hear their squeaks, the gnawing of their sharp teeth. A few times, they had gotten close enough she could see the outline of their bodies. She'd kicked at them as best she could, sent at least one flying.

Her side ached. Her wrists were bound with rope that pinched and burned her skin. They'd given her no blanket, no straw for a bed. Just damp wood and rats.

She breathed deeply, tried to quell her intense nausea. She hadn't suffered from seasickness on the way to England. But then she hadn't been locked in a putrid stinking hole either. Jamie had given her a berth with a bed and a window and ...

Oh, Jamie!

She prayed, not for the first time, that he was safe.

She'd walked into the chapel's backroom, sat in the confessional. "Forgive me, Father, for I have sinned."

But it wasn't Father Owen's voice that had answered.

"I bet you have, poppet."

Her heart had all but stopped and her mouth had gone dry. She knew that voice.

Then the *iarla*'s man had reached in, crammed a cloth inside her mouth so she could not scream, then dragged her roughly out of the confessional and to her feet.

"Gentle, Edward, gentle. I won't have you hurting her." The *iarla* ran a finger down her cheek. "You've led me on quite the merry chase, little one. But it's over now. Oh, don't look so sad. You're going home."

In no time, she'd found herself bound, gagged, and dragged out the back door and over to the *iarla*'s waiting carriage.

"I regret I can't join you just yet, love." The *iarla* lifted her into the carriage. "I have unfinished business with your erstwhile lover. But don't worry. Edward will keep an eye on you in the meantime."

Edward climbed in, sat across from her, his eyes filled with undisguised lust.

The *iarla* started to close the door, stopped. "A word of warning, Edward. If you hurt my prize, if you spoil her, it will cost you dearly."

They'd taken her straight to the *iarla*'s waiting ship and had set sail.

In the utter dark, Bríghid had lost all sense of time. Between the rats and the nausea, she couldn't have slept had she wanted to. Fears darted through her mind, one after another.

What had the *iarla* meant by unfinished business? What if the *iarla* had hurt Jamie? Sweet Mary, what if the *iarla* had killed him?

She'd seen the men with cudgels standing in the alley. They wore some kind of livery. Were they there to arrest Jamie, to punish him for being caught in a Catholic chapel?

And what had become of Father Owen? She remembered what the *iarla* had done to Father Padraíg.

She felt the reassuring weight of the cross against her throat, sent another silent prayer skyward, asked God and all His saints to watch over both Jamie and the good Father.

Jamie would come for her. She knew he would come for her—if he could.

And if not?

A tremor of fear and revulsion passed through her. Tears of helplessness pricked her eyes, ran silently down her cheeks.

She knew what the *iarla* wanted. His prize, he had called her.

His prize.

And then it dawned on her. The *iarla* had not taken her simply to ease his lust, but to hurt and humiliate Jamie. She was a pawn in a game of power.

But then others had always had more power over her life than she. Her parents, God bless them. Her brothers. Even Jamie. They had always had more to say about the way her days unfolded than she.

No, not always.

Hadn't she defied everyone when she'd gone to Jamie's room and given herself to him?

Aye, she had.

She'd grown tired of having her fate determined for her. And so she had defied the Church. She had defied the laws of Britain. She had defied the wishes of her brothers. She had given herself to Jamie without reservation and without regrets. And in his arms, she'd found a greater happiness than any she'd known.

It had been her choice.

But what choice did she have now? She was bound, locked belowdecks. The door, even if she could find it in the dark, was guarded by a man who terrified her, who would hurt her if he could. She had no weapon, no way to defend herself.

There were no choices. She was alone and helpless.

A surge of fury rushed through her.

The last time the *iarla* had kidnapped her, she'd hadn't struggled because she'd thought she was protecting her brothers. But things were different this time. Her brothers were safe in Clare with Muirín and Aidan.

More than that, *she* was different.

This time she would not accept whatever fate the *iarla* handed to her. She would fight him. She would fight him with every ounce of her strength. She would fight with teeth and nails and feet and fists. She would fight him with anything she could find.

And if he beat her until she lay bruised and bleeding?

She would take satisfaction from knowing he was bleeding, too.

The dark shape of a rat approached her, sniffed her skirts. She kicked at it, felt the toe of her shoe connect, heard its outraged squeak as it hurtled through the darkness.

Aye, she would fight.

*T*he clang of iron bars in the distance jarred Jamie into consciousness.

He heard someone groan, recognized his own voice.

Pain split his skull, made it almost impossible to think. He tasted blood, his own blood, felt it thick on the side of his face. Iron bit viciously into his wrists, made his fingers tingle. His shoulders ached, as if his arms were being pulled from their sockets.

Through a fog of pain, he realized he wasn't lying down. He felt cold stone against his back, a floor beneath his feet. And then he knew.

He was chained to a stone wall. His arms, stretched out on either side of him, supported his dead weight.

Thoughts and images drifted through his mind. Bríghid looking out the carriage windows. Bríghid in the chapel crossing herself. Men from the London constabulary.

Sheff.

Alarm shot through him, forced his eyes open.

Sheff had Bríghid. He had taken her from the confessional. He had taken her and set men from the constabulary on Jamie.

Bríghid!

Jamie put his weight on his feet, nearly groaned aloud as his shoulders, suddenly relieved of their burden, shrieked in protest. His entire body ached—his head, his arms and shoulders, his ribs. He savored the pain, used it to bring himself to full awareness.

He looked around, realized he was in some kind of cell. He'd been stripped to his breeches, his chest and feet bare. Straw was scattered on the floor. A crudely hewn table sat in the middle of the tiny room. A window high on the wall let in a weak stream of light. A door of thick iron bars opened to a dark hallway beyond. The stench of human waste, damp stone, and despair permeated the air.

He was in a gaol.

The full reality of the situation hit him. He was in chains, behind bars, a prisoner. And Sheff had Bríghid.

How long had Jamie been here? How long had Bríghid been at Sheff's mercy?

Long enough.

Jamie forced his numb fingers open, closed them around the chains that held him, tested the strength of his bonds. Even when he used his full strength, he could not make them budge. He had no hope of pulling the chains from the walls. Even if he could free himself, there was still the iron door and the guards beyond. The window would be of little use, as it, too was barred. His only hope was to bide his time, wait for a chance to escape. But that might takes days, weeks, even months. He could only imagine what horrors Bríghid would endure in that time.

Damnation! Bloody hell!

Anger at his own helplessness surged white-hot through him. Anguish. Regret.

He should have followed his gut instinct and kept Bríghid at home, asked Father Owen to come to the house. He should have gone to the back of the chapel to make certain it was safe. He'd known there was another entrance. He'd seen the back door during his visits with Father Owen. He should have realized Sheff might have hired another man to follow him and might have known he visited the chapel regularly.

If he had done but one of these things, Bríghid might well be safe at home right now.

But he hadn't. He had failed her, as he had failed Nicholas.

Be strong, Bríghid. I will come for you.

He heard voices, the sound of a key in heavy lock, the squeak of iron hinges, the flicker of light.

"He's just down 'ere, my lord. Are you sure you want to take 'im, my lord? We know how to deal with traitors, my lord."

"I'm sure you do." It was Sheff's voice. "But, as I've already explained to your superior, this is a personal matter."

"As you wish, my lord. Thy will be done, as I always say."

So Sheff had gotten him arrested to subdue him and had now come to take him … Where?

Then Jamie remembered what Sheff had said in the chapel.

I will take her before your very eyes, and you will be helpless to stop me!

Jamie had a feeling that wherever Sheff was taking him, he would find Bríghid. An idea half-formed in his mind, he forced himself to go limp, ignored the screaming agony in his shoulders.

S heff held the handkerchief to his nose, waited for the turnkey, a small man with an equally small allotment of intelligence, to unlock the door. "Hurry up, man!"

Sheff couldn't abide the stench of this place. He'd have been wiser to have the constable's men carry Jamie directly to the hold of his ship, but the constable might have found that odd. Instead, he'd paid good coin to have them subdue Jamie and bring him here, thinking it might teach Jamie a lesson.

Sheff had already planned what he would say. "See what I can do to you? See where I can put you?"

But now he felt Newgate might be too vile a place, even for the likes of Jamie.

The bolt clicked into place.

The turnkey opened the door, held up the lamp. "There 'e is, my lord. I'll stay 'ere in case you need 'elp."

Sheff ducked through the low doorway, glanced around the pitiful cell. There, against the wall, was Jamie. He was still unconscious, his chin against his chest, his body covered in bruises and welts. Blood covered one side of his face. Both of his eyes were swollen.

A feeling akin to regret welled up inside him, but Sheff battered it down. Jamie had brought this on himself. Hadn't Jamie broken into his manor in the middle of the night and threatened his life? Jamie hadn't shown regret. He hadn't acted sorry when Sheff had seen him days later in the House of Lords.

Sheff wouldn't be sorry, either.

"He's still unconscious." Sheff turned to face the gaoler. "Can you wake him?"

"Aye, my lord." The gaoler strode forward and slapped Jamie's face.

"Stop, I say!"

"You wanted me to wake 'im, me lord."

"Yes, wake him, but not by injuring him further!"

Then Sheff saw Jamie begin to stir. Jamie moaned, tried to lift his head.

"Wake up, you!" The gaoler shouted in Jamie's face. "'is Lordship wants a word with you!"

Jamie slowly opened his eyes, let his gaze fall first on the gaoler, then on Sheff.

Sheff pushed the gaoler out of the way, stepped forward. "Jamie, can you hear me?"

Jamie brought his gaze into focus, stared into the eyes of the man who used to be his friend. How long ago that seemed. "Where ... ?"

"You're in Newgate."

Jamie did his best to look confused—unfortunately, not a difficult task. "New ... gate?"

"Aye, the gaol. In London. Don't you remember?"

Jamie said nothing, let his eyes close, his head drop.

"Oh, bloody hell!" Sheff lifted Jamie's chin with a gloved hand. "The constable's men seemed to have done their job too well. At least I know you're not invincible, old friend. My men will take him to my ship now."

"Aye, my lord."

Jamie heard the shuffle of more feet, felt the gaoler begin to unlock his wrists and ankles. When the shackles gave way, he willed himself to stay limp and let himself fall forward, certain he would hit stone.

Rough hands broke his fall, seized him, and he soon found himself being carried between two men like a corpse.

Stay strong, Bríghid. I am coming for you.

*R*uaidhrí heard the key in the lock, sat up.

Light appeared at the top of the stairs. Ailís.

"It's my angel come with manna from heaven."

She handed him the basked. "Hush! You know very well 'tis but bread and water."

Though he was used to her chiding, it was somehow different this time. She seemed troubled. Ruaidhrí took the basket, careful not to tip it, and sat it in his lap. He pulled back the napkin, uncovered a chunk of stale bread and a cup of water. "Sure and it's a feast."

She said nothing.

"How are you and the babe farin', Ailís? Do they feed you well, now you're with child?" Ruaidhrí took a bite, chewed, grateful for anything to fill his rumbling belly.

"I eat fair enough, better than I did at home."

Then he said what he'd wanted to say for days. "Come away with me, Ailís. When I get out of here, come with me."

She shook her head. "Nonsense. Why would I take up with a boy who's always gettin' himself in trouble?"

"I can give you a home."

"I have a home."

"When I get out, I'll take you to my cousin's home in—"

"You're not gettin' out of here, Ruaidhrí! Don't you understand? When the *iarla* gets back, you're going to be hanged!" Her voice took on notes of despair.

Ruaidhrí set the basket aside, stood, lifted a hand to her cheek. He expected to see tears on her face, but instead he found the lines of anger.

"I'm goin' to do all I can to free myself when the time is right. Come with me, Ailís. I promise I'll take care of you."

"You can't even take care of yourself!" She spat the words at him, stepped back from him. "It's not the way you think. I wasn't brought here against my will like your sainted sister. I came of my own choosin'. I wanted a better life, and the *iarla* gave it to me. And when he wanted me in his bed, I went freely."

Stunned, Ruaidhrí, gaped at her.

She laughed, a cruel, high-pitched sound. "Aye, and all that I've done to make your life easier I've done for a reason. Did you ever wonder why I was so interested in the *Sasanach* who had helped your sister? Ever wonder why I asked so many questions? No? Silly boy! I passed every word you spoke on to the *iarla*'s men."

For a moment, Ruaidhrí could do nothing but stare at her. Then, his thoughts began to come together again, and he tried to sift through his memory, recall everything he'd told her. They had nothing on him, no information that could harm him. Nothing but—

The pistol!

She knew who the pistol belonged to, who had taught him to shoot, what he'd planned to do with it.

"Aye, Ruaidhrí, when they hang you, it will be my doing." She was smiling, but tears poured down her face.

His mind buzzed with fury, and a shard of pain pierced his chest.

She had betrayed him. She had given herself to the *iarla Sasanach*, had done so of her own will. And she had helped the *iarla* dig Ruaidhrí's grave.

Ruaidhrí reached out, grabbed a fistful of her hair, forced her head back until she had no choice but to meet his gaze. "Get out of here, *Alice*, before I end your worthless life and that of your bastard child!"

He released her with a little shove.

She turned and fled, forgetting the basket and her candle.

Chapter Thirty-one

*B*ríghid didn't know when she'd ever been this tired. The two-day journey in the ship's hold had seemed an eternity. Seasick and afraid, she'd slept little if at all. Now her eyes felt heavy, lulled by the rocking motion of the carriage, and her mind ached for lack of sleep. Still she fought to stay awake. She dared not sleep.

Across from her sat the man from her nightmares. Edward—that's what the *iarla* had called him. So far the brute hadn't touched her, his restraint no doubt the result of the *iarla*'s promise of punishment. But she could see the lust in his eyes—lust tinged with malice. He'd slept for part of the journey from Dublin, his deep snores giving Bríghid some respite from her fear. But after they'd passed through Baronstown, he'd awoken, and he now sat in silence, watching her like a predator, his face hidden in shadow.

But worse than anything—worse than fear or nausea or exhaustion—was the anguish of not knowing what had become of Jamie. Did he yet live? Was he hurt? Was he held captive in some reeking gaol? Was he on his way to free her? Did he even know where they had taken her? And then it struck her.

Sweet Mary, what if she never saw him again?

The thought nearly forced a sob from her throat.

Let him be alive and safe!

Unwilling to show any part of herself to the monster who sat across from her, she fought back her tears and looked out the window. Clouds blocked the late afternoon sun. The familiar Irish countryside rolled by, starkly beautiful in its winter sleep. More than once today, she'd felt the impulse to force open the door and leap to the ground, but that was no more than a fantasy born of desperation. She'd only succeed in hurting herself. Her wrists were still bound, giving her no way to brace her fall.

How she wished she were going home—home to Finn, to Ruaidhrí, to little Aidan, to her father.

"Is that my Bríghid come ridin' in so fine a carriage?"

"Da'!" Bríghid giggled, felt her father's strong hands lift her out of the horse cart and safely to the ground. She threw her arms around his waist, hugged him tight. Her throat grew tight, and tears pricked her eyes as she clung to him. It had been so long since she'd seen him, so long. They had taken him away, but he was here. He was with her now.

"Aisling ghael." He stroked her hair. "It's grateful to you I am for bringin' her home safe, Mac Tréinfhir."

"She's been a great help to us, with my wife bein' so sick and all. 'Tis I who am grateful to you, Uí Maelsechnaill. I must say I wouldn't mind seein' her as wife to my Torcán one day."

Bríghid came awake with a gasp, heard Edward's hissing laughter.

"Wake up, poppet. We're home."

She fought to clear her mind, her throat tight with unshed tears— tears from a dream.

Da'.

She looked out the window of the carriage at the *iarla*'s hulking manor, ugly and grey against the grey Irish sky.

The carriage stopped, and the door was opened from outside.

Edward lifted his bulk from the seat, climbed out, then turned back for her.

Bríghid met his gaze. "Don't touch me! I don't need your help."

Edward scowled, but he stepped back.

Unable to lift her skirts, she clasped the doorsill with both hands, felt carefully for the steps with her feet, then stepped to the cobblestones.

They crossed the courtyard, Bríghid aware that people were staring at her. Edward led her inside and up the stairs. But instead of taking her to the small servant's room on the third floor, he led her to a familiar room on the floor below.

The room that had been Jamie's.

A lump formed in Bríghid's throat.

Jamie, please be safe!

Edward motioned for her to hold out her hands. With a small knife, he cut the ropes that bound her. Then he opened the door to the room. "Get in. They'll be bringin' in bath water soon. You'd be smart to do as you're told."

The door locked behind her.

The room was as she remembered it, except for the copper tub that sat in the middle of the floor, waiting for water. Then she saw the gown lying draped over a nearby chair. It was the same one she'd been forced to wear that night.

A shudder ran through Bríghid, and she understood.

The *iarla* wanted it to be just like it had been that night.

But this wasn't going to be like last time. Things weren't going to go the way the *iarla* planned. She was no longer the helpless peasant girl he'd frightened half to death a few months ago. Last time, he'd used Ruaidhrí to force her into submission, but Ruaidhrí was safe. This time she would resist the *iarla*. She would fight.

And if she failed?

Bríghid felt nausea and fear well up inside her, reaching not for the cross at her throat, but for the dragon brooch.

He might violate her body, but he could not change who she was. There was nothing the *iarla* could steal from her this time—not her virginity, nor her dignity, nor the love she felt for Jamie and her brothers.

If she failed tonight, she would still find a way. She would survive.

S heff was grateful when his manor came into view. He'd had as much of the confounded carriage as he could stand for one day. What he needed was a brandy. The bottles he'd brought with him for the journey were empty, and he'd had precious little to drink all day.

He stepped out of the carriage, just as the second carriage rolled into the courtyard. This one was barred and closed up tight—a prison cell on wheels. A handful of sterling had persuaded the gaoler at Desmond Castle to let Sheff borrow it for a few days.

Sheff was taking no chances where Jamie was concerned. Jamie would kill him if he escaped—Sheff was sure of it. Of course, he'd have to regain consciousness first.

Sheff's men had been checking on him throughout the journey from London. Though Jamie had awoken a few times along the way, long enough to drink some water or eat a crust or two of bread, he still hadn't come fully awake. This presented a certain problem, as Sheff needed

Jamie awake if this evening were to go as planned. Jamie would be bound to a chair, still shackled, and he would watch as Sheff enjoyed himself with the pretty little Irish baggage. Sheff got hard just thinking about it.

And then?

Sheff didn't like to think about this part. He couldn't very well let Jamie go, could he? Jamie would surely kill him, as he'd threatened to do more than once. This left Sheff no choice but to kill Jamie—the man who had once been his friend.

God, how he needed a drink!

Of course, Sheff needn't do the killing himself. He need merely turn Jamie back over to the authorities. Given the seriousness of the laws Jamie had broken, he'd be hanged. Jamie would have no one to blame but himself. He, not Sheff, had broken the law by arming and training an Irish rebel. He had stolen the girl, betrayed and threatened Sheff. He had forced Sheff's hand against him, and Sheff hated him for it.

Edward's voice intruded into his thoughts. "My lord, the men are asking what you want done with him."

Sheff turned back, caught a glimpse of two of his men carrying a prostrate Jamie between them. He quickly looked away. "Put him in with our other guest. And, Edward, see to it that he's treated. I want him awake by nightfall."

Edward grinned. "Aye, my lord."

*Jamie forced himself to remain limp as the two men carried him indoors and down a flight of stairs. The past two days had given him time to sleep and to heal. He had a broken rib or two—of that he was certain—and likely a concussion, as well. Not all of his unconsciousness had been feigned. When he had been conscious, he'd pretended to be asleep and had allowed himself to be awoken only when they offered him food or drink. He would need both if he were to regain his strength and free Bríghid.

Because they'd thought him asleep, his guards had spoken openly. From among the tawdry details and useless information that made up their idle chatter, Jamie had gleaned one important fact: Bríghid had been taken in a separate ship straight to Ireland. He and Sheff were several hours behind her. Jamie had taken some comfort from this, knowing that as long as Sheff was not near her, he could not hurt her.

But Sheff was not the only man who posed a threat to Bríghid. His toady, Edward, had abused her before, and Jamie had no reason he wouldn't do the same again given half a chance. Jamie had not heard his voice aboard the ship.

"He's bloody heavy."

"That's because he's bloody big, you idiot! Keep movin'!"

Jamie heard a voice from down the hall, presumably a guard. "Another one?"

"Aye. Open up, and be quick about it!"

A jangle of keys. The click as a key slid into place. The creak of a heavy door on iron hinges.

"More bloody stairs!"

"Watch out for that one. He's nothing but trouble. Get back, you!"

Jamie heard a familiar voice let loose a stream of curses in Gaelic. *Ruaidhrí.*

Sheff had been telling the truth about holding him captive.

Then Jamie felt himself being carried downstairs and dumped unceremoniously onto the floor. He fought not to react as bruised flesh met cold stone. He heard Ruaidhrí gasp and knew the boy had recognized him, then heard the footsteps of the men who'd carried him retreat back up the stairs, the door creaking on its hinges as they closed it behind them. Only when he heard the click of the lock did he drop his ruse.

He opened his eyes—found himself staring straight into Ruaidhrí's.

The boy gave a gasp, leapt back. "I thought you were dead!"

"Do you mean just now—or when you tried to shoot me?" Jamie sat up, ignoring the pain in his ribs.

"What are ravin' on about? I never tried to shoot you—not that I never thought of it, mind."

"That's an honest answer." The surprise in Ruaidhrí's voice was genuine, and Jamie knew his instincts had been right. Sheff had lied about that.

"No insult."

"None taken." Jamie took in his surroundings. There was little to see. With no windows, the room was all but pitch black.

"But if you're here, then ... " The boy's voice trailed off, then took on an angry tone. "Where is Bríghid, *Sasanach*?"

"She's here—upstairs, I think. The Earl bribed men from the London constabulary and kidnapped her from the confessional."

"Confessional? What—"

"Keep your voice down. They mustn't know I'm awake."

Jamie then told Ruaidhrí the whole story from the night he'd taken Bríghid to London to the moment Sheff and his hired thugs had stormed the church.

For a long moment, silence filled the darkness.

"Well, that's bloody grand. We've made a mess of it, haven't we?"

Jamie leaned back against the cold stone wall. "Aye."

"It explains those black eyes and all that blood on your face."

"It's not as bad as it looks."

"That's good, because you look like bloody hell."

"Thanks."

"They're going to hang me."

Though the boy had tried to sound undaunted, Jamie could feel the tense undercurrent of fear. "Don't give yourself up for dead quite yet. Tell me what you know about this place. Tell me everything."

"You have a plan?"

"Not bloody yet."

"Fine. I'll tell you what I can. But first, one question, *Sasanach*. You're in love with my sister, aren't you?"

Jamie closed his eyes, mulled over the consequences of telling the truth. But, in the end, there was only one answer he could give. "Aye."

Ruaidhrí groaned. "Bloody grand."

*A*ilís turned the key, unlocked the door.

She did not want to do this. She wanted no part of this. For the first time since she'd left Dublin, she wished herself back on the streets again. Anything to be away from this place. Away from the *iarla*. Away from *him*.

Away from Ruaidhrí.

Why had she told him? Why had she pretended to be proud of herself when she felt such shame for what she'd done? Why had she rubbed it in his face?

She'd seen disbelief in his eyes, then hurt, then hate. She was nothing to him now. She was less than nothing—an Englishman's whore, a traitor, a Judas.

And wasn't she every one of those things? Aye, she was.

The pain of regret nearly forced the air from her lungs.

No one had ever been as sweet to her as Ruaidhrí. No one had ever made her feel precious, like someone to be cared for. Not only had she hurt him, she'd helped condemn him to a painful death. And the other Englishman—the kind one with the lovely green eyes, golden hair and handsome face—she had helped to condemn him, as well.

Hand trembling, she turned the knob and opened the door.

Ruaidhrí's sister sat in a chair before the fire, asleep. Clearly, she was exhausted. And still beautiful. Ailís had hated her for her beauty when she'd first seen her. But now she felt a little sorry for her. She knew what the *iarla* had planned.

Ailís hated to wake her.

She didn't have to.

At the sound of the closing door, Bríghid's eyes flew open in obvious alarm.

Ailís watched alarm turn to disdain as Bríghid recognized her, saw her rounded belly.

Bríghid stood, and even though they were roughly the same height, Ailís felt small, worthless. She tried to remind herself that Bríghid was no saint, no pure virgin, no matter what Ruaidhrí believed. Ailís had seen the bloodstained sheet with her own eyes.

Bríghid spoke first—in English. It was an insult. "Here to do your master's dirty work?"

It wasn't a slap across the face, but it felt like one. "I've been sent to help you with your bath and—"

"I'll not be takin' a bath."

Ailís swallowed hard. "Don't you remember last time? Don't you know there's no point in resistin'? He'll get what he's after in the end. He always does."

"Not tonight." Giddy from exhaustion, Bríghid picked up the familiar and hated blue silk gown, ripped it from its transparent lace bodice to its hem, dropped it on the floor. "I will not wear this. And I will not take a bath."

The servant girl gaped at her in horror. "Are you mad? He'll punish you! He'll punish *him*!"

The note of panic in the girl's voice made Bríghid's stomach knot up. *Jamie*. "Punish him? Punish who?"

"Ruaidhrí! The *iarla* has him in chains down—"

It wasn't the answer Bríghid had expected, and the shock of it sent her into a rage. Her fists clenched at her sides. "You lie! Ruaidhrí is safe! He is far from here!"

"She's telling the truth."

Bríghid's breath caught in her throat, fear a hammer in her breast.

The *iarla*.

He stepped into the room, shutting the door behind him. "Your brother doesn't know how to stay out of trouble. It seems he had some plan to kill me, isn't that right, Alice?"

"Aye, my lord."

There was a buzzing in Bríghid's ears, the panicked rush of her own blood. The *iarla had Ruaidhrí*. But where was Jamie?

"You see, Brigid, once again, your brother's life depends on whether or not you please me. Only this time, Jamie won't be here to take you from me."

The buzzing in her ears became a roar. "Wh-what have you done with him, with Jamie?"

"It's really a question of what the London constabulary did to him, my dear. They got word of a Catholic chapel in the heart of London that was harboring traitors. It's good I arrived when I did. They'd beaten him rather badly, I'm afraid. They locked him in chains in Newgate Prison."

Her head began to spin. *Jamie*! "No!"

"Yes." The look on the *iarla*'s face told Bríghid he was enjoying this. "Of course, I didn't leave him there. I'm not heartless. He's here keeping your brother company."

"Jamie is here?" For the first time in days, Bríghid felt a ray of hope.

"Aye, he's here. I doubt he knows that, however. I think he took one too many blows to the head. My men tell me he was unconscious all the way from England."

He was hurt. Jamie was badly hurt. "Let me see him. Let me care—"

"You will see him soon enough. But first there is the matter of your obedience, Brigid."

Her hope in tatters, she said the first thing that came to mind. "That's not my name."

The *iarla* took a step toward her, let his gaze travel over her. "You are a little spitfire, aren't you? I can see why Jamie—"

The *iarla*'s gaze dropped to the floor to where his foot had caught in folds of torn blue silk. He bent down, retrieved the shredded gown.

Bríghid took a deep breath, lifted her chin, and met the *iarla*'s gaze. Though a faint smile played on his lips, she could feel the anger within him.

He held up the gown, tossed it to Alice, spoke in a mild voice. "If the gown was not to your liking, Brigid, you need only have told me. I'd have found another."

The blow—a backhanded slap across the face—came so suddenly Bríghid was wholly unprepared for the pain. All but knocked off her feet, she struggled not to pass out. Spots danced before her eyes. Her cheek stung like fire.

No one in her life had ever hit her.

It was the *iarla* who kept her on her feet. He hauled her up against him, dug his fingers into her hair, and forced her to look up at him. His breath reeked of drink. His brown eyes held darkness. "Disobey me again, Brigid, and I shall take it out of your brother's hide—and Jamie's!"

He thrust her from him and ordered Alice to find a new gown, then stormed out of the room, Alice behind him.

Alone, Bríghid staggered backwards, sank to the floor, and wept.

*F*inn moved quietly through the trees, his gaze on the little squatters cabin. He wasn't sure what had brought him here. He had searched along the road all the way from County Clare for any sign, any word of Ruaidhrí, and found nothing.

He knew well enough his brother was up to no good. He'd discovered the missing pistol the morning he'd left Clare. He'd opened the wooden box and found only Muirín's saved coin. Muirín had packed the box when they'd left her cabin in County Meath, and though she'd noticed the pistol wasn't in the box, she'd thought Finn had taken it.

Finn had known from that moment that Ruaidhrí had gone off either to avenge their family on the *iarla* or to bring Bríghid home. But he'd found no sign of Ruaidhrí, no innkeeper who'd seen a lad matching his description. Finn had even checked with sheriffs along the way. Nothing. His search had led him back here, back to the squatters cabin.

There was no scent of smoke in the air, no sign of anyone lurking nearby.

He tied the reigns of his horse to a strong branch and moved quietly forward. As he drew nearer, he could see the front door had been kicked in. Inside the cabin, all was dark, the rays from the winter sunset not strong enough to cast their light inside.

He crept along the outside wall, listened for any man or beast that might be hiding nearby. When he reached the door, he looked in and found the cabin empty and in a shambles—a sure sign the *iarla*'s men had been there.

He glanced around him, certain he knew what had happened here. Guided by Finn's misleading advice, the *iarla* had ridden here with his thugs, found the place newly deserted and set about to destroy everything left behind. Finn supposed the bastard enjoyed destroying things. Perhaps it made him feel powerful. Perhaps he—

Something beneath the table caught Finn's eye. He bent down and retrieved the old sack they'd used to store potatoes—the sack Ruaidhrí had been carrying when he'd left for Clare.

Ruaidhrí's winter cap and a shriveled apple, nibbled by mice, were all that remained inside it.

Finn felt the blood rush to his head.

Another set of images flashed through Finn's mind.

Ruaidhrí heading up the road toward Clare early in the morning.

The *iarla* and his men riding down on Finn as he worked to repair the fence.

The *iarla's* men beating him silly.

The sound of his own voice.

The forest south of there shelters a few abandoned cabins. He must be hidin' in one of them.

Finn had thought Ruaidhrí safe on the road to Clare. But Ruaidhrí had doubled back, had gone back to the squatters cabin for shelter, perhaps on his way to fetch Bríghid, perhaps after revenge against the *iarla*.

And Finn had sent the *iarla*'s men straight to him.

"God, no! Ruaidhrí!"

Chapter Thirty-two

*B*ríghid sat before the fire, stared into the flames, unseeing. She would not cry. She could not. She had no more tears to shed.

She had bathed in water grown cold, dressed in the emerald green gown Alice had brought her, even nibbled from the tray of food the *iarla* had sent up for her supper. Now there was nothing to do but wait for the *iarla* to claim his prize.

Had she really thought she could fight him? Had she truly thought to resist?

Aye, she had.

What had happened to her courage?

It had vanished the moment she'd learned the *iarla* held both Jamie and Ruaidhrí prisoner. While she'd gladly take a thousand blows like the one that had bruised her cheek, she could not bear to be the cause of their suffering. Jamie was already hurt—the *iarla* had said so himself. She would not bring him more pain.

She would submit, and she would survive.

A sound in the hallway made her jump to her feet, heart pounding, but it was just someone passing by her door, no doubt a servant on an errand.

She walked to the window, fought to calm the fear that made it hard to breathe and filled her belly with writhing snakes. Outside, the last rays of winter sunlight turned the horizon pink. It would not be long now.

She tried to tell herself she was strong enough to bear this. Last time she'd been here, she'd known little about what happened between men and women, and her mind had been filled with fears about the act itself. But she was no longer a maid. There was no barrier of tender flesh for the *iarla* to break, no innocence for him to abuse.

But, in some ways, that made it all the worse. Bríghid knew exactly what it meant to lie with a man. She knew what his invasion of her body would entail. She knew she would have to open her body to a man she loathed. She knew she would have to bear his touch in the most intimate places, have him inside her, take his seed. And she knew there were unnatural acts, ways he could humiliate her, hurt her.

What had been with Jamie an act of love would be twisted by the *iarla* into a form of torture. For this was not about love or pleasure. It was about control, dominance.

And afterwards, when the *iarla*'s hatred had been spent—what then? Would he let her go? Would he let Ruaidhrí and Jamie go?

She opened her hand, looked down at the dragon brooch that lay in her palm. Garnet eyes flashed defiance. Gold glinted in candlelight. The sight of it comforted her.

The sound of footsteps.

The click of a key in the lock.

Heart in her throat, Bríghid dashed to the bed, slipped the brooch under the pillows next to her iron cross. She would not let anyone take them from her again.

The door opened.

The same young girl who'd brought her supper hurried into the room to retrieve the tray.

Nerves frayed to a single thread, Bríghid tried to stop her own trembling, tried to breathe. *Not yet.* The *iarla* had not come for her yet.

She turned back toward the window, toward the vanishing light.

"I see you decided to cooperate."

Bríghid gasped, whirled about.

The *iarla* stood just inside the doorway. He wore no wig, and his waistcoat and shirt were unbuttoned at the throat. His gazed slid intimately over her. "The gown looks lovely on you—not as lovely as the one you destroyed, but you are still quite beautiful."

A shiver of revulsion ran through her as his gaze fixed on her breasts. She fought the urge to cover herself. She would not give him the satisfaction of seeing her fear. "I-I have done as you wished," she said, remembering to add "my lord" only as an afterthought.

He stepped further into the room, and when the maid had left with the supper tray, kicked the door shut with his heel. His gaze did not leave her. "Your words speak of surrender, but I see defiance in your eyes."

She lifted her chin, fought to find her voice. "I only do what I must to protect my brother—and Jamie."

He smiled. "That's what you say now. Later, you'll be greedy for my attention."

She struggled to hide her disgust. "Never."

"Is that revulsion I see on your pretty face, my dear? You did not want Jamie's hands on you at first. But now you seem quite enamored of him. So it shall be with me."

She looked down at her feet so that her eyes would not give her away. "If I lie with you willingly, will you release my brother and Jamie, too?"

He took a step toward her. "So now you wish to broker a deal, is that it?"

"Aye." She buried her hands in her skirts to hide their trembling.

He slowly walked toward her, a predator stalking cornered prey. "You must believe yourself to be quite extraordinary to demand so high a price—two men's lives for the sport to be found between your thighs."

She backed away from him, sickened by his words, by his very presence. "N-no, my lord. I am but an Irish peasant girl. 'Tis you who have gone to great lengths to have me."

He tossed back his head, laughed, a cruel sound. "True enough, but now that I do have you, there's no need for me to bargain."

She felt the windowsill behind her, knew she had no place else to go.

He stopped mere inches away from her, cupped her bare shoulders with his hands. "Why should I bargain for that which I can simply take?"

She shuddered at his touch, realized he meant to kiss her, turned her face from him. "Y-you promised they would not be harmed if—"

"Oh, I've made no promises, my dear." His hands slid slowly down the bare skin of her arms. "The truth is I cannot release them. If I let Jamie go, he'll surely pay me another little midnight visit, and I'll find myself asleep in my bed with my throat slit."

"Wh-what?"

"Oh, don't tell me you didn't know." He took her hands in his, raised them to his lips. "Did Jamie not tell you? No? Not long ago, he broke into my London manor painted like a savage and threatened to kill me. If I let him out, he'll make good on his threat. I can't let that happen, now can I?"

"Wh-what will you do with him?"

"Shouldn't you be more concerned about what I intend to do with you?" The back of his hand brushed the bruise on her cheek. "I can see that you're not. Very selfless of you. Since I can't dissuade you from this topic, come sit with me, and I'll tell you a story."

He took her hand, pulled her along behind him, sat in one of the overstuffed chairs before the fire, pulled her into his lap.

She felt the press of his thighs against her bottom, and her stomach turned.

"That's better, isn't it?" His fingers toyed with the strings of her bodice, one arm around her waist. "Once there was an English lord and a colonist. The colonist had all the advantages of wealth and learning and counted among his friends the English lord, a peer of the realm. His noble friend showed him every hospitality, treated him as if he, too, were of noble birth.

"One night the colonist stole away with a girl from the nobleman's household, insulting his friend's hospitality. The colonist knew his noble friend was searching for the girl, so he lent his pistol to her brother and taught him to shoot so that her brother might go and kill his noble lord. And, well, to make a long story short, both the colonist and the Irish miscreant became guests of the hangman."

Bríghid's breath left her lungs in a rush. Her heart beat hard so hard it nearly burst. Before she knew what she was about, she sank to her knees before the *iarla*. "No! My lord, I beg you, spare them! Let them go to the colonies far from here! Let them go, and I shall willingly do whatever you ask!"

"Brigid, my dear, you'll do what I ask regardless." He cupped her cheek in his hand, leaned forward. His breath stank of drink. "As for Jamie and the rapparee, they pose too great a danger. I cannot take that risk."

"But Ruaidhrí is just a boy, and Jamie was your friend!"

Bríghid found herself jerked roughly to her feet, as the *iarla* leapt up and hauled her with him. His fingers dug painfully into her arms, his face an enraged scowl. "He *was* my friend. And he betrayed me—over you!"

"Then blame me, my lord, and spare him! Give me to the courts, and let them go!"

He thrust her from him, crossed the room, poured himself a drink, then tossed it down his throat with hands that trembled.

Bríghid shook from head to toe, her mind reeling. The *iarla* planned to turn them over to the courts. They'd be tried. They'd be hanged.

She had to stop the *iarla*. She had to free them. She had to do something.

The *iarla* turned to face her, his expression once again calm. "You nearly managed to spoil my good mood, love. Still, your feelings are understandable, so I'll not blame you. But enough talk. It's time for me to claim my prize. Come."

He walked toward Bríghid, shouted. "Edward!"

Edward opened the bedroom door, grinned. "Aye, my lord. Is it time?"

"Aye. Fetch our guest."

"*B*y the time I'd reached their village, he was dead. They'd tied him to a post and burnt him alive." Jamie didn't know why he was telling Ruaidhrí this. Perhaps those blows to his head had rattled his brains more than he'd realized.

Ruaidhrí's breath hissed from between his teeth. "Bugger me! I guess there are worse ways to die than bein' hanged."

"Aye." Jamie squeezed his eyes shut against his own imaginings of Nicholas's pain and torment. "If I had but gotten there an hour sooner …"

"You did more than any man I know could have done."

"I did nothing."

For a moment, there was silence. Then Jamie heard a snort of laughter.

"What a mighty burden you carry, *Sasanach*."

Jamie felt his temper flair, tried to remind himself he was talking with a boy. "I don't know what you find so funny."

"'Tis none of it funny, *Sasanach*—except you expectin' yourself to be as powerful as the Almighty."

Now Jamie truly was angry. "Watch yourself, Ruaidhrí."

"First you survive the attack. Then you track a band of Indians back to their camp. Sure and you're a lazy bastard!" Ruaidhrí laughed harder.

"If I'd left sooner, moved faster, I might have been able to save him."

"Like as not, you'd have gotten yourself killed."

"He was my nephew!" Emotion roiled like hot pitch in Jamie's gut.

"He was a grown man! Do you think he was unaware of the dangers?"

"You don't understand! You've never—"

"Never what, *Sasanach*? Lost a brother? Aye, that I have. And a father, too. I watched while the *Sasanach* bastards put my father in chains, beat him and dragged him away. I tried to stop them, but I could not."

"You were only a boy."

"And you were only one man against God knows how many Indians."

Ruaidhrí's words hit Jamie with the force of a blow. He found himself speechless.

"I've tried hard to hate you, *Sasanach*, and for a while I was good at it. But I've come to think you're not all that bad. Oh, I can't believe I'm sayin' this!" Ruaidhrí groaned.

Jamie felt his anger drain away and chuckled. "Painful is it?"

"Aye, *Sasanach*. But think on this: You truly believe your nephew would be wantin' you to blame yourself when you did all you could?"

Jamie felt a shaft of pain shoot through his heart. *Nicholas*. "No."

"Then let it be."

Let it be.

Could it be that easy?

A key slid into the lock.

Jamie lay down on cold, stone floor and feigned unconsciousness. He heard the creak of the door on its hinges, saw a weak light, perhaps a candle, through his eyelids. Then he heard Ruaidhrí's snort of disgust.

"If it isn't the little traitor. I wonder—when they stretch my neck, will you watch? Will you cheer, *Alice*?"

Ruaidhrí watched her walk down the stairs, bowl of water cradled in the crook of her arm. He could tell by the pained expression on her face his words had hit home. Good.

She walked over to where Jamie lay like a corpse, set her candle down, but Ruaidhrí pulled her away from him.

"You'll not be touchin' him."

She looked up at him, tears in her eyes. "I must! The *iarla* has sent for him, and I'm to wash the blood from his face and wake him."

"I won't be lettin' you near him."

"But he'll punish you! He'll punish you and me like he punished your sister!"

Ruaidhrí felt rage flare up from his belly. Before Ailís could react, he pulled her hard against him, held her chin between his fingers. "What did he do to my sister?"

Her eyes showed fear, but she didn't resist. "He hit her—hard. I warned her not to resist him, but she didn't listen!"

"What the bloody hell is going on down there, Alice!" A deep voice—the voice of the *Sasanach* who had first kidnapped Bríghid— echoed down the stairs.

Her eyes grew wider, and her voice was a whisper. "Please, Ruaidhrí! He'll beat you!"

"Don't tell you me care, *Alice*."

"Is that rapparee giving you trouble?" The ugly *Sasanach* stuck his head through the doorway, swore. "Let her go, you Irish bastard!"

Instead, Ruaidhrí wrapped his arm around Ailís's throat and backed deeper into the darkness—away from Jamie.

He heard Ailís' frightened whimper and felt a twinge of regret.

The *iarla*'s man swore, stomped down the stairs.

Ruaidhrí had forgotten how big the bastard was, too big for one man to fight alone. "*Sasanach* pig!"

"I'm going to rip your head off, boy!" The *Sasanach* bastard strode menacingly past Jamie's prone form, toward Ruaidhrí, fists clenched.

Ruaidhrí had meant to provoke the *Sasanach*, but now he found himself wondering whether this had been such a good idea. Ruaidhrí saw the fury on the *Sasanach*'s face and swallowed hard. He clapped a hand tightly over Ailís' mouth to silence her, holding her fast. "Go to hell, you son of a whore!"

Then Ruaidhrí saw Jamie rise like an apparition—silent and deadly—behind the *Sasanach*. Before the bastard could react, Jamie threw the chains that bound his wrists round the *Sasanach*'s neck, jerked them tight.

The *Sasanach* made a choking sound, clawed desperately at the chains, his eyes wide with terror.

Ruaidhrí watched, transfixed, as Jamie yanked the chains tighter still, growled into the *Sasanach*'s ear.

"I warned you that I'd kill you if I saw you again! It's your unlucky day!"

Then Ruaidhrí saw Jamie wrap one arm around the *Sasanach*'s head and jerk it hard to the side. There came a loud snap as the Sasanach's neck broke.

The *Sasanach*'s arms fell to his side. His legs gave way, and his head lolled. When Jamie released him, he fell to ground in a twitching heap, then lay still.

Astonished by what he'd just seen, Ruaidhrí gaped at Jamie.

Jamie stepped over the body, his gaze on Ailís.

Ruaidhrí could feel her trembling and released her.

Her breaths came in ragged gasps. She backed away from them, her hands pressed protectively against her belly, her pleading gaze darting from one to the other. "P-please don't! Don't kill me! Don't hurt me! My baby!"

Ruaidhrí was torn between rage and regret. Why should he listen to her pleas when she had betrayed him to the hangman? She had not shown him mercy. Still, her fear and her helplessness cut at his conscience. "No one is going to hurt you, Ailís."

Jamie put a calming hand on her shoulder. "We won't harm you, but you are going to help us. Do you understand?"

"Come, Brigid." The *iarla* motioned Bríghid toward the bed. "Lie down."

She shuddered, looked away. The icy claws of panic closed around her heart, and her mind raced for an answer, some way out of this. She could not lie with him. She could not.

"Come, my dear. There is no point in such stubbornness."

But her legs refused to move. Had she believed she was saving Jamie and Ruaidhrí, she might have been able to bear it, but now? The *iarla* was going to condemn them no matter what she did.

"No." She heard her own voice before she realized she'd spoken.

"No?" He laughed.

She forced herself to meet his gaze. "No."

He looked genuinely taken aback. "I'm fast losing patience with you, wench. You'd best do as I say."

She could scarce hear him over the pounding of her own heart. Her thoughts came in fragments, scattered shards. The door. It was behind her. It was unlocked.

She turned, darted toward the door, grabbed the knob.

Arms shot out from behind her, seized her. Though he was not as muscular as Jamie, the *iarla* was still much stronger than she. He pinned her arms to her sides, jerked her away from the door, dragged her toward the bed.

She screamed, tried to kick him with her heels, felt herself flying through the air. She landed on her belly on the bed, tried to crawl to the other side, but he was too quick.

In a blink, he'd grabbed her legs, pulled her back toward him, forcing her onto her back. He pinned her with his weight. His face hovered inches from hers, his breath foul, his eyes ablaze with fury. "You little bitch! Do you really think you can get away from me?"

"God scorch your soul!" She twisted, wrenched one arm free, and raked his face hard with her nails.

His fist hit her cheek, sent her swirling to the edges of darkness. "Whore!"

She heard herself whimper in pain, struggled to stay conscious.

He was shouting at her, filthy words, terrible words.

She felt his fingers begin to tug on the laces of her bodice and realized as if from afar that her struggles had only served to arouse him.

She had failed.

Then her hand touched something cold, something metal. She closed her fingers around it, felt its familiar shape, its weight.

She opened her eyes, saw him above her, blood on his cheek where she'd scratched him, his eyes alight with a mad hunger as he worked to bare her breasts. Her fingers clenched the brooch. With all her strength, she drove its thick iron pin deep into his chest.

He howled in pain, stared in disbelief at the bloodstain that bloomed like a rose against the white linen of his shirt. He grabbed the brooch, pulled it free, and threw it.

She took advantage of his surprise and pain to twist away from him. Frantic, she rolled off the bed and started to run.

But pain now fueled his rage. He grabbed a fistful of her hair, jerked her roughly backwards onto the bed. "You stupid whore!"

She screamed, lashed out at him blindly with her fists and feet, but she was no match for his strength.

His fingers closed around her throat, cut off her breath. "I warned you not to defy me! Try to fight me now, fucking Irish bitch!"

Fight she did. She struck at him, struggled in vain to pry his fingers loose until her lungs ached from lack of air and she grew weak. The world around her fragmented into spots, became distant—a world of shadows. And she knew she was going to die.

Pain. Surrender. Darkness.

As if from another world, she heard a familiar voice.

"You're a dead man, Byerly!"

Jamie!

Chapter Thirty-three

*H*e was too late.

Jamie saw blood on Bríghid's face and gown, saw the pallor of her skin. A rage borne of anguish and hotter than anything he'd ever known ripped through him.

Sheff released her, whirled about, eyes wide, terror on his bloodied face. "How—"

Jamie raised the sword he'd stolen from its rest above one of the hearths downstairs. "It's time you fought a man."

Jamie stepped slowly forward, blade pointed toward Sheff's heart. "Ruaidhrí, get your sister and Ailís out of here!"

Ruaidhrí rushed in behind him, and Jamie heard him speaking softly to Bríghid in Irish.

A cough. A whimper.

She was alive.

Jamie caught a glimpse of Ruaidhrí lifting his sister into his arms, heard his heavy footsteps, followed by Ailís's softer ones, vanish down the hallway.

He willed himself not to think of Bríghid, focusing his wrath on Sheff. Slowly, he moved forward, the blade pointed at Sheff's chest. "It's just you and me now, old *friend*."

Sheff raised his arms in a gesture of supplication and took another step backwards. "I'm unarmed. I know you, Jamie. You wouldn't kill a man in cold blood."

"I hardly call this 'cold blood,' Sheff." Jamie moved closer. "You murdered one priest, perhaps two. You had me beaten and locked in chains. And you have twice tried to rape and kill the woman I love."

Sheff's eyebrows jerked upward in surprise.

"Aye, I know it wasn't Ruaidhrí's bullet that nearly ended her life, but yours."

Sheff took another step backwards, stopped, his back now pressed against a chest of drawers. "I-It was Edward's doing!"

"Edward is dead." Jamie enjoyed the look of fear and shock that crossed Sheff's face. "Why would he want to kill Bríghid unless you ordered him to do it?"

"He was supposed to shoot your horse, not the girl! It's his fault!"

"My horse?" Jamie heard himself laugh, a cold sound. He stepped forward, pressed the tip of the blade against Sheff's chest. "Why should you want to kill Hermes?"

"It would have been a blow to your insufferable superiority about horseflesh!"

With a flick of his wrist, Jamie sliced the front of Sheff's shirt open. "So you attack helpless animals and defenseless women to get at me. How like a coward!"

"Defenseless? The little bitch stabbed me!" Sheff tore at his ripped shirt to bare his wounded chest.

Jamie saw the deep puncture wound where something had penetrated skin and muscle, was relieved to realize the blood on Sheff's shirt—and probably the blood on Bríghid—belonged to Sheff.

But blood wasn't what caught and held Jamie's gaze. "Holy God!"

Sheff's chest was pitted with scars that could only come from one thing—the pox.

And then it all made sense. Sheff's changed manner. The strange light in his eyes. His sickly pallor. His drinking.

Sheff followed the line of Jamie's gaze. "Now you see. Now you know."

"Syphilis." Jamie looked into Sheff's eyes and felt pity.

"Aye, syphilis." Sheff spat the word. "One of the whores at Turlington's gave it to me about a year after you left—the little bitch!"

"Did you not seek treatment?"

Sheff's eyes widened. "And let them poison me? Do you know what they gave me? Mercury ointment. Arsenic tonic. I tried it all, but it made me sicker, so much sicker."

"Why didn't you tell me? I would have tried to help you."

But Sheff didn't seem to hear Jamie. His eyes filled with tears. "Oh, Jamie, you have no idea. The pain at night—it shoots through my arms and legs like lightning. My headaches—I feel it's eating at my insides, eating me alive. It's killing me, Jamie, but I'll take them with me, I swear it!"

"Take whom with you?"

"All the little whores—sluts like the one who gave this to me. I pass it to them to keep it from my wife. They'll die, too."

A shiver ran down Jamie's spine, and he realized without a doubt that the man who had been his friend was insane. "And all the young servant girls you've tupped, Sheff—the women you've bent to your will—do they deserve to die, too?"

Sheff sneered. "They're whores, all of them. They spread their legs for next to nothing—a bite of food, a trinket, a pretty dress. I give them what they want—and something more."

Jamie struggled to control his anger, sickened by what he heard. "You were going to rape Bríghid, to infect her, too—an innocent woman."

"She's Irish! There are no innocent Irish! But that's not why I wanted her." Then a strange look akin to satisfaction came over his face. "I wanted you to watch, to see who had the power. I wanted you to watch while I took her, as I watched you."

"You didn't see what you think you saw that night."

"I saw you unwrap your gift. I saw how randy you were. I watched while you took her maidenhead. I listened to her scream."

"You saw me undress her and pretend to take her. That was my blood on the sheet, Sheff—my blood, not hers."

"You lie! I saw—"

"You saw and heard what I wanted you to see and hear, nothing more!"

Sheff looked stunned. "You knew?"

"Aye, I knew you were in the next room, watching through the wall. I remembered what you told me about your father all those years ago, so I pretended. I wanted you to think I had claimed her so you would leave her alone. She left this house a maiden still."

Sheff shook his head in disgust. His eyes narrowed. "What kind of man are you?"

"One who still knows the difference between right and wrong."

Sheff laughed, one long howl. "You? You're a criminal, my friend. Or have you forgotten the bit with pistol, the papist church, your being a traitor?"

"The sickness has driven you mad, Sheff. You need—"

Jamie realized he'd lowered his sword arm the instant Sheff hurled the candelabra at him, but that was an instant too late. Hot wax burnt his bare chest. Flames licked his skin. He deflected the worst of the blow with his arm, sent candles flying onto the bed and floor.

Fire leapt up the damask, instantly setting the bed curtains and mattress ablaze.

The room began to fill with smoke.

With a howl, Sheff dashed toward the fireplace, grabbed the poker, and brandished it like a sword. He swung, tried to force Jamie back into the fire.

Jamie easily turned aside the blow. "Don't make me do this, Sheff!"

"You're the one who's going to die tonight, Blakewell." Sheff coughed, thrust the point of the poker at Jamie's abdomen.

Jamie sidestepped, countered the blow, felt the heat of the flames behind him. "Let me take you someplace where you can get help."

"An asylum? I'll not be left to die like some leper in a colony." Sheff glared at him, began to thrust and cut in earnest.

Jamie's throat stung from the smoke, but he parried Sheff's blows with ease. "A poker is poorly weighted for swordplay. Your arm will tire."

"Not before I've watched you burn!" Sheff tried to force Jamie's blade down.

Jamie circled his blade, freed it, raked several quick cuts over Sheff's forearm in hopes he could force Sheff to drop his makeshift weapon.

"You bastard!" Sheff jerked his arm back, hissed in pain, looked down to where ribbons of blood welled up on his linen shirtsleeve. He struck again, rained heavy, driving blows down on Jamie from above.

Jamie parried, hooked his blade over the top of the poker, forced it down, then slammed his fist into Sheff's face.

Sheff's head snapped back, and he nearly fell to the floor. But he didn't drop the poker.

Flames skittered across the carpet near Jamie's feet. Searing heat pressed against his back. The room was quickly being consumed by the blaze.

Jamie knew they had only minutes before they would be engulfed in fire. "We must get out of here!"

Sheff pulled himself upright, coughing, his forehead dripping with sweat from the heat. "Let it be your funeral pyre!"

With that, Sheff stood upright and swung—hard.

Jamie deflected the blow, but the blade of his sword snapped.

Sheff saw his chance, swung again.

Jamie tossed his useless weapon aside, grabbed the poker as it arced through the air toward him, and pivoted with the force of the blow. Though he had intended only to rip the weapon from Sheff's hands, the power of their combined actions sent Sheff hurtling past Jamie into the flames.

Sheff screamed, an animal sound of agony.

Jamie shielded his eyes from the heat and smoke and tried to reach in to pull Sheff free. But Sheff panicked, ran past him out the door and down the hallway, shrieking, his clothes ablaze.

Jamie started after him.

All around him, wood groaned like a tortured beast.

Out of the corner of his eye, Jamie saw the bedpost, a pillar of fire, wrench itself with almost supernatural force from the rest of the burning bed and fall toward him.

He leapt back, flames missing him by inches.

The post crashed against the bedroom door, shutting it, blocking his path.

He was trapped.

*B*ríghid heard Ruaidhrí's voice, felt cold air against her skin. From the pain in her throat and head she knew she was still alive.

"You did it, Bríghid." Ruaidhrí stroked her cheek. "You fought him off just long enough for us to get to you. And from the looks of him, you did a bloody good job of it."

A woman spoke—Alice, the Dubliner. "She's comin' round."

Bríghid heard someone moan, recognized her own voice.

"Open your eyes, Bríghid. Talk to me."

She struggled to do as he asked, said the first word her lips could form. "Jamie."

"He's here, Bríghid. He's inside helpin' the *iarla* pack for his trip to hell."

Gradually, the fog began to lift from her mind. She remembered fighting the *iarla*, stabbing him with her brooch. She remembered the feel of his fingers as they closed around her throat. She remembered hearing Jamie's voice.

Jamie was here. He was inside. He was with the *iarla*. He was—

Her eyes fluttered open. *Jamie!*

Ruaidhrí's face swam into view above her, beyond him bare tree branches and the night sky. They were outside. And though Ruaidhrí was doing his best to keep her warm, holding her close to his chest, it was bitterly cold.

She tried to sit, felt the pain in her head explode, couldn't help but cry out.

"Easy now." Ruaidhrí helped her slowly to sit. "Irish girls who go about brawlin' with *Sasanach* lords should take time to rest."

"Where … ?" She rubbed her fingers across her swollen throat. "Where is he?"

"After we found you, he told me to carry you out. He stayed behind to finish the *iarla*."

Finally, she understood. Jamie was inside the manor still, locked in a battle with the man who had once been his friend. "What if—"

"He'll be fine, Bríghid. After what I saw tonight, I'm surprised he's not already out here. He killed near half of the *iarla*'s men, so he did— with my help."

"And mine!"

Bríghid stared in surprise at the Dubliner.

"Aye, Ailís, with your help, too. You fetched the key to our shackles and managed not to scream. We're all grateful." Ruaidhrí's voice was thick with sarcasm.

"I thought it was 'Alice.'" Bríghid met the girl's gaze.

"My name is Ailís Ní Riagáin."

Ruaidhrí nodded toward Ailís. "She's decided she's Irish after all."

Bríghid was too tired, too worried about Jamie to do more than notice the tension between her brother and Ailís. Her head throbbed fiercely, and she felt more than a little dizzy. She rubbed her temple, felt her brother's reassuring touch.

"That was very brave of you, Bríghid."

She met Ruaidhrí's gaze, saw deep tenderness in his eyes.

"When I first saw you lyin' there, his hands at your throat, I feared you were dead. I thought—" Ruaidhrí looked beyond her toward the manor, leapt to his feet. "Bloody hell!"

Bríghid followed his gaze, gasped.

Fire!

The room she'd been kept in was ablaze.

"Oh, sweet Mary! Jamie!" Bríghid tried to stand, but even had she found the strength, Ruaidhrí would not have let her.

"You're not goin' anywhere, Bríghid! Stay here! Ailís, watch over her. If you betray her, if you harm her in any way ... " He never finished his words, but let them hang in the air.

"Ruaidhrí!" Bríghid looked up at her little brother, reached out, gave his hand a squeeze. "Please be careful!"

"Aye."

Then he turned and ran toward the manor.

*J*amie realized his peril. He could not escape through the window, as that side of the room was engulfed in flames. He could not open the door, as it was blocked by the burning bedpost. The air was full of smoke, making it hard to breathe, and the fire was spreading. Already, nearly the entire room was ablaze, and the heat was all but unbearable.

Unless he escaped in the next minute, he would die, burned alive.

Like Nicholas.

No, he was not going to die, not if he could help it.

He had few options. Seek shelter in the fireplace—a decision that would only delay his demise—or find some way to move the bedpost.

He saw Bríghid's cloak begin to catch. He pulled it from the chair where it lay, beat the flames out, then held it to his face to keep the smoke from his lungs.

Coughing hard, he leapt over veins of fire to reach the fireplace, grabbed the fire tongs, then dashed back. If he could only shift the burning post so that the door could open wide enough for a man to pass through, he could escape.

He tried to grasp the post with the tongs, but it was too big and the flames burned so high his hands were scorched in the attempt, the pain excruciating.

Next he tried to use the tongs as a lever, thrusting them behind the end of the post where it pressed against the wall. But the wall had caught fire, and the heat was so intense against his bare skin he could last only a moment or two at a time.

He sank to his knees coughing, aware he was beginning to suffocate.

On the floor beside him, he saw a glint of gold.

Bríghid's brooch. The pin was covered with blood, and he realized she'd used it to stab Sheff.

My brave Bríghid.

Jamie picked it up and slipped it into his pocket, determined to try again regardless of how badly the heat burned his skin. He'd be a hell of a lot hotter if he didn't get out—now.

He forced himself to his feet, hung the cloak over his shoulder like a shield, gritted his teeth against the blistering heat. Then he drove the tongs between the post and the wall.

Something crashed against the door, made it shudder.

The flaming bedpost rocked.

Jamie leapt back as far as he could lest it fall on him.

From the hallway beyond, he thought he could hear shouting.

He tried to shout back, but his words were lost in a fit of coughing.

This time whoever was outside hit the door even harder.

Again, the bedpost rocked, but did not roll out of the way.

Dizzy, Jamie knew he had precious few moments before the place he stood was swallowed by flame. He pressed the cloak closer to his face, willed himself to stay conscious.

Wood splintered.

The bedpost shuddered, rolled.

The door fell inward, landing atop the flaming post like a bridge.

On top the door lay Ruaidhrí. The boy looked up at him. "What are you waitin' for? Let's get out of here!"

Jamie followed Ruaidhrí out the door into the hallway beyond. Dizzy, he struggled to stay on his feet, sucking cool, sweet air into his lungs.

"God's blood!" Ruaidhrí gazed at the flames that had followed them into the hallway. "We've got to get out of here now!"

Like living creatures, flames skittered up the walls and across the ceiling.

"Sheff." Jamie's voice was hoarse, and he struggled not to cough. "I need to find him!"

"Curse him!"

Jamie shook his head, tried to explain. "He's badly burned. It was the pox. It's driven him mad."

"The Devil can take him, for all I care! Come!"

Jamie shook his head. "I must try!"

He could see fire from down the hall where Sheff had fled. He held the cloak to his mouth, tried to follow the trail, Ruaidhrí behind him, cursing up a storm.

But they'd gone only half the length of the hallway when Jamie realized it was hopeless. The fire before them was thick, impenetrable. The manor, its walls weakened by tiny peepholes, was quickly becoming an inferno. If they didn't get out now, they never would.

"It's no good!" Jamie shouted over the groans of the dying manor. "Let's go!"

"Now you're makin' sense."

They turned back, stopped.

The way they had come was a barricade of fire.

*B*ríghid watched in horror as the manor went up in flames. Window after window showed the orange glow of fire, then shattered. Sparks shot into the night air, smoke rising black against the black sky. Soon the blaze cast an unnatural light upon the night, a false dawn.

And with each passing moment, her fear, her hopelessness grew.

Her teeth chattered from the cold, but she didn't feel it. Tears fell unheeded down her cheeks. Beside her, Ailís wept openly, but Bríghid didn't hear. She knew only one thing: Jamie and Ruaidhrí were in there, and she might never see them again.

Somewhere in the distance, a bell rang in belated alarm.

Men and women shouted, screamed. Some seemed to be trying to fight the fire, while others stood by in shock and did nothing.

Then a great rumbling shook the night, and part of the ceiling collapsed, sending a shower of embers skyward.

Jamie! Ruaidhrí! Their names where a whispered prayer on her lips.

"Mother of God! Bríghid?"

Bríghid turned her head, found herself staring into Finn's worried eyes. "Finn?"

Finn could tell his sister was in shock. Her eyes seemed to look through him more than at him. But she recognized him, said his name, reached for him.

He shed his coat, wrapped it around her shoulders. Then he drew her into his arms. "Bríghid! I thought you were safe in London."

The girl whose weeping had drawn Finn to this stand of trees began to speak almost uncontrollably, rattling off words that made no sense.

"At first I told the *iarla* everything because I thought he'd help me now that I'm carryin' his child, but then I started to care for Ruaidhrí, and then, when the handsome *Sasanach* was brought in, I helped them escape. I got the key, and the *iarla* tried to kill Bríghid. He beat her badly, and they saved her, but now they're inside!" The girl ended on a wail.

Finn lifted his sister's chin, saw the bruises on her cheeks and her throat. If the bloody *iarla* wasn't dead yet, Finn would kill him with his bare hands. "Bríghid, talk to me. Where is Ruaidhrí?"

She met his gaze, then looked toward the manor, pointed. "He went after Jamie. He went to save Jamie. Finn, they're in the fire!"

Finn looked at the manor as another portion of the ceiling collapsed. The entire structure was in flames. His mind told him no one could possibly still be alive in that conflagration. But his heart dared to hope.

He turned to the weeping girl. "What's your name, love?"

"Ai-Ailís." She sniffed.

"Ailís, listen carefully. I'm going in after them. If I don't come back, I want you to watch out for Bríghid. I think she's hurt and needs to see a doctor. Take this." He grabbed the last of Blakewell's coins from his pocket and placed it in her palm. "Head to County Clare. I have family there who will take you in and make certain you're cared for. When Bríghid is herself again, she'll be able to guide you. Do you understand?"

Ailís gazed in apparent disbelief at the coin in her hand, nodded.

Finn bent down to kiss Bríghid's cheek. She sat as if transfixed, watched the manor burn. "Bríghid, I'm going to go get them out if I can."

Then her eyes grew wide, and she pointed.

He looked toward the manor, watched as a two men leapt through a seeming wall of flames. Something heavy was draped over the shoulder of the taller one.

Blakewell. Running beside him was Ruaidhrí.

"Mother of God!"

Bríghid heard Finn swear, heard Ailís begin to sob afresh. She felt relief wash through her, an elixir of joy. She could not see their faces, but the firelight behind them was enough. She'd recognize the catlike grace of Jamie's stride—and the cockiness of Ruaidhrí's—anywhere. She drank them in with her eyes. Jamie wore no shirt. His face and chest were bruised. Both of them were covered in sweat and soot. But they were alive.

Finn rushed forward, helped Jamie lower the heavy bundle to the ground.

It was no bundle, but a man wrapped in her cloak.

"He's dying." Jamie coughed. "Badly burned. It was the pox. Drove him mad."

Bríghid did not hear Ailís' distressed cry. Her eyes were fixed on the man shivering in her cloak. At first she did not recognize them. Then she gasped.

It was the *iarla*.

Jamie looked down at the man who'd once been his closest friend, the man who had tried to destroy him, the man who had almost murdered Bríghid. He didn't know what to feel. Relief? Rage? Grief?

The only thing he knew for certain was that Sheff would be dead in a matter of moments.

They had found him face down on the servant's stairs, surrounded by fire, and had pulled him out. But it had been too late to save him. The flames had burned his body far beyond a doctor's skill to heal, and the smoke had ravaged his lungs.

Sheff's eyes opened. "Jamie, old boy."

"Sheff."

"We've gotten ourselves in a bad spot, haven't we?" He took a long shuddering breath, coughed. "Was it a brawl?"

Jamie realized Sheff's mind was gone. The fire, his burns, had robbed him of any true awareness. Or perhaps the pain had sent him to another time, another place. "Aye, a brawl."

"You look like hell, old friend. It looks like they got the better of us this time."

In Sheff's eyes, Jamie could again see the shadow of the man who'd once been his friend. His throat grew tight. "Aye, they got the better of us this time."

"And me, I've had too much to drink, else why would I be flat on my back?" Sheff gave a week laugh, shivering. "Will you get me home, Jamie?"

Jamie forced a smile, a pang in his chest. "Aye, old friend. You're going home."

"Knew I could count ... on you." Sheff took one long, rattling breath, then lay still, his eyes open, lifeless.

Bríghid watched the war of emotions on Jamie's face as the man who'd been his friend, the man she hated and feared above all others, breathed his last. She wanted to go to Jamie, to comfort him. She fought her way to her feet, took one unsteady step.

And then he there, standing before her. "Bríghid!"

He pulled her into his arms, pressed his lips to her forehead, whispered her name.

He smelled of smoke and sweat, and she savored the feel of him, alive, strong. She had almost lost him, and she felt she might never be able to let go of him again. She let herself sink against him.

She heard his quick intake of breath, felt his body jerk.

He winced, his eyes squeezed shut. "Burns, love."

It was then she saw the redness of his skin, the raw blisters on his chest and hands.

"Oh, Jamie!"

He cupped her face in his hands, wiped the tears from her cheeks with his thumbs, tilted her face upwards until her gaze met his. "I'll be fine, love."

And then there were no words.

His mouth found hers, or hers found his.

It was a kiss of release, a kiss of deliverance, a kiss of prayers answered. Tears of happiness trickled down her cheeks as their lips met, caressed, as their tongues twined, tasted. Salty tears, smoke, sweat.

Her legs, already trembling and weak, gave way. He steadied her, lowered the two of them until she sat in his lap, his arms around her.

He ended the kiss, nuzzled her ear. "When I opened that door and saw you lying so still and covered in blood, I thought you were dead. My God, Bríghid, I don't know what I would have done."

She savored his words, turned her face up to him. "I watched the manor burn and feared you and Ruaidhrí had died in the flames. Oh, Jamie, I died a thousand times thinking I'd never see you again."

"Ruaidhrí saved my life." He pulled her against him, kissed her hair. "You're not going to be rid of me so easily, *a Bhríghid.*"

Behind them, she heard her brothers talking.

"So this is the way of it." Finn didn't sound too angry.

"Aye, so it is." Ruaidhrí didn't sound angry at all.

Chapter Thirty-four

*J*amie guided the horse with his thighs, holding Bríghid as she slept. He didn't think he'd ever felt anything as precious as the weight of her in his arms. He knew she was exhausted, and felt certain the terror of this night had wounded her in places the eye could not see. But if he had anything to say about it, he would be there for her from now on to protect her, to care for her. If it were up to him, they would never be apart again.

They were now on the road to Drogheda, where Jamie hoped to prevail upon Alec's shipping connections to grant them free passage back to London. The plan was for Jamie, Bríghid, and Ruaidhrí to leave for Virginia as soon as possible, before news of Sheff's death caught up with them.

Finn had agreed his sister and brother were no longer safe in Ireland or England. He'd promised to follow them to the Colonies as soon as he was able. When Ruaidhrí had opened his mouth to protest, Finn had sworn to box his ears and worse if ever again Ruaidhrí defied him. Jamie thought it must be a measure of how much Ruaidhrí had grown up these past days that Ruaidhrí actually shut his bloody gob.

Bríghid had slept through the entire discussion, but Jamie was certain she'd have a thing or two to say about it all when she awoke. He knew how much she loved Finn. Leaving her older brother would be hard for her.

They'd had only Finn's horse between them. When it had become clear Bríghid would not be able to walk far—the blows she'd taken together with exhaustion and shock had left her dizzy and weak—Finn, Ruaidhrí, and Ailís had insisted Jamie ride with her.

Revived by the joy of their escape, she'd asked him a hundred questions. He'd told her about his midnight visit to Sheff's bedroom. He'd told her about Newgate and the journey to Ireland. He'd told her about how he and Ruaidhrí had worked together to escape. And he'd told her the things Sheff had revealed before he'd died.

"It was his lackey who shot you. They were trying to kill Hermes."

She'd shaken her head. "Bad aim."

Then she'd taken him to task for not telling her Sheff had captured Ruaidhrí. "He's *my* brother, not yours. It's my right to be worryin' about him. Blame yourself for Nicholas's death if you want, but you've no right to be carryin' my burdens without me."

Jamie hadn't realized she'd known anything about Nicholas's death. "How—"

"Elizabeth told me all about it. It wasn't your fault, Jamie."

Her words, spoken in a sleepy voice into the silence of the night, seemed to crack through the shell of pain that had surrounded his heart for so many months, lifting his heart free. "I know."

Then Bríghid had given into exhaustion and fallen into a deep sleep. She'd awoken only when Jamie had dismounted to bathe his burns in the cold water of a spring.

Jamie glanced down at her face, saw the darkening bruises on her cheeks, felt a torrent of raw emotions. Rage at Sheff for the harm he'd done her, for the hurt he'd done them all. Pity for the man who'd lost his mind to sickness. Grief for his lost friend. But most of all, he felt love for the woman who slept in his arms.

He could not live without her.

Then he heard it—horses' hooves.

"Off the road. Now!"

He guided the horse into the trees, woke Bríghid.

She was sleepy and confused. "Jamie?"

"Someone's on the road, love." He dismounted, gently lifted her to the ground.

"I can't hear it." Ruaidhrí frowned.

"Quiet." Jamie motioned to them to get down, took a fast hold of the horse's bridle.

The stamping of hooves grew louder. From the sound of it, Jamie counted at least four riders. Then came the squeak of a carriage. Almost immediately, a carriage rode into view, drawn by a team of four horses. Behind it came a lone rider.

Jamie and Finn gaped in amazement.

Then Jamie grinned, ran through the trees to the road. "Travis!"

Travis whirled about, pistol drawn, then stared in astonishment. "Master Blakewell? Is that you?"

"Aye, it bloody well is."

The carriage rolled to a stop. The door opened.

Out stepped Matthew.

"Jamie? God be praised!"

"*D*riven mad by the pox." Matthew shook his head. "Such a pity."

"Aye." Jamie adjusted the furs beneath Brighid's chin.

She was fast asleep again, snuggled against him. Ruaidhrí and Ailís slept, too—seated as far apart as possible on the cushioned bench—while Finn had opted to ride behind the carriage with Travis.

Matthew looked at Brighid, his concerned gaze traveling over her bruised face. "And did Byerly ... ?"

"No. She fought him and fought hard. God, Matthew, he nearly killed her."

"And you." Matthew took a deep breath, released it. "Poor Elizabeth. She's out of her mind with worry."

"I'm sorry to—"

"Sorry? It's not your doing, Jamie. Besides, this penchant for unseemly adventure runs in your family. This isn't my first midnight rescue ride, you know."

Jamie laughed, remembering the story of how Matthew and Cassie had ridden through the night to save Alec from the hangman's noose.

"*The Three Sisters* is docked at Drogheda, ready to sail at a moment's notice."

"You brought my ship?" Jamie was amazed.

"Aye." Matthew rubbed his thigh absentmindedly. "It stood to reason you'd need to leave here quickly. I can book passage back to London on any rat-infested crate."

"But how did you know to come here, or did you simply guess?"

Matthew recounted how a battered Father Owen had shown up on his doorstep, bloodied and beaten, with the news that Lord Byerly had taken Brighid from the confessional and had Jamie beaten and arrested. The chapel had been destroyed by the mob, and the good Father, who'd been knocked unconscious by Sheff's men, had barely escaped with his own life by making use of Jamie's carriage.

Matthew had immediately ridden to London and inquired with the constabulary, which informed him Lord Byerly had taken Jamie from Newgate back to Ireland to be prosecuted.

"When I'd discovered you'd already had your ship made ready to sail, I decided it would be the fastest way to reach you—and to ensure you set sail immediately for Virginia. I had your remaining possessions taken aboard—aye, Hermes and Niamh, too."

"And how is Father Owen?"

"You can ask him yourself. He's on board."

"He's on the ship?"

"Aye. But there's more Jamie." Matthew reached into the pocket of his waistcoat, withdrew a letter. "This arrived the afternoon you were taken. You can't read it in the dark, so I'll tell you what it says. Nicholas lives."

There was a buzzing sound in Jamie's ears. Surely he had not heard correctly. *"What?"*

"Aye. It's a long story, but suffice it to say, he escaped his captors and gave Alec and Cassie quite the shock when he showed up on their doorstep two days before Christmas. Alec wrote that Nicholas was badly hurt but is recovering."

How could this be? "But I saw—"

"I know what you think you saw, but Nicholas is *alive*."

"*W*ake up, love."

Brighid heard Jamie's voice, awoke from a deep, dreamless sleep, and looked around her, confused. Ruaidhrí and Ailís sat across from her, Matthew to her right, Jamie to her left.

Beyond the window, the first light of dawn glowed in the eastern sky.

"How do you feel?" Jamie looked down at her, concern plain on his bruised face.

"Happy to be with you."

He smiled. "That's not what I meant."

"I've a wee headache." She felt sick to her stomach, too, but she kept that to herself. "Where are we?"

"The port of Drogheda."

The carriage rolled to a halt. Outside, Brighid could see the flank of a large sailing vessel. Her heart lurched.

He was leaving. He was sailing back to Virginia.

She should have known. She should have realized. This day was destined to come. Last night, she'd been so tired, so upset she hadn't bothered to ask him where they were going.

"Come, love." Jamie alighted, turned, and lifted her to the ground.

The air was cold and smelled of the sea, of faraway places, of farewell.

Jamie shouted, waved to a man on deck, who smiled and shouted back to him.

Bríghid scarce heard their words, aware only that her heart was breaking.

He was leaving.

The gangplank was lowered.

"I'll see that all is made ready." Travis turned and went aboard.

Jamie turned to Finn, Ruaidhrí and Matthew. "We ought to make sail quickly. I doubt much time will pass before word of the earl's death reaches town."

Finn nodded gravely, met Bríghid's gaze, and rested his hands gently on her shoulders. "Bríghid, you and Ruaidhrí are goin' with him."

Stunned, Bríghid stared at her brother, her heart a riot of emotion. How could she explain to him that she did not want Jamie to leave, but neither could she go to Virginia with him? She loved Jamie and would not be able to bear watching him marry an Englishwoman. Nor could she stand to leave Finn behind.

She started to protest, but Finn press his fingers to her lips.

"The English will come for Ruaidhrí. They might well come for you, too." There was grief in his eyes, but also strength. "Had I sent you both away the first time Jamie offered to take you, we might all have been spared great pain. I'll not risk either of you again."

"But Finn, we cannot go without you!"

Finn closed his eyes for a moment, took a deep breath, met her gaze. "Aye, you can. You must. I will follow with Aidan and Muirín when I am able."

"Muirín?" Bríghid and Ruaidhrí asked the question at the same time.

"Aye, she's my wife." He smiled.

Bríghid heard Matthew and Jamie offer their congratulations, but she could do little more than gaze, amazed, into her brother's blue eyes.

Beneath the exhaustion, beneath the worry, she saw deep contentment. He was in love. "Oh, Finn! Why didn't you tell us?"

"Last night didn't seem the right moment."

"My brother a married man!" Ruaidhrí chuckled, slapped Finn on the back. "Of course, there's no explainin' Muirín's choice."

*A*ilís stood to the side, fingered the coin Finn had given into her keeping, watching as he told them of his wedding. Inside her, the baby kicked.

The pox. The *iarla* had been sick with the pox. And now she likely carried that dread sickness, too, and would die or go mad like him. She'd shown no sign of it, but maybe that took time. Or perhaps she had been spared.

Either way, Ruaidhrí would not want her. He hated her now, even though she had helped him in the end. He would never forgive her. He didn't understand what it was to live on the streets, no shelter from the wind and rain, not even straw to sleep on, a crust of bread a luxury. She'd only done what she'd needed to do to survive.

She held the coin to her mouth, bit it.

No one seemed to notice she was there. They had forgotten her already. They had each other. Tears fell down her cheeks, but she dashed them away.

"*Ná tóg orm é, a Rhuaidhrí.*" *Forgive me, Ruaidhrí.*

With one last glance at his handsome face, Ailís slipped away.

"*T*hat's why I can't go with you now, Bríghid. They're waitin' for me in Clare."

Jamie saw the grief on Bríghid's face, wished for the world she didn't have to go through this. She'd been through enough already.

Her voice trembled with emotion. "But why must Ruaidhrí and I go? Can we not also stay with Seanán? With the *iarla* dead, is that not far enough away?"

Finn shook his head. "No, little sister. I won't take that chance."

Jamie knew he'd have to ask her soon. One question. Five words. What was the worst she could do?

Laugh at him, as Sarah had done.

Turn away from him.

Reject him.

She turned on Ruaidhrí. "Have you nothin' to say about this?"

Ruaidhrí shrugged. "It's the right thing, Bríghid. Besides, Finn said he'd box my ears if I defied him."

"So that's it. We're off to America. Finn's off to Clare." Bríghid turned to face Jamie, met his gaze, her eyes bright with unshed tears. "And what is to become of Ruaidhrí and me? Will Ruaidhrí work in your fields? Will I peel potatoes in your kitchen, wash your floors, darn your stockings?"

Jamie was about to tell her he hoped she would, indeed, do some of those things, but as his wife, not as a servant. But the next thing she said stopped him.

"I'll sail to America, but only if we live in Maryland with other Catholics."

Maryland.

She didn't want to be with him. She wanted to be with people of her own faith. But then he hadn't told her. She didn't know. If he told her, would it make a difference?

There was only one way to find out.

"You won't have to go to Maryland to find other Catholics, Bríghid." Jamie took her hands in his. "You're looking at one."

Jamie heard her brothers' surprised gasps, heard Matthew mutter something that sounded suspiciously like, "It's about bloody time."

She looked up at him, clearly confused. "What?"

"I found a way."

Then Jamie told her how, when she'd been fighting for her life, he'd made Father Owen a promise. If she lived, he would convert and become a Catholic. Jamie had kept that promise, had spent many an hour meeting with the good Father in between sessions of Parliament. "The deed was done to the good Father's satisfaction two days before the earl took you from London."

She gazed up at him, her eyes full of worry. "But, Jamie, is it not against *Sasanach* law? Is it not a kind of treason?"

He smiled, lifted a strand of hair from her face. "Aye, love. I'll never hold a seat in the House of Burgesses. I could be stripped of my lands, though I have taken measures to prevent that. I could find many doors closed to me that previously were open."

"You did this for me?" Bríghid stared at him with wide eyes. "Such a price to pay!"

He cupped her cheek in his palm. "Nothing they can do to me could equal the price I would pay if I had to live my life without you, *a Bhríghid*."

Bríghid could scarce believe what she was hearing. Jamie was a Catholic. He'd converted so they could be together. He wanted to live his life with her.

Was this a dream?

Then, bare, blistered chest and all, Jamie knelt on the frozen ground before her, pressed her palm to the pulsing beat of his heart. "*Mo ghrá thú, a Bhríghid*. I love you. I've loved you since the moment I saw you in that clearing, and I'll never stop loving you. Marry me."

Joy beat like a bird's wings in her breast. Warm tears slid down her cheeks. She sank to her knees before him, her hand still pressed to his beating heart. "You are everything to me, and you have been since the night you chose not to take what you were given. Aye, *Sasanach*, I'll marry you."

Matthew cleared his throat. "I'll go wake the priest."

It was only when they went to board the ship that they noticed Ailís missing. And though Ruaidhrí called for her and searched the length of the pier, they did not find her.

Chapter Thirty-five

*F*ather Owen would later remember it as perhaps the hastiest wedding he'd ever performed, and likely the most unusual. Both bride and groom were bruised, yet glowed with happiness. The bride had a gown, but everyone agreed there was no time for her to put it on. The groom smelled of smoke and had managed to slip a shirt over his painful burns by force of will alone. The bride's brothers—one of whom was bruised and scorched and the other of whom was not—looked both stunned and pleased. And the guests—Lt. Hasting and a motley group of crewmen—watched with smiles on their faces, some of the crew weeping openly.

But for all its haste and strangeness, it was perhaps also the most joyous wedding Owen had performed. As he stood on the deck of the ship and spoke the words that would bind Jamie and Bríghid together, he knew they would each do whatever it took to ensure the safety and happiness of the other. Bríghid had found a man willing to walk through hellfire for her sake, and Jamie had found a woman whose love for him would always be his salvation.

It was enough to make an old man believe again.

*B*ríghid was sure she must be dreaming. She was marrying Jamie. In a moment, she would be his wife.

"Do you have the ring?"

"Aye, Father." Jamie turned to Matthew, who held out the most beautiful rings Bríghid had ever seen.

Poised on the band of gold was a deep blue sapphire.

She could scarce more than whisper. "*Oh, Jamie!*"

Jamie slid the ring onto her finger, clasped his warm hand reassuringly over hers.

"*In nomine Patris, et Filii, et Spiritus Sancti. Amen.* You may kiss the bride."

A slow smile spread across Jamie's face. His gaze met hers. His eyes filled with heat.

And then Bríghid was lost in him, lost in the feel of his lips against hers, lost in his scent, in the press of his hard body. She knew people were watching—her brothers were among them—but she could not get enough of her husband.

Her husband.

Then through a mist of joy and desire, she heard Ruaidhrí whisper. "Can we get some breakfast? I've had naught to eat for weeks but bread and water. I'm bloody hungry!"

Her gaze met Jamie's, and she saw the amusement in his eyes. Her laughter joined his as the sun shot shafts of golden light across the morning sky.

"*I*t's time. You cannot tarry, Jamie. The town has begun to stir."
"Aye."

Matthew and Jamie embraced. "Any word for Elizabeth?"

"Give her both my love and my thanks. We could not have gotten through this without you both."

"She's going to kill me when she hears what she missed. You know how Elizabeth is about weddings—weddings and babies. You're like a son to her, to both of us. I'm damn glad to see you safe—and happy."

Bríghid stood on her tiptoes, pressed a kiss to Matthew's cheek. "Give Elizabeth my love and my thanks. You were both so kind to me."

"You're welcome, my dear. It was our great pleasure. Take care of Jamie for us."

"I will."

Matthew's peg leg clicked against the gangplank as he walked ashore to await Finn.

Bríghid fought to sort through her tangled emotions. Such joy and such grief on the same day—it was almost beyond bearing. She couldn't remember the last time she'd cried so much or for so many different reasons.

She looked up into her older brother's blue eyes. "Promise, Finn, you'll come as quickly as you can."

"I promise." Finn pulled her into a tight embrace, kissed her forehead. "Be strong, little sister. Know that I love you, and I'll see you again soon. All will be well. You've got a good man and a good life ahead of you."

Then he held her out before him, lifted her chin, and looked into her eyes. His voice broke as he spoke. "Da' would be right proud of you if he could see you today, Bríghid—aye, and Ma, too. *I* am proud of you. Never forget that."

She fought to hold back the sobs that welled up inside her. "Thank you, Finn, for everything. Give Muirín our love. And tell Aidan I miss and love him."

"I will." He released her, then took Ruaidhrí in a fierce hug. "Stay out of trouble, Ruaidhrí. Watch your temper and your tongue."

Ruaidhrí's voice was tight. "Aye."

Finn turned to Jamie, shook his hand. "Take care of them, Blakewell."

"I will."

"I know."

Then Finn and Jamie embraced, and Bríghid could see the affection and respect that had grown between them.

With that, Finn turned and walked down the gangplank.

Bríghid fought her grief, felt Jamie's arms enfold her. "Farewell, Finn! May God keep you!" she called.

"And you!" He blew her a kiss.

The anchor was weighed. Sails snapped, filled by wind. The ship lurched forward.

On the pier below, Finn and Matthew stood, hands raised in farewell.

Bríghid could hold back no longer. As the ship sailed out of port, she stared at the vanishing landscape of her homeland, at rolling green hills and sandy shore, and she wept. She wept for Finn and Aidan and Muirín. She wept for the grave of her mother she would never see again, for the sacred wells she had visited that would know her prayers no more, for the holly and hawthorn she would not bedeck with ribbons come spring. Most of all, she wept for the bittersweet dream that was Ireland.

She felt Jamie's reassuring touch on her shoulder, felt Ruaidhrí's hand take hers.

Together, they stood in the wind, watched as first Finn, then the shoreline, vanished from view.

"You'll see him again soon. Matthew will see to it." Jamie kissed her hair.

"And Ireland? Will I see it again?"

"Perhaps some day—when it is safe." He turned her to face him. "Meanwhile, I've got a gift for you."

Ruaidhrí had wandered off and was talking about the ship with Father Owen and one of the crewmen.

Brighid sniffed, couldn't help but smile. "Where did you find time to buy a wedding gift?"

He shrugged, grinned. "It's just a little something I picked up."

"Show me."

He reached into his pocket, placed something hard and metal in her hand.

The dragon brooch.

All trace of the *iarla*'s blood had been washed away. The gold and garnets had been polished until they sparkled. She looked up at him, astonished. "How...?"

"There was a moment in the fire when I was all but certain I was going to die. I was suffocating and could scarce stand—then I saw the brooch on the floor. The fire had not claimed it. I grabbed it, thought of you, and knew I'd do anything I had to do to get out of the fire so that I could be with you again. My brave Brighid." He wiped the lingering tears from her cheeks with his thumb.

Brighid gazed at the brooch in her hand, looked up at her husband. "I've got a little somethin' for you, too."

The lusty look in his eyes told her just what he thought she meant.

She smiled, took his hand, placed it over her womb.

For a moment, he looked puzzled. Then his eyes widened, and the air left his lungs in a rush. "A baby?"

"Aye."

"Already? Are you sure?"

Her flux was a good two weeks late. Her breasts felt sore and heavy, and she was ever sick to her stomach. "Aye, I'm sure."

His gaze softened, and he looked at her with such tenderness it made her heart ache. "That's twice today you've made me the happiest man in the world."

Then he took her gently in his arms and held her.

She closed her eyes, nestled her head against his shoulder, felt the sea air in her hair. Grief and fear began to melt away like frost in the sunlight.

His Majesty's Commonwealth of Virginia
Blakewell's Neck, Lancaster County
March 31

*E*verything was different—the trees, the shape of the land, even the smell of the air.

Bríghid stood on the deck, watched the pier draw nearer. She could see them clearly now, recognized Cassie and Alec from the painting. Beside them stood a man who looked very much like Alec. That must be Nicholas.

In a few moments, she would meet them all.

She felt Jamie's reassuring presence behind her. "You've nothing to fear, love."

She let herself lean back against him. "I'm not afraid."

He kissed her hair. *"Bréagach, thú."* Liar.

The anchor was dropped, the gangplank lowered.

Jamie took Bríghid's hand, motioned to Ruaidhrí and Father Owen, and led them ashore.

No sooner had they set foot on land than Cassie took her brother in a fierce hug. "Oh, Jamie, when we got your letter, I feared the worst! It's so good to have you safely home!"

"It's good to be home, Cassie. I'd like you to meet my wife, Bríghid."

Cassie kissed Bríghid on the cheek, embraced her. "You are even more beautiful than Elizabeth described, Bríghid."

Bríghid felt warmed by Cassie's words, and her fear faded away. "And you're as pretty as the painting."

Cassie and Alec looked just like the painting, if a bit older. Cassie's curls were now shot through with strands of silver, Alec's dark hair now touched with white.

"I'm charmed to meet you, Bríghid." Alec stepped forward, lifted Bríghid's hand to his lips, and kissed it. "We've heard so many wonderful things about you. Welcome home."

"Am I to have a chance to meet the lovely bride?" A man who looked like a younger version of Alec stepped forward and lifted her hand to his lips. His dark hair was tied back with a ribbon. The sparkle in his blue eyes could not fully mask the shadows that hid in their depths. "Jamie has done well for himself."

Bríghid couldn't help but blush.

"Nicholas." Jamie's voice was tight with emotion.

Bríghid stepped aside as Jamie and Nicholas grasped one another in a fierce embrace. She could feel the emotion between them, the deep bond, and found herself fighting tears.

"I thought you were—"

"I know."

The moment passed. The men parted.

Nicholas slapped Jamie affectionately on the back, winked at Bríghid. "Why do you always get the prettiest women?"

Then Jamie introduced Ruaidhrí and Father Owen. Both were welcomed in the same friendly fashion. Bríghid had to fight not to giggle as Ruaidhrí shook Alec's hand, looking up at Alec as if he were meeting royalty.

"'Tis an honor to be meetin' you, Sir."

Ruaidhrí had changed these past weeks. Gone was the angry boy who'd always been one step away from being shot or hanged. In his place was a capable young man and hard worker. He'd taken to life at sea, proving himself an able hand at the rigging. Already he was begging Jamie to let him join the crew of one of the family's ships, and Jamie had promised to talk it over with Alec.

As soon as the introductions were completed, Jamie took Bríghid's hand. "Now if you don't mind, I'd like to get my wife home. She's had a long journey and needs rest. I'd like Takotah to see her as soon as possible."

Takotah. The Indian woman Jamie found so beautiful.

Bríghid told herself she had no reason to feel jealous. Even if Jamie had once cared for Takotah, even if he had loved her and taken her to his bed, he was Bríghid's husband now.

"Are you sick, Bríghid, dear?" Cassie looked at her with concern.

"Sick?" Bríghid shook her head. "No, not exactly."

Then Cassie's eyes widened in delight. "A baby!"

"Aye." Bríghid felt herself blush to the roots of her hair as Jamie's family offered their congratulations.

As they rolled along in the carriage, Jamie, Nicholas, and Alec lost in a conversation about the French, Bríghid, Ruaidhrí, and Father Owen stared in wonder out the windows.

"'Tis a blessed land, that much is certain." Father Owen nodded gravely.

"Aye." Bríghid had no idea what to expect. Jamie had described his estate during their weeks at sea, but as they rolled along in the carriage, even his most fanciful descriptions seemed put to shame. The land was vast beyond imagining, with trees of evergreen that reached to the heavens. The cries of strange birds filled the air. Even the sky seemed wider, the sun brighter.

Jamie gave her hand a reassuring squeeze. "It's just around the next bend."

Already they were passing outbuildings and fields. Bríghid could scarce fathom that all of this land was Jamie's, that she would be mistress here, that her children would grow up and know this land as their home.

As the carriage rounded a curve in the road, Bríghid braced herself for her first view of the manor—the great house, as Jamie called it. She hoped it wasn't so great that she was afraid to touch anything or got lost in a labyrinth of dining rooms, salons, ballrooms, and sitting rooms. She was just a poor Irish—

She gasped.

Rather than the enormous manor she had expected, there was a charming two-story house of stone. On the front facing a cobblestone courtyard was a porch painted white. On all sides there were wide windows of precious glass, and Bríghid counted four—four!—chimneys. As they drew nearer, Bríghid could make out the climbing rose bushes that twined themselves around the porch. Soon their branches would fill with buds, and the air would become heavy with the scent of their blooms.

"Oh, Jamie, it's lovely!"

The carriage rolled to a stop in front, and Jamie helped her alight.

Men, women, and children began to gather in the courtyard, shouting greetings to their master and casting polite but curious glances at Bríghid. Their faces, white and brown, seemed genuinely happy. Jamie smiled, returning their greetings with a confidence and ease that bespoke both affection and command.

Bríghid couldn't help the feeling of pride that welled up in her heart for him.

"Who's the pretty lady?" The question, once asked, was picked up and repeated.

When they reached the top of the stairs, Jamie turned back to face the growing crowd. "This is my good wife, Bríghid Blakewell, your mistress. I know she's looking forward to meeting all of you, but we've just finished a long journey, and she needs to rest."

Gasps and whispers buzzed through the crowd, then became cheers.

Then, to the delight of onlookers, Jamie scooped Bríghid up into his arms and, kicked open the door with his foot, and carried her across the threshold.

But once inside, he didn't put her down. Up the stairs they went, down the hall to what was the master's bedroom. There, Jamie placed her gently on her feet.

His eyes looked deeply into hers. He brushed a strand of hair from her cheek. "I know you will always miss Ireland, Bríghid, but I hope someday you will come to love this land as your home."

Bríghid smiled up at the man she cherished. "Silly *Sasanach*, I already do."

Epilogue

March 9, 1756

*B*ríghid rocked in the porch swing, hummed a lullaby to the babe at her breast, and gazed out at the place that had become her world.

Aidan and the other children played with a ball in the cobblestone courtyard. The delicious smell of baking bread wafted through the air from the beehive ovens behind the whitewashed cookhouse. The smell of spring was in the air, and the plantation buzzed with activity.

Cassie, dressed in a plain gown and apron, planted seedlings in the nearby kitchen garden with the questionable help of little Emma Rose, who dug her chubby fingers into the dark soil, then piled it on top of her pretty red-gold curls.

"Emma!" Cassie laughed, brushed her tiny daughter off. "You daft little girl!"

Bríghid smiled.

Normally, Cassie stayed with Alec at nearby Kenleigh Hall, but with their husbands gone on mysterious business and Ruaidhrí again at sea, Cassie had come to Blakewell's Neck to help Bríghid and Muirín, who had welcomed her company.

Bríghid smiled to herself, recalled all the silly things she'd feared a year ago when she'd first arrived on these shores. She'd worried the neighbors would reject Jamie for marrying an Irish Catholic or for being Catholic. And while some had turned their noses up at him, most didn't seem to care, not even when Jamie had a small Catholic chapel built on his estate, his way of thanking Father Owen, who was now busier than ever saving souls.

She'd feared, too, the redemptioners would reject her as their mistress, as she was little more than a peasant herself. Yet they had embraced her quickly, showing her great loyalty. Jamie insisted it was in part because they knew she had once been one of them.

Most of all, she'd feared Jamie's family would not approve of his decision to become Catholic and marry a poor Irish girl. But those fears had been groundless, too. She and Cassie had fast become like true sisters. They shared a love of children, flowers, herbs, and healing lore. Bríghid had spent many hours with Cassie and Takotah, improving her knowledge of herbs and her healing skills.

Bríghid almost laughed aloud as she remembered the first time she'd met Takotah. Jamie had wanted the Indian woman to examine Bríghid to make certain she and her unborn baby were well. Bríghid had tried not to feel jealous, but had been unable to forget Jamie's words when first he'd mentioned Takotah's name.

She's a beautiful Indian woman.

Then an impossibly old woman had entered the room, her long hair grey with age, her face wrinkled as an old apple and covered in strange designs. She had a kindly manner about her, the air of one who had lived and loved and lost.

"Takotah, this is Bríghid, my wife."

Bríghid had gaped at the old woman. "*You're* Takotah? But Jamie said ... "

Takotah had raised one grey eyebrow and given Jamie a look that demanded an answer.

Jamie had seemed confused for a moment, then grinned. "I spoke so affectionately of you that Bríghid feared she had reason to be jealous. But in truth, Takotah, love, I would have married you if you weren't so old."

Takotah had laughed, a warm cackle, and patted Jamie on the cheek. "You couldn't handle me."

Since then, Bríghid had developed a strong affection for Takotah and had felt deep satisfaction the first time Takotah had complimented her knowledge of herbs.

Bríghid heard the squeak of the door on its hinges behind her.

"I think my little Róisín is finally asleep." Muirín stepped out onto the porch and drew her shawl over her shoulders. She looked tired but happy, as any new mother should.

Róisín had been born three weeks earlier, and the birth had been so quick Takotah had scarcely arrived before Muirín pushed her baby daughter into the world.

"You should try to get some sleep, too."

Muirín smiled. "I miss Finn. I hate sleepin' without him."

Bríghid understood only too well. "Aye."

Alec, Jamie, and Finn had sailed away right after Róisín's birth on some important business they refused to discuss. At first, Bríghid had feared the English authorities were again after Jamie, but he had assured her that was not the case. The terrible nightmare with the *iarla* had come to an end when his widow, aware her husband was mad with the pox, had blamed him for the fire and refused to prosecute.

Still, Bríghid had no idea when the men would return, and, in this time of unrest, it was hard not to worry. Last July, the troops Parliament had sent at Jamie's urging had been massacred along the Monongahela River, General Braddock slain. As Jamie had predicted, the British had been ambushed and hadn't even seen the enemy who fired upon them. Almost one thousand men, and most of the officers, had been killed. Though Parliament had approved the building of a few ships on the Great Lakes, it had not yet declared war on France, and sea travel was becoming increasingly perilous.

Muirín yawned, her thoughts clearly elsewhere. "'Tis such a lovely spring day."

"Aye, that it is." Bríghid turned her mind away from darker matters and looked down at her son, expecting to find him drowsy.

Ciarán smiled up at her, her nipple still in his mouth, milk pearling at the corners of his little lips. His green eyes were alert and full of interest. His tiny fists pressed against her milk-swollen breast.

"You're supposed to be fallin' asleep, little one." Bríghid stroked his dark, downy hair with her hand, unable to hold back a smile.

Ciarán giggled.

Bríghid tickled his cheek. "So that's to be the way of it. Not sleepy at all?"

Five months old, Ciarán had arrived on starry night in early October, when the world had smelled of ripe apples and coming rains. Jamie had asked her if she wanted him with her during the birth, as Alec had always been at Cassie's side. At first, Bríghid had been shocked by such a strange idea. Takotah, Cassie and Muirín would be with her, and that had seemed enough. But when her pains had grown fierce, she'd found she desperately wanted Jamie beside her. And so he had stayed with her. He had been her anchor.

And when Ciarán James O'Neill Blakewell had finally slipped into the world, wet and squalling, she had seen tears in Jamie's eyes.

The memory drew a smile to her lips.

Cassie walked up the stairs, Emma Rose on her hip. "Well, that didn't accomplish much. I'll have to try again later, when this little one is asleep. Oh, Emma, you are a mess!"

There was a smile on Cassie's face, but it didn't reach her eyes. And it was no secret why. Nicholas was gone.

Haunted by his ordeal with the Wyandot—an ordeal he refused to describe even to Jamie—Nicholas had left home one night and ridden alone into the wilderness, leaving his mother to grieve and worry for him. He hadn't been heard from in six long months. Alec and Jamie had gone after him, but hadn't been able to find him. And it had become clear that he didn't want to be found. Now they could do nothing but pray for him.

"Sails! *The Four Sisters!*"

The shout came from down the dirt lane that led to the dock.

Bríghid called to one of the stable boys to have the carriage made ready and driven to meet the men and bring them home.

The household sprang into action. By the time the carriage was rolling into the courtyard, Bríghid had arranged for tea to be served on the porch along with a light meal of fresh bread, honey, and cheese.

She pointed to the carriage as it rolled to a stop, crooning to her son in Irish. "Your da' is home."

The door opened, and Ruaidhrí stepped out. How like a man he looked, his skin bronzed from the sun, his body strong from working the rigging. He grabbed Aidan, ruffled the boy's red hair. "Have you been a good lad?"

Alec was next to alight. His gaze sought and found Cassie, then rested on his little daughter. He smiled. "You've been trying to garden again, I see."

He climbed the stairs, took his wife in his arms and kissed her.

Next out was Finn, who all but bounded up the stairs to Muirín and pulled her against him. "Oh, how I've missed you! How's the baby?"

"She's fine. She's asleep."

Then Finn left his wife's side, strode over to Brighid, and pressed a kiss to her cheek. "You're looking lovely, little sister."

He shared a meaningful glance with Ruaidhrí, then met Brighid's puzzled gaze. "We've brought someone, Brighid."

Ruaidhrí leaned through the carriage door and said something to Jamie, who was still inside. Then Jamie stepped out of the carriage, turning back to help someone behind him.

A pair of boots, breeches of plain brown, a head of white hair.

Brighid's heart exploded in her breast, her breath leaving her lungs in a rush. She felt Muirín take Ciarán from her as her knees gave way, Finn's strong arms reaching out to steady her. She could scarce speak, her voice a whisper. *"Da'!"*

The old man who emerged from the carriage was frighteningly thin. His new clothes hung from his bones. His skin was baked brown by the sun. His hair was white as snow. But she would have recognized him anywhere.

His gaze met hers, and his blue eyes grew bright with tears. *"Mo Aisling ghael."*

For a moment, Brighid could do nothing more than drink in the sight of him.

"Da'!" Then the strength returned to her legs. She rushed forward, threw her arms around the man she'd thought she would never see again. The tears she'd held back for five years, tears she hadn't let herself shed the day he was taken, poured down her cheeks.

His arms surrounded her, held her fast. His cheek pressed against the top of her head. *"Mo Bhrighid.* You're all grown up—a woman beautiful and strong."

Pine. Tobacco. Her father's special scent.

"Oh, Da'!" She heard muffled weeping, realized Muirín and Cassie were both in tears.

Then she felt her father sway on his feet and looked up into his eyes. She could see he did not feel well. She could see, too, the shadows in his eyes that told of another kind of suffering. "Are you ill?"

"He's been fighting the ague." Jamie took her father's arm, helped him up the stairs to the porch swing. "But we'll have him strong again in no time."

Brighid poured her father a cup of tea with trembling hands and gave it to him, but he set it aside.

"Come, Bríghid, sit beside an old man." He patted the swing. "I've a gift for you, a father's gift to his daughter."

She did as he asked, confused. "A gift?"

"Of all the things that pained me these past years, do you know what hurt me the most?" Her father looked deeply into her eyes. His voice broke as he spoke. "I regretted most that I had not been able to take you to the fair as I had promised, that I had not been able to buy you the lace and ribbons every maid deserves."

Bríghid watched as her father reached into the pocket of his frock, pulled out a handful of wrinkled ribbons in blue and white, together with white lace.

"Oh, Da'!" Fresh tears spilled onto Bríghid's cheeks as she took his precious gift in her hands. "I'd have gone my life without ribbons if it meant you were safe at home with us."

"I'm safe now, thanks to your husband. You found a good man, Bríghid." Her father smiled, then lifted his tea to his lips, his gaze on Ciarán. "Now I wish to be seein' my grandchildren."

While Muirín placed Ciarán on his grandfather's lap and went to fetch Róisín, Bríghid stood, turned to Jamie.

She met his gaze, saw the warmth in his eyes. "How did you do this?"

It was Alec who answered. "Jamie has been looking for your father since before you left London. He hired a barrister and a number of others to help him track your father down and buy his freedom. It wasn't easy."

Bríghid felt such a rush of love for her husband she thought she might burst. "Oh, Jamie! Thank you! What you have done for us … "

There weren't words.

Jamie placed his hands on her waist, looked deeply into her eyes. "I thought that with your father here and the chapel completed, you might consent to wear the gown I had made for you last year and marry me all over again. Of course, we'll have to wait for Elizabeth and Matthew. She'd never forgive me a second time."

Everyone laughed, a warm sound, like happiness itself.

But Jamie gazed steadily into Bríghid's eyes. "What say you, wife? Will you again be my bride?"

Her heart overflowing with joy, Bríghid answered him with a kiss.

*Watch for the next book in the Kenleigh-Blakewell Family Saga—Nicholas's story—to be reissued by Berkley Sensation February 5, 2013...**RIDE THE FIRE***

*Read on for an excerpt of **Ride the Fire** and an excerpt from **Surrender**, Book 1 of the MacKinnon's Rangers Series!*

An excerpt from…

Ride The Fire

Kenleigh-Blakewell Family Saga Book III
Copyright © 2005, 2011, 2013 Pamela Clare

Nicholas awoke with a jerk, caught between the nightmare and wakefulness, his heart pounding, his body covered with sweat. He struggled to open his eyes, found himself lying on his stomach in someone's bed, his head on a pillow. His right leg throbbed, burned. His head ached. His throat was parched as sand, and a strange aftertaste lingered in his mouth.

From nearby came the swish of skirts, the sound of a log settling in a fire, the scent of something cooking.

Where was he?

Through a fog he tried to remember. He'd been attacked. The Frenchmen from the fort. He'd lost a lot of blood, had ridden in search of help. The cabin. The woman.

Bethie was her name. Elspeth Stewart.

She'd helped him, cleaned his wound, cauterized it—not altogether willingly.

Nicholas lifted his head, started to roll onto his side to take in his surroundings, found he could not. His wrists and ankles were bound to the bedposts.

Blood rushed to his head, a dark surge of rage, of dread.

"You're awake." Her voice came from behind him. "You must be thirsty."

"You little bitch!" He pulled on the ropes, his fury and dread rising when they held fast. "Release me! Now!"

"I-I cannae do that—no' yet. I've made broth. It will help you regain—"

"Damn your broth, woman! Untie me!" He jerked on the ropes again, outraged and alarmed to find himself rendered powerless. Sharp pain cut through his right thigh.

"Stop your strugglin'! You'll split your wound open and make it bleed again."

Infuriated, Nicholas growled, a sound more animal than human, even to his own ears. He jerked violently on the ropes, but it was futile. He was still weak from blood loss, and the effort left him breathless, made his pulse hammer in his ears.

Damn her!

He closed his eyes, fought to subdue the slick current of panic that slid up from his belly, caught in his throat.

She was not Lyda. This was not the Wyandot village.

His heartbeat slowed. The panic subsided, left white-hot rage in its wake.

"Why did you do this? I told you I meant you no harm." He craned his neck, saw that she stood before the fire, ladling liquid into a tin cup, a brown knitted shawl around her shoulders.

"Is that no' what the wolf always says to the lamb?" She carried the cup to the bed, sat. "Drink. It will help to replenish your blood. Careful. 'Tis hot."

Tantalized by the smell of the broth and suddenly aching with thirst, Nicholas bit back the curse that sat on his tongue, drank.

Bethie held the cup to his lips, watched as he swallowed the broth, her heart still racing. For one terrible moment, she'd feared the ropes would break or come loose. She'd known he would be angry with her, but she hadn't expected him to try to rip the bed apart.

Truth be told, she feared him despite the ropes. Although he'd given up for the moment, she could feel the fury coiled inside him. She could see it in the rippling tension of his body, in his clenched fists, in the unforgiving glare in his eyes. He made her think of a caged cougar— spitting angry and untamed. He was not used to being bested.

The arrogant brute! Did he imagine she would grant him warm hospitality after the way he'd treated her? It served him right to be bound and helpless!

As if a man of his strength were ever truly helpless.

Her gaze traveled the length of him as it had done many times while he'd slept, and she found her eyes focused of their own will on the rounded muscles of his buttocks where the butter-soft leather clung so tightly.

Mortified, she jerked her gaze away, felt heat rise in her cheeks. Her stepfather had always said she was possessed of a sinful nature.

"More." His boorish command interrupted her thoughts. He glowered at her through eyes of slate.

"Aye." She stood, hurried to the fireplace, ladled more broth into the cup, uncomfortably aware that he was watching her.

"How long do you intend to keep me a prisoner?" His voice was rough, full of repressed rage.

She walked back to the bed, sat, feigned a calm she did not feel. "'Tis your own fault you lie bound. You cannae be expectin' to be treated as a guest when you behaved like a felon. Drink."

He pulled his head away, his gaze hard upon her, held up the ropes that bound his wrists. "This isn't necessary."

"You threatened me, held your pistol to my head, forced me to do your will and admitted to killin' two men. Do you truly expect me to trust you?"

He frowned, his dark brows pensive. "I didn't mean to frighten you."

"As I recollect, you seemed quite bent on frightenin' me."

"I didn't have time for social graces. My need was dire."

"So is mine!" She stood in a surge of temper, met his gaze. "I cannae risk you regainin' your strength and then, when you no longer need my help, hurtin' me or my baby or takin' what is ours and leavin' us in the cold to starve! I dinnae even know your name!"

For a moment, he said nothing. "Kenleigh. Nicholas Kenleigh."

She repeated his name aloud.

"Now that we've exchanged pleasantries, Mistress Stewart, you will release me."

"Nay, Master Kenleigh. I willna—no' just yet." She lifted her chin. "You'll stay as you are till I'm certain you pose no threat to me and my baby."

He gave a snort. "And how will you determine that?"

"Drink." She held the cup once more to his lips. "Perhaps I shall have you swear an oath, a bindin' oath."

He drained the cup, looked up at her. "And if I am a murdering liar, a man with no honor, the sort of man who would harm a woman ripe with child, how would this oath prevent me from doing whatever I want the moment you cut me free?"

Bethie stood, walked back to the fireplace to refill the cup once more, the truth in his words dashing her sense of safety to pieces. "Are you sayin' I should never set you free, Master Kenleigh?"

"No, Mistress Stewart. I'm saying that unless you plan to keep me a prisoner forever and care for me as if I were a babe untrained in the use of a chamber pot, sooner or later you have no choice but to trust me."

She walked back to the bed, felt her step falter. In truth, she hadn't thought about how or when she would release him when she'd bound him to the bed. Nor had she considered what keeping him bound would mean. She'd been thinking only of a way to restrain him and deprive him of his weapons, and she had accomplished that.

A babe untrained in the use of a chamber pot? Good heavens!

She reached the bed, sat, held the cup once more to his lips. "Very well. I shall cut you free. But you shall first swear to me by all you hold sacred that you willna do anythin' to harm me or my baby or to deprive us of our hearth and home."

He swallowed, licked broth from his lips. Then a queer look came over his face. He stared at the tin cup, then gaped at her. "You drugged me!"

How did he know? "I-I gave you medicine to ease your pain—and make you sleep."

He laughed, a harsh sound. "You drugged me so that you could bind me and take my weapons."

He stated it so plainly that Bethie could find no words to soften the truth of what she'd done. She rested a hand protectively on her belly, felt her baby shift within her. "Y-you left me no choice."

Nicholas saw the defiant tilt of her chin, noticed the pink that crept into her cheeks. He noticed, too, the way her hand softly caressed the swollen curve of her abdomen as if to calm the small life inside her.

What would he have done in her place?

He dismissed the question—and the irritating impulse to defend his previous actions toward her. There was only one rule in the wild—survival. He'd only done what he'd felt he had to do to stay alive.

And so had she.

An excerpt from ...

Surrender

Book 1 in the MacKinnon's Rangers series
Available Now

It seemed to Annie she'd just fallen asleep, when Iain nudged her awake again. Her body achy, her mind dulled by fatigue and hunger, she sat up and saw that it was not long past dawn. Had she ever been this tired? What she wouldn't give for just one more hour of sleep! Or a hot bath. Or porridge and a cup of tea.

How could Iain look so alert and vigorous when she felt listless and painfully weary? They were alive only because of his labors. 'Twas he who'd borne her through the forest on his back, he who'd rowed the boat through two dark nights, he who'd kept watch while she'd slept. 'Twas he who should be worn with fatigue.

Humbled by her own weakness, she sat up straighter, tried to force the cobwebs from her mind. The least she could do was to press herself as hard as he pressed himself and to endure without complaint. She was no squeamish, spiritless lass, and although she might not have been born to this rugged life, she had her wits and at least some courage.

If she'd understood him, they had most of a day's journey before them over land to Fort Edward. She could endure another day.

Iain handed her the leather pouch of cornmeal. "Bide here a wee."

Then he headed off toward the lake with the tin bucket in his hand.

She took a handful of cornmeal, chewed it, and washed it into her empty stomach with a mouthful of cold water from his water skin.

It had been a long night. Wary after their encounter with the French ships the night before and determined not to fail Iain again, shed made certain to stay awake and had watched the darkness glide past, reluctant even to breathe.

Yet, he'd seemed angry, his voice gruff the few times he'd spoken, his face hard. Perhaps he was in a temper over the things she'd said earlier about Culloden and the war. Or maybe he was still vexed with her for giving them away to the French on the ship. Or perhaps it was the poisoned rum, though that certainly had not been her fault.

You take more lookin' after than a bairn.

She'd wanted to be helpful and had offered to take up the other set of oars and row, but he'd shaken his head.

"A pair of oars in your hands would make a bloody din."

She'd felt ashamed to know he was likely right. And so the perilous, long watch of the night had passed in frosty silence, with Annie feeling useless and angry and afraid.

Oh, how he confused her! One moment he held her and comforted her to help her nightmares pass. The next he belittled her, humiliated her.

At least he hadn't kissed her again.

Why hadn't he kissed her again?

Each time she thought of it, her heart seemed to trip. The hot feel of his lips against hers. The scorching shock of his tongue in her mouth. The hard press of his body.

Oh, Annie, I knew you would taste sweet.

The memory of his words made her breath catch in her throat, and she realized she'd taken pleasure in it. She'd taken pleasure in his kiss.

Even as the truth of it came to her, she rejected it. She'd been asleep and caught up in a dream when he'd stolen that kiss from her. 'Twas a deception of her dream that she'd enjoyed it. How could she, who'd been raised a lady, find any pleasure in kissing a traitor, a rough Ranger, a Highland barbarian?

She looked up and saw the man who bedeviled her thoughts walking toward her. The shadow of beard on his chin had grown thicker and darker, and his black hair still hung, long and unbound, lending him a wild appearance. His shirt had come open at the throat, revealing a wedge of dark curls. She remembered what he'd looked like without his shirt, how it had felt to be held against that chest, and her breath caught again.

He moved almost silently, his motions sure, agile and smooth despite his size. He was, she realized, quite graceful. The very idea surprised her. Male grace was a quality she'd never thought of beyond the ballroom; either a man could dance a quadrille with skill and without stepping on her feet or he could not. But here was another kind of grace altogether — an untrained grace, an instinctive grace, an animal grace.

He set the bucket down before her, then knelt beside his pack and took out the soap and cloth she'd seen yesterday, together with the little jar of salve. "The cold water will soothe your feet. Wash them if you like and put on more salve."

Surprised by his thoughtfulness, Annie took the cloth from his hand. "Thank you."

Be quick about it. I'm goin' scoutin'." He rose and strode silently into the forest.

She felt the water with her fingers, found it ice cold. She removed the moccasins, exposing her battered feet. Then she dipped the cloth in the water, squeezed it out and rubbed the soap against it. Although she had every intention of washing her feet, she found herself pressing the cloth to her face instead.

She almost moaned. It felt wonderful. The cold water made her skin tingle, washed away the grime, brought her back to life. Careful not to waste a drop, she washed her face, then her throat, water running in icy rivulets down her neck and beneath her gown. Next, she washed her feet and ankles.

But it wasn't enough.

She glanced about her to make certain Iain was nowhere near. Then she sat up on her knees, let the bearskin coat fall to the ground and slipped her gown and shift down her shoulders to her waist. All she needed was a few moments.

She'd never been naked in the open air like this, and a part of her could scarce believe she was doing something so reckless. She dipped the cloth into the bucket, squeezed it, then stared in astonishment at her own body. Purple bruises stained her skin, caused by her tumble down the embankment. One of her breasts was scratched, and there was an angry red welt above her right hip. Death had made its mark on her.

She shivered.

Eager to put it all behind her, she washed quickly, first her breasts and belly, then her arms and shoulders. The breeze raised bumps on her wet skin, but the cold water soothed her bruises. As dirt and mud and dried blood washed away, she began to feel like herself again.

"You'd tempt a saint, lass. But I am no' a saint."

Annie gasped and covered her breasts with her arms.

He stood not ten feet away, the butt of his rifle resting on the ground, his hand around the barrel, his gaze sliding blatantly over her.

"Y-you ought no' be watchin'!"

"You ought no' be naked."

Iain was surprised he could speak. At his first sight of her kneeling bare-breasted and wet-skinned, the breath had rushed from his lungs. His thoughts had scattered like ashes in a gust of wind. He'd found himself rooted to the spot, his cock painfully hard, his anger and frustration from the past few days merging into sharp sexual need.

Even scratched and bruised, she was bonnie. Her cheeks glowed pink with shame, her apple-green eyes wide with a maid's innocent wariness. Her breasts were round and full, their rosy tips pinched from the cold. Her skin was creamy, her shoulders soft and curved.

Iain had been raised to treat women gently, but he did not feel gentle just now. His mother's Viking blood burned in him, ancient and hot, urging him to fist his hands in her hair and bear her onto her back, to claim her in the most primitive way a man could, to plant his seed inside her again and again.

One arm still shielding her breasts, she fumbled for her shift and gown.

"Leave them off."

She stared up at him, clearly alarmed, and reached again for her gown.
"I said leave them." He closed the distance between them, knelt down beside her, only one thought on his mind: He had to touch her.

Her breathing was ragged, and she trembled. Her eyes were huge and round.

He reached out, took her wrists in his hands, and drew them one at a time to his lips, exposing her. "Dinnae hide your loveliness from me, lass."

Then he feasted on the sight of her. Her creamy breasts rose and fell with each rapid breath, their weight enough to fill his hands. Her puckered nipples looked as if a man had already sucked them to tight, wet peaks. One was marred by an angry red scratch. Behind her breastbone, her heart beat fluttered like that of a wild bird.

Desire lanced through him, sent a bolt of heat to his already aching groin, made it hard for him to breathe. He wanted to cup the weight of her breasts in his hands, to taste her, to draw her nipples into his mouth and tease them with his tongue and teeth.

He ducked down, pressed his lips to the scratch, kissed it.

She gasped, and her body jerked as if his lips had been a brand. "P-please dinnae—"

Lust roared in his ears like the raging thrum of a heartbeat. His cock strained against the leather of his breeches, claiming the right to mate. "You've naugh' to fear from me, Annie."
'Twas an outright lie. If she knew what he was thinking, she'd likely slap him soundly—or scream and run.

You're a bastard, MacKinnon. Can you no' see the lass is an innocent and sore afraid?

Fighting to defeat his need for her, he released her wrists, picked up the cloth and dipped it in the bucket. "Turn 'round. I'll wash your back."

Covering her breasts again, she seemed to hesitate, then did as he asked.

He squeezed out the cloth, lifted the heavy weight of her tangled hair over her shoulder, and pressed the wet cloth to her skin. He heard her tiny intake of breath, felt her shiver, saw the rapid beating of her pulse against the column of her throat.

And the fire inside him grew hotter.

For more on the MacKinnon's Rangers series, visit Pamela Clare's website.

Also by Pamela Clare

Romantic Suspense

I-Team Series

Contemporary Romance

Colorado High Country Series

Historical Romance

Kenleigh-Blakewell Family Saga

Sweet Release (Book 1)

Carnal Gift (Book 2)

Ride the Fire (Book 3)

MacKinnon's Rangers series

Surrender (Book I)

Untamed (Book 2)

Defiant (Book 3)

Upon A Winter's Night: A MacKinnon's Rangers Christmas (Book 3.5)

About The Author

USA Today best-selling author Pamela Clare began her writing career as a columnist and investigative reporter and eventually became the first woman editor-in-chief of two different newspapers. Along the way, she and her team won numerous state and national honors, including the National Journalism Award for Public Service. In 2011, Clare was awarded the Keeper of the Flame Lifetime Achievement Award. A single mother with two sons, she writes historical romance and contemporary romantic suspense at the foot of the beautiful Rocky Mountains. To learn more about her or her books, visit her website at www.pamelaclare.com. You can keep up with her on Goodreads, on Facebook, or search for @Pamela_Clare on Twitter to follow her there.

CPSIA information can be obtained
at www.ICGtesting.com
Printed in the USA
LVOW11s1501141117
556256LV00008B/936/P